THE CADUCEUS

Lucie Dudley

ISBN: 978-0-244-20412-9

PublishNation
www.publishnation.co.uk

For Marianne and Charles

'Man is not born, and he never dies. He is in Eternity: he is for evermore. Never-born and eternal, beyond times gone or to come, he does not die when the body dies.

'As a man leaves old clothes and puts on new clothes, the Spirit leaves his mortal body and then puts on one that is new.'

Bhagavad Gita II, chapter 20-22

Introduction

Dartington Hall, near Totnes in Devon, is a place where all kinds of strange and slightly wonderful things can happen. It's an arts and education centre, and, although much learning and skill-acquiring is done there, perhaps its chief delight is that people previously unknown to each other collide there, and subsequently become useful, significant, or just plain entertaining to each other.

So it was to happen with me in October 2012 when I went down there to give a speech for, of all things, their Happiness Weekend – lectures and workshops about what we've since learnt to call 'wellbeing'. What I was able to contribute to such a gathering was always something of a puzzle to me, but there we are.

The layout of Dartington is a bit like a sort of solar system. The craftshops, classrooms, and spaces for music, painting, and pottery are scattered about the place and these are its planets. At the centre of the site, surrounded by walled gardens, lawns, and shrubberies, is its sun: a two-storey, part-medieval quadrangle which resembles an Oxbridge college but with one side missing. Whether it was removed in times gone by, or never built, I've never quite found out.

At one end is a restaurant and bar, and it was outside this, having given my talk and eaten a meal, that I stepped into the autumn gloom to have a cigarette.

As I stood there, two women emerged on the same mission, and one soon spoke to me. The evening was dark, the lights ineffective, and I could not make out much more than that she was youngish, slimmish, tallish, and darkish. There may have been more ishes, but I don't now recall them. She asked me about how I started as an author, and I told her as best I could, and that I'd just started doing a few e-books. She then – a bit sheepishly and tentatively – told me she was writing a novel, adding, as people invariably do in these circumstances, that it was only half written, probably not very good, and rather messy in places. It was not what you would call a hard sell. But, since this was Happiness Weekend, I offered to have a look at a synopsis, and gave the young woman my email address. It was all so casual I didn't even get her full name.

Within a few days, a text file arrived, together with a few hopeful words from its writer, now revealed as Lucie Dudley. The story centred on the semi-autobiographical main character, Dinah, and her experiences with magic and the world of spirits. Its subject matter couldn't have been farther removed from my knowledge and interest than if it had been a book on basket weaving written in Sanskrit. But Dinah seemed intriguing, the story original, and Lucie could undoubtedly write well. There was promise here.

And so I, Sherlock Holmes-style, agreed to take the case. As a hard news specialist on national newspaper, who at all times dealt in the concrete and whose own books were determinedly non-fiction, I thought I might be able to bring a bit of practical organization to the bubbling ideas factory that was Lucie's head. And so began a process of toing and froing by email, texts, phone calls, and one visit to Lucie with my wife, that would go on for seven years until the book now before you reached fruition.

My inbox records the scores of exchanges between us as chapters were sent, and my sometimes brusque comments and suggestions returned. I asked for the more spiritual passages to be explained to cloddish readers like me, we injected some pace here and there, and, memorably, I succeeded in persuading Lucie that sex on the page is better dealt with by going easy on the detail – and the ecstasy. Early on, she could never quite believe that this middle-aged, full-time Fleet Street writer and book author with four married sons and a not inconsiderable social life had the time and inclination to read and reply. "Hopefully hear from you" (her uncertain email of 22 October 2012); "I hope you don't mind me getting in touch, but I just wanted to check you were still interested in working with me." (her more nervous message of 19 December 2012); "I'm on a knife-edge waiting for your view – cringing, actually…" (2 January 2013) etc etc. But I was interested.

The more I read, the more Lucie responded with revisions, improvements, break-throughs, then the more I believed in her and her story.

And so Lucie worked on, and I, like some football coach on the sidelines, would call out encouragement and, very occasionally, make the odd plea for clarifications and precision. Lucie never flagged. A finished draft was sent, back it went with my sometimes insensitive comments picked out in red, another one came back, and so Lucie shaped and polished until we were both happy.

The title was perhaps our biggest trial. The book's first was 'Seeking The Magic Within', which never seemed right to me (and soon didn't to Lucie either). We traded alternatives, and, finally, settled on 'The Caduceus' – fittingly magical and mysterious.

Letter to agents and publishers were written, and, in a handful of cases, replies actually received (a lack of courtesy to those who write to them being something of a hallmark in the world of publishing). I'm not sure Lucie received many outright rejections, but I told her not to worry about the few she did. After all, among books turned down by multiple publishers are: 'Animal Farm' by George Orwell, 'The Wind in The Willows', 'Little Women', 'Catch-22', 'The Great Gatsby', John Le

Carre's 'The Spy Who Came In From The Cold, 'and J. K. Rowling's first Harry Potter book, spurned by 13 publishers before finding one.

This, then, is the story of Lucie's book, and how it is that you can now have the pleasure of reading the story of her main character Dinah, and her adventures in the world of spirits and love. It is a beguiling and inspiring one. Enjoy it, as I have enjoyed my small part in making it happen.

David Randall, *Universal Journalist*

Dinah:
'Judgment and Vindication'

One

Ten chairs were arranged in a circle around the edges of the room, all except one, taken by her companions for the evening. They made an eclectic group of women. Old and young, some smart, some casual. Working women, full-time mothers and those with a decidedly free-spirited approach to life. Excitement simmered in the silence, as they each secretly hoped to discover something of significance during the night ahead.

Making her way to the free seat, Dinah smiled at the lady on the chair opposite, taking in the young face, short mousey hair and sharply tailored suit. Her own skirt felt tight and restrictive and she shifted uncomfortably as she sat down. I should've changed, she thought, struggling out of her work jacket, but it had been a rush to get there as it was and she hadn't had time to stop at home. Anyway, it was too late now to fret over such things.

Tonight they were gathered at Sheila's house. Sheila was far older than the rest, of undecipherable age, maybe early to mid-seventies. A well-known and respected clairvoyant and healer, her home was filled with the same calm and serenity she emanated herself. With thick glasses and crinkly, grey hair swept into a bun on top of her head, she looked every bit the archetypal psychic. She had a kind face, deeply lined, marked by years of struggle and joy. But more than anything, when Dinah looked at Sheila she saw a wise woman, someone who had learned to accept the challenges of life with graceful equanimity. For Dinah, Sheila, her home and this circle of women provided the peaceful haven she needed.

"Make yourselves comfortable," murmured Sheila softly.

She was lighting the thick white candle sitting on a square of black cloth on the floor in the centre of the circle. The candle acknowledged the sacred element of fire, while next to it a silver dish freshly filled from the tap represented the water element. A heap of

3

white feathers were for air, and a pile of colourful stones and crystals for earth. The arrangement made an altar to spirit, the subtlest of the five elements.

"We'll be still for at least half an hour, probably more, so find a position where you can really relax," Sheila advised. "Lie down on the floor if you prefer. There are blankets if you want to wrap up." She pointed to a neatly folded pile of blankets in one corner. "Help yourselves."

Two of the women stood to get a blanket before lying down in the middle of the circle, spreading the blankets across them. Dinah stayed where she was.

"For the benefit of the new people, we'll go around the circle and give our names and anything else we would like to share," said Sheila.

Dinah had been coming to Sheila's psychic circle near her home in south London for two years now and so already knew most of those present. Only the woman in the suit and another younger girl, who looked no more than twenty, were new faces. Tonight was to be an evening of past-life regression: an opportunity to delve into previous lifetimes and uncover the hidden secrets as to who they had been before.

The suited woman sounded anxious when it came to her turn to speak. "I'm Camilla," she said, her voice breathy with nerves. "I've always known I was psychic. Right from the beginning I felt different and knew others found me weird." A lot of the women, including Dinah, nodded in sympathy. "I work in the City as an analyst, but I've always known I've lived before. I've gone back many times already. I seem to journey back spontaneously in my dreams and even while conscious, without any ritual or formal preparation. I know when I meet someone if I've known them before. I see other faces over their physical face and I recognise who they've been."

There was surprise amongst the other women at Camilla's admission and Dinah too was intrigued. This was not a phenomenon she had come across before.

Camilla hesitated before continuing with her story. "It's my secret, one I've never told anyone else, not a single living soul." She glanced shyly around the room. "I'm happy to be here, to meet others who are curious and open and willing to explore." She stopped and looked down at her hands fidgeting nervously in her lap.

There was a brief pause before the next woman spoke. The twenty-year-old was called Amy and she was fascinated by the very notion of past lives. Her mother was a firm believer she said, and, with her encouragement, Amy had decided to investigate her own strands to the past and was amazed at what she had discovered.

"It teaches me about who I am today," she enthused. "My behaviours and reactions to certain situations, and it explains some of the connections to particular people I have in my life, why we are how we are with each other. Going back into my past has made me look at who I really am and all the opinions and beliefs I have about the world – ideas I've been holding onto so tightly and yet have no substance to them at all."

She paused for breath, eyes shining. "I get such insight with regression, in a way I've never found elsewhere."

Now it was Dinah's turn. "Hi, I'm Dinah," she smiled at Amy and Camilla. "I'm also pleased to be here and excited to journey back and see what comes up." She spoke with a self-assurance she rarely felt anywhere else. With Sheila and these women there was no need for her to hide, no need to pretend, or to try and be anything at all. Here, safe among like-minded people, she could relax and simply be herself.

"I've also always been aware of other lives, of the other worlds and the spiritual beings. I come to Sheila's group every week and it's my anchor, it's what keeps me sane in what often feels like a world in chaos." There were nods of agreement from some of the women. "I'll stay open to whatever comes up tonight. I've no idea what, but it feels important."

Everyone spoke in turn, after which Sheila smiled and nodded. They were to begin. "If we can join hands we'll pray to God for divine protection."

The woman in the suit, Camilla, blanched at Sheila's words, her expression one of utter disbelief. The eyes of all the other women fell upon her.

"I apologise," Sheila said and smiled reassuringly. "I should explain." She was addressing Camilla directly. "The word 'God' is difficult for some and understandably so. It has been used to justify atrocities, to keep us in chains, small and afraid, ashamed of what we are and believing we are sinners. And for many it holds a masculine leaning, ignoring the feminine completely." A sigh of agreement swept around the circle. "But to me the word God is a beautiful word. It speaks of the male and the female as one. It is a perfectly good word, nothing wrong with it and nothing to be scared of. But it has certainly been hijacked by the dark over time, by those with lower intentions, so has become tainted. The dark would have us believe that God is an angry and vengeful power, a being so merciless that we must bow in fear or face the consequences. This is not the God I know. The God I worship is pure Love, beyond duality, who wishes only joy and happiness for humanity. I stand by the word, and for myself I feel it is time to reclaim it, to bring it back into the light where it has always been in truth. But please, if necessary, replace 'God' with your own word, whatever it might be, in accordance with your faith or beliefs."

Camilla nodded, clearly relieved.

"Wonderful," said Sheila. "Let us begin."

Gentle music filled the room as Dinah closed her eyes. Sheila was still talking, but Dinah could no longer fathom the words. Before Sheila had even finished counting down from ten to the luminous ring of a perfect zero – which they were meant to step through into the past – Dinah was in the other realms. She found herself floating in soft grey light, immersed in a giant cloud of dense warm mist as images jumbled across her mind's eye so fast she could not grasp them. Lights and colours flashed beneath her eyelids, faces swam before her and changing landscapes swirled all around. And then slowly, everything was settling. The surroundings steadied and she felt herself treading on solid ground. Sheila and her house were gone. The women were gone. It was just Dinah in a forgotten world from long ago.

Sunshine was streaming through the trees. Green leaves dancing in a light breeze and soft green grass underfoot. Her feet were bare she noticed, but clean and well cared for. A pair of dainty white shoes lay among a pile of other shoes in the grass nearby.

Those are my shoes, she knew, and smiled. *I am very happy.*

6

Long golden hair hung loose down her back and a pale shift gown brushed her knees. The trees and flowers, the birds and insects around her were alive with chatter, and Dinah understood that this girl, herself from an earlier age, knew the natural world well. *I commune with nature and nature communes with me.*

There were others around her. *My brother and sisters.* How many sisters? *Two,* she heard. *We are out walking and playing. We come from a wealthy family. It's a beautiful day and we love each other very much. We love being together.*

A boy's face appeared, at first vague and blurred, but then she made out his tousled dark hair and twinkling blue eyes. He was young and handsome and when he smiled at her, her heart filled with warmth. *My beloved!* The dirty rough shirt and scruffy trousers he wore told her he was not affluent like her. *He works on the farm. He works hard for his keep and is my secret love. Yet my family do know of him. They do not interfere, they let us be.*

Suddenly she jolted. Another energy was making itself known, an unwelcome intrusion, ugly, harsh. Another presence was coming through, another man, much older. *I am scared of him. I don't like how he watches me. He wants me as his wife even though he knows I love another. I refuse him again and again, but he is persistent. He will not give up.* Although she couldn't see him she could feel him, and he did not feel good. Something about him filled her with dread. *He is angry with me.* This unwanted suitor had position in the village, Dinah understood, a man of wealth and influence. A face was becoming clearer, probing eyes and a slight downward turn to the mouth.

He is not used to being refused by anyone. He will be my downfall.

Dinah was aware of someone talking, as if from a distant place. It took a moment for her to register what was being said, soothing words, reaching for her, summoning her back from her altered state. She watched herself drifting up through layers of consciousness, aware that she was leaving the past and returning to her physical body.

There was a strange hush as gradually she was able to take in her surroundings. Her attention was drawn to the hardness of the seat beneath her, then the backs of her hands resting on her thighs.

The voice was counting, she realised, "seven…eight… nine…" A pause. "Ten."

Once more all was quiet. Taking a long deep breath, Dinah focused on bringing herself back to the present.

"When you are ready, slowly open your eyes," said the voice.

'Sheila,' remembered Dinah in relief. She was glad to be back.

Lifting her eyelids was difficult. They were heavy and refused to cooperate at first. It took a few attempts to get them open. When at last she did Sheila was watching her, smiling questioningly.

Dinah nodded and tried to smile back, but her mouth wouldn't work, she was still too groggy.

"Everyone stamp their feet on the floor a few times," said Sheila. "I don't want you leaving bits of yourself behind anywhere."

A murmur of laughter echoed round the room, and Dinah remembered there were other women here. Standing up, she stamped her feet hard.

* * *

The regression of a few evenings back had left Dinah unsettled. She had woken early again this morning having slept restlessly – her pattern for the last few days now. She lay on her bed with her legs propped against the headrest.

Vivid nonsense dreams danced through her mind while she slept, leaving her uneasy the following day. Like a bad movie she couldn't switch off. The past-life emotions had been so strong and the feelings so vivid, but what haunted her was the sense of the sinister man. 'He came through so forcefully,' she fretted, anxiety creeping into her bones.

Shaking herself, Dinah steered her mind in the less threatening direction of how she was going to change her life.

Boredom had been creeping up on her for a while now. The feelings of excitement and accomplishment she had when she first joined the smart London public relations agency had slowly given way to frustration, as she discovered not all was as exciting and alluring as she first imagined.

Over the past few months the fidgety feeling had been getting stronger, becoming more insistent and harder to ignore. Something had to give, but she didn't know what.

"Urrgghh," Dinah groaned at the thought of going into work.

At that moment, the air to her left began to almost imperceptibly thicken, the sensation becoming more and more powerful until turning her head she found herself gazing into two radiant warm eyes. Dinah smiled. Her Guardian Angel.

She had been aware of the Angels and spiritual beings from as early as she could remember, and for her they were more familiar, more real, than any living person.

"This world or the other? I will always choose the other."

Her ability to see and feel into dimensions outside the human earth plane was a private source of joy. To reach away from the mundane and into the magical worlds, free from the restraints of modern material living, knowing that God was always there and would never let her go.

To Dinah, God was beyond the confines of the religions of the world. The word God could easily be replaced with Goddess, or Brahma, Allah, or Yehova. To her, the source of all that is, the ultimate Supreme Being, was not restricted by gender or creed, by different paths or faiths. Church, synagogue, temple or mosque, out in a field or under a tree, it made no difference.

"I feel you strongly today," she whispered to the Angel. "I must be on the brink of something?" Her Angel smiled and a burst of warmth fizzed through Dinah's heart.

What amazed her was how few people were aware of their divine companions, how few knew their own divinity, and refused to consider the possibility that there might be something more to the world than meets the eye.

"People living in fear," she mused. "Believing in fear and chaos, turmoil and destruction and yet not letting themselves believe in love. They won't acknowledge how easy it is to step out of fear and into magic."

Dinah's great-grandmother, Muzzie, had been an exceptional clairvoyant and encouraged her three children, including Dinah's grandmother, to develop their own gifts. In their family line it was normal to acknowledge the spiritual. Telepathic connection between family members was a preferred way of keeping in touch – particularly if a relation was far away. So for Dinah, an only child growing up in the New Forest, it was perfectly acceptable to ponder the metaphysical laws. While her father was a wine broker and her mother owned an antiques shop in nearby Lymington, at home the spirits and elementals were openly welcomed. Deceased family members were included in family gatherings and if anyone was in need of insight or guidance, the tarot was consulted. The line ran unbroken for generations, though whether this was personal to the souls involved or simply because the family had been raised in an open environment, she didn't know.

Dinah's gift of intuition and sensitivity enabled her to instinctively communicate with unseen beings, and allowed her to read people's energy – seeing straight beneath the image or persona being presented.

As a skilled energy reader, she would get a sense of someone from their auric field – just by being near them, seeing a photograph or watching them on TV. A person's aura, Dinah discovered, is a trustworthy blueprint of who someone is beyond the persona and shows any influences hanging over them or which they carry within them. She could detect the subtlest of nuances, whether the person was in balance or off-kilter, in integrity or not. This ability, which she consciously nurtured and cherished, was a mixed blessing. In harsh environments or around devious personalities she would frequently experience extreme discomfort and sometimes a desire to flee. Dinah learned that when people were carrying intense emotion or hiding underhand intentions, they felt volcanic, as if on the verge of eruption.

As a child, Dinah had thought her gift normal, assuming that everyone was aware of spirit and walked between the worlds as she did. She assumed others saw the things she saw and felt what she felt. So it was a shock as she grew up to realise it was not considered usual to converse with other beings in this way, nor to travel into the other realms so easily. In fact it was considered distinctly strange. She soon learned not to talk about such things outside of the home.

Dinah couldn't feel her Angel any more but she spoke to her anyway. "The human world feels so lonely and disconnected. People misunderstanding each other, existing in their own little bubbles of existence. We may live in one of the most populated cities in the world, beautiful, beguiling London – eight million people, jostling together, but so many feeling cut off and isolated, even from those who are closest. The ache of loneliness runs deep."

Sadness washed over her.

"I'm surrounded by people, yet can hardly relate to any of them."

"Don't be sad," said a voice, and Dinah could feel her Angel again. It was like this with the Angels, they would come and go, in and out of awareness. Yet they were never far away and always knew when they were needed. "We are here, Dinah."

As far as Dinah could tell, there was a secret language that others knew and she did not. It enabled mothers to chat at the school gates with ease, and work colleagues to captivate important people at the business events and lunches she had to attend. It was as if they were born knowing this talk, how to pass the time of day and what to say at the right moment to keep the other person engaged.

"Small talk it seems is the name of the game – a game I don't know the rules to and one I find tedious and awkward."

In such situations she would either helplessly glaze over mid-conversation, drifting away to other places no matter how hard she tried to feign interest, or would freeze, her mind racing as it desperately scrabbled for appropriate words. In contrast, the people around her seemed brimming with confidence and self-assurance – wide, empty smiles, impressing the impressionable with extravagant stories of people met and places been. "My brain refuses to get into it all, Angels. It won't pretend and then I offend, or scare people away."

As a young girl, Dinah had lived for being outside. The trees, wind and rain, the bugs and butterflies, birds and wild animals, were the ones she confided in. For hours and hours until darkness fell, she would roam the woods and fields, climb the trees and talk to the sky. Nature she valued above all the human world had to offer a girl of her age, more than party dresses and dolls, more than ballet lessons or birthday parties. The sense of an animal was as clear to Dinah as her mother's mood. And the language of the spirits of the trees and flowers were as easy for her to understand as reading a book. These feelings and sensations, the connection and knowingness that arose from within reached far deeper than any words.

"Of course, now I'm all grown-up and should be okay, shouldn't I?" she whispered. "Now I'm an adult it should all make sense and I should know exactly who I am and what I'm doing."

She smiled sadly. Although still unable to make any real sense of the world, the feelings of difference and aloneness had softened as she got older.

Yawning and stretching, she glanced at the bedside clock. Time to get ready for work.

* * *

Dinah and Solus had been divorced for five months when he had arrived on her doorstep to tell her he was moving to France. A talented singer-songwriter and pianist, he'd been offered a recording contract in Paris with his guitarist friend, Marko. They were flying out next month.

"It's too good a chance to miss, Dinah. They say we're good, that we have a unique sound. Can't you see?"

Yes, unfortunately she could.

In the wake of Solus's departure, Dinah had set about looking for regular work to support her and their two boys, Daniel and Luke. Anything would do as long as it paid enough to cover their expenses, and she had prayed daily, almost hourly, for a miracle. And one had come.

While waiting for the teacher to arrive at yoga one week, the woman on the next mat unexpectedly started talking to her. They had never spoken before, but within minutes she was telling Dinah about a receptionist job at a public relations agency in north London. The woman offered to put Dinah in touch with the managing director, the husband of a friend of hers. Within a fortnight, Dinah had been interviewed and offered the job. Accustomed as she was to the miraculous results of divine intervention, even she was amazed at the speed of this turn of events.

Although her days were filled with the usual receptionist duties of answering phones, greeting clients and making teas and coffees, working at the agency was unlike anything Dinah had ever known. It was as if a doorway into a glamorous new world had opened before her, seemingly filled with long lunches at restaurants, celebrity photo

12

shoots, and awards ceremonies at top London hotels. The managing director was a shrewd man in his late forties called Manny and he soon recognised something in the new receptionist. She had a certain air about her as well as a canny ability to get the job done and done well. So when an opening for a junior executive appeared three months later with one of the busiest teams in the agency, Dinah's name was top of the list.

Again grateful for her good fortune, she made the most of every chance that came her way, often taking work home to get ahead for the following day. The results she achieved saw her rise quickly through the ranks, eventually earning her the title of director on some of the company's most important accounts.

Initially Dinah was delighted, but the thrill of the challenge had now worn thin. She was bored and disinterested and feeling a pull for change that was as frightening as it was exhilarating.

'This job served me well enough,' she reflected. 'I've earned good money and learned a lot. I own my flat, support my children and have savings, so materially and financially I've done well. But now I want something more.' But whatever the something was it was staying hidden.

She knew the answer was somewhere, that the angst she felt was guiding her way. "I just need to look in the right places, ask the right questions. Something inside is screaming for freedom." She was living the wrong life and she was not happy. She could not rest, she could not accept. It was time to move on.

Two

The relationship with Solus had been wonderful in the beginning. They had met in the pub across the road from her London flat. When she walked into the pub that evening she'd noticed him immediately. He was leaning on the end of the bar, messy dark hair and a wide grin, laughing. She had wanted to kiss him right then and there, and, as if magnetically drawn, he had looked straight at her. A few shy smiles and furtive looks later and he was by her side.

"Hey…" A low whisper in her ear.

Amidst the chatter in the pub, Dinah found herself staring into grey kaleidoscope eyes. He had already taken her hand. "I wanted to meet you," he said, a soft voice with a trace of an accent. "I hope you don't mind. Who are you?"

She smiled. His grin was infectious.

"I'm Dinah."

He had gently touched her face then. "Dinah," he repeated, trying out her name. "I'm Solus."

For the rest of the evening, they had only had eyes for each other. Like her, Solus was recently arrived in London. He had been born in southern France to an English mother and French father, but was eager to be in London. "Music is my passion, my whole reason for being." His eyes sparkled. "Perhaps, I will play for you sometime?" At the end of the night, when it was time to go home, Dinah scribbled down her phone number before he'd even asked.

Right from the start she was smitten, and it was mutual. Dinah thought Solus the most perfect man she could ever have imagined – handsome, funny and kind, with warm eyes and a generous heart. With his adamant refusal to get weighed down by the day-to-day grind, he shone with lightness. Whenever Solus sang and played his piano for Dinah, she found his voice so achingly beautiful, the words

14

so hauntingly touching, it brought tears to her eyes. They were soon inseparable and just six months later they moved in together.

Although Solus found Dinah's spiritual side intriguing, spirituality was not something he was interested in himself. It wasn't that he didn't believe in God, he said – he wasn't sure about that either way – it was more that God was not a focus. They would often stay up into the early hours discussing the whys and wherefores of life, and her ideas and inclinations made him smile.

"So all the suffering in the world," he would question. "All the pain and horrors – the killings, wars, child abuse, the cruelty and hatred. Where is our all-loving God then?"

"We cause our own pain," Dinah responded, wide-eyed. "It's humans that do these things, not God. It's humanity. We cause the hurt. We hurt each other. We hurt ourselves. We hurt animals and nature... It's at our hands these things happen, not God's."

"What about the natural disasters then? We don't cause those and it would seem then that God doesn't care about us at all. If he did, he would prevent them surely."

"God does care," answered Dinah. "It's us destroying Earth. Humans plundering Earth for resources, which we could quite easily do without – leaving her damaged and aching. We upset the natural order with our take, take, take. Disturbing the balance of Earth until she cannot help but respond. She doesn't want to cause us harm, but we've become so off-kilter that she can't help but react.

"As a species we always want someone else to blame so we don't have to admit responsibility ourselves. So we blame God. Humanity fell into darkness a long time ago, but it was our choice, and one we made collectively. And now it has got so bad, now we feel the pain of our actions and see the consequences around us and we can't bear it. We can't bear that we brought it on ourselves and so we want to pin it on something else. God is a safe place to offload the blame, to direct all our guilt and anger, so we don't have to carry it inside us. But God doesn't judge us, *we* judge us. Do you see?"

Solus only shook his head.

But still, he was as devoted to her as she was to him. The way she would become entranced by a flower, gazing into its depths, stroking its petals as if seeing something there he could not. Or how sometimes in the early morning he would find her in the garden,

15

crouching in the grass entranced by the light catching on a single dewdrop. Sometimes Solus would wake in the middle of the night and find her gone from their bed. Creeping downstairs he would find the back door flung open and knew she was outside again, standing alone in the quiet, looking up, searching for the stars, the moon, hidden in the dense smog of the London sky.

"Dinah," he would call softly. "Dinah, are you coming in?" But she was away somewhere else, unable to hear him. Disappeared into herself. He knew she would be there a while and with a shiver he would head back to the warmth of their bed. He called it her zoning out time. "Dinah's off with the faeries again," he would say affectionately to their friends. She didn't mind. He didn't need to be like her and he didn't need to see things her way.

He loved how pleased and excited she became at the smallest thing – dancing to a favourite song, the still of the early morning, a rainbow, a warming conversation with a friend or standing out in the pouring rain. Her eyes would sparkle for hours after. But he found the sorrow within her harder to bear. A story on the news, an animal lying dead on the roadside, the homeless people sleeping on London's hard streets, even a tree being cut down. Solus would catch the pain in her eyes and then she would go quiet, withdrawing to a place he couldn't reach. She would close her eyes, muttering to herself; praying, she said. He couldn't see the point of praying. But he would feel sadness coming off her in waves. He learned to steer clear of turning on the news, and stopped bringing the newspapers home.

Dinah knew he sometimes worried for her. "I'm fine, Solus," she would try to reassure. "It's different for people like me. Life is different, intense, but it's a beautiful intense. It just means I feel deeply; it's a filter, if you like, for the buried emotion of the world. For people like me everything is amplified, we process the emotions and feelings around us in the world through our bodies. But prayer helps. It brings positive energy into me and directs it to whoever or whatever I pray for. It's heightened awareness and I wouldn't change it for anything."

When Dinah became pregnant a few years later, they were married in a registry office before the birth. Daniel was born and their lives evolved to another level.

16

Three years later and a second son was born. Solus and Dinah were thrilled. They named him Luke.

She wasn't certain exactly when the cracks between them had first appeared. She couldn't quite put her finger on it. It had been more of a gradual awareness that something was not altogether right, followed by a recognition that it had not been right for a while. But even in the depths of denial, the itch of discontent only got stronger and more entrenched with each passing day. Dinah found herself retreating further into the spiritual as Solus vanished into his world of music. People were starting to take notice of him and his unusual sound. He was playing more often and getting paid for his work, and had begun writing for other musicians. He had no desire to explore himself any further, he was too excited about this world, too excited with the way things were going.

"We don't seem to connect anymore," Dinah remembered crying to a friend on the phone. "We may as well be housemates rather than husband and wife. It's as if something has disappeared between us. We're just pretending to be together and I'm not even sure who we're pretending to. Ourselves? Each other? The world?"

"I'm sure if you talk to him you can work things out," her friend comforted. "If you tell him how you're feeling, Dinah. All relationships have difficult times."

There had followed many more such conversations. Dinah and Solus had not been able to let go of each other easily. In the end it had been a two-year process of trying to ignore the rifts and hurts, ignore the pain of careless words and indifferent behaviour, trying in vain to make everything good.

But slowly, slowly the gradual acceptance that things were not going to work out was taking hold. They seemed to be inevitably separating. Things were going so well with his music, while at home they were falling apart.

Now when she reflected on the last year of their marriage, she saw they were simply no longer meant for each other, that it was simply time to part. It was a difficult time, the death rattle of a relationship, with sadness and resistance on both sides. The discord finally came to a head after an angst-laden dinner with friends. It was the evening after Luke's fourth birthday that they agreed to divorce, a difficult conversation, which ended with Solus walking out, slamming the front door, leaving Dinah sobbing on their bed.

"What will I do, Angels?" she wept, clutching her chest as her body heaved. "How will I survive?"

Only as her sobs began to quiet, as she lay in the silence of emotional exhaustion, did she notice something else filling the room.

She breathed into her pillow. "Who's here?"

A thickening gentle presence filled the space around her – so familiar, comforting.

"It is all happening as is meant to be." The words poured into her mind.

Dinah stilled.

"You were destined to share your lives for a while," whispered her Angel. "Yet the purpose of you coming together has now been served."

A glimmer of hope flickered inside her as the words flowed. "Souls need to move on to resolve other karmic ties and this is the problem with a rigid belief of relationship forever. The mind believes it must make things work in an outworn relationship, when in truth the energy of the partnership has altered and the purpose of the union is resolved. Society conditioning makes many stay together, clinging so tightly, when in truth they know it is time to move on. That's all. This is the only thing, which creates unhappy relationships – fear of losing the familiar and embracing the new."

In that moment Dinah understood. What she was experiencing as a devastating ending was simply a timely new beginning.

It was over the phone from Paris that Solus explained he had met someone new – an American woman called Lila. They were in love and already living together. Dinah hadn't seen this coming and the news startled her.

"You'll like her Dinah, and she can't wait to meet the boys."

Dinah had nodded, suddenly inexplicably sad. The absolute cut was here.

The Angels soothed her heart, guiding her through the unexpected confusion, which rose up. "You see only a small fragment of the picture, Dinah, and it is this limited vision which creates fear and pain. Life experience is a tool, an opportunity, nothing more, nothing

18

less. The things which happen to you flow perfectly to help you return to what you really are. Don't give them any more value than that."

Dinah sighed. Their relationship had followed its course and come to a natural conclusion. Now their souls needed to disentangle. Solus was moving on and so must she.

"Know this is your soul choice as well as his," the Angels reassured. "It is born from love. Let go willingly, with love."

Having made the decision to transform her life, Dinah asked the Angels for a sign to guide her forward. She'd had enough of London and knew she wanted a different way of living.

Switching on her computer at work one morning she spotted an email from a local spiritual community, devotees of a mystical Indian teacher. They often sent out updates and news of their events, but Dinah never usually read them. Today however, she did. And within the text one word stood out – Porrick.

The name sounded familiar, but she couldn't place where she might have heard it. "A small country town near Dartmoor," informed the newsletter, where the community were hosting their annual festival.

Dinah typed 'Porrick' into the computer and images of a medieval English town appeared, surrounded by hills and fields. In one, the ruins of a once grand, grey-stone castle with crumbling arched windows overlooked the town's winding lanes and narrow streets. Half-timbered cottages stood amongst rows of neat, brightly painted stone houses with grey slate roofs. Porrick was between the moor and the sea, and had a strong bohemian culture. It was home to healers and psychics, and spiritual seekers of all paths, a place where craftspeople and artists, traders and writers lived side-by-side with the mainstream crowds and holidaymakers. Dinah was warmed through just reading about it.

Dartmoor was a childhood holiday haunt and one of her most favourite places. The wide-open spaces of heather and bracken suited her. It was a mystical landscape of ancient hills strewn with twisted trees and secret valleys flowing with magical streams.

When the words, 'new home' popped into her mind, she jolted.

It had been a long day at work and now Dinah was gently rocking in the Tube carriage back to her flat in a corner of south London. Not one of the capital's most beautiful parts to be sure, but it was home and she honoured it for that, grateful to have a place to call her own.

The faces of her fellow travellers this evening looked tired and grey.

"Is it only me who longs for freedom?" she wondered, gazing at the people sharing her journey. The carriage was packed tight. Next to her a middle-aged man in a crumpled suit was reading a newspaper. Two teenage boys lounged on the seats opposite, hands in pockets, staring glassy-eyed into nothing, as in the aisle between them a young woman in a big coat and heels clung to a hand strap, swaying silently back and forth.

"Am I the only one who finds this way of living so intolerable?"

The train pulled into a station and for a moment there was a flurry of activity as people got off and more people crammed on. The man in the crumpled suit abruptly folded up his paper and pushed his way to the door. He just managed to jump off before the doors slammed behind him, and Dinah watched him hustle his way down the platform, weaving in and out of the other commuters to be on his way.

"How does everyone else accept this life so effortlessly, while I could shatter into a million pieces from the sheer effort of trying not to scream?" The restlessness was bubbling inside her again.

The train continued before stopping at another station. Again the doors opened, and a few got on and a few got off.

"What the hell are we all doing?" murmured Dinah aloud. The woman holding the hand strap looked down at her in alarm. Dinah smiled.

She couldn't stifle the urges pressing for change any longer.

No more trying to force herself into accepting her lot. The voice inside was refusing to collude with the lies anyway. "There is more to life, Dinah, and you know it. If you only dare reach."

Three

Heading to Oxford Street on the bus one afternoon to buy coats for Daniel and Luke, Dinah absentmindedly picked up a newspaper that someone had left behind.

It was a drizzly day and as she stared out of the window into the gloomy streets, she couldn't help but reflect on how dull life in London had become: long hours in the office, never-ending housework, treadmill cooking. It was all so routine and day-to-day. "I've fallen asleep while still awake!" She realised and the thought horrified her.

Turning her attention back to the paper she half-heartedly scanned the headlines, but nothing grabbed her until she came to the travel section. To her astonishment she saw the town being reviewed was Porrick. The writer was clearly a fan, enthusing about the town's merits and all it had to offer, referring to it as 'a real gem' near Dartmoor. The emphasis was on the town's 'alternative' lifestyle and free-thinking culture and as Dinah gazed at the pictures, she once again felt a pinprick of hope and possibility.

"What is it you want, Dinah?" whispered a voice as the bus lurched to a stop. Thrown forward, Dinah clutched the handrail, bemused. "What do you mean?" she asked. And then it dawned on her that she had been assuming the Angels would give her the answers, tell her what to do and open all the doors while she need not make any effort at all. "Have I actually got to work it out for myself?" she panicked. "And more crucially – can I work it out?"

The word 'Trust' flashed into her mind.

"Oh!" she exclaimed. "Trust that I'll find my way no matter what appears to be happening." It suddenly seemed hilarious that the answers were inside her. No need to search outside for clues, frantically trying to solve the puzzle of life in a desperate hunt for happiness.

"But that means I'm fully accountable for myself and that if things don't go how I want, if my actions bear no fruit – then there's no one else to blame. My destiny rests in my hands alone."

Following one's dreams means risking getting it wrong and losing everything. Not the most reassuring of prospects! To follow the inner nudges can be uncomfortable when accompanied by fear, but to deny the inner voice leads only to stagnation and frustration.

"Porrick..." Dinah sensed something in that name. She was peeping over the precipice and nearly at the point where all there was to do was jump. Like the archetypal 'Fool' in the Tarot, who takes a leap of faith into the unknown, while looking to the heavens for guidance. He trusts and believes, innocently oblivious to the fact that while one side of his path is solid ground, the other is a sheer drop into the abyss.

The bus was now in Oxford Street. Dinah got off and merged into the crowds, wending her way through the tourists, shoppers and office workers, dodging buses and taxis as she crossed the road to the department store. The bustle agitated her.

"Away from nature, away from fresh air." She ducked into the relative calm of the shop. "Is this what I want for Daniel and Luke? The way of living I want to show them? My example of how to live a life, when I feel as if my soul is dying?"

"The inner spark never goes out, Dinah," whispered her Angel. "It burns inside, no matter how dulled it may feel. The time is now."

All at once, Dinah knew the right path was the one that made her excited about life. There were no guarantees, but the alternative of staying as she was would be a living death. With clarity descending the uncertainty was evaporating.

"I must show my children to never be afraid," she said aloud, not caring who overheard. "To never believe in the limits and restrictions society puts on us, or that we put on ourselves. To believe in yourself enough to follow your dreams."

Her Angel gently touched her cheek. Porrick was calling.

* * *

The roads were even busier than usual as Dinah went to collect the boys from after-school club. She had taken the bus rather than the

Tube, but traffic jams brought them to a standstill. Realising how late she was already, she got off a couple of stops early and ran the rest of the way. By the time she arrived, everyone else had gone and she was met with two cross faces.

"Sorry," she apologised to a woman, who was tidying away some colouring pencils and paper. "The roads are chaos tonight." The woman tilted her head but didn't reply.

"I know you hate it when I'm late," said Dinah, turning to face Daniel and Luke. "But sometimes it can't be helped."

"Everyone else left ages ago," complained Daniel accusingly.

"There was nothing I could do. Sometimes things get in the way, but I'm here now so get your coats and let's go."

The boys shot off so fast that by the time Dinah got across the playground to the pavement, they were already far ahead and she had to call them back so they could stop at the grocer's.

Putting a head of broccoli in a paper bag, she unintentionally tuned in to a discussion between the two women ahead of her in the queue. They were deep in a conversation about schools.

"Amy hates school. We have tears every morning," an older woman with pink tips on the ends of her hair was saying to her companion.

"You poor thing," said the other sympathetically, a blonde in a fluffy coat. "Listening to you and other parents, I'm dreading Tom starting. No one seems happy with how things are."

"Amy is behind with reading," went on her friend, "She says she's always getting told off. She's miserable."

The blonde lady nodded in sympathy. "We've delayed Tom starting for as long as possible and now we're thinking about something different," she said. "David wants us to look at alternative schooling; they seem much more relaxed and softer with how they treat the children. It's not so much expected that they must fit in, be 'good' and sit quietly all day."

"I can't believe you've said that," cried her friend. "I was reading about alternative schooling and there's a big one near Porrick."

Dinah started.

"We're going down there next week to have a look!"

23

That was the third sign. Dinah could have kissed the two women but whispered a thank you to the Angels instead. An unseen hand brushed her cheek.

Porrick was the place then. God was confirming and she could feel it for herself now. The magic was beginning to flow and the message couldn't be any clearer. After paying for the broccoli, Dinah rounded up Daniel and Luke and the three of them skipped back home laughing and dancing all the way. Daniel and Luke loved it when mum was happy like this.

Now Dinah was realising it was only her stopping herself, everything seemed more tolerable. Even the faces on the tube didn't appear quite so drawn or resigned. Walking from the Tube to the office, she noticed she didn't have the dreadful sinking feeling that usually accompanied her to work. Liberation was calling and it felt good.

Up the steps, through the doors and into the office that had been her workplace for the past few years. Manny was in reception as she went in, wearing an immaculately pressed suit and with smoothed back hair. His back was towards her and he was barking instructions at Natalie, the furrow-browed receptionist.

"Hey, Manny," Dinah smiled.

In one seamless movement, he swivelled on his heel and flashed a bright white smile before striding into the meeting room, where three other similarly suited men and a young sombre-looking woman were sitting round the glass-topped table. Now they could begin the moneymaking business of the day.

The way Dinah was feeling, she wasn't sure she'd be able to sit through even one more of those meetings ever again. Nobody else yet knew her plans. It was her secret and one she was relishing. In her elevated mood the day turned into one of the best she'd had for years. She wooed a new client over the phone and then, between phone calls, managed to produce an impeccable document to be presented to one of the company's biggest clients. These tasks were carried out carefully, but without any attachment to the outcome because the outcome wasn't important any more.

Tidying her desk at the end of the day, Dinah reflected on how her relaxed, happy approach had produced such successful results. If only she could hold onto this lighter attitude when faced with potentially life-changing events, everything would flow so much better.

Even Daniel and Luke were full of chatter and jokes when she collected them from school, as if mirroring her own carefree mood. They were overflowing with life and excitement. It's how we're all meant to be, she thought.

After dropping the boys at school the following morning, Dinah called the office from her mobile and told them she wouldn't be in that day. As she already knew would be the case, there were no questions asked. The Angels were at work, smoothing her way. She headed straight for Paddington station.

By mid-morning the train had passed through Exeter. As it skirted the coastline, the sea sparkled blue and white, sunshine bouncing off its surface. Dinah was excited.

"Thank you for showing me the way, Angels," she sent out, and felt the soft Angelic hand on her hair and then her cheek.

There was a lightness to the air as she got off the train at Porrick, in complete contrast to the density of London. She felt happy and peaceful, which was a good sign, as feeling uplifted from a place indicates positive energies are present.

A sign pointed to the town centre and she began walking along the footpath up to the main road. When she came nearer to what she presumed was the high street, Dinah was drawn towards a small side street on the right. Curious, she wandered down only to find herself standing in front of a run-down looking estate agency called Sunflower Lettings. Despite the peeling paint and faded house pictures in the windows, a jump in her tummy propelled her forward and so pushing the door open she went inside.

It was just one small room with a man sitting at a desk overflowing with papers and half-drunk cups of coffee. He was on the phone, but raised a hand towards her and mouthed that he'd be done soon and so Dinah studied the houses displayed on the wall while she waited. The pictures were slightly faded and curling at the edges, as though they'd been up awhile.

Eventually the man put down the phone and got up with a smile.

"How can I help?" He ran a hand through his hair.

"I'm looking for a house to rent in Porrick." The words came out by themselves. "Somewhere for me and my two boys. At least three bedrooms, with a garden – we've got two cats and a dog – and ideally within walking distance of the town centre."

"Well, you've come to the right place," said the man, going to a grey filing cabinet in the corner of the room and delving into a drawer. "I've got a few properties on at the moment and I know one of the landlords accepts pets. I'll have to check with the others, though." He pulled out a file.

Dinah's heart leaped. "We're moving down from London, so if there's anything suitable I could see today that would be great."

"Two of them are vacant at the moment, so you can certainly have a look today." He handed her some house details from out of the file. "I'll see if anyone's free now. Can you give me a minute?"

"Of course," nodded Dinah, grinning, as he picked up the phone again.

The first house was nothing special, but had a small terraced yard, where they could sit out in the summer, and the rent was cheap. The second house was modern but run-down, in need of serious redecoration with a third bedroom that had barely enough room for a bed and a chest of drawers. The area didn't feel as nice as the first one either. She felt a bit deflated after the initial excitement. Neither of these properties were right – they weren't what she was looking for at all.

The estate agent's mobile rang as they were leaving. It was one of his colleagues, phoning to say that the tenant from another property was in for the next half an hour if Dinah wanted a quick look round.

"It would be perfect for you," enthused the agent. "Lovely house, a bit more expensive but worth it. You'll love it and it's only a short walk from here."

From the moment she walked into the sitting room and saw the open fireplace and the views from the window over the town to the moor, Dinah knew she'd found their new home.

Officially it was a maisonette, but with two floors it felt just like a house, and was filled with old beams, wonky steps and crooked corners. She was buzzing with excitement.

"No house has ever felt like this before, Angels," she sent out. "It feels so right!"

There were the necessary three bedrooms and the kitchen was large and bright with space for a table and chairs. Off the kitchen the utility room doors opened onto the garden, which, when Dinah saw it, chased any doubt from her mind. It was mainly lawn and walled all the way round in old Devonian stone and there were even a couple of fruit trees and a vegetable patch.

She clapped her hands in delight. She couldn't have dreamed up anything more perfect for her and the boys. She took the house on the spot.

After returning to the office to fill out the forms she had a quick look around the town, and what she saw made her even more certain that it was the right thing to do. A warren of twisting cobbled lanes ran off the high street, secretive corridors with mossy stone walls begging for exploration. Turning down one to see where it led, Dinah went on a winding excursion past small stone cottages with peephole windows and hooded doorways, before re-emerging back on the high street only slightly further up. The high street itself was lined mainly with medieval buildings, some Tudor, but all immaculately cared for, and without the chain stores to be found in most English towns. There were bookshops, crystal shops, vegetarian cafés and more than a couple of healing rooms, as well as the usual town stores, banks and pubs.

At the top of the high street the market square was overlooked by the town's ruined castle. It was an impressive sight despite crumbling walls and a tumble down tower.

On the train back to London, Dinah felt like a child again, elated and unencumbered by a set path to follow. She hadn't planned this at all, it was entirely spontaneous, but now she was doing it she knew it was right. They would have fresh country air, more time outside and a gentler pace of life all round. She was leaving behind what was expected, what social conditioning would have her believe. Now it was time to start doing things her way, regardless of how others might react.

The thought sent a shiver of excitement straight through her.

When the train had drawn clear of the station, Dinah pulled out her phone and taking a deep breath called the office and asked for

Manny. After a long pause, he finally came on the line, sounding rushed and impatient. Her heart thudded in her chest.

"Manny, it's Dinah." She couldn't conceal the happiness in her voice. "I'm handing in my notice. I'll give you my resignation in writing tomorrow but I wanted to let you know as soon as possible."

Manny was shocked, and even more so when she explained what she was doing. He was horrified and immediately tried to talk her out of it. To him, it was incomprehensible that anyone would leave London, leave the security of a job with the guarantee of a regular pay cheque, to head off to the wilds of the country, without any idea of what they were actually going to do when they got there.

"Are you mad?"

"But you have two children who depend on you."

"You'll never work in the industry again if you take a break now."

"In a month... but you can't just do that, you can't just leave, now..."

"I can," she replied gently. "Because the Angels have told me that this is what I must do and so I'm going to do it."

The stunned silence on the other end of the phone made her smile.

"What do you mean, Angels? Angels! For crying out loud, Dinah, you're one of our best directors. You can't leave. You need some time to think things through. You're having a funny turn."

"No, no, I'm saner than I've ever been in my life," she replied. "Insanity is spending your life in a job which means nothing, surrounded by people who you don't really know, pretending to be happy when inside you are dying, and being too frightened to do anything about it."

More silence.

A stilted goodbye and "we'll talk about this tomorrow" concluded the awkward conversation.

Dinah felt bad for Manny but nothing could dampen her spirits. She had found the courage to speak her truth to someone she suspected would have no idea what she was talking about. Or perhaps he was more of a someone who would pretend they had no idea what she was talking about because they too were in that very position, but as yet were not ready to do anything about it. It reminded her of something she had read, about how when prisoners

28

are set free, many reoffend just to get back into prison, where they feel safe and are taken care of.

They don't want the freedom or can't cope with the freedom and it's not just prisoners, she thought. So many of us live like that. Accepting the comfort zone even though we are unhappy. Refusing to take a risk to break free for fear of failure. That's no way to live.

The train rocked along the track and Dinah gazed out to sea, delighted to know that very soon this landscape would be on her doorstep. Moor and sea, greenery and trees, nature right there before them. She wouldn't have to seek it out as she did in London, looking for the odd patch of grass or heading to the cultivated parks for her fix of nature. Here it was wild and real and raw, as it was meant to be, as God intended.

Only a month left at work. She'd just leaped off her own personal cliff. She couldn't quite believe it.

That night Dinah dreamed of an amber Angel with enormous feathered wings, stretching to take her hands. The Angel had long flowing hair and the most gentle, loving face. It took her to the higher worlds, the worlds beyond the physical plane, where Angels dance in joyful jubilation.

As she looked down on her life from up high, Dinah saw clearly the pure potential within her, of what she could yet become. Viewing herself from this place of expansion, soaring across heaven and earth, she had total clarity of what was so, seeing all and feeling all. Nothing was hidden.

A new life was on offer, one filled with possibility and as she held it in the palm of her hand she vowed to do whatever it might take to follow her heart, to reach her destiny. She vowed that from now on she would meet all experiences with grace, both the good and the bad to be greeted as treasure.

"From now on nothing will deter me," she promised. "I will follow my intuition, trust it to guide me to wherever I need to go."

Four

*'When you have come to the edge of all light that you know,
and are about to drop off into the darkness of the unknown,
faith is knowing one of two things will happen. There will be
something solid to stand on, or you will be taught how to fly.'*
Anonymous

Work was strange now she was leaving, as though she no longer had any right to be there and should have gone already. There was an aloofness from her colleagues, including Manny, as though by moving on she was somehow betraying them. Dinah didn't mind though; she felt more alive than she had in years. Having given in her notice she began to close down other areas of their London life as well. The flat was on the market. The boy's school informed and the local Porrick school contacted. Farewells were arranged, memberships cancelled and possessions packed into boxes – each step taking them further away from the past and closer to a new future.

Dinah prayed daily for a suitable person to come and buy their home. And she prayed they would offer a fair price, without trying to beat her down to the lowest possible figure.

"Why are you selling?" more than one person asked.

"You should rent it out. Somewhere to come back to – just in case," another advised.

"It's not a good time to sell, the market's down. You'll lose money."

The well-meaning advice came thick and fast but Dinah refused to be swayed. "I'm selling," she tried to explain, "because I know I'm doing the right thing by going to Porrick. I'm willing to trust that where I'm going is where I'm meant to be. I'm not listening to doubt because I don't need to, and although I sometimes feel uncertain and

30

can't see exactly what lies ahead, I know I am being guided. That God won't let me fall because I'm following my heart."

She knew any hesitation or fear in her actions, like keeping the flat 'just in case', would affect the energies of the move. It would send out a message to the Universe that she was not so sure after all, that she did not fully trust her own guidance. Ultimately it would let in the fear. Dinah was determined to stay strong. No doubters or sceptics would sway her.

* * *

When the business lunch finished, Manny said she might as well go home. Grateful for the unexpected afternoon off, Dinah decided to walk to the school to pick up the boys rather than taking the Tube. The exercise and air would clear her head. She had been feeling somewhat frazzled with all the activity of the past few weeks.

Daniel and Luke were delighted not to have to go to after-school club and chased each other home laughing all the way. It put a smile on Dinah's face to see them in such high spirits. The innocence and wonder of children never failed to move her. The shining light in their eyes a constant reminder of who we really are, of the lightness and joyfulness and vast potential available to us all.

It was really only for Daniel and Luke that Dinah made such an effort to adapt to the world, a world she found perplexing. If not for them she might have set off for the Indian ashrams a long time ago for a life of renunciation. The path of a solitary spiritual seeker held a kind of romantic appeal for Dinah, and yet she never fully wanted to let go of the world. The warmth of a good friend, a shared moment or supportive hug, a good book, trees and flowers, a tasty meal, beautiful music – she would miss these things too much. It was the simple things that made life so valuable and beautiful.

The boys were playing a game involving the wrought iron railings and dodging in between unsuspecting pedestrians.

"Boys, slow down," Dinah called after them.

They both turned and waved, Daniel giving her the thumbs-up sign. Determined, lively and always on the go, nine-year-old Daniel had a ring of blond hair running all the way around his head like a halo. He was always up to something, always full of chatter and it seemed to Dinah, easily able to get whatever he wanted. His younger brother, six-year-old Luke, had large blue eyes, which seemed to penetrate into your heart, and a mop of dark, almost curly hair. He was the quieter of the two and was always ready with a hug or a pat when anyone was hurt or upset.

Dinah was also pleased that her boys, too, were showing a connection with the spiritual dimensions of life. Luke saw people's auras, as well as elementals and spirits; and his older brother could see and feel energy, just like her, and was acutely telepathic, often reading her mind word for word. Daniel once told her, when she was angry over some now-forgotten misdemeanour, that he saw flames of fire around her. Dinah was appalled by the sudden insight into the effect of her emotions on others, and pledged to take more care with her own energy. It was a pledge she struggled to keep under the strain of living in London.

* * *

Tonight was another night of regression at Sheila's. There was no way of knowing what would surface and after last time, Dinah was filled with trepidation. It was also the last evening she would be part of the group. The thought saddened her. These women had been her main support during the last few years and Sheila's house was the one place that she could truly relax.

Dinah met Camilla at Sheila's front gate and they greeted each other warmly.

"It's good to see you, Dinah, smiled Camilla. "I've been looking forward to this all week – couldn't get away from work quick enough."

"I know the feeling," said Dinah. "It's exhausting trying to pretend you're something you're not, trying to fit in."

"We missed you the last few weeks," the other woman said. "And Sheila mentioned you were leaving London."

Dinah nodded, biting her lip as it hit her with full force how much she would miss Sheila and the group.

Inside was as warm and familiar as ever. Candles cast a soft glow into the room and gentle music enhanced the peaceful atmosphere. People were finishing cups of tea in the kitchen and so, taking a chair,

Dinah waited for the others to come through. Her palms were damp and she wiped them on her trousers. She was nervous. The Angels were encircling her, a cloak of comfort, and she realised just how reluctant she was about revisiting the incarnation with the young girl.

During the sharing ritual, Dinah was subdued and when it was her turn to speak, emotion welled up.

"It's my last night and I want you to know how much I've valued my time with you. You're amazing people and I'll miss you all. I hope I find friends like you in Porrick."

"You will, Dinah," said Sheila. "I'm sure of it. Like attracts like after all. We all have to say goodbye sometimes and it can be sad, but when the sadness passes you're left with fresh new start."

Dinah smiled gratefully. When everyone had spoken, Sheila motioned they were to begin. On the chair, Dinah pulled up her legs and crossed them underneath her.

"Blankets in the corner for those who want them," reminded Sheila. "Does anyone have any questions before we start?"

Nobody spoke.

It happened as before. As soon as Dinah closed her eyes she was adrift. Vaguely aware of Sheila counting down from ten she had already entered another world.

"Where am I?" she questioned. "Who am I?"

Flora, came the reply. An image of a grand-looking man in a powdered wig came to mind. *George III.* She was in eighteenth-century England once again as the young woman, about fifteen years old with golden hair that fell just below her shoulders. Her dress was vivid blue, her favourite colour, long, billowy and expensively embroidered, and looking down at her feet she saw dainty pale shoes. Nearby, a woven basket lay on its side in the grass and peering inside she saw it was filled with orange flower heads and strands of a sweet-smelling plant she didn't recognise. The aroma was strong though and she breathed it in.

It was a dreamy summer's day, hazy and peaceful, and Dinah understood she was tending a little garden of shrubs and herbs in the corner of a much bigger garden. She had real care for what she was doing, talking to the plants as she worked, lovingly plucking the blooms, stroking the leaves and pulling weeds from the soil. This girl could feel the plants as if they were a part of herself – the gift of unspoken communication with the natural world. The garden was long and wide, rich with green grass and bordered by rose bushes in full glorious bloom. A towering tree dominated the centre of the lawn with branches spread wide. Along one side a wall ran the full length of the garden, only interrupted by an archway, leading to a mysterious unknown space she was yet to explore.

Peals of laughter and shouting came from close by and although they were out of sight, Dinah knew she was hearing her younger brother and sisters. They sounded happy and carefree.

We are a close family. My parents allow me to be who I am. Without knowing exactly why, Dinah sensed this was particularly important for her. She had a sense of being different in some way – that she was not altogether the same as the other girls. At the thought of her parents, of her brother and two sisters, warmth spread in her chest. *They are protective of me. They love me dearly but also worry. Something about me concerns them.* For the moment, Dinah was unable to reach what this thing might be. Now the scene was shifting and a face appeared, a face that also warmed her through and made her heart flutter. Here was the young man with sparkling eyes filled with love. Love for her and her alone. *My beloved.* She smiled as she saw how dusty and dirty he was, as though he had just finished a hard day's work.

The boy, nearly a man, was poor, but she loved him with the whole of her heart. He was someone who had heard all the stories about her, which circulated the town every now and again, but other than being sure to set people straight he had no care for what others might say.

They were pledged to each other that someday they would marry, and if necessary, would leave the town and go elsewhere. Nothing would stand in their way. *'I love you so much,'* she called to him, and he reached out his hand. She stretched for him, but as their fingertips neared, almost touching, she was lifted away.

The light darkened now and the happy feeling was gone. The garden was gone, her beloved was gone and she was somewhere else. She had moved forward in time, possibly just a few months and found herself in a darkened room, seated at a wooden table with just a solitary flickering candle for company and many jars and small pots spread out before her. It was night-time, quiet. In her hands a stone cup was filled with berries and leaves from some kind of herb. She was pounding them with a heavy pestle, crushing the berries until their deep red juice spread into the bottom of the bowl. The girl was entranced with what she was doing, muttering under her breath as she worked. The words were barely audible, strange, guttural sounds from an ancient and long ago language. Dinah knew that this girl, herself from long ago, was talking to Spirit.

'This is why people stay back from me. This is what causes the whisperings in the village. I do not hide myself as well as I should. It is why my family keep me separate. I don't yet understand that others do not like what I do, that they are frightened of me and my family are frightened for me.'

The scene was fading. Again Dinah was travelling and again time was shifting. Now she was dancing barefoot in the sunshine for her beloved. She could feel him near, and when she turned she saw him lying on his front in the long meadow grass, head propped in his hands, smiling as he watched her. *He knows my gifts, he knows what I am and does not mind. He is not fearful of me like the rest.* She could see his face quite clearly, a handsome young man with a strong jaw, wavy dark hair and a twinkle in his eye. *We are in love. Nothing will come between us.* They were in a meadow under a tree, a beautiful oak. Sunlight filtered through the branches and leaves above them, casting patterns of dappled light on the ground. Around them long grass waved in the breeze, dotted with meadow flowers in reds and purples and yellows. The air was sweet and she felt contented and free, delighted to dance for the one she loved. He got up and came to her, slid his arms around her waist, his cheek resting on hers. The soft prickle of his jaw brushed her skin and she threw her arms around his neck. They were moving together, their bodies pressing into each other as his lips found hers. *Nothing will part us. Not ever.*

Still she danced, but now it was night and she was alone in the moonlight, twirling to the earth and stretching to the sky. Overhead the moon was in crescent, its rays catching her hair as hundreds of stars sparkled across the darkened sky. She was in the woods near her home, trusting the silhouetted trees to stand guard, while in the house her family slept on. Others came to join her, all women, holding hands and dancing, skipping and swaying, spinning round

35

and around. There was a mysterious hush in the air, the only sounds their stifled laughter and the swishing of their skirts. This circle of women, maybe eight or nine altogether, were moving to a soundless rhythm all of their own. Their rapturous faces hovered before her, one after the other, giving her the chance to see them more closely. They were all under thirty and all wore their long hair loose, but one woman especially stood out from the rest, appearing up close and lingering, with long red hair, pale white skin and piercing blue eyes.

She is my friend and confidante. She defends me in the town, among her family and neighbours. They do not suspect that she connects with Spirit also, that she is the same as me. She is more careful. More adept in how she presents herself.

In time to their silent dance, the women were chanting, almost a whisper. Those strange noises being made by the girl in her room with her mortar and pestle were now amplified by many voices, calling in the elementals – the faery folk – inviting them to join the dance. From the power being generated, Dinah sensed many beings were indeed present, coming forth to rejoice with the women in the essence of life itself. Swirls of effervescent light were appearing, encircling the group, flickering between the women with flashes of luminous colour. Dinah's ears pricked when she heard music playing, only just audible above their chants. A peculiar high-pitched music not of human creation, but a mesmerising elemental melody drifting through the veils – pipes or bells, she couldn't tell. But Dinah knew that only these women could hear the otherworldly tune, that it was a gift for their ears only and as the music played and the dance wore on, her heart began to soar. The celebration was a sight to behold, a thing of such beauty and power – a uniting of humanity with Nature's higher beings. A prayer to the Source of all as together they gave thanks to the Higher Power.

When the scene began to fade, Dinah found herself staring into darkness. Everything was hazy and she felt herself light-headed and starting to drift. This time when the dimensions shifted, she lost her balance completely with the unexpectedness of the change and called the Angels to steady her. She wasn't jubilant any more. She was scared. The moon and stars had disappeared and all around her was black. Squinting into the shadows Dinah thought she could make out the vague outline of a man moving around. As she watched he seemed to be coming towards her, and the nearer he got the faster and tighter her breathing became, her terror growing with every step he took until she was rigid with fear, as if the devil himself was licking her soul. She recognised him as the sinister figure from before, and as his face came close she recoiled from the coldness surrounding him. Dark intent fired from this man like poisoned arrows aiming straight for her. *He wants to hurt me.* Her body shook and her heart thudded until she thought it would burst through her ribcage. The girl she was then – Flora – began to cry. *Leave me alone. Please don't hurt me.* She was pleading, begging, but his eyes glittered with malice. She knew then that there was nothing she could do to save herself. Nothing would stop him.

She was falling. "Help, Angels," she cried. "What's happening?" With a stomach-turning jolt she found herself sitting bolt upright and when she opened her eyes, groggy and confused, she was startled to find herself surrounded by women all with their eyes closed. An older woman crouched next to her.

Dinah gasped, trying to catch her breath. "Who are you?"

"Breathe, Dinah, breathe," instructed the woman. She sounded familiar.

"Sheila!" Dinah grabbed her hand.

"You're alright, Dinah," said Sheila, her voice low so as not to disturb the others. Getting to her feet she beckoned Dinah to follow.

In the kitchen, Sheila poured Dinah a glass of water and opened the back door to let in some air.

"You came back abruptly," she said. "You went deep quite fast. I think you were pulled out for a reason. Maybe not quite ready?"

Dinah's hand shook as she took the water. She felt unsteady, as if she were floating.

Sheila rubbed her arm. "Go outside for a bit and stamp your feet on the ground, on the grass not the terrace. It will ground you." She looked concerned.

"Thank you, Sheila," Dinah whispered, squeezing the woman's hand. "I'm fine now, really. It just shocked me, that's all. I think my Angel brought me out." A soft hand brushed her head.

Sheila gave her a hug. "I must go back in. Come through when you're ready."

A nearby streetlight illuminated the garden. Dinah stamped her feet, enjoying the sweet night air. It was obvious Sheila loved her garden. The lawn was perfectly tended and the line of pots against the wall brimmed with flowers. In one corner a holly tree was adorned with colourful ribbons and tinkling chimes, reminding her of a Christmas tree.

By the time she went back in, everyone was up and talking. They all sounded uplifted as they shared their experiences, and Dinah listened with fascination to the different accounts.

Jenny, who'd been coming to Sheila for years, told of an exotic land and of finding herself in man's body. "I was somewhere in South America. My name was Jacob and it was very hot. I was sweating and had to work hard, long hours in grinding heat. I had a wife and children, and one son in particular seemed familiar." She frowned.

"He felt like my brother in this life. It was his eyes. And my brother knows me better than anyone. I had so much love for this son. He was with me when I died, holding my hand and crying. None of the rest of my family was there. I was heartbroken to leave him behind."

The stories were all quite ordinary and mundane; no tales of fame or fortune, but the experiences were rich indeed.

"Dinah, would you like to share?" Sheila eyed her quizzically.

"No. Sorry. I'd rather not," said Dinah. She felt uncomfortable, anxious, telling the story. "It feels undone somehow. I was a girl in a loving family, but I felt unsafe." Involuntarily she shuddered.

"I'm afraid it got a bit bleak towards the end and I came out spontaneously. I didn't recognise anyone from this lifetime."

Sheila nodded quietly.

The women were silent for a while, each lost in quiet reflection, considering the events of the evening. The group was coming to an end.

"Until next week then," said Sheila gently. She blew out the candle closest to her. "It is time for farewell."

There were tears and smiles as Dinah said goodbye. She hugged them all and they wished her well. Suddenly she didn't want to leave. "If only the whole of my life could be as it is here," she said wistfully to Sheila at the door.

"I wish that, too, but the world isn't quite ready I don't think."
Sheila stroked her hair fondly. "It's getting there though."

"Thank you so much, Sheila, for everything." They hugged.

"I wish you so well, Dinah. I'll be sending you thoughts and blessings in my prayers. And there is always the phone too."

"I'll think of you too, Sheila. And when I come up to London I'll be sure to call. I'd love to join you again one day."

Looking back at Sheila's little house for the last time, Dinah was sad. But I still wouldn't change it for anything, she thought, pulling the gate shut behind her.

Five

By the time the train pulled into Porrick station, London felt a lifetime away. Daniel and Luke had bounced excitedly on the train seats for most of journey, occasionally disappearing up the corridor to explore. Dinah had managed to coax them back to their seats with a pack of playing cards and they had spent the rest of the time bickering over who had shouted "snap" first. Luckily the carriage was more or less empty.

As their furniture wasn't due until the following day, the three of them were booked into a bed and breakfast for the night. Edenfield B&B was only a short walk from the station, but trundling suitcases over cobbled stones was not easy, especially for Dinah, who was being pulled along by their excited spaniel, Sophie, while also carrying the cats in their travel box. Seeing his mum struggling, Daniel took Sophie's lead as Dinah tried her best not swing the cat box around too much, but inside, Topsey and Smudge were furious with the disturbance and meowed continuously until at last they arrived at the B&B.

The owners, a hippy-looking couple called Ros and Chris, took pity when they saw Dinah's frazzled state and offered to call a taxi to take the cats to the cattery.

Ros was tiny with a puff of blonde hair and bracelets that jangled all the way up to her elbows. "The Elm Tree restaurant has glorious food, and it's only round the corner so you could eat there and walk back afterwards."

"Sounds perfect," said Dinah. "We're starving and it's been a long day."

"I bet it has," said Chris, who wore round moon glasses and had long frizzy grey hair. "You've moved down from London you said on the phone?"

"That's right."

"Always stressful moving. Especially with little ones and animals too!"

Dinah nodded. Ros was petting Sophie affectionately. "Do you want us to look after this one while you're out?"

"Oh, yes please," said Dinah, gratefully. "That would make things much easier!"

"Pleasure. I'll go and call a cab." She disappeared through a swing door into what Dinah presumed was the kitchen, while Chris showed them to their room.

The B&B itself was tatty and worn, but it was clean and had a warm homely feeling about it. It felt good here already and despite being exhausted, Dinah felt peaceful and right. They just had time to freshen up before the taxi came.

The restaurant was quiet. Daniel ran to a table by the back window closely followed by his younger brother, where they pulled out chairs, scraping them on the floor, and reached for the menus.

Dinah noticed a woman at the next table watching Daniel and Luke with an amused expression. A cup and saucer was pushed to one side, while a notebook and pen lay open in front of her. Their eyes met. Dinah smiled and the woman smiled back.

Having ordered their food, the boys began to argue about who should get the top bunk at the bed and breakfast. As they became progressively louder their voices carried across the room, disturbing the hush.

'Sssshhh...' reprimanded Dinah. "You don't have to shout."

"You've just arrived in Porrick then?" It was the woman from the next table.

There was something distinctly familiar about her, although Dinah was certain they'd never met before. She had a perfectly heart-shaped face, with clear creamy skin, framed by shoulder-length black hair, so dark that in the subdued lighting of the restaurant it shimmered blue-black. The woman was attractive, there was no doubt about it, but it was her piercing blue eyes that really captivated Dinah. The irises were the palest ice blue, sharply outlined in deep indigo, and the effect was so startling that Dinah wondered if they were contact lenses, but something told her they weren't. Her clothes were unusual, too. A long dress made from layer upon layer of sheer

41

violet fabric with wide trailing sleeves and a low-cut, square neck. At her throat hanging from a heavy silver choker an oval pendant of royal blue glinted in the candlelight every time she moved. Around mid-forties, guessed Dinah, a slight flutter in her stomach.

"Yes, this afternoon," she eventually replied, wondering how the woman knew. Had the boys mentioned it? She couldn't remember. "We've moved down from London."

"Ah. That's good. That's exciting. Porrick is a special place. What brought you here, if you don't mind me asking?" She had a slight accent, although Dinah couldn't place it.

Although the woman was friendly enough, Dinah wasn't yet ready to reveal herself by mentioning the signs she was following, or the Angels.

"Fresh air," she smiled. "And the beautiful countryside. Lots of things, really."

"I see," said the woman. "Do you have family here? Or friends?"

"No, no. We don't know anyone here. We hope we'll make new friends though, don't we boys?"

Daniel and Luke were too busy examining the pudding menu to respond.

The woman appeared suddenly thoughtful. "There are some good people in Porrick, but also some to take care with. Like everywhere else in that respect, I imagine."

"Yes, I suppose." Dinah wasn't sure where this was going.

"It can be quite cliquey here, I think, for some people's tastes, but you seem like an experienced person, someone who knows how to find their way around." She smiled warmly. "I'm Ambrika by the way," she said leaning over and proffering one hand.

Formal, thought Dinah, as she reached to take it.

"This is Daniel and Luke." The boys looked up and said hello.

"I'm Dinah." Their eyes met and the woman started, before leaning in towards Dinah as if for a closer look. Their hands were still pressed together and the palms were hot, too hot. Healing energy.

"Sorry," Ambrika smiled and retreated slightly, though she still seemed mesmerised by whatever she saw in Dinah's eyes.

Dinah's stomach fluttered again. *Angels, who is this woman?*

The woman dropped Dinah's hand. "You know Spirit?"

"Yes," answered Dinah, matter of fact.

42

The question didn't surprise her. She could sense this woman and her energy was strong, powerful even. It told her immediately that Ambrika also was on her path. What startled her was that the woman had recognised it in Dinah. Not many people had the gift of reading energy this way, but this woman clearly did. Ambrika held her gaze. Silence.

"Sorry." She smiled this time and looked down. "I was meditating before I came here. I must still be half there."

"It's fine, I understand." Dinah wasn't entirely convinced by this explanation.

"So, Dinah, may I ask what path you follow?"

"Well, my own path really. No labels to put on it or teacher to call my own." She paused. "I hear the Angels." With no reaction from Ambrika, she added: "I practise yoga, meditate, follow the signs and my heart as best I can."

"Ah – I feel that in you. Following your heart. You've come to the right place. You're meant to be here. I know it."

The comment buoyed Dinah's spirits. "That's good to hear from someone else."

Ambrika smiled, a slow mysterious smile. "I run groups if you're interested, and do past-life work." Her eyes fixed on Dinah, who suddenly felt tingling on the back of her head. Angels urging her to pay attention.

"I'm a healer. I channel Spirit, work with the land."

A pause. They stared at each other as the air shivered around them.

Then without warning, Ambrika began gathering her things from the table and piling them into a small velvet bag. "I must go."

"Oh, okay," said Dinah, taken aback by the suddenness of the woman's departure. Ambrika took something from her purse and gave it to her. It was a business card. "Call me if you need anything."

Taking the card, Dinah was abashed at this odd turn of events, but smiled nonetheless.

"Thank you."

Ambrika rose and moved away, but when she got to the door she hesitated and looked back to stare at Dinah, as if examining her even more thoroughly. Dinah shifted uncomfortably until Ambrika, realising she was behaving strangely, gave herself a shake and with a wave disappeared into the night.

Interesting, thought Dinah. "Angels, what was that about?"

"Patience," whispered a voice.

* * *

The shortening days of October found the three of them gradually settling into their new home. The weather had turned and they were properly in autumn, with interminably wet grey days and leaden skies. In the mornings they were woken by the haunting cry of seagulls, an immediate reminder they were no longer in London, and what with unpacking, organising furniture and getting to know Daniel and Luke's new school, Dinah was busier than she had expected.

During the day, Dinah wandered the streets of Porrick, getting to know the shops and cafés and the people who worked in them, getting a feel for the place. A network of cobbled alleyways and passages encompassed the main street, with tucked-away houses and hidden doorways in moss-covered walls. The main street ran up a slight hill and, between all the usual stores one might expect in a market town, there were other more unusual shops, and these were the ones that drew Dinah. Windows filled with intriguing displays of crystals and wands, statues of deities, and decks of oracle cards, expertly fanned.

One shop was tucked off the high street and mysteriously named The Golden Gateway. There was a cauldron in the window and above it a large silver pentacle hung from the ceiling – the symbol of the quest for divine knowledge. Curled up next to the cauldron a large grey tomcat was fast asleep, supposedly oblivious to the goings on around him. Dinah admired him and, as she did, he opened one yellow eye and stared at her, stretching out a long slim paw and yawning languorously. He watched her with the penetrating feline knowingness cats have, following her every move as she marvelled at the chalices and crystals on show, the coloured silks and candles, and an impressive arrangement of feather fans.

Blowing the cat a kiss, which it received with a regal blink of its one open eye, Dinah went into the shop. A bell rang above the door as she entered. It was dark inside and she was surprised to see that most of the shelves were in fact filled with books.

A young woman with bobbed red hair sat reading behind the counter. She looked up briefly as Dinah came in, before returning to her book. "If you need any help just ask," she said distractedly.

The books were all spiritual in theme, exploring different religions and paths as well as various practices of magic. Dinah was impressed as she examined the titles, running her hands along the book spines, feeling the energy of ancient wisdom and knowledge emanating from them. "You have a wonderful selection," she told the shop assistant. "Everything I could possibly think of."

The woman put down her book. "We pride ourselves on being able to get hold of most titles even if we don't have them in stock. Were you after anything particular?"

"Not really," said Dinah. "Just browsing."

"We have music too, if you're interested. And through there" – she nodded to a doorway – "crystals, candles, oils, cards, that kind of thing."

"Okay, thanks."

Time disappeared for Dinah in places like this and she happily immersed herself in exploring everything on offer. It wasn't long though before she was back at the bookshelves again, pulling out one after another and flicking through the pages until something caught her eye. Then she was lost in the words until another title grabbed her attention. It was only when she happened to glance up from an intriguing text on the Hermetic secrets of alchemy, that she saw the clock on the wall and realised she'd been in the shop for nearly two hours. The woman behind the counter was still reading, though, and didn't seem concerned.

The Hermetic book had a number of interesting principles around magic that Dinah hadn't come across before so she decided to buy it. She approached the counter and while the woman rang it up, she spotted a large noticeboard on the wall, covered with leaflets of events happening in the town and services on offer. Dinah was amazed at the scope of activities, workshops and courses available.

"Something for everyone in Porrick," said the woman, seeing the surprise on her face.

"I can see," said Dinah, putting the book in her bag.

There were healing gatherings and meditations, chanting and psychic development groups, Tantra classes and moon circles, men and women's empowerment classes, sweat lodges, art therapy, counselling, different styles of yoga, retreats and dancing circles. The list was endless. Dinah felt happiness wash through her as she wandered back out into the high street. She was at home, really at home, in a way she'd never felt before.

Amongst the day-trippers and holidaymakers still flocking to Porrick even at this time of year, she was becoming more aware of the locals. A man with a long brown beard passed her, wearing a purple pointed hat and wide-bottomed stripey trousers. A young woman with a shaved head and dressed head to toe in orange robes bustled into the newsagents, and a group of women with feathers in their hair and brightly coloured skirts and jackets poured out of one of the cafés.

Porrick feels like magic, thought Dinah, contentedly. It's in the air.

That afternoon she joined the library and bought some scones from the bakery. Strolling to the bottom of the main street she noticed a narrow side alley and decided to see where it went. After passing a line of terraced cottages, their gardens still alight with colour, she eventually came out by the river. The sun was bright. The water still and smooth as a mirror, perfectly reflecting the flaming orange trees and crisp blue sky. The sight made her stare and she sat on a bench to take it in.

They would need a car down here. In London it wasn't necessary, with the trains and buses, but in Porrick she wanted to go to the beach and the moors and a car was the only practical way to get there. Things were coming together and with the money from the sale of the London house in her bank account, she could enjoy some free time until she began her new work – whatever that was going to be. This was a proper new beginning, a blank page with which to do whatever she wished, and from now on she would try her best to make sure that everything she did was something to be enjoyed and which made her sparkle. Walking Sophie,gardening and yoga. Even the household chores she found therapeutic nowadays: cooking, cleaning, making the house tidy and cosy.

"The only thing missing is romance," she told the Angels. "I'm ready though, to share my life again."

A small brown bird landed on the bench beside her. Not daring to move or draw breath, Dinah simply watched it. It hopped a little closer until she could almost have reached out and touched it. It was so tiny and dainty, with such detailed markings, a slender black beak and thin twiggy legs. "Are you trying to tell me something?" she asked. "Telling me not to give up on love just yet?" She knew the Angels often used birds as a way to communicate hope and support, and that the elementals, the faery realm, will shape-shift into a feathered friend so as not to alarm unsuspecting humans. She also knew that when a bird behaves strangely, trying to get your attention, it pays to take notice. This one had puffed up its feathers so that it was round and squat and Dinah couldn't stifle a chuckle. The sudden noise startled it and it immediately flattened its feathers, poised on full alert. A moment later it tipped its head and flew off.

"Bye," Dinah called after it. "Take care." The encounter had warmed her through and she thanked the Angels. It was just what she needed.

Walking back she picked up a pebble and sent it skimming across the top of the water, satisfied to see it bounce three times.

Dinah hoped the bird was a sign for love.

Since her divorce she'd had a few dalliances here and there, nothing serious. It simply hadn't worked so far. She hadn't wanted to go any deeper with anyone and didn't want to upset the status quo with Daniel and Luke.

"I want someone faithful and loyal, kind and trustworthy. Who'll love me and the boys and treat us well." She had leaned heavily on the Angels during the past few years. Relying on them to carry her through, and during times when she really struggled, she would simply pray harder, trusting in divine resolution.

"What would I do without you?" Dinah was breathless at the thought. "What if I'd never bothered to open up? If I had no belief – what then?" She felt quite distraught. "How do they cope? Those who only recognise the material plane, who scoff at the spiritual and psychics and have no faith. How do they get by?" It was as if some people survived on minimum capacity, with no inner nourishment and without feeding their souls, accepting their lot in spite of the discontent and pain. Dinah wondered if it was because they were too fearful to question, because the vast unknown with all its possibilities can appear frightening and dark at first.

"It can be frightening," Dinah conceded. "I get scared, without really knowing why. Even when I know there is nothing really to be afraid of. Is this just the nature of fear?" The air shifted about her followed by a trail of tingles on her skin.

"Do we just scare ourselves into staying small and limited, rather than risking the familiar to reach for our dreams – even when we sense the unknown could fulfil all our hopes and desires, and make us whole again."

Six

The newspaper advert was small and unremarkable and yet her eyes fell upon it as soon as she opened the page. The library was deserted apart from the old female librarian, who with piles of books scattered around her feet was reorganising the fiction section. There must be hundreds of books there, thought Dinah. Chaos! But from the serene expression on the woman's face there was to her at least order within the chaos.

Turning back to the advert, Dinah saw it was for a yoga class. Nothing special about that; in this town you could find a different yoga class for nearly every hour of every day. But something about this one stood out and that needed to be honoured. It was a Vinyasa Flow class, a challenging, dynamic form of yoga, not Dinah's usual way to practise. There was a blurry picture of a man sitting in lotus position and next to it a telephone number and the name Tony.

Jotting down the number Dinah headed outside where she tapped the number into her mobile. Eventually someone answered. It was a man and he sounded annoyed.

"Yes!" barked a voice, not shouting exactly, but not far off.

Dinah blanched. She realised the phone hadn't clicked on to answerphone as was usual nowadays and she had distractedly let it ring. It must have been ringing for quite a while, sparking the man's irritation. Although taken aback by the curtness of the greeting, she politely asked to speak to Tony.

"That's me. What d'you want?" said the voice, rudely.

Dinah hadn't counted on this, an impatient and obviously bad-tempered yoga teacher making no effort to mask his hostility, but she refused to be rattled. "I saw your class advertised in the paper. I wanted to come along."

Silence, followed by a sigh. "It's a closed class usually, but I've space for two more, hence the advertisement. Do you have a regular practice? It's not a class for beginners."

"Yes, yes—" She began to tell him her yoga background, but he clearly wasn't interested and cut her off mid-sentence.

"Fine. Come Thursday. 7pm. The hall off St Bartholomew's. Bring your own mat."

Clunk! He'd put the phone down without bothering to wait for a response.

With the phone still pressed to her ear, it took Dinah a few moments to register that he had indeed hung up on her. Indignation welled in her stomach. Now she was unsure. Was this not the thing to do after all? It had felt right when she read the advert, as though she was being guided, but maybe not. Had she got it wrong? His manner made her reluctant to follow through. She closed her eyes.

"Go," came the whisper, accompanied by a stroke to the back of her head.

Her Angel had responded so quickly and clearly, that Dinah knew she must go, no matter how bothersome the teacher sounded.

Ah, she thought. Maybe this class has something for me, disagreeable teacher or not.

* * *

The room was warm and quiet. The heady smell of incense filled her nostrils, its evocative fragrance clearing her mind.

There were at least twenty people here. Should be a good class, Dinah thought hopefully.

A white candle flickered at the front of the room by the teacher's mat. The teacher. He sat cross-legged, unmoving, eyes closed. In spite of herself, Dinah was intrigued and slightly nervous. Rolling out her yoga mat, worn through in parts from years of practice, she seated herself and waited. As she did, she examined him more closely.

Messy, dark blond hair tucked behind his ears, and pale skin with a delicate pinkish hue. The stubble around his jaw, not quite a beard, suggested more than a few days' growth. With his thick, unkempt eyebrows, the overall impression was of someone who cared little for

50

external appearance. Although he was sitting, his red shorts displayed the muscular toned legs of someone committed to yoga, as did the green t-shirt, stretched tight across a wide chest and broad shoulders. Dinah found something about him a little intimidating.

Yoga had been part of her life since she was fourteen years old. The ancient art had captured her from the start as she discovered the calm and peace to be found within each posture. Over the years the way she practised changed, adapting to the twists and turns in her life, but always staying with her, a constant companion. Dinah had experienced many teachers and attended countless retreats, but while grateful for any direction they offered, it was her own inner wisdom which spoke the loudest.

Still more people were flocking into the hall. No one spoke. They came quietly, putting their belongings at the side of the room before finding a space to roll out their mats. Most lay in savasana – on their backs with their legs apart. Such a seemingly simple posture, and yet for some, where complete surrender is the goal, one of the most challenging.

The yoga teacher still hadn't moved and hadn't opened his eyes once. Dinah followed the others lead and also lay on her mat. As she began to release and let go, she sank deeper and deeper within, calm engulfing her. And then all thoughts were gone.

The voice came from close beside her. The teacher was by her mat. Although he was speaking, she couldn't make out precisely what he was saying, but he spoke in such lulling tones that she was drawn from her inner worlds. His voice flowed in and around her, something inside absorbing the words as they carried her into the deepest parts of herself. With the minutest and most silent of footsteps he began to encircle her mat. Dinah was on full alert, eyes closed but all other senses heightened and vigilant. She could feel with startling clarity the moment the sole of each foot made contact with the ground, the gentle reverberations echoing through the wooden floor.

What is he doing? She lay frozen, heart pounding as discomfort flooded through her. Her limbs were so heavy that she couldn't move a single muscle, not lift a finger, nor stretch a toe.

Right now, she couldn't even recall what he looked like. Blondish hair perhaps, solid build? But she could feel him. He was radiating power and dominance and it seemed for the time being that he was concentrating his attentions on her. His feet came to a standstill by her head and Dinah knew he was looking down at her, his stare searing into her skin.

As her face flushed red she felt panic rising. This was too much, too intense and her breath came short and fast. She was starting to feel crushed and knew she must act fast to break the spell.

He wants me to know he's in charge, intuition told her. He wants authority. Dinah had met men like this before, men who need submission from women and take power through dominating others.

"Is he one of these, Angels?" she asked. "A self-proclaimed, spiritual teacher who diligently masters the invisible energies then uses the knowledge for personal gain?"

No reply was forthcoming, only waves of calm soothing her beating heart. Perhaps she was wrong?

Through the confusion came an irresistible urge, a pull from inside urging her to show her own strength, to prove she was no novice seeking a guru.

I've my own powers, she communicated to him silently, almost sure he could hear. *I've honed them during many lives and I know how to use them. I'll show you, teacher – you are worthy of the effort.*

Gathering the full might of her inner force, Dinah focused all her intention on building her auric field. By drawing her awareness deep inside, she strengthened the energy within and around her physical body. The transformation was beginning and she sensed him flinch, ever so slightly, in response.

Not many would have felt that. She was delighted and smiled inwardly at his reaction. *Now you are starting to understand.*

Dinah was flexing a psychic muscle she not often had cause to use and was aware of how much she was enjoying it, how alive she felt, how vibrant. This man was a master, she could feel it.

But now he is meeting a high priestess – she brimmed with confidence as the thoughts meandered through her mind – of equal strength and power. I think this may be his first such meeting!

The teacher was definitely giving her his full attention now. It was piercing into her and very nearly, but not quite, throwing her off balance.

Her energies were receding and she had lightened herself to the point where, energetically, she was barely present. It didn't matter what psychic intentions he sent out now – she had made herself safe and beyond reach.

She felt him hesitate, momentarily bewildered, before he quickly recovered and abruptly walked away. The psychic cords forged between them during this encounter snapped shockingly apart and hit Dinah hard. He had pulled away too fast and her body jerked in response. Something told her he had done it on purpose, punishing her for her show of strength and refusal to bow.

"He isn't ready to acknowledge you."

The whole episode had lasted only seconds.

From then on, the class continued as normal. The teacher didn't pay her any more attention as he led the students through the yoga postures. It was a strong class, but flowing, and Dinah willingly succumbed to the postures.

"No need to strive, to do anything or be anything," the teacher instructed as he walked around the room, weaving between the mats. His voice was hypnotic.

"Allow the asana to do what it was created to do. Relax more with every out breath. Let go. Breathe deep, breathe slow."

Dinah stretched longer and deeper, feeling her body melt and unravel under his instruction. She was starting to find her own pace again, her own inner rhythm against the backdrop of his teaching. Everything was starting to soften as she dissolved into the ecstasy of the stretch. By the time they got to shoulder stand she was free from all thoughts and concerns, the only consciousness being the bliss of surrender.

"Aaahhh…" Only the smallest noise escaped her lips.

They sat for meditation at the end, and Dinah had never reached such depth before; so clear, so sharp. There was no Dinah. There was nothing except a pure state of being, where all the worry, pain and tension, all the emotions, plans and racing thoughts simply drifted away as if they had never been. They were dissipated in a fuzz of warmth. It was like taking a much-needed holiday, only this was a holiday where the mind and body could truly rest, a holiday away from the blur of life. Freedom.

From the clear empty space inside. All will come to you.

The class ended in the same unassuming manner it had begun. People quietly rolled up their mats, some dropping money into the pot beside the teacher, and then leaving. No words spoken.

Dinah approached his mat. She intended to introduce herself, but as she got closer he turned away and engaged another student in conversation. It felt deliberate. Or was she being paranoid?

With his back firmly towards her, he obviously had no desire to talk with her and so she put her money into the pot. He feigned not to notice and this made her feel odd. She realised she had been expecting some kind of verbal acknowledgement from him, but when she said goodbye, he didn't even bother looking up; indeed he seemed not to not have heard at all. How strange. She left.

Re-entering the everyday world was always to be done gently after visiting the deeper places inside oneself and so Dinah cautiously walked back out into the high street. It was already ten o'clock. The moon was particularly luminous, nearly full, and she could feel its energy pulsing down onto Earth. The stars appeared exceptionally bright and she stopped for a moment to breath it all in. There was something unusual about the sky tonight. It felt different, more intense, even accounting for tomorrow's full moon. There was a hush of anticipation in the night air as though something was shifting.

Dinah walked home in a haze of blissful peace. Letting herself in she did her best to hold this higher state while paying the babysitter. Kate was a local girl who worked in the town nursery and boosted her earnings with evening childcare. With long black plaits and an elfin face she didn't look a day past twenty, but was so sweet-tempered that Daniel and Luke had taken to her immediately.

With Kate gone, the house was completely silent apart from the crackling of the dying fire in the grate. The boys were asleep and so making some tea, Dinah took it into the sitting room to watch the remaining embers burn to ash.

Seven

The beach was deserted. It was one of those gusty autumnal days, with wind so strong that Daniel and Luke could lean into it without falling over. The tide was low, further out than she'd ever seen, and they'd walked for what seemed an age before finally reaching the water's edge. When she dipped her fingers into the sea it was so icy it took her breath away.

Yemaya – Mother of the ocean, guardian of women and children and teacher of ultimate surrender. Dinah called to the Sea Goddess and pulled three small and now slightly crumpled paper boats from her pocket, which they'd made from newspaper that morning.

"Daniel! Luke!" She had to shout to be heard over the wind. "Come here."

They came running, excited and full of sea air, with Sophie scampering behind them, all wet fur and flapping ears.

"Have you thought of something to ask for?" asked Dinah, passing them their boats. "A blessing from the Ocean? It can be whatever you like."

"I want a computer," said Daniel immediately and taking his boat waded into the sea, protected from the chill by wellington boots.

"What about you Luke? Have you thought of something to ask for?" She turned to her youngest son.

"Yes," replied Luke, and without another word followed his brother into the waves with his boat.

Dinah walked into the sea behind them as far as her boots would allow. Lowering her own boat into the water, she asked Yemaya for a blessing for each of them, as well as for every person mentioned in the newspaper pages they had used to make the boats. The three of them then stood back and watched the little sea vessels being tossed on the water, before they were swallowed by the waves – a sign that Yemaya was happy to grant their wishes.

"Yes," shouted Daniel, happily punching the air. "I'm getting a computer!"

"Looks like you are Daniel," laughed Dinah. "But Yemaya delivers gifts in her own time, so forget about it for now and be patient."

A quality I still struggle with, she sighed to herself.

The river, which flowed into the sea along this stretch of beach, was now a mere trickle and the dinghies that normally bobbed in the water lay abandoned and forlorn on the wet sand. Staring into the wild, grey ocean, stretching before her, Dinah thanked God for bringing them to this place they now called home.

The three of them had then played dizzy men together. Stretching their arms out wide as they turned round and round in circles, trying to keep their feet on one spot, twirling faster and faster until they either fell over or stumbled off to one side. The wind made Sophie high-spirited too and she darted between them, barking enthusiastically and jumping into the air to catch their sleeves. With the gale whipping in her ears, Dinah relaxed as she turned, easily losing herself in the rhythm of her spinning body, knowing she wouldn't fall over herself. She knew just how to place her feet to stay balanced and as she spun she began to feel like one of the long-skirted whirling dervishes from the mystical Sufi tradition, the peaceful, esoteric faith often associated with Islam.

When she finally opened her eyes, it was just in time to see Luke lose his balance, and after a few wild and wobbly steps, land on the wet sand with a thump. It was starting to drizzle now and the air was heavy, charged. Everything was rugged and raw down here on the beach and Dinah felt elated by the sheer force of the natural world around her: the blasting cold wind, which made her ears rattle, the heaving ocean throwing itself onto the sand, and the magnificent landscape of bleak rolling hills against the slate grey sky. Pulling her hood tighter, Dinah called to Daniel and Luke that they should be getting back. Heads down, unable to hear each other over the roar of the wind and the crashing of the sea, they made their way back to the car.

As they drove up the winding lane to the main road, Luke leaned over and whispered into her ear. "I asked for a turtle."

Home was Dinah's sanctuary, away from the external influences of the outside world and somewhere she could really relax. In the kitchen, she lit some incense and purposefully began to slow her breathing as the exhilaration of the walk melted into a softer feeling.

The antique pine dresser, which stood next to the fridge was the first piece of furniture Dinah had bought purely because she loved the look and feel of it. The grainy, knotted pine was deeply polished and waxed, showing its age and the love people had felt for it over the years. The wood was intricately carved with curves and curls, alluding to its German origins, and the ornate metal inlay hinted at flowers and nature. The dresser housed all the books which had touched her and taught her, spiritual authors past and present, the famous and the lesser known. It was where she kept her oracle cards, angel feathers, pebbles and crystals, candles, incense and sage. Propped up in a row were images of Angels and deities, who inspired her and who she called on for protection and guidance. The dresser held everything required for spiritual contemplation.

Opening a drawer, Dinah reached for her tarot cards, used infrequently now but always treasured. They were a gift from her father when she was thirteen years old, and every so often she would draw a card just to see. The colourful, vivid images still gave her a warm feeling of familiarity and to hold them brought back memories of sitting at the kitchen table with her father, while he smoked his pipe and explained the meanings and symbolism hidden in the pictures. She learned about the twenty-two cards of the Major Arcana, and how each depicts a stage of the human passage through life. Then the four suits of the Minor Arcana – wands, pentacles, swords and cups – each relating to a different aspect of the everyday.

The tarot had captivated Dinah from the start. She recognised them as a mystical place where pictures come alive and share hidden truths with those who seek. The cards could answer questions and explore possible paths, highlighting current influences the querent might be under and any challenges or successes to be met. The tarot speaks of possibility, the potential of life and how we create our path with our thoughts and attitude to the now. It was this subtlety that had ignited her all those years ago. That the world is illusion we create individually and collectively; that we exist in a place where reality, as most people know it, is not truth. The truth is found behind the veil, which falls between this world and the next, and where the only way to exist is in openness and surrender. This is the place where Dinah was most comfortable.

Shuffling the deck, she focused on the cards passing through her fingers. The heat inside her, directing her to the card she needed to see. And as she already knew it would be, the card she pulled was 'Death'.

The Grim Reaper eyed her, scythe in hand, a sinister smile stretched wide across his skeletal face.

The Death card, mistakenly feared by many, is a powerful omen of impending and unavoidable transformation. *The time is now* it says. *Time for rebirth*. The skeleton's face, peering from beneath a black hooded cowl, seemed to allude to darkness and malevolence.

"Our own death, death of another, the threat of death, death of a way of being, death of a relationship, of an identity, or of a job," Dinah mused. "It seems the fear of death holds many of us in bondage."

She knew that for now the card spoke of death of a circumstance. Everything had changed and was changing still and she could either flow with it, or cling to the outworn as it broke apart regardless. Resting her gaze on Death's face, Dinah was gradually drawn into the picture. Slowly, slowly she entered the image until she was standing directly before the foreboding figure cloaked in black. Dinah stared at Death, and Death stared back.

She was surprised at how calm she was, looking into the empty black eye sockets, at the hard yellowing face and menacing claw-like brown fingers wrapped tight around the scythe. "You don't scare me," she said firmly. "There is nothing frightening about you. It's only change and I accept your presence in the world in all your forms."

In response the skeleton face began to quiver, gently at first, merely a tremor. But as Dinah watched, the trembling became stronger and faster until, to her alarm, the whole figure was jerking violently. Pieces were breaking off. First a finger, then another and another, followed one by one by the ribs, dropping to the ground as the pelvic bone crumbled to dust. In horrified fascination, Dinah heard the spectre's jawbone crack and slacken, revealing even more of its large yellowing teeth, before this too fell to the floor and shattered. The neck went next, the head lolling to one side as the scythe clattered to the ground to join the mounting heap of bones at her feet. Then in a puff of grey dust the whole thing sharply caved in on itself.

When the air finally cleared, Dinah saw in its place a vast pillar of shining white light, so bright that she had to turn and shield her eyes. It was only as her vision adjusted that she could make out the figure of a male Angel within. He towered above her, enormous and strong, with magnificent wings spread wide. Yet there was a tenderness to him and although unable to see his face, Dinah knew he was radiantly beautiful. Waves of warmth and love emanated from him and somehow he felt familiar. Dinah wondered who he was. The Angel smiled and opened his arms to her, softly introducing himself as Azrael. The Angel of Death.

'Men fear death as if unquestionably the greatest evil,
and yet no man knows that it may not be the greatest good.'
William Mitford

It had been just two days shy of Dinah's eighteenth birthday when her father died while out shopping for her present – a platinum choker with a heart-shaped pendant. The heart attack that killed him was as fast as it was fatal, but was also strangely timely she remembered thinking, in that his passing coincided with her official 'coming of age' – marking the end of her childhood and the transition into adulthood.

She and her mother had rushed to the hospital, but he died in the ambulance on the way and no amount of resuscitation could persuade him to return. "So stubborn," her mother remarked tearfully. The events that followed were hazy. The hospital returned his belongings, including a parcel of pink tissue paper tied with pink ribbon. A stream of family and friends gathered to visit the body and make funeral arrangements. And a heap of white feathers appeared on the front lawn the day that he died, and remained until the funeral was over before mysteriously disappearing. There were strange dreams and an unseen hand soothing her brow as she tried to sleep, and the sweet smell of pipe tobacco that followed her through the house.

That year her birthday passed quietly by. All celebrations were cancelled by Dinah herself, including the planned dinner for forty and the music and dancing that was to have followed, despite her mother's plea that "Dad would want you to celebrate. He would want you to be happy." Dinah wasn't having it. Angry that he'd left without warning, it was here that she began to falter on her path, now viewing her life in two halves – before his death and after. The old Dinah had gone, perhaps with her father to exist elsewhere, and left floundering in her place was a new, bereaved Dinah, a wounded and furious version of her former self.

Life became an uncharacteristic whirl of clubs and parties, where her only concern was what to wear, the latest partner by her side, and the greeting of the mildest of acquaintances as long lost friends. Everything revolved around the pursuit of escapism – anything to blot out the turmoil within. It seemed the dark night of the soul was upon her and with faith put to one side and all spiritual inclinations discarded, the grip of isolation and fear was beginning to tighten.

It was that summer she met Jamie.

When her mother announced she was moving to rural Spain, wanting a new start and brighter climate, Dinah chose to stay behind, taking a waitressing job in a local restaurant instead. Jamie had come in for lunch one day with his cousin and sat at one of her tables. Dark and good-looking and outrageously flirtatious, he was a fashion photographer from London, and to Dinah's innocent eyes exuded glamour and charm. While she served their meal he chatted her up, eloquent and confident and all the while cajoling for a date. Although cautious at first, Dinah found him so persuasive that her resolve soon weakened. And so, before handing him his bill, she scribbled her number on the back. The other waitresses gasped with envy when they saw the size of her tip.

The king of romantic gestures, Jamie swept Dinah right off her feet. He was seven years older than her and showered her with gifts and flowers right from the start. He wanted to see her as often as possible and to know everything about her. On those days when they weren't together he would call morning and evening, wanting to know everything she had done while they were apart. Dinah was flattered. It was nice to be pursued by such a handsome and ardent admirer. He was attentive and thoughtful, often driving the miles from London to Lymington to surprise her at work and whisk her back to his flat in Hampstead, and he never tired of taking her to fashion shows and galas, parties and restaurants. His was a dazzling world filled with rich, successful people and Dinah was enthralled.

But, as their relationship progressed and the initial euphoria began to subside, she noticed things starting to dwindle. The calls became shorter and less frequent. The gifts stopped completely and he seemed more irritable than charming. More worryingly, she noticed how things were only well between them when they were doing what he wanted. If she dressed to impress, was sociable and entertaining and, most importantly, followed his lead, then they were good. But if she felt tired, vulnerable or in need of a hug, if she wanted to leave somewhere early or disagreed with him in any way, he quickly became distant and sulky. Behind closed doors the jovial, appealing charmer was controlling, critical, and moody. There were actually two Jamies, and for him life was about image, status and money. He was fun, but it was a hollow fun. Dinah saw how he drew people to him, and how they basked in the glory of his attention, just as she had. But his turnover of friends was high and, with alarm, she saw he only gave people time if they could do something for him. While Dinah came to terms with the fact that Jamie's only concern was himself, it was her mother who pointed out that he sounded "as if he has more than a touch of Narcissus about him, darling". And it wasn't just Jamie. With the rose-coloured glasses removed, Dinah detected similar energy in those who crowded around him. This connection needed to end before it went any further.

In a futile attempt to escape her own despair, she had been seduced by the most superficial trappings of the material world, and now found herself existing in a place where the light is devalued, and love and compassion considered worthless in the shadow of status and wealth. Yet even in her bleakest moments the Angels still called, reaching for her as she fell into the darkest of pits, reminding her that the flame of God always burns bright within. Dinah was aware of the inner flame they spoke of, yet sensed hers smothered in dense black fog.

It was during this time that she woke in the early hours to find something heavy pressing down on her chest. Caught between slumber and wakefulness, Dinah was blurrily aware of a terrible presence pinning her to the bed, as groggy with sleep she blinked her eyes open to find a grotesque old hag sitting on her chest. The old woman was bearing down so close that Dinah could make out every speck of dirt on her twisted grimy face. With stinking greasy hair and filthy pointed teeth, the hag was the thing of nightmares – radiating malevolence, small and hunched, yet heavy as a lead weight. The more Dinah came round the more she sensed evil in the room. She wanted to scream but no sound would come. Struggling for breath, she found she couldn't move a single part of her body. Trapped in the horror of sleep paralysis, desperate to escape but unable to move, Dinah was starting to panic. This only seemed to excite the hag even more, as squeaking with delight she bent closer to drool over her petrified prey.

Suddenly a bolt of light came from the left, fast and accurate. It knocked the hag off Dinah's chest sending her hurtling through the air with a screech of rage. Freed, Dinah shot bolt upright just in time to see the old woman disappear into thin air. With the hag's eerie wail ringing in her ears, she pulled up her knees and hugged herself tight.

Something extraordinary had occurred. Despite her recent neglect of spiritual practice her spiritual helpers had rescued her from the darkness. They had come in her time of need to fling evil back to the darkest depths of the etheric realms.

Dinah quickly fell back to sleep and her Guardian Angels entered her dreams. "No matter how far you stray from the path of love, nothing will turn God away from you."

The epiphany, which ultimately freed her from melancholy, came a few months later in a bookshop in London. Dinah was temping at a solicitors' in the east of the city and on this particular day had stopped at a bookstore on her way home. Wandering around the shop she was surprised to find herself in the spirituality section, and began absent-mindedly scanning the titles before half-heartedly pulling one out. The book had a pale blue cover, she didn't register its name, but when she opened the pages a word leaped out from the text:

'Self-love'.

"Oh!" The word struck something and for a moment she froze, unable to take her eyes off the letters. Self-love. What did it mean?

"It means to fully forgive and love myself," the revelation came. "To let myself off the hook for any self-perceived misdeeds, and to love myself as I wish others to love me."

It was so simple. The word was freedom – liberation from guilt, regret and sorrow, from anger, self-hate and unforgiveness. It was tempting, yet could she truly put all her burdensome baggage down?

God never left, Dinah understood. It was me who left. The Angels were singing and clapping their hands. Happiness is a choice. I can choose darkness and misery, anger and upset, or I can choose to be happy regardless of what goes on around me or what others may think I have or haven't done. I can choose joy and peace for myself because it's my decision to make.

Dinah's heart, long-since closed, blossomed and glowed with warmth. As heat spread through her chest, tears stung her eyes. Tears of forgiveness – for herself and for the ways of the world.

Not long after, Dinah was brushing her teeth one evening when the air shivered and her Guardian Angel was by her side, in an unusually solemn mood.

"You bear wounds from previous lifetimes, Dinah. And only by healing these wounds will you rediscover the truth of how life should be. Your descent into darkness was the very thing to initiate your return home and in this way you can know the dark as your friend. Through meeting the pain and going beyond it, the armour encasing you was shattered. You believed it protected your heart, yet it was a barrier to love, merely holding you in fear. When the armour is dissolved, when you are fearlessly open and exposed, then you are open to the wonder of life.'

Those sorrowful years spent in the abyss had seen Dinah grow in many ways – the qualities brought back from the depths of devastation now embodied in her being. As she emerged from the shadows back into the light, she saw these most difficult years were her greatest teacher. The journey through suffering, through the darkest valleys of her soul, had proved a necessary if uncomfortable springboard to greater self-knowledge. Such journeys have no guarantees, but those who face the demons within and conquer will be transformed.

* * *

From hereon, Dinah became aware of one particular male Angel often around her. He was protective and comforting and she talked to

63

him frequently, wanting to forge a stronger connection. He told her his name was Azrael and she felt safe with him, enjoying his soft presence and light-hearted touch. As their bond strengthened, Dinah understood Azrael was the Archangel who helps souls transition between the earth plane and afterlife and brings reassurance and healing to those left behind. And so, whenever Dinah heard of a tragedy or loss of life, either personally or on television or in the papers, she would request his help. By invoking Azrael this way, she knew that a recently released soul would receive all the assistance they needed for a smooth passage into the light, for a safe passage home.

Even when small, Dinah found death mysterious, like an unsolvable conundrum. What happened to the person or animal? Where did they go? Her first close experience was when their dog, Annie, died. Annie was old. They all knew it was coming, but it was a shock nonetheless to find her stiff and cold, lying in the lavender. Amidst the sadness, what struck Dinah most was Annie's lifeless body. It was now just a carcass, empty and heavy. Something had left and had gone elsewhere.

When she was young, Dinah hadn't associated the spirits she could feel and see with people who had died. It didn't occur to her that the noises, movements and other activities in the house, were linked to those who had left the earth plane. Often, she would be woken in the night by whispering or giggling, or a misty energy passing through her room. Sometimes she was curious and other times she would simply ask whatever it was to be quiet so she could go back to sleep. One night she awoke to find a woman at her bedside, gently stroking her cheek. It was only when the lady caressed her forehead that Dinah heard her mother's laughter coming from downstairs and realised the nice woman in her room was not Mummy. Unexplainable loud bangs and cracks, lights turning on and off by themselves, packs of playing cards splayed on the living room floor when no one was home but herself, putting something down for a moment only to turn and discover it gone. This was all part of the everyday. Nothing unusual for Dinah, it was just how it was. She knew when someone invisible was nearby, and she knew when something unkind was trying to frighten her. Sometimes she would succumb to fear and run away, but usually she would stand strong and demand it show itself to her. And as she knew would happen, in the face of her courage it would lose its power and vanish back to wherever it had come from. She was never sure, where that might be.

Many years later, whilst attending a spiritual convention, Dinah heard one of the speakers telling a story of a professional cameraman, who could also see spirits. He had been commissioned to film a skydiver jumping from a plane. On the day, the cameraman went first, releasing his parachute to wait for the skydiver to follow, but when the skydiver jumped and pulled the cord to open his parachute, nothing happened. To the horror of onlookers he plummeted to earth. Pandemonium ensued as people screamed and ambulances were called, but what the cameraman saw told a different story. While the skydiver's physical body did indeed plummet to the ground, the cameraman saw his spirit leave before he hit the earth. The spirit looked joyous and liberated and realising the cameraman could see him, gave a cheery wave before peacefully fading into the sky. While the cameraman witnessed a jubilant release, the crowd perceived a horrific tragedy.

From the kitchen, Dinah could hear the television going in the next room. Daniel and Luke were watching one of their shows. The death card was still in her hand, once more depicting the skeleton holding its scythe.

Death of an outmoded way of being was what she was experiencing. Change in any form requires emotional readjustment and Dinah knew this was the time to increase her spiritual practice: yoga, meditation and prayers, to stay in consistent communion with the Divine – God, the Angels and the Spirit Guides. She felt them easily in the quiet of her home, their soft loving touch, which always came when needed. When going through a period of upheaval, the Angel way is to light up the path ahead, one step at a time, each step requiring faith that she was going in the right direction.

"I've taken the biggest leap, Angels," Dinah sent out. "I'm here in Porrick. I've left my old life. I've done it." She was suddenly amazed. "I wonder what else can I do?"

Eight

With stooped shoulders and hands pushed deep into his coat pockets, Nathaniel cut a pensive figure as he strode to the shop for cigarettes. The previous night had taken an unexpected turn and he wasn't exactly sure why he had behaved as he did. He'd only planned a quick drink after work before going home for an early night.

The music wasn't up to much in the bar they'd been in, too folky for his taste, but the two women vying for his attention soon distracted him. Both were attractive in different ways. The curly haired brunette, Cassie, was petite and flirtatious, making it clear from the outset that she was interested in more than just conversation, taking every opportunity to brush against him. Her friend was tall and quiet. With elegant long limbs, doe eyes and sleek blonde hair, she initially gave the impression of being rather reserved. Yet as the evening wore on and the drinks flowed, the glances she cast him became increasingly seductive, her hand lingering on his arm, and under cover of the table, her leg pressing against his.

When the women first approached his friends were quick to show their wedding bands, and as the evening progressed they disappeared one by one back home to their wives and children. But Nathaniel had no such commitments and fuelled by alcohol he was starting to enjoy Cassie stroking his face and the way her friend hung on his every word.

Cassie won out in the end, kissing his neck as they danced, before pushing her tongue firmly into his mouth. He hadn't objected. And when at the end of the evening she had wrapped her arms around his waist and asked if he lived nearby, his only thought was, "Why not?" He was happy to go along with it. She was nice enough, entertaining company and he was a free man.

They bantered easily as they walked to his place, Cassie proving a worthy match for his gentle teasing, her eyes alight with anticipation.

Once inside, she insisted he put on some music and then in perfect time to the melody, removed her clothing piece by piece. Fluidly slipping off her dress she deftly unhooked her bra and dropped it to the floor. In just her knickers, she had given a coy flourish before bending over to wriggle out of them and stand naked before him.

As he emerged from the shop with his cigarettes, Nathaniel stopped short. A woman was coming up the high street pushing an old bicycle and heading straight for him. He couldn't take his eyes off her and each step she took was bringing her closer to him. Drawn by his scrutiny the woman glanced at him with a friendly smile, but as their eyes made contact, the smile froze and then wavered, before finally giving way to a frown. He wasn't behaving normally he knew, staring like a fool, but he couldn't help it, he couldn't move. Even as she scowled at him the deep blue of her eyes appeared lit from inside.

All his focus was on her and now she was agitated, impatiently brushing her hair from her face and pointedly turning her back on him. Only a few feet away from where he stood, she propped her bike against the wall and taking a bag from the basket, slung it over her shoulder before stalking past him and heading down the alley that led to the library.

Despite a powerful impulse to reach out and touch her as she passed, Nathaniel sensed this was not a good idea. Instead, he drank in everything about her, every tiny detail from her oval face and slim frame to her pale skin and the way her smooth chestnut hair fell to her shoulders. Why had he never seen her before? He would remember, surely? So she must be new in the town or maybe on holiday or visiting friends?

The woman had disappeared through the library doors without bothering to lock up her bike and without giving him a second glance. He went after her. Later, when reflecting back on the day, he was amazed how he had pursued with no regard as to what he would say or do when he got to her. All consideration for social etiquette vanished as he rushed after her.

Inside the library, in the studious stillness, an old man with fluffy white hair sat at a table poring over a newspaper. There was no sign of her though. Wandering the aisles of bookshelves, Nathaniel scanned every face until around a corner he found her settling at one of the computers. She turned as he approached and looked directly at him. Their eyes locked and she started, before sharply turning away. As if drawn by an invisible thread, Nathaniel found himself standing behind her chair, his hands resting on its back. They didn't speak, but for a moment were held captive in some strange ball of energy. Nathaniel couldn't think straight. It was as if they were adrift underwater, a force much stronger than them in play, binding them together.

Her fingers clutched the keyboard as she regarded him sideways. The scowl was back, but Nathaniel only cared about the dark tendril of hair falling across her cheek and how he wanted to touch it. Instead he felt a jab of anxiety and sensing it came from her, he stepped back. She's threatened, he realised. Another step away and she twisted in her chair, displeasure shadowing her face.

The people nearest them were starting to stare, sensing something going on in their corner of the library. Reluctantly, Nathaniel knew he must go. He was sorry to have frightened her and regretful at making such a clumsy approach. At the door he turned to see she had gone back to whatever she was doing as if nothing had happened. His heart dropped a little.

Once outside, Nathaniel made a snap decision to go to the café opposite and wait for her to reappear. He'd never considered himself a watching and waiting type before, but he wanted to get another look and as luck would have it there was a free table in the window.

Hanging his coat on one of the chairs he ordered an espresso at the counter – all without once taking his eyes from the entrance to the alley.

It turned out he didn't have long to wait. Just as he sat down with his coffee, the woman gingerly emerged, looking cautiously around. Nathaniel smiled. She looked relaxed again, but was blatantly scanning the street, looking up and down, eyes searching. When her gaze fell on the café she froze. Nathaniel held his breath. She was staring at the café window with a bewildered expression, at the very place where he sat. Then with a shake of her head she climbed onto the bike and cycled off down the high street.

Dinah's heart thumped ferociously as she pedalled. What on earth was that? she wondered.

The unexpected meeting had thrown her, but undeniably left her exhilarated. At the bottom of the hill she stopped to catch herself, to catch her breath. She was certain the mysterious man was watching as she came out of the library. She could feel him. Applying the brakes, Dinah took her feet off the pedals and hopped off the bike.

"Damn! Who is he, Angels?" she muttered, starting to walk. "And why did I shut down at that precise moment?"

The whole world had disappeared apart from the two of them. Two people connecting in the library of all places, but he hadn't felt like a stranger, not at all.

Energetic connections could feel intense, but this one was like walking into a wall. As she crossed the road Dinah wondered if she would see him again. He could easily be passing through. People came and went all the time in Porrick.

In her mind's eye she could picture his clear brown eyes, and the way his sandy brown hair was streaked with grey and curled around his temples. All other facial features eluded her, but there was an air about him, a confidence, and he was tall, more than six foot. "Would I know him if we met again?" She needed somewhere quiet so she could hear the Angels.

Back on the bike again she headed for the river meadows. Despite the chill she was hot and flushed as she cycled along the path that ran along the water's edge.

There was a bench at the end of the path, a peaceful spot to sit as not many walkers ventured this far up. Dinah propped the bike against a tree and sat down on the riverbank, gazing across the stark landscape, over the water to the hills on the far side.

"Who is he, Angels?" she asked, deliberately focusing her attention inside.

"He meant no harm," came the reply. "He was sorry to scare you and would like to know you."

Dinah sat patiently, quietly, willing further information to come. But after ten or so minutes with nothing else forthcoming, she had to concede she'd had her lot. It seemed trust was the only option.

* * *

69

Romance had been lingering in Dinah's thoughts for a few days now. She'd been feeling slightly despondent, wondering if she should take action to attract a meaningful relationship or if it really was a matter of leaving it to destiny.

Daniel and Luke were with friends for the afternoon and so with some time to herself she had cleaned the kitchen and mopped the floor. Now she was looking forward to an afternoon of meditation.

In the sitting room Dinah lit some incense and placed a cushion on the floor. Settling onto it she called to the Angels. "What can I do to attract romance?"

The air chilled and she was surrounded by many Angels, each one sending out dazzling radiant light. As they drew near it was like being engulfed in a soft blanket. Warmth spread through her, obliterating her cares and worrisome thoughts.

"I will meet someone special soon," she said firmly, but without conviction. "A genuine bond of intimacy and sharing. A relationship that brings growth through joy and happiness. There is someone coming, Angels? Surely?"

"Patience." The reply came through strong, and she had to stifle a groan.

They were stroking her hair and she knew they didn't like seeing her so doubtful. A whisper. "Ask Ambrika what she saw."

Dinah let the message sink in. When she finally bowed her head and came out of meditation, the incense was completely burned away. Thanking the Angels for their protection and support, she mulled over the message.

"Hmm. Ask Ambrika..." She was intrigued.

Getting up, she went into the hallway to find her bag which was hanging on the bannisters. Rummaging inside, Dinah located her mobile and purse and sat on the bottom stair to look for Ambrika's card. It was tucked inside one of the side pockets. She hadn't seen or heard anything of Ambrika since that first night in Porrick. She'd assumed they would cross paths eventually, but it hadn't happened yet, which was surprising in such a small town. The golden card had a white feather in one corner and was written in swirly black writing.

Ambrika.
Divine Teacher, Healer and Communicator
Group work and individual sessions catered for.
Please call to discuss

There was a telephone number on the back. Dinah fingered the card thoughtfully. Her Angel had told her to ask, but it felt odd phoning up a virtual stranger to ask her what she had seen.

There was a strong connection between us and Ambrika was behaving very knowingly, she told herself. And she did say to call if I needed anything at all.

Steeling herself she dialled the number anyway. There was a reason for all this she was sure. As the phone started ringing her stomach lurched.

"Hello." It was Ambrika's voice.

"Ambrika, it's Dinah."

Silence.

"I met you in the café the day I moved to Porrick, a while back now. I had my two boys with me... We chatted. You gave me your card."

"Yes, yes, Dinah, I know who you are. How could I forget?"

"Oh!" said Dinah, taken aback. "I was wondering if I could come and see you? It feels important. That sounds silly I know but..."

"Not silly, Dinah. You're right. It is important. When can you come?"

"Oh!" Dinah was surprised by Ambrika's directness. "As soon as possible, when's good for you?"

"I'm full for the rest of this week but could do next Thursday, ten o'clock? We'd have about two hours."

"Perfect," said Dinah, not entirely sure what she was committing to.

"It is perfect, yes," said Ambrika matter-of-factly, before giving Dinah precise directions to her house.

"Do you know what you would like from the session? Or are we allowing Spirit to lead?"

"Well, I wanted guidance on a few things," said Dinah, feeling desperation rising. She wanted reassurance from someone else that

71

her faith was justified. That she was on the right path and that there was cause to be hopeful.

"I need direction I guess. It would ease my mind and—"

"Dinah, Spirit looks after us," Ambrika interrupted abruptly. "When a door closes on us it is for good reason, and if you keep knocking on that door, persisting, you'll find when it opens again that there's a monster behind it!"

"Oh!" exclaimed Dinah again, not sure what else to say.

"I'll see you Thursday then," said Ambrika, cheerfully. "Take care." She'd gone.

Dinah rested her chin in her hands. That was strange. The Angels always urged her to take heed when doors closed and to allow them to shut with grace. To try and force them open again was never a good idea. You were supposed to be open to new beginnings instead, which was fine in theory, except when it came to matters of the heart, where traditionally she struggled. Dinah had lost count of the number of times she had ignored all the warnings and red flags and tried to reignite a failed relationship. Hopefully giving it just one more go, bending over backwards to try and make it work, while deep down knowing it was futile. Intellectually she could grasp the wisdom of allowing a flawed relationship to come to its natural end, but her emotions often got the better of her, encouraging her to keep going.

In the sitting room, Dinah picked up the cushion from the floor and flung it onto the sofa. As it sailed through the air, a face flashed in her mind's eye – a girl, laughing and carefree, with long golden hair. She was smiling, happy. Two hands holding onto each other, a man and a woman, fingers intertwined. The cushion landed and the vision stopped.

Dinah froze. A memory was surfacing. I know that girl! She searched inwardly, but there was only the still.

* * *

With the directions scribbled on the back of an old envelope, Dinah set off for Ambrika's. It would take no more than ten minutes to walk and, despite the amount of rain they'd had and the lingering dampness of the past week, today was fresh and sunny.

Crossing over the bridge she turned right at the corner store and followed the road to the end. Rows of old stone terrace houses lined the streets and there were plenty of trees and bushes, giving this part of town a rural feel. At the end of the street, Dinah turned into Somerset Crescent and found number three on the right. She hadn't been here before and noticed the clear, welcoming feel of the street. The residents obviously took pride in their homes and the love and positive energy was tangible. Nearly all the houses had window boxes, filled with plants and flowers even though it was November. The front-gardens were well tended, some of them transformed into vegetable plots filled with cauliflowers, leeks and Brussels sprouts.

A beautiful street, thought Dinah, wondering how much this had to do with Ambrika.

The front door to number three was dark green with a gleaming brass knocker, which Dinah rapped a few times before standing back. From inside there came the sound of footsteps scurrying down a corridor before the door swung open to reveal Ambrika in a flowing red dress. Again Dinah was struck again by the intensity of her smiling blue eyes and how with her sleek black hair she looked every bit the archetypal Goddess. She pulled Dinah into a hug. "Good to see you. Come in."

Everything inside was as neat and welcoming as out. The stripped wooden floorboards shone and a colourful stripy runner ran all the way up the stairs, at the top of which a magnificent ornately framed gilt mirror hung. After taking Dinah's coat and hanging it on a peg by the door, Ambrika led her into the sitting room. The fire was lit and the air was sweet with the smell of patchouli oil. On the windowsill a sizeable sphere of pearly white crystal sat next to a large pot of pink cyclamen.

"Selenite," said Ambrika, following Dinah's gaze. "To bring balance and mental clarity." She motioned for Dinah to take the sofa nearest the fire.

"So how have you been?" she asked.

"Well," said Dinah, "happy to be in Porrick."

"I knew you would be. The energy here can be difficult for newcomers, but you feel a fit. I knew it as soon as I saw you. Porrick has something for you. I feel it. You've got reason to be hopeful."

Dinah grinned. "I feel a fit. I know we're in the right place." Slipping off her shoes she folded her legs underneath her on the couch. She already felt at home.

They smiled at each other and again Dinah felt the same surge of familiarity she'd experienced when she talked to Ambrika in the restaurant. They had only met briefly a few weeks ago, but there was something else, something more.

"I know you," she said, surprising herself.

Ambrika's smile widened. She was watching Dinah with such love and understanding that Dinah was confused. She had known this woman before, she was suddenly sure of it, and yet she didn't know when they would have come across each other or where. The air in the room thickened.

"Dinah, I recognised you immediately. The minute I saw you. We've been together in other lifetimes."

Dinah was speechless.

"I know you recognise your gift," Ambrika went on. "You were born knowing and it is part of your purpose here and mine. It's part of our reason for being, but you have yet to fully discover who you are. Perhaps I can give you another piece of your jigsaw puzzle?" Seeing the confusion in Dinah's eyes, she hesitated. For a moment they gazed at each other in silence.

Dinah could feel tears coming. They were tears of having found something important which she hadn't even known she'd been looking for. They started in her belly and then welled into her heart, constricting her throat, catching her breath, until overflowing they spilled down her cheeks.

Ambrika didn't move.

"I've always felt different," whispered Dinah. "But I never knew why. I see and hear and feel things that others don't seem to. I know how to do things without being taught; rituals and healing that no one has shown me. I hear the natural world speak and I feel people's energy."

The tears halted as suddenly as they had appeared, but she was shaking. "I'm burning inside. The heat is so strong – it's all I can do not to burst."

Ambrika nodded understandingly.

"It feels as though nobody wants what I have to offer. They don't recognise me or see me. They don't want to hear. I carry my gifts, I honour and treasure them and want to share, but I don't know how. I feel frantic with this need to speak and be heard."

Ambrika got up and came to sit beside her. "You're right where you need to be, Dinah. You don't need to worry. God is with you all the time." She took her hand. "And you've lots of Angels around you."

Dinah couldn't help smiling. "God and the Angels carry me through," she replied. "I don't know what I'd do without them." The Angels were crowding round her now, pressing into her, and from the look of wonderment on Ambrika's face she could see them. "They say it is time for you to live your truth," Ambrika said haltingly. "To summon your courage and step out into the world, and to trust that the Divine will always comfort and lead you, to trust that you are eternally held and protected and no harm can befall you."

From the soothing momentum of her words, Dinah sensed they were coming from spirit.

"But why is there so much fear in me, Ambrika? Why do I feel so unsafe and unsure?" She was shocked to realise that she was begging for answers – again that feeling of desperation. "Why do I care so much about being accepted, about not wanting to upset? Why am I so terrified of anger and negativity?"

Ambrika put an arm around her.

"The world has been dark for a long, long time and for people like us, and there are many, it has been a hostile place to be. We speak of Spirit and connection, we know the ancient wisdom, the keys to existence, and many have been frightened of us through the ages. Frightened of our power, which they did not understand. They lived in fear, while we lived in love, and for a time we were hated for it."

Dinah's breath quickened.

"You are a seer, Dinah, a wise woman, as am I," continued Ambrika. "Yet we have suffered for our craft. For centuries the world has repressed the divine feminine. She has been crushed and almost destroyed, burned as a witch, tortured for heresy, condemned as a madwoman or labelled a whore. She was considered dangerous to those in power, a threat to the male rule, and an influence to be eradicated or beaten into submission."

There was a twisting in Dinah's gut, a wrench tugging at her insides and she leaned forward to ease it, one hand clasping her belly.

Ambrika's voice was gentle. "Woman has been forced to deny her true self in fear for her very life. Her natural gifts of intuition, healing and prophecy were devalued during the patriarchy of the last few thousand years, when the masculine values of intelligence, logic, strength and power reigned supreme. The masculine shunned the subtler qualities of the feminine throughout this period, choosing instead to demean and belittle her. Woman has been kept small and insignificant as sister was pitted against sister in a battle for survival, but many of us refused point-blank to stand down and this is why we carry such depth of pain."

The burning sensation in Dinah's stomach was building, a cauldron of fire spluttering in her belly. Every word Ambrika spoke confirming what she already knew to be true and now the fire was raging; bubbling and growing, hotter and hotter until it crackled sparks across her chest. She shuddered and clutched her sides, gasping for air.

"Life after life, Dinah, we held firm in our beliefs and life after life we have paid for it – many times." Ambrika's voice dropped as she squeezed Dinah's hand. "On many occasions, we paid most brutally."

Unable to hold herself any longer Dinah bent double as a screech of anguish exploded from between her lips. She was sobbing and shaking as grief wracked her body. Feelings and images swam through her and Dinah trembled as vivid and real, brutal and harsh, they told the tale of the persecution of Woman down through the ages. And it was a barbaric tale – one of repression and terror, of misunderstanding and of being misunderstood, of betrayal and accusation, fear and humiliation.

Everywhere Dinah now looked she saw the devaluation of Women. It was in the deadened heart of the prostitute as she lay down to sell her most precious gift. It was in the faces of clever shining women, ignored by their society or battered into submission. It was in the young girl's hunched bodies as they cowered in fear, unable to protect themselves against the burly men who come for them. It was in the scream of the innocent – burned, stoned or drowned for witchcraft. It was in the monotonous routine of the housewife, forced to cast aside her identity and depend on her husband, to be subservient to his every whim.

And it was in the self-loathing of modern Western woman, conditioned to perform for the male hierarchy, to deny her natural self and believe her face, body and hair were never good enough, that she must cover her skin in strange fake colour, be cut open wide to grow her breasts, shrink her thighs or smooth her skin, to smile and pout, shimmy and giggle, all the while subduing and denying her wild, instinctive, creative self.

It was in the agony of female genital mutilation and in the terror of young girls forced into wedlock with much older men.

It seemed that contempt and disgust of Woman was embedded in the psyche of the world.

The revelations flowed like a horrifying history lesson and Dinah jerked in pain and disbelief, an unwilling pupil witnessing the truth of humanity; the agony, the torture, the terror and the perpetrators' glee, the broken hearts, the wounding, her wound, buried deep inside but now ripped open, ragged, bleeding and raw, time and time and time again. Throughout the turmoil, Ambrika stayed near. Holding her hand, waiting for the chaos to subside.

The burning pain in Dinah's chest was lessening and she was starting to regain control of her breath. Her eyes were red and sore and she was exhausted, but jubilant. The dramatic explosion of spiritual insight had come from nowhere and taken all her strength, yet confusion and fear was now replaced with clarity.

Ambrika stroked Dinah's hair. "Have hope Dinah. Things are changing. There is no more persecution for people like us, not as we have suffered in the past. We are untouchable in this world and the time has come to shine our light. It is our reason for being alive. It is no longer only a man's world. Women are slowly regaining their footing, finding their strength and living their truth, and although there is still a way to go, the pendulum is swinging and Woman is rising again, reborn from the ashes of her destruction. She has endured and survived and is alight with potential. The world, the planet, is reaching for a higher way of being now and it is Women who will save us all.

"God made the masculine and feminine equal in all ways and Women are hearing the call to embrace their power. It is instinctive and cannot be denied. The feminine energy of gentle unyielding nurturing power will save humankind and the Earth. Woman will bring balance to the out of control male energy, soothing the archetypal ego-led male warrior and bringing peace to Earth once more. There may be disturbance as the old is shaken off and the new world emerges from the darkness, but when the darkness does release its grip, joy will follow."

Dinah was glowing. "I know you're right and I know I'm safe. I've never felt so safe before, not in this life."

The woman who had knocked on Ambrika's door only moments earlier was no more, and in her place was someone strong and courageous. Someone who had seen the traumas and cruelties, inflicted without mercy. Now she was being offered a gift, an opportunity to accept and forgive. This understanding gave her power and quite suddenly Dinah was no longer afraid. She would never go back to what she was before. Now she could see.

Nine

With a brown paper bag in one hand, Dinah selected six of the plumpest oranges she could find on the stall. Porrick market was always busy but today was exceptionally so, and having paid the stallholder she turned to find a queue of people crowding behind her. Tucking the oranges into her bag, Dinah manoeuvred her way to the bread stall next door. It was then that the back of her neck started to tingle and her face flushed hot. Someone was watching.

Spinning around she scanned the throng of Saturday shoppers hoping to pinpoint the source, and eventually spotted Ambrika standing just a few feet away and staring at her with a mischievous grin. The pull to go to her was so strong that Dinah's feet walked towards her as if they had a mind of their own. By the time she got to Ambrika, her cheeks were flaming red. Ambrika smiled and put down her bag to open her arms for a hug.

"How've you been?" she asked, laughter sparkling in her eyes. "I thought I'd see you sooner than this. I wanted to make sure you were alright."

"Everything's good, thank you," said Dinah, fanning her face with her hand. The heat was starting to diminish. "I feel different since we talked, more settled and peaceful. It's as if knowing something of my past, where I've come from... I don't know... I just feel better."

Ambrika took her hand. "Tea?" she suggested.

"Yes please," said Dinah.

"I have something to tell you actually. Shall we meet at my house in an hour? I've still got few things to pick up in town."

Mystified, Dinah agreed.

The door was ajar when she arrived and, pushing it open, she saw Ambrika peering round the kitchen door. "Come in, come in. I'm just boiling the kettle."

Once more Dinah was drawn into the warmth and comfort of Ambrika's house. The fire was blazing in the front room and this time the scent of lemons filled the air. Taking off her shoes, Dinah snuggled into the squashy sofa. A blanket was folded over the arm and Ambrika unfolded it and floated it over her. "It's a blessing to be cosy when it's cold and grey outside, don't you think?"

While Ambrika went to make tea Dinah sat quietly, pulling the blanket snugly around her and gazing idly into the fire. It was so tranquil here and she was so relaxed. The heat from the fire was making her drowsy, her eyelids growing heavy, wanting to close. The flames were getting bigger; brilliant oranges, reds and golden white, twisting and leaping in the fireplace, and the longer Dinah watched, the more she imagined she could see shapes appearing – vague outlines of hazy forms dancing through the flames. She sat up sharply, rubbing her eyes and blinking before looking back into the flames. Now the figures were even clearer, indeed, they seemed to be solidifying within the blaze. Fire faeries! The salamanders! She was transfixed. There, just for a moment, a young woman's face beaming out of the fire at her with a kindly expression, as behind her a long writhing dragon coiled between the logs, twisting and turning, until with a flick of its tail it darted into the embers. Dinah leaned nearer. A group of little people were circle dancing, men and women and children too; miniature folk with flaming yellow hair, burning red clothes and pointy fire faces. Holding hands they spun around and around, bobbing and skipping, their echoing laughter shimmering into the room. Completely entranced, Dinah crept closer to the hearth until she was kneeling before it. She wondered if she dared send her own energy into the fire, knowing well that fire faery magic is a force to be reckoned with, capable of great destruction as well as creation, and with potential to wreak havoc if not treated with due care.

Having never met a fire faery before, Dinah tentatively introduced herself before asking if they were willing to communicate. She knew she had been graced with a connection when a surge of fiery happiness pulsed through her and one of the womenfolk looked up and waved.

Salamanders are playful and cheeky by nature, intelligent and quick and with a touch of disdain for their cumbersome human counterparts. These salamanders however, were giggling excitedly, causing sparks to crackle in the depths of the flames and making Dinah laugh out loud. The smile on her face grew wider still as they gleefully continued their dance, glancing her way every now and again, as if inviting her to come further into their fiery world. Their curiosity at this human contact was tangible and she shivered with delight. Dinah remembered that with the faeries it is better to communicate with emotion, as words can easily be misunderstood and prove a block to successful relations. So, she sent her feelings into the fire, politely requesting that they inflame her passion for life and ignite her creative spirit. These most enigmatic of elementals have the power to bestow inspiration and motivation on a human soul, often with spectacularly speedy results. Where apathy has set in or the sparkle of life has dulled, they can bring forth creative solutions and the desire to live life to the full.

While Dinah basked in their warmth she sensed another presence beside her, a human form. Ambrika had returned and was joining her in communion with the faeries. Dinah saw rays of silver light spilling from the fire and engulfing them both, sparks of merriment and love so strong that it can penetrate the darkest of hearts and most closed of minds. Powerful surges of life force pulsed through her. "Ahhh…" she sighed, closing her eyes.

Who knows how long they stayed this way. It felt like an age and when she eventually opened her eyes again the faeries were gone and only the crackling flames remained. Dinah silently bade them farewell, and knowing that it never pays to slight a fire faery, thanked them most profusely.

"That was magical," whispered Ambrika, her eyes glittering with light. "They don't often show themselves, I think they find us humans rather slow and clumsy!"

After an appropriate pause to readjust to their earthly surroundings, they got up from the floor and moved to the sofa.

It was Ambrika who broke the silence. "I told you about the spiritual gatherings I hold?"

81

Dinah nodded.

"Well you'd be welcome to join us. I've a feeling you might find it helpful."

"I'd love to! Thank you!" replied Dinah, thrilled.

"Good." Ambrika looked pleased. "I've also been told something of what is coming up for you and wanted to share. It came through quite spontaneously while I was washing up, so must be important."

Dinah nodded again, curious.

"I was told that two possible opportunities are coming your way and it is for you to choose, which is right for you." She closed her eyes. "One will be a battle, offering the chance to experience hard-won love through inner conflict and external struggle. The other could easily be disregarded, but has subtler qualities, which at present lie dormant. Both bring the chance for learning and growth, but only one has the potential to blossom into something that many only dream of."

Dinah's heart was beating fast. "Are you talking about a partner? About love?"

Ambrika's eyelids flickered. "They say you've given up on romantic love, even though your heart and soul is filled with longing. They say you must be prepared to risk your heart to find what you so desire. Both these energies will be strong and they come for a purpose, to show you something about yourself. Both have something to offer but the outcome is not set in stone. You are in charge of your destiny and the only requirement is to open your heart."

Ambrika inhaled slowly.

"That's amazing, Ambrika, thank you," exclaimed Dinah. "And thank you to your guides or whoever brought the message." Immediately she tingled from head to toe.

Ambrika eyes were open again and she was watching her.

"You are lucky. I almost feel a little jealous," she smiled, slightly sadly, Dinah thought.

"Do you have someone special?" she asked gently.

"Not right now." Her friend looked down at her hands. "But I did have, although he's long gone now. We were together for many years before life moved him on – his choice, not mine. I loved him very much and we did part as friends, but my heart was broken. It still aches" – she put her hand to her chest – "and I haven't met anyone since."

She sounded so resigned and defeated that Dinah took her hand.

"He was a healer." Ambrika stretched her legs out from under her, placing her feet on the ground. "I'm from Croatia originally, and me and Rafael come from the same village. We were childhood sweethearts, went to school together and came to England together to begin a new life, maybe start a family. I was lucky enough to find work quickly and Rafael joined a devotional group with an Indian teacher. They saw his gift straight away and he became a leader at the centre."

Dinah was still.

"He was very involved, but for me it had no appeal. Lots of people passed through their doors and then a girl from Russia arrived, Sima, a little younger than me and quite beautiful, warm and friendly, a truly open heart. Often she would come for supper and I liked her, she felt like a sister. You can guess what happened."

Dinah nodded, serious.

"It took a while for me to admit they had become lovers. When I confronted Rafael, he was distraught, they both were, but they said it was love. I would have forgiven him if he had let her go, but it was not to be. They left together a few weeks later. I never saw him again."

Her eyes met Dinah's.

"That's when I left London and came to Porrick. I have tried to be with other men, to make it work, but it never has because it wasn't real. Do you see?"

"Yes," said Dinah, sadly. "Letting go when you're still in love is painful, as is the sting of rejection when another's involved. It's hard not to blame, not to hate. I'm also disillusioned with romantic love and no matter how I try to stay positive, nothing worthwhile seems to materialise. I've had disappointment after disappointment since Solus and it's always the same – lifted hopes and soaring spirits, and then crashing down into the reality of dysfunction or plain incompatibility. Now I want someone who is truly meant for me and nothing else will do – though I sometimes wonder if this means I will stay single for ever."

Ambrika looked wistful. "Well, from the sound of things you'll be having fun soon enough. And with a choice to be made!"

Ten

Standing on her yoga mat, Dinah invoked the Devas – tiny elemental light beings who oversee health and wellbeing – to oversee her practice.

The new yoga class had renewed her enthusiasm for her own practice and was reawakening her wonder at the magic to be found inside the human body. As she gently moved through the postures, she reflected that despite her concerns about the teacher and his odd manner, her practice was flowing beautifully and she was enjoying the depth of self-discovery to be found at his class.

Just as she was descending from a headstand, Dinah heard the front door slam followed by the clatter of feet coming up the corridor. Daniel and Luke burst into the room.

"Hi Mum," they chorused.

Perfect timing!

That night, Dinah dreamed she was wandering through a forest, a beautiful, pine forest where dappled sunshine fell on the path at her feet. It was soft and still and she was happy to be in such a place, gazing around and breathing in the warm air and woody aroma of pine resin. As she walked along the pathway, drifting through the trees, she was at peace with herself and the beauty of her surroundings.

Then with a start she saw a figure on the path just ahead of her. Though he wore a dark green cloak, which reached to the floor and his face was concealed by the hood, she knew it was the yoga teacher. He was completely still and yet his presence seemed to obscure everything else, as if of no consequence. Dinah was puzzled. Now the dream was all about him.

For a moment they were both unmoving until quite suddenly he threw back his hood to show his face. Dinah was frozen to the spot as their eyes locked. Incapable of looking away, warmth exploded in her heart and body, a sensation so strong it was almost overwhelming. He was smiling, more to himself than at her, with a veiled expression she was unable to read. And when he opened his arms she went straight to him as if propelled by some external force. With every step she took she noticed the energy getting stronger, the strange pulse of connection washing between them, drawing her to him and leaving her breathless until finally she fell into his arms. As Tony pulled her close, the energy intensified; an erotic charge building, stronger and stronger until she was writhing in his arms, powerless to prevent herself from moaning in pleasure.

In her dream state Dinah knew she had lost control, that something bigger was in charge and there was no option but to succumb. Yet the next moment she was falling, legs turned to rubber, unable to speak or stand as she slipped from his arms. Desperately she grabbed at him, clutching at his cloak to try and stop her fall, but nothing could be done, the material only slipped through her grasp.

Tony held her hands as she fell. Controlling her descent as, bereft of all thought, she slumped to the ground.

Sitting bolt upright in bed, Dinah gasped for air. Wide-eyed and heart hammering she looked wildly about her.

In the darkened room she could just make out familiar objects – the bedside lamp, the chest of drawers, the wardrobe. She was in bed. Reaching for the lamp she switched it on, and as light illuminated the room she saw Sophie curled up in her basket staring at her enquiringly.

Relief swept over her. Of course it had been a dream, but no dream had ever been so intense, so charged with feeling and emotion. This was of a different quality altogether. Getting out of bed, Dinah rubbed her feet on the carpet to make sure she was fully awake.

Why was Tony there? His presence had been so strong and the whole thing so real, too real, to be only a product of her subconscious. Although souls often meet in dreamtime – to communicate on a higher level than the waking mind allows – this dream felt wrong.

Climbing back under the covers it struck Dinah that Tony may have orchestrated the whole thing. The thought shocked her. While dream travel into another person's psychic space is a healthy and natural occurrence, it becomes more sinister when someone with higher awareness and conscious intent enters another's domain uninvited.

Uninvited being the key word! Dinah thought crossly.

If Tony had intentionally infiltrated her sleep, while she was vulnerable and susceptible, that would make it psychic invasion and that in turn would show his utter disregard for others' privacy and free will. Turning off the light, she lay back in bed. She was calmer, but the suspicion that this had been no accident persisted.

But why would he? She was bewildered. To demonstrate his spiritual prowess? To prove he is a force to be reckoned with?

The notion that he had found a way in, despite her self-professed expertise in psychic protection, made Dinah anxious. But before she had the chance to tip into fully-fledged panic, she was engulfed in warmth.

"You are safe, Dinah," her Angel murmured into her mind. "He sees you, that is all. You are always safe."

With the darkness and warmth of the Angels lulling her into slumber, Dinah recalled how Tony had controlled her within her own dream. Although it frightened her, she could not deny it had felt incredible, like nothing she suspected could even exist.

"I'm not sure of him," she sent out sleepily. "How do I know he is trustworthy?" If nothing else she would take it as a wake-up call to be more scrupulous with her spiritual protection and bedtime prayers. "Trust I'm safe," she reassured herself before drifting back into sleep.

* * *

Nathaniel was in his pyjamas making coffee in the kitchen while he waited for the computer to boot up. It was just after ten at night and he was expecting an email from his business partner giving the schedule for their meeting later that week. The proposal was for a development of thirty eco-friendly houses and a boutique green hotel, an hour from Málaga and set amidst almond groves overlooking the sea. All interested parties were gathering on site on Friday to finalise the figures and sign off the paperwork and Nathaniel was keen to get started. He was excited. It was a big project for him and Ed.

86

Taking his mug through to the office, he sat down at the desk and began to trawl through his inbox. He'd just located the email when the buzzer in his flat rang for the main door downstairs.

Who an earth was that calling so late? He ignored it and started to read. He had high hopes for this project. It had a lot of potential and apart from proving that sustainable building on this scale was viable, it could make them a tidy sum. The buzzer rang again, for longer this time, and again, Nathanial ignored it. Whoever it was would have to come back tomorrow, now wasn't a good time. He carried on reading and found that everything was in place. Hopefully, Friday would only involve tying up one or two loose ends.

A few minutes later the buzzer went for a third time and this time didn't stop. Someone was holding the button down. Infuriated, Nathaniel jumped up to answer.

"Hello!" he barked into the intercom.

"Hi Nathaniel, it's Cassie." A woman's voice. Nathaniel racked his brain.

"Cassie?" His mind was blank. "Errr… I'm busy right now and it's late… was it anything important or can it wait?"

"Well, yes it's important!" The voice sounded agitated.

Nathaniel sighed. "Give me a minute, I'll come down."

Slinging on his jacket he left the front door to his flat on the latch and hurried downstairs. When he opened the main door he found the woman from the bar on the doorstep. The one he'd slept with. He'd forgotten her name and he'd forgotten how pretty she was. Her mass of dark hair fell loose around her face and her full mouth was shiny with lip-gloss. She was beaming broadly.

"Ah, Cassie…" Nathaniel smiled appreciatively.

"Hi!" There was a pause.

"I can't ask you in I'm afraid. I'm in the middle of something."

"Oh!" she frowned, apparently affronted. "I thought I'd call by on the off-chance." And then the smile was back and she stepped further into the doorway, gazing at him expectantly. "I had fun the other night."

"Yeah, me too," said Nathaniel, distracted. He wanted to get back to work.

"I haven't seen you around?" she went on. Nathaniel was holding the door half open, poised to go back upstairs. "No, I've been busy, work and—"

"So, I thought I'd call by instead," she interrupted. "I thought we could go out sometime?"

"That would be great, but I'm going away tomorrow and I —."

"Where you going?" She cut him off.

"Spain, on business."

"Lucky you! How lovely, I'd love to go to Spain…" She stared, the statement hung between them. Nathaniel wasn't sure what to say.

"So, when you're back, then?"

"Yes, when I'm back,' he agreed, eager to get back to work. "Like I said, I'm up to my ears right now trying to get everything done before I go and I really do need…"

"When are you back?" She produced her mobile. "I'll call you, what's your number?"

"Tell you what, let me take yours." Feeling in his jacket pocket, Nathanial was relieved to find his mobile.

A slight scowl clouded her pretty face. "Well…okay."

While he tapped her number into his phone she leaned in closer as if to see the screen and Nathaniel was suddenly acutely aware of her face close to his. Her breath was warm on his face and when he surreptitiously glanced across, he found himself looking into her cleavage, now pressing against his arm. He was half tempted to invite her in after all.

The spell was only broken when he finished taking her number and looked up again. There was a knowing smile playing about her lips. "I'll wait to hear from you then," she said, brushing his chest with her fingertips. "Have a good trip, and don't forget to call me. I'll be waiting."

She was walking away but then stopped suddenly and gave him a coy look from under her lashes. "When did you say you were back?"

For some reason Nathaniel didn't want to tell her, but she just stood there looking at him and there seemed no way around it.

"Well, I didn't, but maybe Monday, possibly later. We're not sure yet."

"Okay. I'll expect your call." She blew him a kiss.

Nathaniel smiled awkwardly and shut the door.

Eleven

The first evening Dinah attended Ambrika's spiritual gathering she was exceptionally nervous. The thought of meeting so many strangers in such an intimate setting was daunting, but she forced herself to go.

She was glad she had. There was such camaraderie within the group. Individuals united in a search for deeper meaning in their lives. Together they meditated and channelled, directed healing where it was needed and read tarot for each other. Ambrika took a spontaneous approach to her gatherings, preferring to see who came before deciding what they should do for the night.

To begin with, Dinah stayed quietly at the back of the room, reluctant to socialise. But they were all so friendly and welcoming that it didn't take long for her to feel at home. Anyone was welcome to offer something to the group if they wished, be it an insight for discussion, a ritual, visualisation or meditation. One evening a tall lady in flowing gowns had requested they dance, and in the face of unanimous agreement Ambrika had put on some music. The music flowed as they moved and swayed. What began as just one song led to another and then another and then "just one more", and before they knew it they had danced the whole evening away.

Dinah had been perfectly content to watch events unfurl from the sidelines, until on her fourth visit when, much to her dismay, Ambrika asked her to guide the group meditation.

"No!" was her horrified response. But Ambrika merely smiled, leaving Dinah to suspect that she would not evade her friend quite so easily. In a state of acute embarrassment and with all eyes expectantly upon her, Dinah looked around at the crowd of faces only to be met with warm eyes and supportive smiles. Without exception everyone was willing her on. "Just speak what comes," soothed Ambrika. "I wouldn't ask if you weren't able."

Apprehensively, Dinah agreed.

While everyone settled, some on the floor with crossed legs, others on chairs with their feet on the ground, she took a deep breath and closed her eyes.

"Start to focus on your breath." Her solitary voice carried across the room, sounding thin and shaky to her anxious ears. "Feel the air on your nostrils with the inhale and again with the exhale." The room was becoming still and peaceful and she found that the more she relaxed and let go, the more her nerves were dissolving, allowing her own natural rhythm to come through.

People were releasing into meditation and Dinah was starting to enjoy herself, and when she furtively stole a glance around the room to see how everyone was doing, she gasped in amazement. Bands of light beamed from each and every person. Brightly coloured rays of purple, green and gold streaming from their bodies and illuminating the room with mystical light. Their faces were clear and peaceful as above them hundreds of golden white Angels filled every conceivable space. It was as if Angels were tumbling from heaven, a never-ending spiral of light joining with the beautiful souls now immersed in divine contemplation. Dinah saw the Angels directing beams of spiritual energy through their hands to different parts of each person's body. They were administering healing and Dinah watched mesmerised, until they wrapped around her too: a woollen cocoon enfolding her, into which she willingly succumbed.

When Dinah eventually resurfaced, peaceful and refreshed, she could no longer see the Angels. As always in meditation, time was obsolete, so who knows how long they'd been adrift in the inner seas. She couldn't even remember her own eyelids closing.

Quietly she cleared her throat before gently calling everyone back, drawing their attention to their bodies, to their feet and hands and to their breath. In response people were blinking and stretching, tentatively wiggling fingers and toes looking rested and happy. Dinah was delighted.

Ambrika's spoke from the other side of the room. "Dinah also channels Spirit, if anyone has a question…"

Once again caught unawares, Dinah stared at Ambrika. Leading a meditation was one thing, but giving readings on the spot was quite another. Before she had a chance to refuse, a young woman with blonde hair was eagerly leaning in. "I have a question." Dinah fully intended to explain she was not ready, that it didn't feel right, but when she saw the pleading in the woman's face she found she couldn't say no. Strengthening her resolve she smiled encouragingly. "What would you like to ask?"

The woman frowned. "I'm worrying about money. I can't stop and I'm not sleeping. It's been going on for ages and I can't get work. I don't know what to do..." Her eyes were filled with worry.

With a deep breath, Dinah closed her eyes and looked inside to see if anything was coming through. To her utter surprise the words came spilling out of her. "A job will become available early next year, end of January or around that time. It's something new, something you haven't done before and you won't have to go looking, it will find you. Though it won't seem much to begin with, a few days here and there, things will quickly take a turn for the better. You'll enjoy this work and will be rewarded financially. It's important to stop the relentless worrying. It doesn't help, it only blocks you."

The woman was clearly delighted and Dinah saw the worry in her eyes replaced with relief. "Thank you so much," she said breathlessly. "That's really helped."

"You'll be fine," said Dinah.

It felt wonderful. The words had flowed effortlessly. She hadn't hidden away as was her usual trick and best of all, in overcoming her own fear she had helped someone else climb out of theirs.

* * *

Following the peculiar dream encounter with the yoga teacher, Dinah was curious about seeing him again, wondering if there would be any change in his manner towards her or whether he would show any indication of having entered her dreams. Somehow she suspected not.

With the supper dishes cleared and Daniel and Luke playing a board game on the kitchen table, Dinah changed into her yoga clothes. Although she didn't understand why she was so drawn to Tony and his class, she knew that for the moment it was important to keep going. The man was having the strangest effect on her and she couldn't fathom it at all. In spite of reassurance from the Angels, she

91

felt strangely panicky at the thought of him, scared even. She didn't know why and she didn't like it. There was something else too, that almost frightened her more. Beneath the fringes of doubt lay a powerful longing, a longing to know more of him and go further. It was like the most intense push and pull inside her soul. She was experiencing something different with him, a strength of desire she hadn't experienced before, but what concerned her was that it was him who had opened the door and him leading the way.

"I want to go deeper, Angels," she admitted. Yet there was something about him, which made her anxious, uncertain, but there was no way she could turn back now. She needed to go further, and without Tony to point the way it would all come to an end. 'Why does this terrify me so much?'

When Kate arrived ten minutes later in a flurry of good spirits, Dinah kissed the boys goodbye and with a churning stomach headed off to class.

Inside the hall she was immediately engulfed in a sweet cloud of incense and soft music. It was busy tonight and the atmosphere was charged, heavy with expectancy. Most people were deep in meditation, lying on their backs in savasana or like Tony, who was positioned at the front of the room, in lotus position with crossed legs, a straight spine and forefingers and thumbs touching. He certainly knew how to create a sacred space – entering the room was like entering a different dimension.

As Dinah moved past Tony she was intensely and uncomfortably aware of him and this feeling only increased as she dropped her bag and mat on the floor. She was certain his eyes were on her but didn't have the courage to look. It was extremely unnerving. It's as though every movement I make is being noted, she thought crossly.

Determined not to show she was flustered, Dinah feigned indifference by sitting down as calmly as she could and stretching out her legs to wait for the class to begin.

* * *

Although his eyes were closed, Tony knew she had come. He felt her enter the room, sensing her even when she first appeared in the doorway, her energy disturbing his quiet contemplation. Now he was alert. He had easily entered Dinah's sleeping world and had no qualms about doing so. He was intrigued by her and wanted to reach her in a way that was simply not possible on the physical plane. Yet he hadn't counted on the direction the meeting had taken or the strength of the energy between them. It had taken him unawares and while it was true that he'd been somewhat distracted ever since, barely able to think of anything else in fact, he hadn't dared visit her again in the same way.

He was irrationally pleased she was here though and opening his eyes just a fraction watched her walk across the room. She seemed to glide before him and he recognised she was in a state of meditation. The way he could feel into her had surprised him initially, but now he was aware of the connection and was sure she felt it, too. This knowledge made him confident of being a little more direct. Far more so than he would normally be with a new student and anyway, he reasoned, she had pretty much challenged him to show her what he could do.

Tony quietly assessed Dinah, watching as she took off her shoes and socks and straightened her mat. Nothing particularly startling to look at. The thought made him feel better. Pretty enough face, but there was something else, an ethereal quality, which gave her a mysterious air. He wondered what her secrets were and whether it would be possible to find out. After fussing with her mat she finally sat down, rather self-consciously Tony thought, before realising with satisfaction that she knew he was watching her. He'd never known such connection with a woman and not wanting to miss the moment he experimented by directing his thoughts at her.

Something bigger than us took over the other night. Wouldn't you agree?

With a scowl she looked straight at him. There was a disturbing charge as their eyes connected, but Tony deliberately did not move a single facial muscle. He didn't look away nor avert his eyes even for a moment. In fact he gave absolutely no outward acknowledgement of any kind other than silently holding her gaze. Something like fear flickered across her face and yet she also did not look away. They were staring at each other across the room, the tension gathering as currents of electricity burned the air. The charge was getting stronger, so much so that Tony wondered if the people sitting between them would leap out of the way to avoid being burned. Strong sensual feelings were stirring. It was like being sucked into a vortex. They were falling into each other, into each other's eyes, merging into each other's souls and nothing could save them.

"Excuse me..." A disembodied male voice alerted Tony to the fact that someone was beside him. Without missing a beat he pulled away from Dinah to find one of his long-term students crouching next to him.

"I didn't mean to interrupt..." The man looked slightly confused.

Pasting a self-assured expression on his face, Tony shrugged. "Not at all. How can I help?"

The man had pulled a hamstring and as Tony advised on how to approach tonight's session so as not cause further injury, he stole a glance at Dinah over the man's shoulder. He was interested to see that her cheeks were flushed red.

They made unspoken contact twice more after that and both times the effect was dramatic. The students were poised in a one-legged balance, straightening their right leg out in front of them while holding their big toe. Dinah appeared to be perfectly comfortable and stable in this asana and so Tony decided to test her resolve. Stealthily crossing the room, he quietly positioned himself in front of her mat and stared directly at her. As he hoped would happen, under the heat of his scrutiny she started to lose her balance. Once more her face began to redden and he caught the flash of desperation in her eyes as she wobbled before falling clumsily out of the pose. Smiling smugly, Tony serenely moved on to the next student, knowing that he left her infuriated behind him.

Then as they sat for meditation, Tony noticed that a female student wearing a large headscarf was blocking Dinah from view. The stab of disappointment was unsettling, more than it should have been and he deliberately shuffled back slightly until she was again in his line of vision. Their eyes locked and the flash in hers matched the ping in his heart. Again they were falling into each other, bound together by something he couldn't control and despite feeling unexpectedly vulnerable and exposed, Tony found it impossible to look away. His heart hammered in his chest and he was finding it hard to concentrate. The woman was a siren and he couldn't seem to keep his eyes off her. It was causing chaos with his equilibrium. She's a magnet, he thought.

However, for now he must finish the class and he couldn't do that while he was locked into her. Closing his eyes, he trembled and took a breath, mentally disconnecting. When he opened his eyes again and looked round the room he saw most students were already in a deeper state. It was an advanced class and many found it too intense here, feeling out of place in the deeply connecting energy. But this one, Dinah – was that her name? – she fitted in quite seamlessly. No need to guide her, she knew what to do. Although, Tony sensed he was taking her into unfamiliar territory and this pleased him, made him feel happier within himself.

Recalling their first conversation on the phone, he remembered how rude he had been. The ringing of the phone itself had been an unwelcome intrusion, interrupting as it did a spontaneous meditation, but he'd also been irritated by her manner. He had assumed she was just another one who wanted yoga to keep fit, someone who took it up as a fad but gave up when they realised how much more was involved. These people annoyed him. No commitment or discipline and guaranteed to leave when they hit an inner block – ruining what he was trying to create. Tony wanted students who were willing to stay the course, those he could take to an advanced level and guide through the process. They needed to demonstrate courage, stamina and perseverance, and only then would they be granted the opportunity to go further.

Stealing a sidelong glance at Dinah, he saw a tantalising smile playing around her mouth and it made his heart flutter. What was it with her?

At the end of the evening she gathered her belongings and swept out of the hall. Tony found himself unexpectedly saddened by her departure – that he would have to wait a week, maybe more, to see her again.

Twelve

Lying on a blanket on the floor of Ambrika's front room, Dinah rested her head on a small white pillow doused with lavender. The scent soothed her. Past-life regression was not new to her, but this time felt different and even though Ambrika was holding the space, Dinah was nervous. This was not a journey she would ever do alone anyway, as you never knew what was coming until you were actually facing it.

Throughout her life unpleasant feelings had been her constant companion, always hovering close by, ready to take over at the slightest provocation. She wanted to go deeper, to understand why the unsettling anxiety? Why the fear?

Ambrika's soft voice was calling in the Angels, the spiritual protectors, lulling Dinah into relaxation. They both knew the perils of going into something like this without adequate spiritual support – that undertaking this work without due care can prove a step too far for the psyche.

In her dreamlike state, Dinah saw a path of lunar light winding through an inky dark pool and she began to walk, step-by-step heading into the etheric planes.

"There's a door ahead of you." Ambrika's voice came from far away. And as if by magic a huge arched doorway loomed up before her, reminiscent of an aged church door of darkened wood with iron fixings.

"Open the door and go through," instructed Ambrika. With her arms stretched out like a sleepwalker, Dinah watched her hands land on the metal latch before the door swung open. There was only vast empty grey space beyond and when she stepped through she found herself suspended in nothing. It was most peculiar. The world and everything in it had disappeared. Dinah wasn't concerned, she liked being adrift in the Universe and was starting to enjoy the experience when, with a start, she realised her feet had found ground.

Looking down at her body she saw dirty rags and skinny legs and hands, which were gnarled and grimy. She was an old scarecrow of a woman of undeterminable age and Dinah understood that she lived on the fringes of society. Yet there was a burning love within this old crone, a pure heart that would never refuse help to whoever came asking.

The old woman was busy. She was working by candlelight in a cramped, low room, bereft of comfort save a straw mattress and rough woollen blanket in one corner and a modest fire burning in the grate. Iron pots and pans were stacked around the hearth. One suspended above the flames, bubbling gently and billowing a strange herbal scent into the room. Despite the shadow of squalor and poverty, the walls were lined with shelves crammed with mysterious glass bottles and small wooden pots. The woman was perched at a crude wooden bench. Working deftly, she appeared to be preparing some kind of tincture. Her nimble fingers moved quickly, a pinch of this, a nip of that, into a jar filled with what looked to be coloured water and all the while muttering continuously under her breath. The water had been blessed under the light of the moon and infused with the properties of petals and berries from sacred plants, transformed by ancient wisdom and holy words into potent healing medicine. The woman had just finished pouring the pale liquid from the jar into a blue glass bottle, when there was a quiet knock at the door.

"Come," she beckoned, her voice scratchy with age.

The little door creaked open and a lady entered, tall and grand in an embroidered grey cloak with the hood pulled up so only her chin could be seen. The lady was clearly agitated and fell at the old woman's feet, clutching at her rags as the hood dropped back to reveal blonde hair and a gaunt white face etched with worry. "Do you have it?" She pulled at the old woman's legs, her voice breathy with anxiety.

It was obvious the old woman was expecting this visitor as she didn't quicken her pace one jot, nor seem unduly affected. Calmly she pushed a stopper into the blue bottle and turned to face her guest with a kindly smile. "Everything is as I promised it would be. God gives his blessing." She proffered the bottle to the trembling lady.

"Take it to your child. Three drops under the tongue morn and eve and he'll be well soon enough."

Transformed by gratitude the lady got to her feet, grasping the bottle.

"Thank you." Tears wet her eyes as she clutched it tight to her chest. "How can I repay you?"

The old woman merely shook her head.

"You have paid my fee. I ask only that you never speak of this to anyone. It would cause me grave trouble and your husband must never be told."

The lady shook her head vigorously as the precious bottle disappeared into the folds of her cloak. "My husband would beat me if he knew I was here, even for the sake of his own son. He is a stern man and does not take kindly to such things." She drew the hood back over her head. "I promise no talk will pass my lips. My appreciation is beyond words. God bless you." Taking the old woman's hand she pressed it to her heart.

The old woman rose. She was used to such platitudes from those she helped and she shuffled towards the wooden door to let the lady back out into the night. The lady's son was very ill and despite the best efforts of the physician, he worsened with every day that passed. The family was wealthy and it would have been easy to charge a vast sum to save the son, but the woman only ever asked for a few coins for her services, no matter the customer. The true payment was the lightness in her heart and the satisfaction of using her wisdom to relieve suffering on earth.

There was, however, a real risk in plying her trade and every time was fraught with danger. The lady's husband was the local priest and well known to be ruthless in his desire to crush any person or act he deemed to be sorcery. It was no secret how much he detested the old woman, how deep his contempt and ceaseless his suspicion. His dark eyes were upon her in the market square, watching her every move and making her shudder whenever their paths crossed. Employing her gifts this way certainly left her vulnerable to talk and accusation, but she would continue regardless. It was her duty.

With the lady gone the old woman shut the door and went to the hearth. She knelt awkwardly before the fire with only a pile of rags to cushion her bony knees from the hardness of the floor. She stared into the flames, pressing her palms together and thanking God for his love and for giving her courage. The lady's son would be better before the week was out and she thanked the spirits for their help.

These images were fading as fast as they had come and Dinah found herself floating up through the layers, back to her body into Ambrika's front room.

Blinking she saw Ambrika beside her.

"Well done," said Ambrika. She looked pleased.

Dinah's voice was quiet. "That old lady though...me... I was scared for her."

"I think you've scratched the surface today, but there's more to come. You must absorb what has emerged before going any further."

"I'm not sure I want to go further," admitted Dinah. "I've got a feeling there's something I don't want to see."

"You're in control, Dinah. Your unconscious will never show things you're not ready for. Whatever comes, comes at the right time, but sometimes courage is needed. We need to be strong to face the wounds from our past."

* * *

"It's going to be standing room only soon, if things go on like this," remarked Ambrika to Dinah a few days later. They were washing-up mugs and glasses after the weekly gathering. Tonight had been busier than ever. "We're getting too big a group for my little house."

Every week brought more new faces. Everyone was welcome, no one turned away, but it was becoming a squash to fit everyone in. Dinah handed Ambrika a glass to dry. "The Angels keep telling me to lookout for a bigger space," she said. "But I haven't seen anywhere yet I'm afraid." They had also told her that she would be playing a bigger role soon, that she had a particular message to share and that it was important she be heard.

"They say I'll be teaching people to reconnect with Earth," she confided to Ambrika. "I don't know what to make of that!"

Wiping the glass, Ambrika put it on the sideboard. "Most people live with a severed connection to Earth, cut off from the Mother, ignorant to the disturbance this causes within their psyche. Without that bond we're unable to reach up spiritually and live instead as sleepwalkers, only brushing the surface of existence, neither fully linked to above nor below. This is not a true life. It's fragmented and broken. You'll teach them how to strengthen their cords to Gaia, to stay connected and grounded, so they can continue their ascent to enlightenment."

Dinah was astounded. "But where do I myself learn about all these things?

Ambrika tutted good-naturedly. "The answer is under your feet!'

* * *

Heading up the high street to the market, Dinah was aware of an Angel beside her, gliding in perfect time with her steps. The Angel told her wordlessly that something was about to occur and that she must pay attention.

At the bread stall, Dinah was deliberating between a cottage loaf and a farmhouse wholemeal, when she overheard the woman next to her chatting to the stallholder about a new yoga centre in the town. Once home, without taking off her coat, she settled at the computer and quickly found the yoga centre's website.

'A beautiful, peaceful space available to hire for classes, retreats or one-off events.'

The picture showed a large airy room with clean white walls and pale wooden floor. There was a wood-burning stove in the corner and an altar filled with statues of Hindu deities. The room appeared large enough to accommodate quite a few people and so, with a beating heart, Dinah picked up her phone and rang the centre's number.

When she approached the building and saw the two stone Angel statues positioned each side of the main door, Dinah knew that this was the place. She couldn't help but smile.

A young man in baggy yoga pants and with unruly blond curly hair opened the door and introduced himself as Peter, the owner. He showed her the main yoga studio, the meditation room and the washroom as enticing wafts of incense followed them as they went. He then took her to the studio for hire, leaving her alone so she could properly gauge the atmosphere. The room was as appealing in real life as it was on the website. The altar was draped in red cloth and dominated by a large brass statue of the Hindu God, Shiva, while the alcoves either side were filled with smaller statues of other deities.

With Peter gone, Dinah was free to tune in to the energies of the room and was immediately aware of the calm flowing over her. She grinned.

"Everything okay?" Peter appeared in the doorway.

"Yes," said Dinah excitedly. "It has beautiful energy. It's perfect."

"Good." he grinned back at her. "I knew you'd like it. I'll go and get the diary and we can look at dates."

A loving hand brushed Dinah's head and in reply she blew three kisses into the air for the Angels. There were such strong positive vibrations in Yoga Space and she knew they'd be able to tap into it to enhance their evenings.

"You could be in luck," said Peter, returning with a thick black book. "I had a cancellation this morning for today next week, if you're interested?"

A week from today! Dinah felt a flutter. Despite the nerves, she booked the room. The Angels were clapping delightedly, confirming that this was the thing to do. They were almost jumping up and down with excitement and Dinah beamed from ear to ear. Everything was in place. The venue was secured and all there was left to do was to tell people.

Ambrika was delighted but didn't appear unduly surprised at the news. She merely nodded sagely, leaving Dinah to wonder if she had known all along this would happen.

The word was going round. Ambrika was already known and respected in the community, and Dinah herself was earning a reputation through her work at the gatherings. They gave leaflets to group members and displayed them in auspicious places throughout the town. And Dinah committed to sitting for at least ten minutes every day, solely to visualise the room filled with people who would benefit from attending. Now all that was needed was prayer and trust that the right souls would come.

The first night fourteen people came. What had been a crowd in Ambrika's front room now seemed sparse in the open space of the yoga centre, and although Ambrika was pleased, it was fewer than Dinah had hoped for.

"Slow growth is preferable,'" Ambrika reassured her. "The energy has time to build and it's a gentler way to experience things."

They were waiting for people to settle before getting started. Nerves bubbled in Dinah's stomach.

"No need for fear." A whisper from her Angel. She relaxed, but only a little.

After a group visualisation to carry them into a higher state, where worries disappear to leave only peace and contentment, the dancing began. To begin with the music was deliberately gentle, softly resonating, coaxing everyone to sway their bodies, but as the pace quickened people were getting up, moving vigorously as the melody came faster and stronger. Self-consciousness melted away as each person found their own natural rhythm, whooping and spinning, igniting the sacred inner flame.

The heat was building and the room was a mass of writhing bodies. Sweat poured down Dinah's chest as her own inner fire seared through her, never completely lost as she dipped and twirled, always with an eye on those around her. As the music hit its crescendo people were crying out, primal shrieking and crazed laughter echoing through the room as they leapt higher and spun faster in pure ecstatic release. Now the music was slowing, summoning the dancers back to earth as it gradually reverted to the gentler pace of before.

Dinah sat down, stretching into the ground as she delighted in the hot smiling faces around her. Melting into the calm, the stillness after the storm, it was a shock when she registered Ambrika inviting people to ask questions and then heard her name. The shock turned to horror when she opened her eyes and found everyone looking her way. Dinah stared at Ambrika, who shrugged good-naturedly as if it were nothing to do with her.

The requests came thick and fast. Questions about love and money and work. One man called Adrian was having trouble with his brother. They ran a company together he said, but the business was in trouble and they had different ideas on how to manage things. They were barely on speaking terms, while trying to present a united front to clients, and Adrian was constantly stressed, worrying that matters were only going to deteriorate. He fretted about his mortgage and bills and that his wife would discover how much debt they were in. As he talked, Dinah was shown Adrian as a little boy, about seven years old with a crop of pale blond hair, while next to him was another little boy – younger, maybe only three or four years old. The parents weren't often around and she saw Adrian taking care of his younger brother, getting his food, playing with him and comforting him in the night when he was scared. She understood it was an underlying conflict between the two of them causing their difficulties.

"The source of your troubles goes back to childhood," she said gently. "You looked after your brother, took care of him and he is very grateful. He loves you very much." She saw Adrian's eyes were damp. "But now he's older he wants to look after himself. He wants to make you proud of him, but feels you won't give him the chance. He fights so hard against you because he thinks you don't believe in him, that you see him as weak and helpless and that you alone will be able to save the company."

Adrian looked dismayed.

"It's alright," said Dinah quickly. "If you co-operate with each other then things will soon resolve. The bond between you is strong and if you can show that you trust him and believe in some of his ideas, then you'll see a real improvement, including financially. If you can relax the need to oversee every detail of the business, you'll feel lighter and happier and will see a real shift in your relationship, and the business will begin to stabilise. The two of you will make it a success, if you bring some understanding towards each other, and balance your approach to work."

Dinah responded to nearly every question with a message of comfort or direction. Occasionally, however, she would receive no answer at all, just an empty black nothing inside. Then she knew that the person was either not ready to hear the information, or more likely, that they themselves had the answer and were not yet ready to trust it.

When no more questions were forthcoming, Ambrika rose and motioned everyone else do the same. They were all glowing as they stepped forward to clasp each other's hands.

"Tonight we'll close by dedicating the energies to the Earth Mother," Ambrika said, confident and clear. They made a large circle in the centre of the room. Divine children, brothers and sisters peacefully united.

"All of us know the distress of the Earth and sometimes we flounder in our mission to assist, allowing ourselves to become overwhelmed by the scale of what we face. The destruction of the natural world continues apace and the greed and ignorance of materialism appears ever increasing. Things cannot continue as they are. But we stand united, connected with Earth and with our open hearts the Universal love flows through us. I suggest we channel this love into Earth. For her healing."

There were smiles of assent across the room.

"It's easy to forget that the spiritual forces are with us and that while people like us tread the earth, Gaia has her army. We are the peaceful warriors in our fight to save her. Our fight is all she has and it makes all the difference. Every time we send our love into earth a healing occurs, and every time we remind a sister or brother to take care, to cherish our land, then we act in service of God and the stronger Gaia will become."

Dinah closed her eyes, and feeling the warmth in the hands of the people either side of her, she spoke into the circle.

"Thank you Earth Mother, for holding us, feeding us and nourishing us…" A shiver skirted across her back. "Thank you for bringing us to service in this way, to revere and protect our land and to cherish the sanctity of the natural world. We send our love deep into your centre – for your healing and ours."

Everyone was still, silently channelling energy into the ground beneath them as a deep love for Earth flowed around the circle. Dinah sighed and heard others do the same. It was a while before they carefully released each other's hands.

It was the end of the evening and after farewell hugs and kisses, people were leaving.

Turning to Ambrika, Dinah grinned. "I'll book the room for a fortnight's time then?'

"Absolutely," said Ambrika. She touched, Dinah's arm. "I hope you don't mind. I was told you could answer people's questions and it came through so suddenly, I had no time to ask you."

Dinah couldn't help laughing at the anxious expression on her face. "I know I need a push sometimes and maybe not knowing in advance was best." She gave Ambrika a wry smile. "But next time, if you can, it would be good to know beforehand."

Thirteen

The ease flowing through Dinah's life was all down to her move to Porrick, with the only niggle being her ongoing misgivings about Tony. Yet the Angels consistently guided her to continue with his class and so every Thursday evening she was to be found at the church hall, where she and twenty or so others would stretch their cares away. It was becoming an essential part of her life, an anchor keeping her grounded and peaceful. Even so, before each class and without fail, she called the Angels to be with her.

For the first few weeks, Tony remained distant and aloof. But with such a mysterious connection between them his indifference only piqued Dinah's interest even more. She was paying far more attention to him than she had with any other teacher, even though he never acknowledged her and never said goodbye when the class was over, not even when she spoke to him directly as she passed his mat. He was always looking the other way or talking to someone else and so far had not responded.

Dinah was becoming aware of a close-knit circle of women around him, a sort of inner elite among the rest of the students, and that there seemed to be a couple in particular on whom he focused his attentions – a slim woman with straight auburn hair and a striking brunette with bright green eyes. In fact, Dinah couldn't help but notice that these women were all attractive, all under thirty-five, and without exception, all unfriendly. It was obviously some kind of clique and not something she wished to get involved in. And anyway, having encountered such situations before, Dinah knew how common it was for a group like this to form around a charismatic spiritual teacher. But there was something about this situation in particular that set alarm bells ringing. She vowed to steer clear.

That said, the rhythm of the yoga practice itself was wonderful and as a result her meditation was deepening. A major shift was taking place inside her and at the same time, Tony's attitude towards her seemed to alter. The deeper she went the more attention he paid her, beginning one evening when he called goodbye to her as she left. Startled, Dinah could only nod in reply.

The next week he spent most of the session by her mat and caught her eye several times while speaking, as if wishing to convey he was talking directly to her. Dinah wasn't sure what she had done to warrant such a drastic change of treatment and it was all the more unnerving because as Tony became friendlier, the other women became less so. They went from ignoring her completely to outright hostility.

The woman with auburn hair, who every week religiously aligned her mat precisely in front of Tony's, turned and scowled ferociously at Dinah during a twisting pose. The look was menacing enough to send a dart of anxiety through Dinah's stomach. What was that? she wondered. An Angel touched her cheek, but she received no explanation. For some reason the woman was threatened and Dinah was certain it was to do with Tony's change in behaviour towards her. From then on she avoided all social interaction within the class and other than offering the odd polite greeting, she barely spoke a word.

One evening, Dinah was in a deep forward bend. She sighed. The stretch was delicious and she languished in the release. She flinched when a hand touched her lower back and looking up found Tony staring down at her. The pleasure of only seconds earlier vanished. Now her heart was pounding and she had the distinct impression that he knew exactly the effect he was having. Neither moved, both still, both waiting. Heat from his hand penetrated her skin, as gently he began to massage her lower back with steady rhythmic strokes. The air between them crackled and unable to bear it a moment longer, Dinah exhaled and bent further to escape the sensuous touch of his fingers. Immediately he stopped and backed away, off to attend to someone else on the far side of the room. Dinah wrestled between relief and disappointment. Uh oh!

The next time he approached was during a more advanced posture. Dinah usually enjoyed being adjusted in yoga, but something about Tony made it different. There was a sense of intimacy about him, far more so than was usual, and the frisson between them whenever he came near was getting out of hand. This time he actually sat down next to her and placing his hands on her back gently twisted her round. His breath stroked her neck as he trailed his fingertips down her arm, gently clasping her thigh and pulling her to rest against him. Dinah was embarrassed at the sensuous shiver that ran through her. I'm behaving like a gauche teenager, she thought, not for the first time. And I can't seem to help it, the energy is too strong. But amidst her confusion, she was flattered.

Most weeks now Tony hovered around her mat and in spite of herself she was pleased. Tension hung in the air between them and she could even sense when he was going to come to her before he actually did. Soon the occasional adjustment became an adjustment in nearly every pose, or if not an adjustment, the brush of his hand on hers, a caress to her thigh, always some kind of physical contact. Her skin prickled at his touch and reluctant desire bubbled inside her, an untapped volcano, which could erupt at any moment. It was a struggle to maintain her composure when she felt as if she was on fire. Hot and flushed all she could do was focus everything she had on her breathing. Yet apart from these intoxicating moments and the 'goodbye' when the class was over, he made no other attempt to engage her in any way. It was very peculiar.

Am I imagining it? she frequently wondered. Imagining a connection where there isn't one at all? It was strange, but she couldn't say why.

And the women in his inner circle, as she now viewed them, were getting worse. Icy stares were sent her way when she arrived, and then again as they clustered together at the end of the class. On one occasion, two of them deliberately pushed past her, knocking her off balance as she put on her shoes. Dinah stumbled against the wall, open-mouthed and astonished. They appeared not to have noticed at first, as though she were invisible, as with arms linked and heads together they kept on going. It was only when they got to the door and both glanced back at her that she saw delight in their faces.

Outsiders not welcome, Dinah realised. The upset made her tremble. It was then that she noticed someone beside her and turned to find Tony smiling sympathetically. Dinah was embarrassed but grateful for the support.

"See you next Thursday, Dinah?" He touched her shoulder. There was real concern in his eyes and unexpected warmth flowed between them. He took a step closer.

"Yes," she replied, her voice tight. Unsure of what was happening she clutched the yoga mat to her chest. "Thank you."

Tony rubbed her back gently. He was scanning her face when his forehead suddenly furrowed, his eyes lingering on hers as though he saw something in them. She saw the light in his eyes become something else, something she couldn't read. Regret? Confusion?

Sensing her scrutiny, he removed his hand and looked away. "Good," he said.

They stayed suspended in awkward silence, until Dinah managed to rouse herself. "I better go." She moved towards the door. He watched her walk away and when she got to the door and looked back she saw he hadn't moved at all, but that his shoulders were slumped and his arms hung dejectedly at his sides. Dinah felt inexplicably sad. He looked bereft and dejected, but she kept on walking until she was outside.

Much to her dismay, the following week Tony came nowhere near her. With a stab of disappointment completely out of proportion, Dinah was forced to admit exactly how much she'd been enjoying their furtive encounters, the intensity of the charge, the heat whenever he came near, the subtle suggestion of what might occur. What have I got myself into?

Resentment thudded in her stomach as she watched him languidly adjusting the other students. Worse, she couldn't shake the feeling that he was avoiding her on purpose. "Why?" she wondered. "He wouldn't do that would he, Angels?"

It was very obvious though that everyone was being attended to except her. Was she imagining it or did he smile seductively into one woman's eyes when he lengthened her arm, and when he straightened the leg of the woman in front of her, did his hand remain just a moment too long on her thigh?

This is ridiculous! Dinah clamped her eyes shut. Who cares what he does. I should be concerned about my practice.

At the end of the session when she picked up her mat, Dinah felt someone watching her and looked up to see two of Tony's women with their arms wrapped around each other. They weren't moving or speaking, but one of them was studying Dinah intently. As their eyes met the woman shot her a sardonic smile and pulled her friend closer into the embrace. Quickly Dinah turned away.

The displays of love and warmth were for effect and it made her irrationally cross. It's all for show, but for some reason they want me to see it.

Something about Tony, and this group of women was all wrong. She felt the edge of competition, hierarchy even, as they vied for his interest. The energies of jealousy and rivalry were easy to identify for Dinah. Such distinctive forces hurtle through the atmosphere like flint heads, sharp points of energy firing straight from the perpetrator's auric field. Conscious or not, the negativity is flung out into the world towards the unsuspecting focus of their emotions. For the one on the receiving end it can feel like being blasted by shards of glass that pierce the emotions and psyche, resulting in unexplained physical symptoms such as sudden backache, or pain in the shoulders or neck. The effects on the psyche itself can be even more detrimental, with anxiety, paranoia and depression or feelings of deep unease. Just a jealous thought or angry intention from one person to another, acts as a curse.

People aren't careful enough, thought Dinah. They don't understand the effects of their thoughts and emotions on the world – that we are all connected and our negativity can influence another's well-being.

This way of exercising thought and emotion, known as psychic attack, is a frequent occurrence among the unaware. It causes havoc with a person's equilibrium and chaos in their life, and the attacker also does not escape unharmed. Conscious or not, the negative force will always be returned back to them, only amplified. Spiritual law decrees that whatever intention or energy a person gives out, that very same force will come back to them threefold, either immediately or in due course, depending on where they are in their karmic journey. So while those who send out love, compassion and understanding will receive these wonderful energies back, so it goes that people spreading negativity or abuse of power will receive the same back only amplified. There is no hiding from the consequences of our behaviour. Luckily, once Dinah recognised the energies she could deflect them away from herself.

She called Archangel Michael. Said to be the most powerful Archangel, Michael sits on God's left-hand side and is the Angel understood to have thrown Lucifer out of heaven. Other than God, there is no stronger being in the universe and he was always the first one she called in emergency of any kind. When Michael was present, Dinah would feel him behind her, sometimes with his hands on her shoulders – strong, powerful and protective. Archangel Michael bestows courage and confidence to those who call him, especially those in the clutches of self-doubt and fear. Like all the Angelic beings his love is boundless and unconditional. When he comes to your aid with his sword of light and truth and his shield of protection, you are safe from all psychic and energetic harm. With his presence secured, Dinah then surrounded herself in golden light to deter unwanted lower energies.

It was becoming clear that for the women in his class, Tony was not simply a yoga teacher: he was the guru, the leader, the Master, and they were his devoted followers. When class was over they crowded around him, all wanting to get close, all needing his attention. Under a guise of peace and calm they jostled against each other, each wanting to be the one to get closest. When Tony spoke they hung on his every word. If he laughed they laughed too, and if he found displeasure in something or frowned, they would do the same.

It made Dinah feel odd.

He clearly enjoys it and plays his role well, she mused, being adored by so many submissive women.

She was surprised at the intensity of scorn she felt for them, and quickly sent out an entreaty to rectify the impact of her own negativity; "Angels, help me rise above my ego, please bless these women with love and light." Then, crossing herself she tucked her mat under her arm and left.

It felt good to be away from that stifling energy. Dinah had no interest in competing for this teacher's attentions and was disheartened by the false displays of spirituality. It felt ugly and compromising. Not for the first time, she wondered where this was all leading.

Fourteen

Nathaniel was nervous. This was unusual and he found it disconcerting. He took a deep breath of cool night air. Porrick was abuzz with festive activity. It was a week until Christmas and from early December stalls had been appearing each evening along the pavements outside the shops. They were selling all the usual traditional fare – mulled wine, roast chestnuts and mince pies – as revellers, well wrapped-up in coats and scarves, strolled the high street.

Tonight, however, the Christmas cheer passed Nathaniel by and as he approached the yoga centre the tension in his stomach seemed to grow. Halting he closed his eyes for a moment. "Jesus, just relax," he told himself. "It's nothing you can't handle. There's nothing to worry about." But somewhere he didn't quite believe his own assurance. It was to be a night that promised 'a journey through altered states of consciousness', to 'strengthen your connection with yourself and Gaia', so said the advertisement. He wasn't sure what it meant exactly, what was coming. Something in those words frightened him, but he pushed the fear aside.

Then there was the other fear, one that went deeper. He hadn't seen the woman since they crossed paths outside the library and he was worried she might be hostile towards him again, or worse, indifferent. Maybe she wouldn't even notice him. Then he would have to risk an uninvited approach and possible outright rejection. Nathaniel wasn't sure what he would do if that happened and quickly blotted the thought from his mind.

"Stop it!" he spoke sternly to himself. "There's something between us. She has acknowledged you already – don't start sabotaging yourself!" He walked on determinedly, forcing himself into a confidence he wasn't feeling. He would give anything for a cigarette right now, but there just wasn't the time and somehow it didn't feel right to go in smelling of smoke. The lights were on in the yoga studio and from the number of people gathered outside, immersed in quiet conversation, it seemed he wasn't the only one keen to see this woman tonight.

Once inside, Nathaniel found himself in a small reception area. There was an air of calm expectancy about the place and a lady with long, greying blonde hair in a flowing white dress was welcoming people. She was hugging some, shaking hands and kissing others, and proffering a tray of drinks to each person as they arrived, each glass tumbler filled with a pale green liquid, before directing them through a doorway and into a room beyond. An older man in faded orange robes and with a short white beard, tapped her on the arm. They exchanged a few words and then she picked up a crescent-shaped cushion from a pile on a nearby bench and pressed it into the man's hand. Then taking him by the arm, she led him through the doorway.

Nathaniel stood back, uncertain what to do. She must have felt his gaze because when she returned she came straight to him.

"Hello," she smiled, her voice warm and her eyes bright. Nathaniel relaxed a little.

"Yeah, hi." He feigned a confident stance to hide his discomfort.

"Ah, okay. You haven't been to anything like this before maybe?"

The woman seemed to look at him, or was it into him, even more deeply. He noticed her accent. Sweden? Denmark? It was appealing, in fact she was appealing, sexy even, and as naturally as breathing he slipped into flirtation.

"No, I haven't." The seductive smile, a sidelong glance from under his eyelashes. "I thought I'd come and see what all the fuss was about." He gave her a cheeky grin.

She smiled back, but it was more the smile of a knowing mother lovingly looking at a precocious child, than of a woman captivated by his charm. It wasn't a reaction he was used to from women, and under her gaze Nathaniel felt his self-assurance evaporating. Suddenly, he felt like a small boy. Sensing his discomfort and coinciding crash of confidence, the woman took his hand in hers, laughter dancing in her eyes.

"It's okay." The hand holding his was tender and encouraging. To his bewilderment he felt himself blushing. "You'll enjoy it more if you can just let yourself relax. Ambrika and Dinah are good at what they do, at bringing Spirit to touch people. You don't have to do anything, that you are here is enough."

Although he never usually failed in flirting, and was more practised than most in the art, this woman wasn't the least bit affected by his charm. This unsettled him.

"Help yourself to a cushion. We'll be starting shortly."

The woman dropped his hand and he immediately felt a reflex to cling to her. God, what was going on with him tonight? He never usually felt so unsure, so out of place; he could usually take a leading role in any situation.

"Drink?" She held up the silver tray and Nathaniel took one of the small glasses, automatically lifting it to his nostrils.

"It's an herbal remedy only," she said, sensing his hesitation. "Something to clear the palate and mind." He swallowed it down in one gulp and grimaced. The drink was sweet and pungent and he wasn't used to such flavours.

The woman was watching him closely. Was it his imagination, or did she look momentarily puzzled before breaking into a wide, mischievous smile.

"Dinah is pretty, too, I think you would agree?"

Nathaniel suddenly felt extremely uncomfortable. She couldn't know could she? Know that Dinah was why he had come?

Get yourself together, Nathaniel, he told himself and then had to tell himself again as he headed for the next room.

It was packed and the air sweet and smoky. Gentle music was playing. He had thought he was late, but there were still people coming in behind him. He'd only seen the small non-descript leaflet pinned to the board in the health food shop earlier that day, so it was pure luck he'd been able to come at all. But as soon as he'd seen her picture, alongside a woman with black hair, and read her name, Dinah, he knew he would be here whatever it took. The leaflet had described this evening as an opportunity for spiritually minded souls to come together for a raising of consciousness, whatever that might mean. It offered a chance to meet others on a deeper, truer level, to honour the Earth Mother and to revel in remembering 'the truth of who we are'.

Nathaniel usually dismissed such claims as New Age nonsense, but seeing the picture of this evening's hostess, the woman who had captivated him so in the library, his curiosity was piqued. He had seen her and felt her and something said she was not one for frivolity or pretence.

Could there be something special here, he mused. Attraction was certainly present and he certainly felt nervous enough, as though something unexpected really could happen tonight.

The specified start time was 8pm, and at precisely 8.01pm, the doors to the outside world were closed. The woman with long, greying hair slid the bolt across the door. This prevented any latecomers from disrupting the energy of the group once the evening had begun. The men and women, some local, some not, sat quietly on the floor as the lights were dimmed. The fire crackled in the wood-burner, comforting orange flames visible through the glass door, and there were candles on every shelf and alcove, casting flickering yellow light into the room.

In the small room at the back of the yoga studio, Dinah and Ambrika had completed their preparation of meditation and prayer and were now readying themselves to enter the main room.

"There must be more than fifty people!" Dinah told Ambrika as she peered through the door and saw everyone awaiting their arrival. "I didn't expect so many." She hadn't anticipated such a dramatic increase in numbers and felt the first knot of nerves.

Ambrika squeezed her hand. "Don't forget to breathe!"

Stepping into the main room, Dinah closed her eyes and took a moment to settle into the clear quiet space inside. The Angels had told her that tonight would be significant, which intrigued her. Yet even though she asked more questions the only answer she got was, "Trust."

Ambrika and Dinah wove their way soundlessly around the people on the floor. Some were already meditating, while others watched them make their way to the front of the room. Dinah lowered herself onto the waiting cushion, crossed her legs, and began to focus on the base of her spine while scanning the room. The man next to her picked up the skin drum lying at his feet and, as they all closed their eyes, he began to beat slowly with his hand. With the vibration of the drum reverberating through her, Dinah immediately felt the top of her head weighted and heavy. She trembled with expectation as invisible hands went to work, nimble fingers pushing on her temples, her brow, encircling the top of her head above her crown. They were opening her crown chakra to receive the higher energies: the chakra through which humanity can connect to the spiritual source. Golden light streamed into her body accompanied by a flooding sensation of ecstasy. Her breathing naturally calmed as a beautiful rhythmic pulse ran from the top of her head to the tips of her toes.

It was powerful tonight, possibly because there were so many of them all focusing on the same intention of peace and love. In time to the quickening beat of the drumming, the golden energetic infusion was intensifying. It flowed from the top of her head, to the base of her spine, before spinning up the front of her torso, repeating itself again and again in a perfect rhythmic cycle. A smile spread across Dinah's face as her body shook gently. The energy replenishing the whole of her as heat collected in her tummy.

Nathaniel stared at the woman, entranced. She hadn't yet seen him, even though he found himself positioned directly in front of her. When she opened her eyes he would be the first thing she saw if she looked straight ahead. He could feel warmth radiating from her and the atmosphere in the room had altered completely from when he had arrived. It was soft and heavy.

Dinah was swaying, her body gently vibrating as if releasing some kind of charge. She was not of this world right now and Nathaniel was surprised that he knew it, that he knew she was following her own inner rhythm. There was something more happening though, he could feel it in him, around him, out of his control but something was moving. His head felt fuzzy, the beat of the drum pounding on his brain. The temperature in the room was soaring and Nathaniel was sweating. The urge to close his eyes was overpowering and he battled to keep them open, reluctant to take his gaze off her.

The external world was becoming muffled, he could feel others in the room, could hear the music playing, but it was the drum that had his attention. Heavier and heavier his eyelids became until at last he succumbed and closed them. As Nathaniel plunged into darkness he heard those around him sighing.

In a state of blissful trance, Dinah gently opened her eyes. As her vision adjusted to the outer world her gaze came to rest on a face. It was a man and he looked familiar. Blinking a couple of times to regain focus, her eyes widened in surprise. With a surge of adrenalin she recognised the man from the library sitting right in front of her. His eyes were closed, but his eyelids flickered, as though he had not quite let go.

Throughout the room Dinah could see a glowing hue radiating from everyone in front of her, as if their souls were alight with fire. This man though, his fire seemed brighter than the rest, vibrantly alive. Spirit wanted her to notice him.

He's attractive, she mused, suspecting he knew it only too well. She hoped he knew it merely as a truth rather than from arrogance. She could feel him too, not as powerfully as in the library, but there was something here. A smile played on her lips as she glanced down at her hands in her lap and when she looked up again he was staring straight at her. They flinched in unison, yet neither looked away. They both stayed quietly still.

The drum was slowing, the beats softer and further apart. People were shifting on their cushions and those who had been lying down were now stirring, bringing themselves upright again.

"Dinah," the voice called from inside. Immediately, Dinah snapped back into the present and saw that Ambrika was standing, facing the audience. The drum had stopped. Rising, Dinah placed her bare feet firmly onto the ground.

Ambrika was holding her hands aloft, palms reaching for the sky. The others silently stood to emulate the movement and the man from the library did the same. Dinah stretched upwards too, touching her palms together, feeling the energy spiralling up her body, before she brought them back down. From the place deep within, she addressed the room:

"We here, gathered tonight in peace, love and light, stand firmly on Mother Earth. From the soles of our feet we send our roots deep into the ancient land, into the core of the natural world, for connecting and grounding, centring and healing."

116

A pause. Ambrika was slowly raising her arms upwards again, up to the ceiling until her fingers were touching. Dinah called out:

"We here, call upon the highest energy of light and love that we can comfortably carry at this time, to enter into us, for our healing of mind, body, and our energetic field."

Nathaniel found the words were fuzzy, that he couldn't quite distinguish what they meant. He felt something happening nearby and turning his head was alarmed to see the woman next to him noticeably trembling. He stared, confused by the calm serenity of her expression even as her body shook. And then, a perfectly normal-looking everyday man began to stamp hard on the ground. With his eyes scrunched shut he yelped every time his foot hit the floor, his body jerking in response.

All around him people seemed lost in another world – moaning, grinning, hugging themselves with rapturous faces – and Nathaniel was acutely aware he was the only one who seemed disturbed by the sudden turn of events. It was as if he were in a strange parallel dimension where nothing is real. All he could do was watch, a fascinated and slightly embarrassed observer.

What on earth is going on? he wondered, unsure whether to laugh or get up and leave.

It was weird and compelling at the same time. Something he had never encountered before. The room was getting hotter and hotter and he pulled at his t-shirt, peeling it away from his clammy skin.

As he stared in confusion at the strangeness of the people he found himself surrounded by, Nathaniel suddenly caught Dinah's eye. She was looking straight at him, smiling, hands pressed together as if she were about to pray.

He felt exposed, naked under her gaze and his face flushed. When she began to raise her arms again, not knowing what else to do, Nathaniel closed his eyes.

"We call upon the Divine Mother and Father," her voice rang out.

"The Archangels, Angels and highest vibrational beings,

We ask for your help, that we may be a blessing to all those we come into contact with

We ask for your help, that we may be a blessing for all situations, which enter our awareness

We ask for your help, that we may embody the Divine in this world

We ask for your help, that we may become one"

For the next hour or so, Nathaniel allowed himself to be led by the goings on around him. The two women, Ambrika and Dinah, took turns leading the group through ritual, dance and movement. He no longer had any idea of himself, of where he was or of what exactly was taking place, only that the evening passed in a bizarre haze of dancing and hugging, of stroking and hand holding and looking into the eyes of strangers. There were moments that touched him, as he met each person from a place he had never been to before. He could feel the warmth and tenderness around him. It felt odd and awkward, but was also strangely comforting. He was being shown something that he had somehow missed, caught up as he was in the hustle of life.

Seeing Dinah across the room he watched as she embraced a woman with long red hair. He made his way to them and stood close behind. They stood with their arms wrapped around each other and he waited patiently. When they separated and as the other woman moved away, Dinah was left alone, and seizing the moment Nathaniel caught hold of her hand. He could barely breathe as he slowly moved in front of her. Their fingers clasped each other, hot and damp, his chest brushing her shoulder causing her to fall into him as his arm went around her waist. At last they were facing. The energy between them bubbled and they stood together, silent and unmoving, absorbing each other as the rest of the room disappeared. Nathaniel let his other hand go around her back pulling her close against him. They were held together as if by invisible glue and neither could have pulled away even if they had tried.

The room was quiet. He moved slightly and then his hands felt for hers again as he slowly stepped back. When she lifted her head to meet his gaze he tried to pull her close again, their palms hot, their hands sliding in each other's grasp.

But she was moving away. "I have to finish the evening," she whispered, so quiet he barely heard. He had no choice but to let her go, following her with his eyes as she joined Ambrika at the front of the room.

"Thank you" – Ambrika's voice was soft – "to all of you for coming and giving yourselves to such a beautiful evening. We have come to the end. So please, share this love we have ignited tonight to all those who come your way. Go safely and blessings to you all."

The room was emptying, people drifting away, but Nathaniel stayed. A surge of anxiety jolted through him and he knew for certain it was hers – he could feel it. She was about to flee. In one swift movement he went to her and she looked up, startled. Giving her no time to react he took her hands in his and pulled her close. "Don't start freaking out again. You've nothing to be frightened of in me," he whispered, urgently, into her ear.

To his relief she relaxed at his words and so gently, he tentatively wrapped his arms around her.

"Sorry," she whispered.

"I'm Nathaniel," he grinned. Gently he rested his forehead on hers, staring into her eyes as his heart pounded.

"I'm Dinah," she said.

Fifteen

When Nathaniel returned home later that evening his flat was in chaos. He hadn't bothered tidying up from the previous night and the leftover debris reminded him of Cassie, who he'd been with until the early hours of the morning. Hands on hips, he surveyed the scene. Two empty wine bottles and glasses, an ashtray brimming with dead cigarette ends releasing a putrid smell, discarded clothes lying crumpled on the floor.

They'd hooked up again in the pub. He'd been surprised to see her standing next to him.

"Hey, Nathaniel." She'd smiled seductively and handed him the pint she was holding. "I bought you a drink."

He didn't see any harm in accepting, and then it had seemed rude not to introduce her to his friends and before he knew it she'd joined their party, her hand resting possessively on his shoulder. He did think it slightly strange though, that she was in his local pub and apparently out on her own. He'd never called her after he got back from Spain and hadn't given it much thought, but she didn't mention it. She didn't seem to mind.

At the end of the night she'd snuggled into him, one hand caressing his thigh. "It's good to see you again," she said nuzzling against his neck, making his skin tingle. Her fingers moved up to his groin and, although at first he pulled away, he was aroused in spite of himself. "Let's carry on back at yours. We had such fun last time, didn't we?"

There was a lustful glint in her eye. In the end he hadn't put up much of a fight, but she made it extremely hard to say no.

It was becoming a bit of a habit, too many nights out and too many drinks before bringing a woman back to his apartment. Cassie was just another face, another body. He'd given her no thought, no courtesy. She'd wanted to sleep with him and he had been willing. That suited him fine, or so he had thought.

Nathaniel's heart tightened. The gentleness of the evening, from being with Dinah and from what he had experienced, was dissolving. He felt guilty. As though he had dishonoured the woman he had met this evening and dishonoured the woman he had been with last night. What was this feeling making him squirm? Regret? Shame?

Nathaniel leaned against the sitting room wall, recalling how easily he had carried Cassie into his bedroom. She was light as a feather and a compliant bed-partner, only too willing to fulfil his every whim.

It was only as first light reached through the bedroom curtains that they had finally fallen asleep. Nathaniel had woken first and was showered and dressed before she had stirred. When she did open her eyes, patting the mattress next to her, inviting him back to the bed, he smiled with as much kindness as he could muster.

"I need to go out," he lied guiltily.

Only hours after they had shared their most intimate selves, all he wanted was for her to go, her presence now an unwelcome intrusion into his day.

"Oh." She froze, an expression he couldn't read on her face. Nathaniel looked away.

She sat up without covering her breasts, looking round the room for her clothes. "Right, I see." Her voice was cold, resentful.

"I put them there." Nathaniel pointed to the pile of garments on the chair by the bed. "I'll let you get dressed then." Awkwardly he left the room. A few minutes later as he was making coffee in the kitchen he heard the front door slam. He checked the bedroom and then the sitting room. They were both empty and relief washed through him. He wouldn't have to bother feigning interest or make inane small talk as he politely waited for her to leave.

Tonight with Dinah, however, was an entirely different affair. Nathaniel slumped down into one of the armchairs.

"Oh God," he groaned.

With his head in his hands he felt discomfort sitting heavy in the pit of his stomach. It was something he would rather ignore, but it was nagging and it was persistent, demanding his attention. It was an uncomfortable feeling of having done something wrong and

Nathaniel was not used to such feelings. It made him distinctly uneasy.

The woman from last night was the polar opposite to Dinah in every way as far as he could tell, and something about this made him feel terrible. An image of Dinah swam before his eyes, lost to the music, lost to this world. He remembered her gentle touch as they hugged, the light in her eyes, the softness of her. His heart warmed when he thought of Dinah, but it also increased his self-disgust as he thought of Cassie. With a sigh, Nathaniel went into the bedroom, which now felt more like a crime scene, the location of a questionable encounter, which last night he had believed was fun and passionate and now just felt sordid.

Whenever he closed his eyes, Dinah appeared as vivid as if she was actually there. Something about her delicacy, her openness and vulnerability touched him, and not only that, he was realising things about himself too, about how he behaved with women, how he perceived them and treated them.

"Come on Nathaniel," he reassured himself. "You need some sleep."

Thankfully he had changed the sheets after Cassie left and there was no evidence in the bedroom at least of her ever having been there. Easily banishing the thoughts from his mind, Nathaniel stripped off his clothes and climbed into bed. He was soon snoring.

* * *

Dinah floated home that evening. Both boys were in bed and so having paid Kate, Dinah saw her to the door. In her dreamlike state she didn't feel much like talking, but thankfully it didn't worry Kate when Dinah was quiet. She was happy to chatter about whatever the three of them had been up to, always reporting on how long it had taken her to get them into bed. Unfortunately, the more familiar Kate became the less seriously Daniel and Luke took her attempts at discipline and bedtime was fast becoming something of a battle. Dinah promised to talk to them the next day.

Closing the door behind Kate, she breathed in the stillness. The evening had gone well, way beyond her wildest hopes. Together they had journeyed to rich, inner places and the energies had been powerful. Three different people had sought her out to thank her for the evening and compliment her. One woman had wanted to know more about her, asking where she came from and how long she had been involved in hosting such groups.

On her way home, her Angel had told her that a lot of heaviness had been removed from those who were present and much darkness released. It felt good to finally be of service in some way. And then there was the man, Nathaniel, appearing as if brought by the Gods. "He feels nice, Angels." She hugged herself. "Real and honest. I can't feel agenda or power games, no trying to manipulate or take control. He feels good."

Anticipation buzzed inside her when she thought of him, of his easy wide smile and soul-stirring eyes. The way he held her hand was perfect, so tender, the way a hand should be held. When he stroked her face it was as though it was the most precious of treasures and a current of heat had ignited between them. Nathaniel had glowed with delight, his beaming smile warming her heart. He had asked to see her again.

"Tomorrow?" he had suggested.

Knowing she would need at least a little space, Dinah had made an excuse. Rushing was not the way. So they had agreed to meet the following week, between Christmas and New Year, at a local coffee house.

This night, as Dinah slept, images swam before her, disturbing and intrusive. All was dark and something pulled hard and cold on her wrists. She was trapped, restrained, and panic flooded her body, her breath shallow with fear. Metal dug into her wrists, manacles scraping the skin so it bled. Heavy chains were holding her captive; she was shackled, unable to move. Then through the gloom footsteps were coming, shuffling towards her.

"What do you want?" she was crying, petrified. "I'm sorry, I'm sorry. Forgive me."

A quiet laugh and she felt his breath, warm on her face. The malevolence seeped from him into her, leaving her paralysed with fear. And then his hands around her neck, cold bone fingers, squeezing, gently at first as she squirmed, a futile attempt to get away. His face only inches from hers as he stroked her collarbone, running one finger down her windpipe, teasing her with what she knew was to come. She was already choking, gasping and spluttering even before his grip properly took hold and now those hands clenched her throat tight, squeezing hard, a vice around her neck. "Please," she whimpered, even as the air was denied her, the very life force being kept from her by a faceless monster. Yet she knew him. Those hands were merciless, fuelled by loathing. He wanted her gone.

Abruptly released from the torment, Dinah sat up, wide-awake and shaken. "Where did that come from, Angels?" she cried. "And why have I dreamed it tonight of all nights?"

* * *

Turning on the light in the hall, Tony was feeling good. It was cold in here though, and he shivered, a definite chill in the air. He flicked the switch to start the heating. He was looking forward to this evening, the last class before the Christmas break.

The group had been getting a bit stale earlier in the year, but since the new woman had joined things were improving. Siobhan and the other women he had chosen to initiate more fully had become tiresome recently. They were so eager to please and although a novelty at first, flattering even, there was no fight there – it was all just too easy. This woman though, she was different. She was causing a stir, both with Siobhan and the rest of them as well as with him. He smiled, although maybe for different reasons.

She aggravates them, he thought. He felt unexpectedly bad about that. But a little aggravation brings fire to the inner worlds, something real to work with, he reassured himself.

He glanced at the clock. There was half an hour until his students arrived. Positioning himself at the head of his mat he began his first 'salute to the sun' sequence of the day.

There was a curious energy in the hall tonight and Dinah hesitated in the doorway, trying to decipher the atmosphere. When nothing particular came through she summoned her courage, not sure why she might need it, and propelled herself into the room.

124

There weren't so many people tonight, half the usual number. Probably at Christmas parties or doing last-minute preparations. Finding a place for her mat she slipped off her coat and pulled her jumper over her head. The stillness in the hall always surprised her. Nobody really spoke. They might smile politely, but that was all. Occasionally she would hear the odd mumbled conversation, but as a rule the sessions passed in silence.

It certainly heightens the devotional atmosphere, she thought, lying down, but seems to amplify everything else as well.

Everyone was still and settled. Tony's quiet voice began to fill the hall, cajoling them into deeper stillness. He was walking around the room, weaving silent footsteps between the mats and Dinah's heart began to thump when she realised he was heading her way. Motionless, she kept her eyes closed, but as each step brought him nearer, her breath quickened making her chest heave. To her frustration there was nothing she could do to stop it. Unexplainable anxiety was building and she flushed red.

"This is our last time together before the festive season." Tony spoke so softly that Dinah had to strain to catch the words. Each syllable was drawn out, stretched to maximum enunciation.

There was the subtle sound of a foot on the floorboards close by. All Dinah's calm and peacefulness was gone as she tried to work out where he was in the room. Then came the gentle vibration of a second foot being placed deliberately slowly, on the floor next to her head. Silence.

"Now. Right now," he continued. "Right here, in this room. Here we are blessed with an opportunity to be present – fully present. The gift of going inside is being offered, a chance to discover, to experience, who we truly are."

It's like mass hypnosis, Dinah observed wryly, watching the thought as it flew across the surface of her mind. Even then she was falling deeper, her whole being awaiting his next words. Although his movements were barely distinguishable, Dinah could tell he was slowly encircling her.

"Together, we have shared the gift of a beautiful autumn of practice." Dinah sensed him studying her, watching for a reaction. "New faces joined us," he whispered, his voice directly above her and she jolted. He was speaking straight to her. She was trapped by

125

the energy between them, unable to move her body as her face flamed.

"This class is not the usual yoga class as by now you well know. Here, we go further. We practice true yoga, beyond only asana, beyond the mind."

He was dropping the words into her one by one and in response Dinah's turmoil was subsiding. She was starting to relax and soften.

He knows what I'm feeling, she understood. The states I'm passing through. He senses and controls it. He's playing at being puppet master, knows my confusion and enjoys it. Still, the pull to him was irresistible.

"Some here are advanced and some less so," Tony continued, a hint of accusation penetrating into her. "Maybe" – just a whisper now – "you feel vulnerable?" He paused, assessing her response. "As you draw close to the inner fire, it can feel too much for some. Too frightening. You are filled with mistrust and fear. You are unsure. Perhaps you want to run? But something holds you."

Dinah's heart nearly stopped. It was as though he was revealing all her hidden fears and doubts to the whole class, to a roomful of strangers.

"It takes courage to drop your idea of who you think you are, to drop all your opinions and embrace complete surrender." The words struck like a hammer to the heart. The impact of what he was saying was making her insides curl.

With horror she felt him kneel next to her. The tension bristled between them and when his hand brushed lazily across her forehead, his touch merely gliding over her skin, the sudden contact shocked her right through. Before she could recover he placed his hand firmly on her stomach, unmoving for a moment, before slowly running his palm back and forth across her lower belly. The sharp pang of arousal flared inside her. Helpless to control her body's response, Dinah was ignited with desire. Burning hot and unable to stop a gasp escaping, her longing was only eclipsed by embarrassment.

Delighted, Tony got up and moved away as behind him, Dinah trembled.

* * *

The buzzer jarred him awake. Nathaniel had been up late the previous evening, working on a document for a meeting that day. He often worked at night, finding his concentration was better and he could get more done. It was after two by the time he got into bed. The buzzer sounded again, noisy and intrusive as still half asleep, he stumbled out of bed to the entry phone and picked up the handset.

"Hello?" His voice was groggy. Silence.

"Hello, who is it?" he tried again.

Nothing. He replaced the handset and went back to the bedroom. Just as he was gratefully climbing back under the duvet, the buzzer went again. Frustrated, Nathaniel jumped up and went back to the phone.

"Yes, who is it?" Nothing. "Hello... hello!" He waited. When no response came he slammed down the handset and for the second time went back to bed. The digital clock by his bedside showed 5.39am.

"Urrghh," he groaned. When the buzzer sounded again five minutes later, he ignored it. And when it rang five minutes after that, he was already asleep.

"Bloody hell!" Nathaniel swore as the buzzer once more dragged him from sleep. Stretching, he flung back the covers. It was ten o'clock.

"Who is it?" he said sternly into the handset.

"Hey, Nathaniel, you going to let me in?" It was Sam. Nathaniel pressed the button to unlock the main door downstairs.

By the time there was a knock on his front door, he had pulled on some jeans and a t-shirt.

"Hi Sam." Nathaniel let his friend in. A rush of cold air came in with him.

"Brrrr... It's cold out," remarked Sam. Rubbing his hands together, he noticed Nathaniel's half-dressed state. "You've forgotten we're going to watch rugby?"

"Oh god," Nathaniel groaned, rubbing his forehead. "Give me ten minutes while I shower. "You can make coffee." He pointed to the kitchen.

"Late night or something?" his friend asked quizzically as Nathaniel headed back to the bedroom. "You sounded grumpy on the intercom." He lowered his voice slightly. "Have you got someone here?"

"No, no." Nathaniel's muffled voice came from the bedroom. "I worked late, but someone was ringing my doorbell this morning. Bloody five o'clock! And whenever I answered there was no one there." He appeared in the doorway with a towel wrapped round his waist. "Wasn't you, was it?"

Sam shot him a look. "Hardly," he grinned. "I've got better things to do with my time – new baby and all."

Nathaniel frowned. "It was strange." He disappeared back into the bedroom.

When he finally emerged, dressed and ready to go, a cup of coffee was waiting for him on the kitchen counter.

"So, what happened with you and that woman?" Sam called from the sitting room.

"What woman?" Taking the cup, Nathaniel grabbed his jacket from the back of the kitchen chair and went through.

"From the pub. Wouldn't leave you alone."

"Oh. You mean Cassie." Nathaniel grinned and seated himself on the sofa to drink his coffee. Sam was watching him.

"Well, the usual really." He shrugged. "What you'd expect."

Sam grimaced. "We thought she was going to eat you alive. Bloody hell!"

"Yeah, she does come on a bit strong."

"Bit strong?" Sam was incredulous. "You're joking? I've never seen anything like it. Who is she anyway? You've never mentioned her, she seemed to think you were an item or something."

"She was at a bar in town a while back. Picked me up more or less. I wasn't complaining at the time, but she has a habit of appearing wherever I go. I think she might be lonely."

"Or desperate?" his friend interjected.

"What are you saying?" Nathaniel laughed. "Look, she's nothing really. Gone. There is someone else though, that I've met."

Sam rolled his eyes. "Don't you ever get tired of it?" Finishing his coffee, he put the mug on the table and pulled on his coat. "I don't know how you do it. Come on, let's go."

Nathaniel didn't move. "Dinah's different." The softness in his voice caught Sam's attention and he turned to stare at his friend.

"Dinah?" I've heard that name somewhere, I think. Who is she then?"

An unexpected wave of tenderness swept over Nathaniel.

"She lives in Porrick. She runs workshops in the town. You've probably seen her leaflets up."

"What kind of workshops?" asked Sam, curious about the marked change in Nathaniel's demeanour.

"Spiritual I guess. Dancing, meditation, that sort of thing. It was weird. Good weird. If I'm honest it kind of blew me away."

"You went?" The expression on Sam's face was of such utter disbelief that Nathaniel couldn't help laughing. He slapped his friend on the back as they made for the door.

"Sam, I like her, that's all, and there's chemistry."

"Ah, that's more like it." Sam smiled knowingly. "That's the Nathaniel we know and love. You fancy her then, that's what you're saying and as yet nothing's happened, I take it?"

"Of course, I fancy her, but we've only just met."

"Never stopped you before."

Nathaniel frowned. "Look, we're getting to know each other, but I think... Oh, I don't know. Can we leave it there."

"Sure. Of course." Sam was astounded.

Sixteen

It was pelting with rain as, with head bowed, Dinah walked to the café by the river. The wind was so fierce that she had to clutch her hood to stop it blowing off her head. Arriving at the café she pushed open the door to be hit by a blast of warm spicy scented air. The café was known for its exotic soups and homemade breads. It was crowded. People chatted as they tucked into bacon and eggs and mugs of hot chocolate, as waitresses bustled around clearing tables.

Nathaniel was sitting at a table in the far corner. He got up when he saw her and came to greet her. For a moment they clasped hands, his liquid brown eyes and smile making her heart ping. His hair was windswept and damp, his hands chilled, so he couldn't have been waiting inside for long.

"Hi," he grinned.

"Hi," she smiled, shaking off the rain.

"Come and sit down."

Nathaniel edged his chair closer to hers. He felt so comfortable that she had to remind herself that he was in fact a new acquaintance.

"It's great to see you." There was a slight flush in his cheeks as their eyes met and for a moment she didn't know what to say.

"It's good to see you, too." Now she was blushing.

There was definitely something different about Nathaniel. From nowhere, she was overcome by an alarming urge to reach out and touch his cheek. Instead she hastily wedged her hands under her bottom, relieved that he was trying to get the waitress's attention and so missed her momentary confusion.

"What can I get you?" He faced her.

"Tea, please," she replied, grateful her composure had returned.

A lull fell between them as the waitress went to fetch the tea.

"So…" He was fiddling with his coffee cup. "The library."

"Ah yes. The library." He had nice hands, she noticed, big and tanned, with long fingers.

"I'm sorry if I came on too strong," he apologised. "Chasing after you like that. I don't know what came over me."

"It's okay, really. You took me by surprise that's all. I'm sorry I reacted so strangely. I don't know what came over me either."

They smiled shyly at each other. His smile made him look younger, more innocent somehow, revealing even white teeth and a crease to one side of his mouth.

He wanted to know more about her and, as best she could, Dinah told him. Nothing deliberately kept back or hidden. She talked about her childhood in Hampshire, about family life, a blissful bubble burst only by her father's sudden death. She told him about her marriage and divorce, her two boys, and of an empty life in London before she came to Porrick.

"I felt dead," she admitted. "And I wanted a life worth living – a fulfilling life with happiness and contentment."

It made Nathaniel consider his own life and what he was doing. What am I doing? he asked himself. He wasn't sure.

He watched her eyes as she talked, and her lips. Listening intently as she spoke freely of things he knew nothing about, of matters way out of his usual sphere of interest. She talked about God and of feeling different, of hidden energies, of Nature and natural magic – topics he'd never considered before and, if he were honest, would up until recently have dismissed as 'mumbo jumbo'.

Living in Porrick, Nathaniel was accustomed to such talk. You couldn't move for healers and psychics and there was always some kind of spiritual event or gig on in the town. People singing and chanting as they walked up the high street, peace groups meditating in the square, or devotees meeting for mass prayer and blessings from a visiting guru. There was no escaping it. It didn't bother him. It was entertaining in a way and gave the place character. Maybe it was simply that he hadn't been ready, but he'd never considered the possibility that there could be something in it. Now was different though. Now he was curious. It almost sounded believable when Dinah spoke of such things as Angels and spirit beings, past lives, soul connections and magic.

"I talk to my Angels and guides constantly," she confided, her eyes aglow. "They're around us all the time – guiding, comforting and helping, and there are other worlds too, planes of existence that overlap with the earth plane, which you can tap into if you know how, whenever you need help."

Nathaniel liked listening to her and could tell she was utterly convinced by it all, but some of these things were beyond comprehension. It was bizarre. There seemed no end to the mystery in her world: force fields of coloured energy around people, feathers from Angels, messages from elementals, and back-to-front suns that rise in the West and set in the East.

Everything she says would make her sound mad in different circumstances, he thought, and yet I know she isn't.

A part of Dinah urged her to stop talking, worried she was revealing too much. This part was embarrassed, but there was another part too, a part that felt liberated to be so open and it was this that kept her going. This part was tired of pretending and hiding, tired of the games. It wanted to take a risk with someone, regardless of how they might react – to be fearlessly honest. She was sharing her soul, exposing her innermost everything to someone who was effectively unknown to her.

He's listening, Angels, she noted. He doesn't seem horrified or shocked. The initial uncertainty was disappearing and in its place tenderness was emerging. It felt nice.

"Nathaniel?"

He nodded quizzically.

"Did you feel something that evening at the meditation? I mean, during the music, the drumming?"

He paused. "I did find it a bit odd," he confessed. "I've never been to anything like that before, but I saw your leaflet and thought I'd come and see. I can't really describe it though, what happened."

He stared into his cup a moment, before picking it up to take a sip. Dinah waited.

"I felt uncomfortable I guess – people behaving like that. I'm not used to it – the hugging and staring into people's eyes. I found it a bit strange. But honestly, afterwards, I felt..." He hesitated, searching for the right word. "Peaceful. As if all the noise, the busyness had gone and what was left was clear and quiet." He chuckled. "That sound crazy?"

"No, no." Dinah was delighted. "Peaceful is perfect! Peaceful and clear. That's the whole point. I know it can be unnerving to begin with and I could see you found it uncomfortable. But I was hoping others felt it, too – it's why I'm doing it. When I go inside like we did that night – in meditation, or prayer, through dance or connection with another – it's then I really feel God holding me, and all the confusion and pain falls away."

She was dropping down even now, each word carrying her further inside. "Then I'm light as a feather, fully connected. And I remember that everything is alright after all, that I can live fully in the disconnection that still exists in this world, back in the separateness, because I know more is possible."

Nathaniel stared, confused by her words but struck by the rapturous tone of her voice. Her eyes were closed, one hand poised in the air. It reminded him of how she'd been during the dancing that evening – here, and yet not. Realising she was drifting, losing her footing on the earth plane, Dinah quickly pulled herself back. Her cheeks were hot and red and it struck her exactly how much she cared what he thought. She couldn't meet his gaze.

"So, the Angels, Dinah," he spoke quietly. "What are they?"

"What are they?" she repeated the question, considering. "They're pure spiritual beings, all around us, always, pure energy, pure love. They exist on a higher frequency to us, a higher plane and unlike humans, they have no ego. They come from God, divine messengers if you like, almost a go-between, I think, between us and God. They help us feel God's love, because often we can't feel it by ourselves."

She stopped.

"What do they do?" Surprising himself, Nathaniel found he really wanted to know.

"They guide us," Dinah spoke carefully. "Towards living our lives to our highest potential. They watch over all of us, no judgment, not ever, and whisper guidance, leading us towards the highest level of living that we are capable. They want peace for Earth, for everyone to be happy and carefree, living beautiful lives. They remind us of the sacredness of the world and of life, to value

133

ourselves and each other – the earth, animals, birds and seas, as part of the divine creation. They remind us to show love for all living things, including ourselves, which we often forget."

Nathaniel leaned back in his chair.

"Go on."

"They are the Divine Energy; unconditional love and pure light. They are always with us, whether we feel it or not. We are never alone, nobody is, not as we believe we are."

Nathaniel suddenly felt warm; he didn't know where it was coming from. And something like hope fluttered in his chest. Maybe there was something watching over him, looking out for him.

"Our souls are directly connected with our Guardian Angels, and nothing can taint or break that connection, no matter what we do. The trouble is a lot of us are stuck in our egos – in illusion, 'maya' in yoga. It distorts how we see things, how we see ourselves and the world around us – wanting this, chasing that – but with a conscious intention to communicate, with an open heart and mind, the Angels help us break through, to see the truth of our lives, of ourselves. With their help we open the channels to our soul and strengthen the bond. We may see them or hear them more clearly, but even if we don't they are there regardless."

Nathaniel liked the idea of Angels as all-loving entities. Dinah's certainty was absolute and he found that reassuring despite his own doubts.

"Everyone can talk to the Angels, whoever they are, and you don't need to call them with words." Her eyes sparkled. "They answer your inner states. A call to the Angels comes from the soul. They stand by us through everything, whether we ask or not, holding and protecting us, even when we get caught in the illusion and mistakenly believe we have cause for fear."

Was it his imagination or did everything seem quieter? Stiller? As if something had stopped.

"And when you connect with them," Dinah went on, "you're in direct connection with the Source of all. With love. With God."

They were in their own sphere within the café, as if they had temporarily stepped out of the world. Her words were a balm, soothing his worries, hushing the fears. And Nathaniel was curious. "So, I talk to them – but will they answer?"

"Always. Trust them to find a way to reach you. They always hear us and always respond."

Her bright eyes fixed on his face.

"Ask for guidance, but then listen." Her hand went to her stomach. "Listen to your heart, your feelings, any images or loving words which come through."

Nathaniel looked dubious.

"Do I sound crazy?" Dinah couldn't help herself. "Do you think I'm mad?"

The higher energy was dispersing and she looked at Nathaniel expectantly. His expression was unreadable. She'd been talking for quite a while and he'd barely said a word. Anxiety tightened her stomach.

"I've bored you," she blurted. "Going on too much. Sorry." She suddenly felt nauseous, and sensing her discomfort, Nathaniel took her hand.

"Don't," he said firmly. The twinkle in his eyes put her at ease. "I like hearing you talk."

"What about you?" she asked quickly. "Tell me about you."

Leaning back again in his chair, Nathaniel ran a hand through his hair.

"Not as interesting as you by any stretch, I'm afraid. Born and raised..." he hesitated. "...not raised, grew up I should say, in London, Streatham. My mum was on her own. She wasn't interested in raising children, she preferred men and the bottle." There was an edge to his voice and a sudden hardness around his mouth.

"That sounds tough," said Dinah, sympathetically.

"It was tough." He shrugged and then his face softened. "I've got two sisters and a brother. I'm the eldest. I moved down here five years ago. I'm lucky with my work. It doesn't matter where I live."

"What do you do?"

"I'm a property developer."

"Oh!" Dinah's face fell.

"Eco-homes," he added quickly. "Sustainable buildings, cutting carbon emissions, sustainable materials, that kind of thing." She grinned, relieved. "We're doing a project in Spain. Eco-housing, a hotel. I've got a business partner who lives in London, so I go up there once or twice a month and the odd trip away."

"That's amazing." Dinah was thrilled. "It's what the world needs and you're obviously doing well. Is that what brought you to Porrick?"

"I knew the area. My father's family was from Devon. I've still got an aunt in Exeter and a few cousins dotted around the county and in Cornwall. That's not why I came here, though. It was more to do with lifestyle. I surf and I like being on the moor, swimming, camping, that sort of thing." He paused at her obvious surprise.

"Sorry, you didn't seem the type," she said quickly.

"You thought I was a city boy?" He sounded offended.

"Not at all. I don't know what I thought. Just not that you'd be pitching a tent on Dartmoor and jumping into cold rivers and streams."

Nathaniel laughed.

"I'm happy here. It's a good place for me. Different ideas and ways of doing things, different ways of living, and there are interesting people here. Unusual people like yourself..."

His voice trailed off and he picked up her hand. The charge undulating between them set her insides on fire and when he lifted his head, she saw her own longing mirrored in his eyes.

"I should go," she said squeezing his fingers. "I need to pick up my boys from football." Although she was comfortable with him and felt like she had known him for ever, Dinah wasn't sure if there was anything more than sexual heat present. He appeared sincere, but also had the definite air of the playboy about him. She pushed back her chair to stand.

"Okay." He sounded disappointed. "I'll walk you out."

Rummaging in his coat, Nathaniel left some money on the counter and with her hand clasped in his, led the way outside. He turned to face her. "I'd like to see you again."

"I'd like that, too."

He paused. "Can I take your number?"

Tapping Dinah's number into his phone, Nathaniel was relieved. Now she couldn't vanish.

When he stepped in to kiss her goodbye her arms went around his waist, and when his lips pressed her mouth, his tongue finding hers for the briefest moment, she didn't pull away.

* * *

Tonight was the first yoga class of the New Year. Hugging her coat tight around her, Dinah called goodbye to the boys and Kate as she left, pulling the front door shut. Since the last time she had seen Tony, Dinah had been carefully noting any visions or inner nudges she received. During their time apart he had appeared twice more in her dreams. These were always strangely vivid, filled with feeling and emotion, but nothing overwhelming. She was starting to accept these strange night-time meetings. He seemed incredibly powerful when he entered her awareness this way and she couldn't help notice how blissful she felt afterwards, a feeling that stayed with her into the day. It occurred to her, too, that he was beginning to take up a fair bit of her thoughts, even when she wasn't with him.

"He's getting in my head, Angels," she sent out as she walked to the class. "And I'm still not sure he's to be trusted. He seems to have penetrated my mind without me even noticing. It seems to have taken him no effort at all."

Still, she was pleased the class was starting up again after the holidays. She had been restless during the two-week break, in spite of the festive celebrations. Noticing these feelings, Dinah was compelled to wonder if it was his yoga teaching she was longing for or him? There was something about the wondering that made her not want to answer.

Tony paid Dinah no attention when she arrived and led the class straight into a stronger than usual yoga practice. By the end of the session she was adrift in blissful trance and when they sat for meditation she was already halfway there. Quietly immersed in stillness, it was with a start that Dinah realised everyone was already leaving. Mats were being rolled up and shoes put on feet. In that moment she knew she must speak to Tony, and speak to him now.

Yet something about this man made her nervous. He prodded at her with the sheer force of his will. Dinah rolled up her mat with shaky hands. She couldn't explain her reaction. He triggered something in her and she had no idea what was coming next. Out of control was how she felt and even then the absurdity of it all didn't escape her. He seemed able to read her in a way nobody else ever had.

As she waited patiently for him to finish a conversation with another student, she could sense his awareness of her standing behind him. It was getting odder and odder. The last student left and with no other distractions he finally turned to her feigning surprise.

"Hello?" He was completely expressionless.

Dinah faltered. What is he doing? she wondered, looking him square in the eye. Why is he pretending to not know I was here?

"Yes, Dinah?" Tony wore an enquiring expression.

"Can we talk?" To her mortification, her voice was so quiet she could barely hear it herself. Embarrassed, she tried clearing her throat. A gentle hand brushed her hair and Dinah knew that although it was awkward this man had something for her. The reason would appear soon surely. Kneeling next to him she stared at her hands.

"I don't know why I need to speak to you, all I know is that I do."

Tony smiled lazily and shifted slightly to face her. "We're two magnets, Dinah." His voice was low. "You feel drawn."

She raised her head as a charge went through her. She was unable to tear her eyes from his.

"I can help. You don't need to be afraid." Time evaporated. She was falling into him, feeling the pull, irresistibly drawn by the force in his eyes, his words.

He smiled and gently touched her hand. That one small gesture, and a surge of desire pounded through her.

"Help me with what? I don't understand," she replied. Her voice was clear, but the sudden desperation in it shocked her. "You confuse me. I need to hear more, but I can't seem to grasp what you say. And your energy is so strong… I don't want to lose myself."

"Lose yourself, Dinah? Who is Dinah that she can be lost? Nothing real can ever be lost." He was leaning closer, his eyes fixed on hers and she was a prisoner under his gaze.

"I can help you," he repeated firmly. "What you feel. It is what you yearn for, what you have always yearned for. This craving, this longing, it is a signpost showing you the way, showing you what you have been searching for your whole life. Only now you discover it was here all along."

He slowly reached out and took her hand, resting it in his. "You are realising that what I teach in this class is something more than mere asana. I teach real yoga, not acrobatics, not aerobics; I teach truth." Again, as he talked, Dinah was drifting deeper. Deeper into connection, a delirious connection she had no desire to break. They were merging. "It unsettles you because it goes beyond everything you've ever known."

A pause. He was watching, waiting for something. Dinah couldn't speak and the silence hung between them. Time stretched in all directions as they stared into each other's souls.

"Shall I tell you what I think of you?" Although his voice was soft the words jarred, and just like that, Dinah was free. She snapped back to consciousness as if woken from a stupor. Whereas moments earlier she was lost in dreamy union now she was flustered and uneasy.

Who do you think you are? The thought flashed in her mind.

Tony blanched but went on. "You've been hurt, Dinah. You are scared and resentful and so surround yourself with walls. You imprison yourself while recognising that there is something here in my class for you, something that you crave. You want to come to me, to open and be welcomed and yet you hold back. This inner conflict causes you great distress, Dinah, and this confusion, as you buy into your self-created identity and deny the truth of who you are, ultimately leads only to pain."

Annoyance flared at the audacity of his words, at his arrogance. "I want to come to you?" she demanded, the words laden with contempt. No longer afraid she met his eyes directly as anger frothed in her belly.

"You long to let go into a teacher, Dinah," he said calmly. "It is why you come to my class."

"What teacher?" There was an edge in her voice. "You?"

He didn't react to her withering tone and met her challenging gaze with a smile.

"You mean you're offering me your services as a guru, Tony? What about God? What about life? They are my teachers. They teach me all I need to know far better than any one person could."

"This goes beyond God, Dinah." He was still smiling. Confident.

"What do you mean?" Dinah gasped, shocked. "How can anything go beyond God?"

Silently he focused on her eyes. The impact of his scrutiny made her anxious. It was deliberate and she knew she was being hooked in again, sucked into the vortex. The outrage was loosening and while she was aware of a small voice urging her to flee, she couldn't quite muster the strength to actually get up and leave.

"It's okay," he murmured. "I see you, Dinah." His spoke slow, unhurried, his voice tender. "I see the beauty of you, beyond your idea of who you believe yourself to be."

The palms of her hands were damp as she gripped them, her heart pounding uncomfortably, but try as she might she couldn't look away. It was as though he was penetrating into her, watching her squirm, naked and exposed as he read all the secrets in her eyes – all the fears, hopes and desires laid bare.

It was a battle of wills and suddenly not caring what he thought, Dinah snapped her eyes shut.

"You don't need to be afraid of me." He sounded amused. "But if you really seek truth, Dinah, you must transcend your story. There is no other way."

"What do you mean, my story?"

"Who you believe yourself to be." He was watching her intently. "The story is persuasive and holds us in its grip until we free ourselves – it tells us who we think we are, of what it is we think we need to be, what we must have and do and, of course, who we believe others to be. It's a trap and it is all lies we tell ourselves to make ourselves feel better."

He sounded almost fervent and Dinah frowned, trying to comprehend his meaning.

"Most people go through their whole life in their story. It is familiar and therefore more comfortable and you have to be brave to see it for what it really is, to admit the truth that your whole life is utter fabrication."

"My view of who I think I am?" Dinah floundered, but he continued as if she had not spoken.

"To give up your story is to let go of the struggle. It is not for the faint-hearted, it's true, but those caught up in their own stories live in pain and sorrow. To let go of it, to drop all the opinions and ideas we carry around with us, it is the only way to know the truth, to rediscover the beauty of being. It is found inside us Dinah, not outside, and is the very essence of being."

He took her hands in his, so gently she barely felt his touch, just the softness of skin on skin.

"It is a direct route I offer you, a fast track if you like. You'll have to do it at sometime, Dinah. It may as well be now."

There was so much turmoil inside her and she noticed her hands trembling in his. "But I don't understand. How can a soul grow if it completely lets go of the story? Surely there would be no opportunity to learn, to blossom from its own experience of life. Isn't that how we reach liberation – enlightenment – the very reason for life itself, our only reason for being here at all?"

Tony baulked slightly, his gaze unyielding.

He dislikes being contradicted, Dinah realised, and ever so slowly withdrew her hands.

"This is a direct path," he repeated, with an edge to his voice that made her flinch. "One of the surest routes there is. You are welcome to join us or not. It is as you wish."

With that he turned away and began gathering up his belonging strewn alongside his mat, the money pot, incense, some matches. Watching him tip them into a battered sports bag, Dinah felt a chill wash over her as she realised she had been dismissed. Her palms were damp and she rubbed them together before getting up.

"I understand it can be difficult," he spoke, his voice suddenly gentle and reassuring again, catching her off guard. Touching her arm, he moved so she could not avoid his eyes. "And sometimes painful. The ego is like a vice and will not relinquish its hold easily. But I can help you." They were so close she could see individual stubble bristles on his jaw.

"I won't let you down, Dinah. I won't hurt you and I won't betray you."

The choice of words startled her, even more so as desire pulsed through her in response. She had to leave.

"I must get back for the babysitter," she said grabbing her mat. Her voice sounded strained and harsh to her ears after the poetry of Tony's words, but she no longer cared. The thought of being with him for even one second longer was intolerable.

"I'll walk with you," he smiled, and before she could object, swung the bag over his shoulder and took her elbow, guiding her to the door. While Tony locked up the hall, Dinah had a chance to examine him more closely. He was stocky with a way of holding himself that projected authority. His skin was best described as swarthy, with thick stubble around the chin and dark blond hair that curled over his coat collar. His clothes were practical, grey tracksuit bottoms and a faded blue sweater under an old grey coat. When he turned to her he was nervous and unsure, unable to meet her eyes. Dinah wondered if he knew she had been studying him so acutely.

"I go towards the river," she offered. "You?"

He looked relieved. "No, I go the other way – up the hill."

Relief swept over her too. The energy between them was tense and she had no idea how to ease it, so when he opened his arms to hug goodbye it was a wooden and awkward embrace.

"It was nice talking, Dinah." His confidence had apparently returned as he put a hand on her shoulder and looked her square in the eye. "We'll see each other next week then."

Seventeen

Hurrying home, Dinah scowled. "You're being crazy," she scolded herself firmly. "You're all over the place. You don't want to become one of Tony's followers, do you?"

If she were honest she had felt very ungracious towards the women in his class who fawned over him. Yet here she was tongue-tied and yearning, just another doting yogini to add to his harem. And worse, she was certain he knew exactly how she felt. It made her squirm to think of it and embarrassment was one emotion she thought she had thankfully left behind long ago. Clearly not. Tony seemed to bring it out in her with worrying regularity. He was beginning to turn her world upside down.

"What now, Angels? Am I falling under a spell?"

That night he was in her dream again. They were in a car together; he was driving and she was the passenger. In her dream state she was surprised to be here, but it felt good being with him. The car was going up a hill, it was dark and the road was steep and winding. It felt extremely hazardous, and Dinah gripped her seat, but Tony managed to navigate the road with ease. Then, taking his hand off the steering wheel he reached across and squeezed her thigh. As if by magic, desire flooded through her.

Darkness.

Now she was in a chamber, huddled on a wet, dirty floor. There was no light and it was cold and damp. She was hungry and scared. Something was wrong.

Why am I here?

Through the gloom she could make out stone walls surrounding her, some kind of cell. Looking down at her hands she saw they were pale and thin, and that they were grasping frantically at each other, as if by their own accord. She was rocking relentlessly, back and forth, back and forth. She couldn't seem to stop. Through the darkness

143

came strange noises, things calling out and echoing around her. Primal, animal howls and awful screeches that sent fear rippling through her. Yet she knew these demented sounds weren't coming from animals, but from humans, others like her, locked away in a small and frightening world. Terror was coming for her again. Dinah woke up, sweating.

* * *

Sam's house was a higgledy-piggledy end-of-terrace cottage on the outskirts of town. To get through the porch you had to manoeuvre over the guinea pig cage, brought inside until it got warmer, and then climb over the mountain of wellington boots and shoes. Once you were in there were toys everywhere, and every available bit of wall was adorned with children's paintings and pictures. It was a proper family home, like the one Nathaniel used to dream of as a boy. By stark contrast his childhood home had been virtually empty and unloved. No colourful paintings and pictures, just bare walls, sparse furniture and four unkempt children. Mum hardly ever there, or if she was, locked in the bedroom with another new face, another big, heaving man, or crying in the kitchen knocking back the wine.

Most nights it was Nathaniel going through the kitchen cupboards, looking for something for supper, watched by his brother and sisters. He'd been brave, tried to smile and console, but most often he'd gone knocking to Mary next door, a friendly old lady with a pale wrinkled face. For a time, Mary was the mother figure they needed, feeding them soup and biscuits, and cheese on toast. She taught them to play cards and would brush and plait the girls' hair and wash their faces. It had been a blow when she died, and that night Nathaniel had huddled in bed and cried himself to sleep. It was the one and only time he allowed tears to fall. He was thirteen years old.

It made him cold to remember and he shivered off the memory as he knocked on Sam's door.

When Sam called earlier to invite Nathaniel to supper he had mentioned seeing Cassie in the supermarket while he was doing their weekly shop, or said rather that Cassie had banged into him. "Literally crashed into me from behind."

144

Sam had been in a rush so hadn't had time to explain further and Nathaniel wasn't sure he even wanted to know more details, but his friend had promised to tell him tonight. Nathaniel already felt a twinge of anxiety.

The kitchen table was already laid for supper with cutlery and glasses, napkins and a basket of bread. The three children were in bed, including baby Annie, who was just seven months old.

"Smells delicious," said Nathaniel, handing Sam two bottles of red wine. A big grey pot bubbled on the stove.

"Of course. I cooked tonight," said Sam, producing a corkscrew and proceeding to open one of the bottles. "We're having chicken curry. Ellie's just checking on Annie and the girls. She'll be down in a bit." Ellie was Sam's partner of fifteen years.

"So," said Nathaniel, pulling out a chair at the table as Sam handed him a glass of wine, "as much as I don't want to bring her up, you said you saw Cassie?"

"Errr... yes, I'm afraid I did. She's a strange one, Nathaniel. She banged into me and then tried to pretend it was an accident, but I knew damn well she'd done it on purpose. She wanted to talk and guess what about."

Nathaniel was expressionless. "Go on."

"Couldn't get away from her. She was going on and on, saying how great you are, how she's so glad she met you, that we must all get together and had I seen you recently, that she hadn't seen you for a while..."

Nathaniel snorted. "She sees me all the time, she makes sure of it. Pops up wherever I go." He couldn't contain his annoyance. "You know, I'm wondering if it's her ringing my doorbell at all hours."

"Is it happening a lot?"

"Yes! At least she hasn't got my phone number!"

Sam stopped stirring the curry. "Now I've spoken to her in the cold light of day, it wouldn't surprise me. She was trying to get me to promise to organise a night out for us all. Really pushy, kept insisting, said she'd see us at the pub on Thursday."

"Urrggh" Nathaniel groaned. "Well I know where I won't be on Thursday. Was that it then?"

"Well, yeah." Sam was scooping rice into three bowls. "It was weird. I was going to suggest you back off from her, but it sounds like you're already there!"

He grinned at the serious expression on Nathaniel's face.

"Don't worry about it. Just keep away from her and she'll get bored."

There was the sound of footsteps coming down the stairs.

"Ellie's got the children off," said Sam, putting bowl of curry and rice in front of Nathaniel.

"Let's not talk about Cassie anymore," urged Nathaniel, gulping a large swig of wine.

* * *

Even though it was not yet midday the grey drizzle and darkened sky made it seem like early evening. Dinah was going to meet Tony. The air on her face was cold and she was grateful for the thick mittens and heavy fleecy-lined boots that kept the chill at bay. He was picking her up from the garage just outside town on the road leading up to the moor.

Tony had approached her last Thursday after class. She felt a hand on her shoulder and found Tony crouching next to her. She was even more surprised when he asked if she would like to meet him during the coming week. He had suggested going for a walk somewhere away from the town where they could talk more. Their eyes met and she felt the strange pang of longing that she often had with him, filling with warmth and hopefulness but tinged with an undercurrent of something she couldn't quite decipher. Flattered, she had accepted his invitation and then winced as he promptly informed her that he would help identify and dissolve some of her defences.

"It will be good for you."

These sorts of remarks worried her. Apart from being unsure what he meant it made her uneasy when he spoke like this and she immediately regretted her hasty acceptance.

What does he want? She wondered, agitated. What is he up to? Trying to add me to his harem of women? Trying to prove he has some kind of secret knowledge? What?

She had no idea about this man. He was an utter stranger, someone she knew absolutely nothing about. He could be anyone at all and, frustratingly, being relatively new to the town herself, there was no one she could ask about him. The others in the class were aloof and distant and not open to conversation so she would just have to feel her way.

The Angels reassured her, telling her to trust she was safe, but she struggled nonetheless. If she and Tony had a higher reason for being in each other's lives then she detected no awareness on his part and that made her nervous.

If it's only me aware of a deeper connection, it means I'll have to take sole responsibility for peaceful resolution come what may.

Spotting his car parked by the garage kiosk, Dinah hurried over. The door swung open as she neared and she climbed in, grateful for the warmth blasting from the heater. "Hi," she smiled. "Sorry, I'm late. Have you been waiting long?"

He looked at her without saying a word, the hint of a smile on his lips. Unnerved, Dinah shut the car door and pulled the seat belt across, grateful for any distraction to avoid the knowing in his eyes. It must have been only moments, but it felt an age until he finally took his attention off her and manoeuvred the car onto the main road.

"He always has this effect on me, Angels," she sent out as she plugged in the seat belt. "I'm calm and composed and then the minute I'm in his presence it all changes. The worst thing is I can't seem to pull myself together."

Sitting back she was uncomfortable at the resounding silence lingering between them, but as they drove further onto the moor, as the main roads gave way to country lanes flanked by tall, wild hedgerows she began to relax. The magical landscape of Dartmoor was taking over. The bare branches of winter trees arched overhead giving the impression of travelling through a series of woodland tunnels. They crossed narrow stone bridges spanning wide gushing streams, the waters flowing fast, muddied and swollen from recent rains and pounding hard over rocks and boulders.

Vowing not to be the one to break the silence, Dinah concentrated on the magnificent scenery. She guessed Tony knew she was jangled and so she stared fixedly out of the window, refusing to give in to the mounting tension. They ended up driving the whole way without

147

speaking and it was only when they turned down a narrow side track that he finally spoke.

"I'm taking you somewhere special, Dinah," he said, smiling at the way she jumped at the sound of his voice. "Somewhere dear to my heart." They pulled into a grassy lay-by and he pointed to a mossy, pebble-strewn pathway, which led deep into the woodland. "This way." She followed in his wake as again they fell into the strange silence that Tony so seemed to enjoy. Whenever she looked across at him he only smiled.

Why did I come? she wondered, crossly. He only makes me edgy and uptight. She kicked at the damp earth, disturbing the layers of rotting leaves. But something about him made her want to know more and she kept walking, despite the niggling anxiety.

"Dinah!" She started as he interrupted her thoughts. "You must be alert in life in order to be truly alive. It can feel uncomfortable at first, the alertness, the fire, it can feel disturbing and yet it is key. Those who walk sleepy and dull live in delusion, caught in their stories believing themselves alive, telling themselves they are alive and yet they aren't. They are the living dead." His words came from nowhere, strange and seemingly random and yet touching a chord deep inside. Was he reading her mind? Was it actually possible for him to know all of her thoughts?

"When you fall into the trap of the comfortable, when you succumb to the safety of the familiar and routine; you have fallen asleep. That is the biggest curse to befall a person. A life wasted."

He was speaking quietly, his words provoking strange, new feelings within her that she didn't recognise.

"To live fully awake we must open and receive everything that comes our way without judgment or censor. Welcome whatever comes, without labels of good or bad – by accepting the story for what it is – a story – you find the peace and joy you so desperately seek."

They were gently bumping into each other as they walked, their footsteps naturally adjusting to each other's rhythm. Tony took her hand so tenderly, almost reverently, and in spite of an overwhelming shyness, Dinah let him.

Together they ventured further into the ancient woodland of Dartmoor, a place where the elementals roam, free from accusing

148

human eyes, of hidden mysteries and times of old, and the deeper they went the stronger the unseen energies became. The intensity of the surroundings was starting to affect her. Dinah didn't know if Tony could feel anything but powerful sensations were flooding her body and she willingly opened herself up to receive. The familiar pulse of the natural world and its ever-watchful Guardians was always present for Dinah, but here in the rugged terrain of the moor, far from the nearest town, the energies were strong, penetrating her soul, making her mind and body hum.

Ahead of them the pathway opened into a clearing and Dinah guessed that was where they were headed. Drawing nearer she saw the clearing was encircled by rows of gnarled trees and Dinah felt one in particular calling her – an ancient oak growing near the stream. Its massive trunk was split in two to reveal a gaping crevasse, while beneath, a labyrinth of thick roots stretched out wide before delving into the earth. Without a word, Dinah went to it and laid her palms on its weathered bark. The instant her hands made contact she was pulled into its energy field, waves of timeless healing emanating through her as she pressed against the trunk. The sheer size of the tree told her it was one of the oldest in the wood, a solid presence in a transient world with heavy boughs, laden with mistletoe, which reached in all directions. The branch above her was long and bowed and stretched towards the stream as though reaching for a drink. At her feet, Dinah noticed a wide flat stone covered with moss and she sank down onto it, resting her forehead against the tree trunk and closing her eyes. She was absorbing the oak, its strength and power, merging with its soul, listening as it whispered.

"I hold the energy of the land within me and while I and others like me, stand, All is Well. During the darkest winter months, the harshest, coldest days of the year, I am naked. The winds and rains may batter me, unceasing, but I stay firm. I may lose branches, but my roots, strong and deep, reach into the soil, to the core of Earth giving me nourishment and stability. Earth provides all I need to survive and withstand the most brutal storm. As the sun begins its return it warms the land and spring comes again. New buds appear. I am reborn. To begin with my buds are small and vulnerable, but as the days pass they grow into lush green leaves and bear fruit. In summer I am stronger than ever before. I am vibrant and alive and at

149

the peak of my cycle. In autumn I discard the outgrown. With the shortening days my leaves flame orange and gold, before dying and falling to the Earth. I release them willingly, so that humanity too may release the past. They fall to the ground to become compost, fertilising the soil to feed the new growth, which comes with the new cycle.

"The releasing of the outworn and the weathering of the dark and cold is what brings my rebirth. Tirelessly I repeat the seasons, knowing that every cycle will be different. Some winters will be icy and harsh, some will merely be rainy and dark, but I endure it all. And as the world continues on, my message for humanity is one of encouragement and resilience. I never give up and I never lose hope, because I know that spring always comes again, no matter how long the winter. This is the nature of the Divine cycle of Earth."

A jubilant tinkling reached Dinah's ears and as she lifted her head she saw the stream nearby. It was singing, joyful and free, on its way to reunite with the ocean. Getting unsteadily to her feet, Dinah carefully walked towards the water, slipping down the muddy bank, clinging to tree roots and then picking her way over huge wet boulders to reach the water's edge. The streambed was scattered with brightly coloured pebbles, and huge dark rocks formed bubbling whirlpools as the water coursed round them to the sea. A line of prehistoric looking trees ran along the bank on the far side, their bark all but concealed by lichen, their branches twisted with age. They reminded her of watchful old soldiers, stooping and bent, while faithfully guarding some long-forgotten secret.

The elemental energy here was overpowering. Clusters of rowan trees, holly and elder nestled together, trunks swathed in ivy. Beyond, the subdued fire of long dead bracken gave the landscape an ochre tinge. Cupping her hands she bent and scooped up some water, splashing it on her face, delighting in the cold on her skin.

"A sacred place," she murmured.

"Yes it is." A voice at her side. She jolted. Of course, Tony was here.

"I knew you would appreciate it, Dinah."

She stayed quiet, merely gazing about her, unable to reply.

Before her eyes the landscape was subtly changing. The beauty of the surroundings transporting her to another place as the hidden energies revealed themselves to her willing eyes. Dinah gasped as dancing coloured lights appeared, hundreds of orbs skimming the water, diving playfully through the air and skating across its surface, while beside the stream the minutest silver sparkles darted skittishly across moss-strewn pebbles. The water sprites were showing themselves and Dinah watched captivated.

The wind picked up, making the branches of the trees around her rustle and sway.

"There's a wound inside you, Dinah."

She heard him and closed her eyes. Tony's voice was soft, but was intrusive. "Your wound causes you to close off. I feel it in you and I see deep inside you, to the truth beyond your hurts."

"I don't close off..." she began to protest, but suddenly felt inexplicably tired. His words were touching something inside her, causing her heart to ache.

"You don't know who you are, Dinah. You identify with your personality, your story, so much that you've lost sight of who you really are."

A longing she had never noticed before stirred deep within her. And it was gaining momentum with every word he uttered, as if he were teasing it out of her, demanding it show itself. As the feeling worked up through her body she bent double, sighing, again and again, until finally it came out of her mouth as a long drawn-out groan. The energy coming off Tony was like an ocean wave, but he made no move to comfort her as she scrabbled down to the ground, hand clutching her chest.

Dinah stayed that way, hunching into herself until the sensation started to recede. Now he was lifting her upright and she rose cautiously, disorientated by the unexpectedness of what had happened. It had come from nowhere, as though summoned by his promptings.

"I'm okay," she reassured Tony, who didn't appear the least concerned by her strange behaviour. "I feel like I've put down a heavy weight. I actually, surprisingly, feel pretty good."

He still didn't move or say anything at all and Dinah began to feel foolish. She had a sudden impulse to run away and the thought made her smile. She wondered what he would do if she just took off. The

151

image played in her mind, so tempting in its absurdity, as without a word Tony turned to climb back up the bank to the pathway.

Following behind him, Dinah was happy. She didn't need Tony's validation, *something* had taken place, and nothing could dull her spirits. They trampled along the path and got to the car just as a dense white mist descended, blotting out the hillside. They drove back to the town in silence.

Eighteen

"I love your skirt," exclaimed a voice. Dinah looked up to see a pretty woman with dark hair hovering over her. "You look wonderful in it."

They were outside the cornershop where Dinah was untying Sophie's lead from the post where she had left her while she went in for milk.

"Thank you," she said, pulling the lead free. The woman was smiling but staring so intently that Dinah immediately felt awkward.

"Where did you get it? I'd love to get a skirt like that!" Her enthusiasm was somewhat disconcerting as Dinah's skirt was quite plain and worn and nothing special as far as she was concerned.

"Er, I can't remember actually. It's quite old," Dinah said, unexpectedly flustered. The air around her was prickling and she took an involuntary step back. The woman didn't move, although Dinah was sure she caught a flicker of annoyance in her eyes. "Archangel Michael, protect me," Dinah sent out, without knowing why.

"That's a shame. Never mind." The woman's smile was still friendly and she knelt down next to Sophie to pet her. Sophie was only too happy to be stroked and shuffled closer to the woman, eyes blissfully closed.

"Gorgeous dog," the woman said and kissed the top of Sophie's head.

Odd... thought Dinah.

"I've got one the same," the woman went on, seemingly oblivious of Dinah's discomfort. "A spaniel. She looks just like yours." For no apparent reason, Dinah didn't believe her.

The woman continued stroking Sophie, cooing and gurgling as Dinah stood over them until it went past the point of comfort.

"I must go," Dinah blurted, giving Sophie's lead a tug. She knew she was being rude, but couldn't help it. "Bye." She tried to force a smile, but it was strained and she yanked Sophie's lead much harder than she intended to get away. The woman stood up, still smiling. "Of course. It was lovely talking to you. I'm Cassie by the way." She offered her hand for a handshake. "Maybe see you around?"

The question hovered between them and ignoring the woman's hand, Dinah involuntarily took another step backwards.

"Er, maybe…"

She was already walking away, dragging Sophie behind her. When they got to the corner and Dinah glanced back, the woman had gone.

"Sorry for pulling, Sophie," Dinah apologised, patting the dog on the head. "But that was weird."

* * *

At least once a week, sometimes more, Dinah would go to the moor, to the spot shown to her by Tony. Something about the place soothed her heart and whenever she felt the pull she would go. Wandering through the woods she often wondered if she would ever encounter him here. Mysteriously they never crossed paths outside of his class, not even in Porrick.

Whenever she came she would sit quietly on the stone under the oak, sheltered by its branches, mesmerised by the tinkle of the stream. She was happy here and would spend many hours watching the water, talking to the trees and the nature elementals – the faeries. The energy was strong here and she found it a place where she could voice all her worries without fear of judgment. And in the still of the wilds could more easily hear the reply. Each time she came, her connection with this part of land and its spirits deepened, periods of meditation and reflection forging unbreakable bonds. It was her refuge – a place of safety and escape.

Today Dinah stomped up the path, a tumultuous mood clouding her thoughts as she headed towards the clearing.

Solus had phoned early that morning to talk to the boys before they left for school. Answering the call, Dinah couldn't help but notice how happy and breezy he sounded.

"Work's gone crazy busy and we've moved house. Everything's chaotic."

His elation with life had left her feeling somewhat disgruntled.

Flopping down under the tree Dinah flung her bag to the ground in bad temper. "I want to meet someone, too!" She spoke crossly to the wilderness. "Someone to share Daniel and Luke with."

She had truly believed she didn't begrudge Solus his good fortune in work and love, and felt guilty at the ping of resentment in her belly that things weren't working out quite so well for her.

The relationships she'd had since Solus had all been unsatisfactory in varying ways, and had all hit that point where she knew they could go no further. "And then I come crashing down!" she sighed. Leaning back against the tree trunk, she pulled up her knees and wrapped her arms around them. Nathaniel flashed into her mind's eye. "The chemistry is there, but we're in two different worlds. And is he even capable of a mature committed relationship? With respect, without games, or power struggles, or needing to control?" She tugged at a piece of moss. "And then Tony! I don't understand at all what's happening there. It's strong but it's strange. Nothing ever moves on." She felt better already, speaking her innermost world out loud.

A fuzz of tingles pressed down her side making her shiver. "Trust," she heard. Her Angel had come. "You deserve more than you allow yourself to receive," cautioned the Angel. "We keep those away who would bring distress and it is reason to celebrate when the wrong person leaves." Dinah's mood lightened a little. "Love your life as it is right now, Dinah."

Dinah sniffed. "Thank you," she whispered.

All the while, Dinah noticed the elementals weren't saying a word. "Faeries, please talk to me," she put out a polite request.

Silence.

"Are you here?" She persisted, listening quietly. There was sound of the wind in the trees, the gurgling stream, but there was something else too. The air was charged, a sure sign. They're close, she thought excitedly.

"Faeries, why is it all so difficult?" she asked, encouragingly, fully aware she was being heard in spite of receiving no response. The elementals never adhere to the beck and call of humans. Humans as a collective group have yet to earn the trust and respect of the faery realms, yet individuals with a sincere heart can build a bridge between humanity and the faery kingdoms.

"I struggle as a human," confided Dinah, feeling hundreds of little ears all around and hundreds of watching eyes. They were curious, waiting to see what she might do now she had their attention. She was enjoying the game. "The human world is so tricky to navigate. Faery ways are so much easier. I'd far rather be faery." There was a definite sensation of rummaging in the air and the sound of rustling foliage. She was causing a stir. "Faeries, how do you see humans?" Dinah pushed on, determined to get some kind of response. "Do you think we're exotic and mysterious as I see you? Or do you think we're all daft?"

"Not all of you!" A jovial voice took her by surprise, making her jump, and immediately she heard giggling. Connection! Delighted, Dinah clapped her hands.

Then an unexpected hush fell and something caused her to turn. A figure had appeared beside her. Come so stealthy and silent she hadn't even noticed until he was right next to her. A mighty and formidable presence, so strong that she recoiled slightly, alarmed.

'Cernunnos.' The name flared in her mind as adrenalin fired her body. Horned God of the Wildwood. And although she could not remember ever having met him, she knew him well.

Two magnificent antlers vast and intimidating adorned his head. Dinah hardly dared breathe and was only aware of being completely overawed by the force of this mysterious being. Instinctively she called Archangel Michael, instantly feeling his soothing presence urging her not to be afraid.

"What does he want?" Dinah asked the Archangel.

Cernunnos shifted slightly, slowly easing his weight from one solid muscular leg to the other, and Dinah saw how exceptionally long his feet were, with toenails that grew over each toe like claws. With the torso of a man and legs covered lightly with fur, he was unlike any elemental Dinah had ever seen. He radiated warmth but the potency of his energy was intimidating: a solid and incorruptible masculine force, which Dinah sensed not much would overcome.

I brought you here. His voice was gruff, somewhere between a growl and a drawl and despite communicating telepathically, the

156

words boomed into her, strumming her bones. Dinah was afraid, even with Archangel Michael by her side.

It is your time of emergence.

This all-powerful God, an embodiment of unwavering strength, made her simultaneously want to shrink away *and* go nearer. Unable to move, unable to speak, Dinah juddered from the impact of connection.

You know me and I you.

He read her faultlessly. *Many lifetimes we have worked together. You are my initiate and for this service you have been hunted many times.* Dinah flinched. Something was awakening, a timeless fondness for this powerful being, a recognition accompanied by profound sorrow.

It is time to remember. His voice softened. *As a bearer of wisdom beyond this world you have duties yet to be fulfilled.*

Quiet.

Archangel Michael was placing his hands on the crown of her head and Dinah felt herself merging with the ancient God at her side, becoming one with Cernunnos as feelings, thoughts and visions flashed before her.

I am Protector and Hunter, Cernunnos told her. *King of the Forest and the Natural world. My kingdom is that which your kind destroys without thought or care for the Divine creation. The forests and lakes, rivers and mountains, deserts and woodland, jungles and seas. These worlds are the foundation of existence.*

As Dinah listened she saw the devastation of the natural worlds. Woods and forests being felled and the unyielding pollution of the land, air and waters. She saw the majestic ice lands melting into the sea, and witnessed tribes of indigenous peoples losing their land. She saw animals, fish and birds treated as objects, a commodity to be bought and sold, and winced as she saw whole species wiped out, and many hundreds more teetering on the brink.

Human beings must consider the implications of their actions, Cernunnos sent into her mind. *As children who eat too many sweets and then feel sick, humanity has been gorging, Dinah, and the sickness is coming. Earth cannot withstand much more.*

She felt his distress and it ignited her own. Melancholy resonated between them.

They know in their hearts it is wrong.

Dinah watched helpless, feeling the Earth at breaking point, buckling under the weight of relentless mistreatment.

Every individual is responsible for the direction the world is heading.

And Dinah saw how if the destruction of the Natural world continued, it would bring about the downfall of human existence.

Here were magnificent ancient cities of long ago, populated by evolved, intelligent peoples able to harness the power of the natural world to bring about comfort and ease. And yet they too succumbed to temptation, misusing their knowledge and working against nature and the natural order and ultimately destroying themselves. These highly advanced civilisations were reduced to rubble and dust by the misunderstanding of humankind.

The misunderstanding of humankind. The words lingered and she knew they were key.

Earlier civilisations destroyed through their own neglect of what is. But never has Earth tasted such devastation as she faces now.

Then Cernunnos took her far ahead into the worlds of possibility, places that had not yet been created and yet might never be. Now she saw a race of beautiful light-filled people, living beautiful light-filled lives on Earth in harmony with Nature and the other worlds.

This is the Divine plan, explained Cernunnos.

Happiness washed over her at the sight of a world with clear air, clean waters and flourishing woodlands. Animals roamed free, living side by side with humans, and nature and people were thriving. The atmosphere was one of radiance, purity and plenty, a place where Angels and Spirits co-existed with humanity, acknowledged and loved for their assistance and guidance.

Communication is through the mind and existence is one of love and respect for all that is. Between human and human, animal and human, plant and human.

Dinah understood the beauty of how it could be, the possibility of perfection next to the ugliness of how it is and where it is heading. Her heart was breaking.

It must be shared, Dinah, said Cernunnos, his words laden with anguish. *The natural world must be revered. Humankind can alter its course. Have hope. By honouring and loving all that is natural, by respecting what is and discarding the falsely created. It is time for Womankind to rise up, for it is She who will save her race. It is time for Her to step forward and show the way. She can no longer hide away and watch from one side. The time has come.*

With a breath, Dinah once more felt the solid stone beneath her.

The veils were coming down and Cernunnos was fading, as Dinah's awareness of her physical surroundings increased. She could just about hear his voice though, urgent.

We are all at the crossroads, all of us together, but it is humanity who has the choice. The elementals do what they can but are powerless without the support of the human race. Ignore the signs and omens and continue downwards. Or awaken. Drop the meaningless and embrace the truth.

Life change is nothing, Dinah. His voice just a murmur. *Not when facing the pain of annihilation.*

Nineteen

Nathaniel had texted Dinah first thing that morning, her phone beeping from inside her bag while she was having breakfast. Usually she would have ignored it but something prompted her to look.

Dinah, how have you been? Wondering if you want to meet up? Nx

She typed a quick reply. *Lovely, when are you free?*

Her phone pinged back immediately. *Tonight?*

Great. When and where?

"Mum, what's up?" Luke was regarding her suspiciously. "Who's that?"

"No one darling," she said, cheerfully, aware she was grinning from ear to ear.

"It can't be no one. Why are you smiling like that?" Daniel was eyeing her too.

"You're right." Tucking her phone back in her bag, Dinah rejoined them at the table. "Of course it isn't no one. It's a friend, that's all." She suspected she wasn't going to get off the hook quite so easily.

"Which friend?"

"You haven't met him yet, Daniel. He's called Nathaniel and we met in the town."

"What did he say?"

"He wanted to know if I'd like to meet. Daniel, can you pass me some toast?"

Daniel didn't move.

"Where did you meet him?" Luke was managing to spoon cereal into his mouth without taking his eyes off her face. Dinah paused. They were picking up something unusual was going on.

"Boys, it's alright. He came to one of my gatherings and we sometimes meet for coffee. He texted to ask if I want to meet later. Daniel, can you please pass the toast?"

"Why are you smiling so much?" Luke this time.

"Well, sometimes when you meet a friend or talk to them they just make you smile."

Both boys were quiet while Dinah spread jam on her toast.

"Mum?"

"Yes, Luke?"

"What if you meet a man and he lives with us and we don't like him. What would you do?"

"I wouldn't live with a man if you didn't like him – that's a promise." They were both still. "Oh boys..." She took their hands. "That will never happen. I would never bring someone to live with us if we weren't all completely happy." They both looked grave.

"Daniel. Luke. You are the most important things in my world and you come before anyone else. When... and if... a nice man does come to share our lives, then all of us will be happy – him too. All of us will love each other and want to spend time with each other, and nothing else will do. Got it!"

Daniel started to giggle. Luke smiled. "Got it."

They both relaxed. Dinah was relieved.

Dusk had fallen by the time Dinah emerged from the alleyway into the high street. Taking a few deep breaths, she put her hand to her belly and concentrated on calm, on really embodying it. She knew it was there beneath the nervous excitement. She had been so embroiled with Tony lately that Nathaniel had been side-lined from her thoughts, eclipsed by what was beginning to feel like a very toxic acquaintance. She had no idea what was going on between them.

"Tonight I am clear, Angels. Tonight I can meet Nathaniel without being distracted, in honesty as he deserves to be met, as we all deserve to be met."

The moon was a perfect crescent, a fingernail sliver of silver white against the blue-black sky. A quick calculation told Dinah the moon was waxing – a period of high energy and a good time to implement new plans and ideas. Gazing into the night-sky she felt as if she were staring straight into heaven. The moon smiled.

They were meeting at the top of the high street by the steps up to the church. Dinah saw him sitting on the steps staring vacantly ahead as he smoked a cigarette, the plume of smoke wafting into the night air. She had forgotten how handsome he was and as her heart fluttered. She was suddenly shy.

"Nathaniel," she said quietly.

"Dinah!" He threw away the cigarette and came to her, arms outstretched. With a grin he pulled her to him, squeezing her tightly before lifting her off the ground and spinning her round so her hair tumbled onto his face. They were both laughing.

When he finally lowered her down he kept his arms around her, and before she knew what was happening he was kissing her on the mouth. She melted into him, his arms tight around her. When they finally drew apart Dinah wobbled, unsteady in his arms and he gently kissed her again.

"Let's go get a drink!" She nodded, sliding her arm around his waist. It felt so normal, as though they had always been this way.

They went to one of the quieter pubs located down an unlit side street. It was small inside with a low ceiling and candles on each table. A fire roared in a wide elaborate stone fireplace. While Nathaniel ordered red wine, Dinah took off her coat and seeing a pile of leaflets on the bar began flicking through them.

One was for a kirtan concert the following week, in a music hall over the other side of town. She picked it up.

"What are you reading?" Nathaniel was holding a bottle and two glasses. "An Evening of Kirtan," he read over her shoulder. "What's that?"

"Devotional chanting," she said, excited. "It's the repetition of sacred sounds and words to music. It's call and response, so the wallah, the lead vocalist, chants a mantra, and the audience chant it back and you keep going like that. It gets you to a higher place really fast. Pure alchemy."

"For three hours?" Nathaniel was aghast.

The leaflet said 6pm–9pm. "Well, they might talk as well, but yes. It's great, really."

"Hmmm," he replied, and grinned. "Let's go and grab that window seat."

Following him to the back of the pub, Dinah squeezed into the bench before Nathaniel slipped in after her. He poured some wine, before handing her the glass.

"So, how've you been?" His smile was so disarming that she felt completely relaxed. "It's been a while. I thought you might be having second thoughts?" His eyes fixed on her.

"No!" she cried. "Nothing like that. I've just had things on and it's been a bit up and down, but all good. Things are settling, I hope. How about you?"

He paused. "Well, work's been busy. I've been in London quite a bit, and in Spain." Absentmindedly, he rested the palm of his hand on the rim of his wine glass. "But that's work for you. It'll calm down, it always does. It's good to see you though."

Warmth spread through Dinah's chest as he studied her through half-open eyes. Tentatively she rested her hand on his, caressing the skin with her thumb as a spark ignited. They both smiled.

"You're beautiful." He was leaning in, staring at her intently.

Slightly taken aback, Dinah hesitated, considering her words. "Thank you. I like you too." She smiled, but released his hand.

"There's something here. I feel it." He looked so sure, so certain.

"We're only on our second date though."

Nathaniel looked perplexed. He was clearly used to women falling at his feet and couldn't work out her reserved response. Dinah deliberately looked away, awkward. "There's no hurry, is there?" she whispered, more of a statement than a question. "No need to rush, to scare each other off."

"Tell me…" He came closer, his face just inches from hers. "What could you do to scare me off? I've already seen what you do – I might not get it completely, but you've told me how it is for you, with Angels and spirits, and I respect that. Unless there's some dark secret you're hiding?"

She shook her head.

"Well then." He sounded sincere.

Without warning the air around them began to disjoint and quiver. She froze, body taut on high alert as she felt something like sharp needles going into her. There was bad energy here, in the pub. Where was it coming from? Startled she looked around, head twisting in all directions, feeling sick as her solar plexus went into spasm.

It's coming right at us, she realised. "Archangel Michael, protect us. Angels, where is it? Show me the source." She clutched her stomach.

Her eyes landed on a woman standing at the bar staring right at them. She was vaguely familiar. Small, delicate with a mass of dark curly hair and glowering at them with what could only be described as white rage. When her eyes fixed on Dinah she bristled, and Dinah almost heard her hiss.

"Ignore her," instructed Nathaniel, slipping his arm protectively around her waist. "She's a past encounter that's all."

Dinah faced him, shocked. "She looks furious." She was shaken. The glint in the woman's eyes was disturbing. But under Archangel Michael's protection her solar plexus was relaxing and the sickness was fading.

"What happened?" she asked Nathaniel.

Nathaniel scowled and then sighed. "I met her in a bar a while back. She made a beeline for me, wouldn't leave me alone and we spent the night together." He shrugged.

An alarm pinged in Dinah's psyche. "Oh no! Angels, is he one of those men?"

"And I'm afraid, I repeated the experience."

Dinah remained motionless as he shot her a look.

"She turned up at my local and again, wouldn't leave me alone. She stayed at my place, a combination of drink and foolishness. It was a mistake. She wants more. I don't." He looked uncomfortable.

"I've seen her somewhere," said Dinah, trying to remember where she might have seen the woman. "Did you treat her well?" She really wanted to know.

Nathaniel squirmed under her gaze. "No, maybe not." His eyes flicked to the bar. The woman had gone. "No, I didn't. I wasn't nasty. I just didn't want to get into anything with her and she has become a little, shall we say, fixated." Now he was angry. "She turns up at my flat at all hours, bothers my friends, follows me if she sees me in town. That kind of thing."

"Oh no!" said Dinah, aghast, her mind spinning. She took a gulp of wine. "Do you do that often?"

"Do I do what often?"

"Use women for sex?" she blurted. The edge in her voice surprised her. Nathaniel looked shocked. The romantic ambience was gone.

Nathaniel stared at her defiantly. "She made herself available and I was happy to go along with it. It was her choice too, not just mine." Dinah looked away and silence simmered between them.

"Sorry," she said, finally. "I don't know why I asked that." She fidgeted with her wine glass. "It's none of my business."

"Look," – he sounded weary – "women have been happy to give themselves to me like that. She seduced me, not the other way around."

Dinah didn't know what to think. The woman had definitely felt out of balance, dangerously so, her mind off-kilter. But even so, no one likes to be used and then rejected. These unpleasant revelations made her feel unsure all over again. That Nathaniel was some hardened lothario. Crashing his way through life, hurting hearts, oblivious to the emotional damage left trailing behind him. Fooling her, drawing her in.

Nathaniel clenched his wine glass. They had crossed a boundary into uncertain territory.

"I know women behave badly, too," Dinah conceded, wanting to salvage something of the evening. "Women using sex to ensnare men, or impress men, or to get their attention. She's coming from her wounded shadow, the part that doesn't feel good enough. It's the wounded feminine acting out, I know, but it's the wounded masculine that responds."

"I'm not wounded," he said sharply and stared at her again. "I have a past. Yes, I've got a history, but who hasn't?" Picking up the bottle, he slopped more wine into his glass before putting it back down on the table with a bump. Tension radiated off him.

Dinah touched his arm. "I shouldn't have commented. Can we just forget about her and get back to our evening?"

Nathaniel eyed her, twisting his glass round on the table. "It isn't just women who get scared and get used you know. Men do too. And for the record I would love to fall in love, to meet the one, but so far it just hasn't happened." He fell silent, expressionless.

Dinah's heart thumped. The hint of a smile danced at the corner of his mouth and the air burned between them. Tingles running down her arms and face alerted Dinah to the presence of the Angels. Nathaniel was quiet, but as she steadily met his gaze, something softened in her chest.

"You know," she said, her stomach undeniably churning, "I want more than just lust, or being in a relationship to avoid being alone. I've done all that, I want more now. I want true intimacy, something deeper, more real." Her voice faded.

The way he was looking at her was confusing. He looked serious and slightly cross. "My past relationships may have been lacking, Dinah, but perhaps I want something more, too."

They had changed the subject after that, moved on to less unsettling topics. Books and food, which countries they had been to or still hoped to visit, and, when the wine was all gone, they gathered their coats and headed outside. It was good to be in the fresh air again. Cleared the head.

Nathaniel offered to walk her home but Dinah declined, needing some space after the earlier strangeness of the evening. He had kissed her goodbye, a brief peck on the lips, which to both their surprise inadvertently became something more lingering, more passionate, as if they couldn't draw away from each other. When they did eventually separate, breathless and unsteady, Nathaniel squeezed her hand. "Okay?" he enquired.

Dinah nodded. Her voice lost.

The town was empty as she walked home, and apart from the muffled sounds of people in nearby pubs she could have been completely alone. One or two shops had lights on, but most were in darkness. It was only the occasional street lamp dotted sporadically along the pavement that lit her way.

The slimmest slice of moon glimmered above the town and she stopped to stare. "How did you become so beautiful?" Dinah asked it, smiling to herself and smiling even more when a passing man looked at her in concern before hurrying on. "Talking to the sky, he thinks I'm mad, Angels," Dinah said laughing. "He doesn't understand that everything is alive, that everything is energy. He doesn't listen to the sky talk and probably doesn't hear the trees and the plants either, the sea and the air. He probably isn't interested in such things and what they have to teach."

She sent the man a blessing.

Returning her gaze upwards once more she lost herself in the stars, in awe of the magical beauty and shimmering light. Casting her arms wide, a mysterious smile twitched her lips as she spotted the pointed turrets of Caer Sidhi, glimmering amongst the stars of the Northern constellation. "Aha!" she whispered. "I see you right there!"

The castle shimmered before her, strong and proud, built of glistening glass and thousands of stars. As the sacred domain of the mighty Faery Queen, Arianrhod, Caer Sidhi is said to be visible only to those of pure heart and mind. Goddess of the Feminine and weaver of magical energies, Arianrhod stood firm in the face of the patriarchy of the past few thousand years – refusing to bend or to be crushed into submission and rejecting with a vengeance the imposed masculine supremacy. A guiding beacon for the Feminine, whole unto herself and with no need for masculine protection, she exudes a primal sexual power which can never be subdued. During the descent into Patriarchy, Arianrhod merely hovered to one side, unseen and invisible, biding her time, poised and waiting for the energies to shift.

"So the time is come Goddess?" questioned Dinah, transfixed by the sight, knowing that the appearance of this potent symbol of Feminine power was a sign. "The Feminine is returning and there is no going back."

The moon seemed to expand at her words, as in turn the castle glimmered brighter and more radiant than before. Her heart quickened. "Thank you for granting me this vision," sent out Dinah. "For blessing me and guiding my path." She hesitated. Dare she ask?

With her hands clasped beneath her chin she stared intently into the mystical castle, and after a thoughtful pause gently sent out a request to the Goddess.

"Arianrhod, please help me discern a lover who is true and respectful, who is faithful, trustworthy and loyal. Please protect my heart and warn me if I am being misled or deceived in any way. Tony confuses me – the draw and yet the resistance, and though Nathaniel feels clear, I'm not sure he would be true."

In the following moments everything fell silent. An eerie still descending before a cool wind picked up and swept around her as the world dropped away. The breeze caressed her skin and through the thick night air she could hear music playing – high, haunting notes straight from the etheric realms. The melody soothed her spirit as unbidden words skirted the fringes of her mind.

I am the Goddess of the Moon, Saviour of the light, Seer of the stars, Queen of the night, moving through the sky, Send me your prayer, For I am Arianrhod, Faery Priestess of the Air.

The trance state retreated as quickly as it had come – only now Dinah was exhilarated. As she continued home, her body flushed with fire and her heart pulsed with excitement. The goddess was with her, supporting her quest for equality and mutuality in love.

It wasn't long before her thoughts meandered back to Tony and Nathaniel. She hugged herself. "They will prove it if they are sincere," she told the Goddess. "Time will tell. I can't help wonder though, in how we met and when we met, if fate is playing a part?"

At the bottom of their road an owl swept low, calling into the night – an acknowledgement she was being heard. "My worry with Tony," she continued, encouraged, "is that he is only after power. That I am just the latest challenge and someone to conquer." Her footsteps slowed. "Whereas Nathaniel seems to have unresolved issues around women, and unresolved issues around women will always block true love."

Up ahead the house was in darkness except for a light shining through a gap in the sitting room curtains. And even if Nathaniel could be true, pondered Dinah, is he willing to travel his own soul path? Because if not we're out of each other's reach straight away. He'll never be able to meet me as I want to be met, nor me him. Two people together, yet passing each other by on two different planes.

She knew it would be no small thing for Nathaniel to commit to his own spiritual journey. The spiritual path, while filled with the joy of self-discovery, always gives way to challenge in some form as you come up against internal blocks. Maybe I'll start to annoy him, talking of God and Angels and the parallel worlds? Things he'll know nothing about unless he explores for himself. We'll simply be unable to connect. Her stomach lurched at the thought.

Pressure at her side as her Angel moved close. She shivered as the words entered her mind. *For many lifetimes, Dinah, you have been stuck in fear. This is the lifetime where it is possible to break free.*

* * *

'Thank you for tonight, Dinah. Let's meet again soon? Nx'

Nathaniel stopped under a street light to text Dinah. Pressing send, he was suddenly acutely aware of being watched. At the sound of a footstep he instinctively spun round. "Who's there?" he called into the darkness.

"So jumpy, Nathaniel," a woman's voice came from the shadows, just out of range of the glare of the light.

"Who is it?" he asked again, although with a sinking feeling he already knew.

"Don't worry, it's me, Cassie." She stepped into the light, a coquettish smile on her face. She was quite beautiful to behold, smooth skin and glossy hair that perfectly framed her fine features. But the sight of her made him immediately annoyed.

"Right, Cassie. So, now you're following me through the night?"

She pouted girlishly. "Who was that woman you were with?" Not waiting for a response, she came nearer, sliding her hands around his waist, pushing herself into him. Just in time, Nathaniel took a step back and caught her wrists to hold her at bay.

"Not your business, Cassie." Nathaniel was regretting he'd ever met her. "Look, I'm not sure what you're up to, but I really think it's time you moved on. I'm getting a bit tired of finding you everywhere I go."

"I can't help it if we keep meeting? Must be destiny bringing us together." She smiled in what was clearly meant to be a seductive manner, only to him she simply looked fake.

"Destiny has nothing to do with it though, has it?" Nathaniel said impatiently. Dropping her wrists he stepped back. "You orchestrate these meetings, Cassie, but bottom line is that I'm not interested. Okay!"

The smile vanished. "Don't talk to me like that," she snapped, her tone razor sharp. "You used me for sex," she spat.

"You came onto me remember?" Nathaniel countered sharply. "You made it perfectly clear what you wanted and I gave it to you, that's all. You asked to come back with me, you even danced for me for crying out loud. We're both adults and we both knew what we were doing. There was never any promise of anything more."

169

She was completely still, her expression frozen. "You used me and now you want to get rid of me. Well I'm not going!" Something in her manner and voice, in the words she used, made Nathaniel shiver. He just wanted to get home and into bed. She was glaring at him.

"I'm too tired for this right now, Cassie. Look, we had sex a couple of times. So what? There is no relationship – nothing to cling to because there was nothing there to begin with. I'm going home. Goodnight." Before he could turn away she was on him, grasping his coat, pawing at his clothes and trying to kiss his face.

"No, don't go." The desperation in her voice shocked him. "I'll come back with you. We'll go back to yours now. We're good together. Come on. I know you want me."

She was pleading, pressing herself roughly into him and kissing his neck before trying to force her tongue between his lips. For an instant Nathaniel was too surprised to react and then suddenly he mobilised into action, grabbing her shoulders and pushing her away. "For God's sake, are you mad?" he shouted. "I said no, for Christ's sake!"

Cassie recoiled. "Don't ever call me mad!" Her eyes flashed, her voice icy. "This isn't finished. You can't just use me and dump me. And I'm going to tell that woman what you are. I see her around the town all the time."

A stab of fury flamed in Nathaniel's chest at the mention of Dinah, but he tried to stay calm, now suspecting Cassie of having something seriously wrong with her. "Dinah already knows." He breathed hard. "I told her what happened with us." He regretted the words immediately.

Malicious delight gleamed in Cassie's eyes. "Ah, Dinah is it?" The spite he heard in her voice made him wince. "Dinah... hmmm." She broke off, tapping her finger to her chin as if thinking hard. "Shouldn't be difficult. We've chatted already – got on really well actually. After all we have a lot in common."

Nathaniel stilled. "What?"

"Oh yes, we had a lovely talk." Jealousy glittered in her face. "And I'm sure she'd love to go for coffee, a nice girly chat. What d'you think, Nathaniel? She smiled nastily. "I'm sure she'd be interested to hear my version of you and me."

170

Nathaniel's chest tightened. "There is no 'you and me' though, Cassie." It was an effort to keep his voice steady. "And like I told you, she already knows we've slept together."

Cassie tipped her head to one side, like a little girl. "But she's only heard your side of the story."

"There is no side! There is no story!" roared Nathaniel in frustration.

"I thought he cared about me, Dinah." Cassie feigned a tearful voice. "He chased and chased, wouldn't give up, but as soon as I caved in, as soon as I fell in love with him, he dropped me."

"Cassie!" Nathaniel was simultaneously astounded and repulsed.

"She looks like an understanding sort of person, I'm sure she'd feel bad for me, make her think twice about who you are." Her eyes narrowed. "Wouldn't it, Nathaniel?"

He didn't try to mask his scorn. "Biggest mistake of my life sleeping with you and one I won't be repeating."

She blanched. "You loved it. You know you did."

"Keep away from me, Cassie." He took a step towards her and was satisfied to see her cower against the wall, the malicious glare now replaced with fear. Shaking his head in disgust, Nathaniel walked away.

Twenty

Night had fallen as Dinah arrived at Ambrika's. By the time she had cooked supper for Daniel and Luke and got their bags ready for school the following day, she was running late. Hurrying the boys through the town she had dropped them at Kate's house. The streets were silent and dark. All the houses had their curtains pulled tight across, only the slivers of light alluding to the life contained inside.

While she waited on the doorstep for Ambrika to answer, a black cat with a white bib appeared from under a nearby car. It trotted towards her, tail aloft and began rubbing itself against her legs, looking up at her with big blue eyes and mewing beseechingly.

"Hey, puss." She bent down to tickle its ears.

The door opened.

"Dinah," Ambrika smiled. They hugged and the cat darted inside.

"He belongs to next door, but seems to think he lives here," explained Ambrika. "Come through and make yourself comfortable. I'll get us some water."

There were no lights on in the sitting room, although it was well lit by candles and the fire in the grate. The cat happily curled up on one of the sofas, wrapping its tail around its body as it purred loudly and stared unblinking at Dinah.

"Have you come to help, puss?" asked Dinah. The cat closed its eyes.

Returning from the kitchen with two glasses, Ambrika put them on the side table, before dragging a heavy black fireguard in front of the fire.

"Ready?" she asked.

"Yes, ready," said Dinah, a shot of adrenalin flaring in her stomach.

"Are you alright?" Ambrika looked concerned.

"I'm fine, really, just a bit anxious for some reason. I don't know why."

Ambrika nodded thoughtfully.

Dinah was going back again to revisit the old woman in her ramshackle house. There was more to this story, she was certain. As soon as her eyes closed she was drifting and, although she could hear Ambrika, she was already on the pathway of golden light, watching her feet as she walked. The same wooden door as before appeared and she unlatched it with one hand and stepped into the space behind. At first there was only blackness, and then streaks of grey-white light swirled about her. Dinah was entranced by the patterns and forms materialising before her.

"Dinah, tell me what you see." Ambrika's voice cut through the reverie at the same time as a solid scene appeared.

"My town," Dinah said immediately. "I am near home. I'm in Norfolk."

"What do you see?" repeated Ambrika.

"I see buildings, small wooden houses, thatched, and a wide market square. There's a stone cross in the middle, but it feels dark – not night-time dark, more energetically. Murky. Heavy. I don't like it." Stirrings of fear gripped her body. "It's market day. I'm trying to get home. There is mischief here. It's taken hold and does not bode well. Not for me." Dinah felt her beating heart quicken.

"There are pigs and goats running loose, and hens in wooden boxes. The people wear tunics and rough weave dresses, hats and hoods. They wear dark colours, subdued. The floor is dirt, and it's muddy and wet, my skirts drag in the mud, water soaking my shoes. Urrgghh," she groaned. "They're flimsy and have holes in."

"Dinah, breath. Breathe, slow and deep." Ambrika's voice was reassuring, hypnotic. "What is your name?"

"Elizabeth, Lizzy. Lizzy Norreys."

"And what is the year, Lizzy?"

"It's 1600 something. Early 1600s or thereabouts."

"Do you have family, Lizzy? Are there loved ones around you?"

"I am widowed, my husband long-since passed. We had not yet borne children. I am alone with the Spirits. They keep me company well enough."

She was scurrying along, head down, clutching a basket in one hand, a wooden staff in the other. The old woman could smell the fear. It was everywhere – stifling her.

The market was busy today, people crowding the ramshackle stalls to buy rye and oats, and vegetables.

Activities had increased recently. The accusations were more prevalent, and rumour was rife. The talk was of heresy, of spells being cast and curses unleashed, of devil worship, and satanic ritual. In this community the most natural occurrences could prompt whispers – a baby born dead, someone falling unexpectedly ill. It was mainly women being outcast for trivial deeds. Those living a solitary life or with too quick a tongue or a too-knowing smile. Even owning a cat could lead to denunciation. In these parts, in these times, it did not take much to be branded a witch. And then came the pointing fingers and bitter condemnation, and it seemed that once those fingers had pointed, there was little chance of escape, no matter how much the poor wretch protested innocence.

It was not a good time for women such as Lizzy to be practising as she did.

She crossed herself as she walked. *Lord, help us.*

The shadow of evil was gaining momentum, lengthening over them all. The undercurrent of persecution might be out of sight of the authorities, swirling beneath the surface of daily life, but Lizzy felt it nonetheless. The stench of terror and panic was pervading.

"Tell me," Ambrika's voice was pushing through, calling her. "Tell me, what is happening, Lizzy?"

"He despises me. He always has."

"Who?"

"I don't know." Dinah was agitated as she lay on the floor, her face screwed into a fearful grimace. "I don't want to see. He is a man of blackened heart."

"Lizzy, you are safe. You are safe here. No harm can come. Who is this man?"

Dinah saw eyes, two cold hard flints, pointed straight at her. She shivered.

"Oh no," she groaned. "He feigns goodness, but his heart is black. I can see it and he knows I see. He is driven by grievance and rage."

The man was tall and stocky, far younger than her. Thick grey hair and a forehead lined deeply with crevices. The skin of his cheeks was creased too, unbridled discontent and self-righteous anger etched into his features. He wore long robes. Dinah gasped.

"I see priest robes, I think. He is with the Church. He pretends to be God's servant, pretends that he serves only the Lord." She whimpered. "Around here it's him who drives the oppression. It is at his behest, at his whim, that the persecution heightens. He spreads talk of witchcraft and pacts with Satan, of devil worship and black magic. He has the people fooled. They believe him to be a pious man, a man of high character, but it is he who uses his intentions for the dark. It is he who wishes ill on others."

Panic swept over her, bile rising in her stomach. "I try to keep away from him, but it does no good. When he comes near I hide in the shadows, but to no avail. He feels me and knows what I am. He talks to people, makes suggestions about me. He will have my skin, he will make sure of it."

Lizzy was entering further into her, filling Dinah's body. "Don't be afraid," whispered the old woman. "He uses great cunning, instigating fear and inflaming it with words and deception. He is skilled and knowing, and uses the dark to achieve his ends."

Faces were coming through, faces of women, young and old, gathering around the man. "They fall for the self-proclamations of piety and purity and believe him to be great – as he tells them he is," croaked Lizzy.

The hairs on Dinah's body stood upright. "It is already begun," she told Ambrika, scared. "It's already underway and can't be stopped. It's only a matter of time. The talk is spreading."

"What's underway, Lizzy? What's happening?" Ambrika encouraged her to delve deeper. Dinah didn't want to.

Now there were other faces, kindly faces, faces that had regard in their eyes. And then a glitch, something occurring that she could not see, hidden beneath the smiles. The faces were changing, morphing into hideous, snarling masks.

Once allies, now enemies. Dinah squirmed.

"Breathe, Dinah," Ambrika by her side.

"There's a turn in people, in how they are with me. I used to go unseen, considered an oddity by most, but treated with respect. Now there's animosity and the feel of the village is different nowadays, unpleasant, no longer safe. People stare at me – they fall silent and watch. Groups gathering, men and women, refusing to step aside as I try to pass, blocking my way so I have no choice but to go around. Two times in the past weeks, I came home empty handed from the market, unable to get past the people I meet as they block my way."

"Lizzy, what are you seeing?"

"I feel anger and fear and I call the Spirits for protection. There is trouble coming for me," said Dinah. "It's everywhere as I walk round the market. The energy is bad."

Elizabeth was shuffling ahead, leaning on her staff for support. She was leaving the market square to take the road out of the village, over the bridge and back to her house, a mile or so to the east.

"There are women up ahead, three women on my path. They are waiting for me, although they pretend we meet by chance. They are churchwomen and they stand in my way."

One had long black hair tightly secured in a bun. No more than thirty-odd years with a sharp nose and darting black eyes. She called out, stern, vicious, "Oh Lizzy Norreys, this is no place for the likes of you." Lizzy halted. "This town is for those who obey God's laws. And we know well what you do. Everyone knows what takes place in your house, communing with the devil, that he teaches you his ways, bringing the darkness of evil down on all of us."

The three women were closing around her. Lizzy stayed mute.

"Friends, only last week my pail of milk turned when Lizzy Norreys walked by. Left no good, soured by the devil's helper."

It was only then that Dinah noticed the woman carried a small wooden pail covered by a cloth. For no reason that she knew she was afraid of that pail. Lifting the cloth the woman's eyes glittered in triumph. "And see here..." She held the pail aloft for the fast gathering crowd to see. Under the cloth, a mess of curdled milk was revealed. "She has the devil's hand. Be sure of it."

The other two women gasped theatrically, covering their mouths with their hands, feigning shock and fright. The crowd was starting to mutter.

"Proof she's a witch," someone crowed. It was a small bird-like woman of angular frame and prim dress. She was immaculately presented. Not one fair hair out of place and, despite her skirt reaching the ground, not a spatter of mud to be seen.

"Something must be done! We ignore her doings at our peril."

Dinah's heart thudded against her ribs, and then a hand caught Lizzy's elbow.

"Leave it alone." A man's voice.

As one, Dinah-Lizzy breathed with relief. It was the blacksmith, a kindly man and she knew he would see her well. His wife had come for help some years past, driven near mad with fear of being barren and tormented with desperation to give her husband a child. With the guidance of the spirits, Lizzy had prepared a remedy for the woman to drink and one lunar cycle after, she was with child. A few years passed and the woman sought Lizzy again. It followed the same as before. One month after the drinking of the remedy, nausea and fatigue came, announcing the conception of a second baby.

"She's a witch, we all know it," the black haired woman cried to the crowd, the two by her side nodding eagerly.

The old woman shook her head. Dinah felt sick. Their spite came at her in waves, their delight at her terror spiking into her.

"Lizzy, what's happening, who do you see?"

"These women, their mouths are unclean, tainted by the dark. They follow his prompts, accusing me of the black craft and knowingly speaking the untruths he feeds them. People are listening now. The seeds he sows taking hold and flourishing. They are starting to believe. It won't be long."

There was nothing to be said. Nothing would make any difference. Nothing could tide the gossip and unfounded speculation.

"This is madness," exclaimed the blacksmith. "Madness and no more than that."

Dinah froze. A presence hovered close by, menacing, dark. She knew he had come before he showed himself, before he even uttered a word.

"God will be her judge."

The voice sliced into her. Cold eyes piercing her, a vicious smile twisting his mouth.

The blacksmith stiffened by her side. His hand circling her scrawny wrist as he slowly pushed her onwards, slowly on up the road, away from the crowd. He turned to face her, kindness in his eyes, but also sorrow.

"He knows what is coming," whispered Lizzy.

"Be on your way, Lizzy. It isn't safe for you here." His voice was low, so only she could hear. "Best not visit the market awhile. I will bring you out vegetables and bread."

Bent over her staff, Lizzy's hands shook as basket in hand she began to walk away. Those eyes were on her back again, digging into her soul.

"I want to come out." Dinah was fully back in her body, back to consciousness and Lizzy had gone. "Ambrika, bring me back."

It was important when accessing past lives through visualisation to come out the same way you go in, but even as Ambrika led her through the door and back along the pathway of light, she was one step ahead. And when she blinked her eyes open there was no disorientation. Dinah was immediately returned. She sat up.

"How you doing?" Ambrika was by her side, offering her a glass of water. She took a sip.

"There's something horrible there, Ambrika. That man, not the blacksmith, the other, the priest. He lurks, almost to one side of the story, but he's important. Something else is going on, something is about to happen to Lizzy."

"I agree," Ambrika stroked her hair. "That's my feeling too, but there's no need to rush. We shall see what unfolds and it will unfold as it does."

Dinah exhaled hard.

Twenty-one

Winter held Porrick tightly in its grasp with short dark days, damp and cold. Dinah dressed carefully, wrapping up with layers of clothing under a thick jumper. She and Tony were meeting again to walk through the woods along the river.

Taking her scarf from the hook on the back of the bedroom door she wound it around her neck before pulling on thick fingerless gloves. Glancing through the window she saw rays of watery sun piercing through the clouds, casting golden streaks of light to the earth. The sight lifted her spirits.

Tony was resting against the gate gazing at the river as Dinah approached, but as she drew close he turned, opening his arms wide to her. Although uncomfortable she greeted him warmly enough and they met in a hug. Tony had been delighted when she had agreed to this walk. It felt like a significant step forward and for some reason this made him peculiarly pleased. As a rule he kept himself beyond this kind of inconsequential attachment, but it was impossible to deny he was feeling more anticipation than usual, keen to forge a deeper bond with this woman.

Initially he had found these unexpected feelings disconcerting. Tony was not used to seeking out the attentions of another. It was more comfortable, safer, when people came to him. Dinah, however, was different somehow, there was a knowingness about her which put her slightly out of his reach and this made him curious. The way she kept herself back slightly, maintaining a barrier between them, which he wasn't yet sure how to break. Still, he felt good in her company, despite her relentless questions and contradictions. Tony breathed her in as they embraced, holding her tenderly as though she would shatter if he clasped too tight.

She lowered her eyes as they parted and with a smile he took her hand. They began to stroll up the river path.

Dinah broke the silence first. "I always feel so uncomfortable around you and I don't know why," she blurted.

"It is because I don't do story, Dinah." Again that smile playing around his lips. "It can and does, make people uncomfortable. They don't know how to respond to someone who simply won't play the game, who won't acknowledge the illusion."

Dinah often wondered about 'story', a word frequently used in spiritual circles to refer to the illusion of the drama and fears of life, and the various roles we play. The term alluded that a soul incarnate on Earth is far more than our physical and mental reality would have us believe.

"I don't understand how you don't do story, Tony. How can you exist in this modern world and not?" Dinah felt unease surfacing again.

"And I ask you, Dinah. How can you exist in this world in your story and find the peace which you crave?"

They fell silent, their steps slowing as they synchronised to one another's pace.

"I don't always have peace. Often I'm thrown by what goes on around me, and I often get caught up in the drama and have to catch myself and pull back. Sometimes it's too late and I'm already immersed and have a journey to get back on track. But I don't see how this can be avoided. Isn't it just the nature of life?"

"It's how you choose to be, Dinah. It is your choice, nobody else's. The story will always suck us in and will always pull us down. You're right though, the very nature of the story is to distract us from who we are. And to exist inside it will always bring pain."

Dinah paused, thoughtful. Tony knew she was absorbing his words, while simultaneously seeking something to refute him. It seemed she was incapable of just accepting what he said. There was always a resistance to work through.

"You're a difficult student, Dinah." He stared at her, impassive.

Ignoring the remark, Dinah pressed on. "Surely it's about balance? To stay completely outside of my story, to truly live outside of my identity but function in the world, is impossible surely? I am not a sadhu living in the woods or a mystic in a mountain cave. I live

180

in this town, Porrick, in this country. I have children at school and I have to find a way to relate with people around me in a way they understand and find acceptable, or they would think me mad. I would be an outcast, Tony, and not just me, my children too..."

A shadow crossed his face. "Most people spend their whole lives trying to be a something, Dinah," he interrupted. "Trying to make themselves into something *acceptable*." His words were loaded with scorn.

"They desperately mould themselves and it's a constant battle, trying to be a someone, or something they feel will fit with the people around them, fit their environment, something to make them feel better about who they are. It is all the ego of course. But when we do this, when we attempt to live this way it is a lie, and we only betray ourselves, selling ourselves short, and for what? Money, status, power – being accepted? So what? Being accepted by others who are also living a lie?"

Dinah scowled, struggling to keep up, to grasp the words.

"Living a lie," continued Tony, relentless. "Is a falsehood, a fake. It's empty, it is untruth and means nothing and never will. Seek happiness in the ego, in the story, and you will never succeed. You are destined to misery and to failure. The story is merely distraction away from the truth. It is why all of us – the busy, the successful, the wealthy, the arrogant, the famous, the comfortable – until we seek truth, feel empty inside. And if we dare to stop, even for a moment, then we find ourselves lacking inside and that, Dinah, the pain of that alone, is just too much to bear."

"You make it sound terrible!" cried Dinah, shuddering. "Dark and unhappy, phony and miserable, unfulfilled. Life isn't like that for everyone."

"Yes it is, Dinah. The pain is too much, even for a moment. Until we find the courage to drop the illusion. And not everyone finds themselves ready. For some it is simply overwhelming and so they must keep pushing on, striving and forcing until they become exhausted. Until they tire of the story they must keep going with it, believing it, or they will shatter into pieces, but when the break does come and it always does, this is when an opening appears. It is maybe the smallest crack in consciousness, but it is there nonetheless

181

and once it has appeared it can never be closed. Once it has been seen, it can never be denied."

"I don't understand you," said Dinah, frustrated, hands clenched at her sides. "You're going too fast, speaking in riddles. I'm getting left behind."

Far from heeding her request to slow down, Tony sped up. "When we take time to stop and take our awareness inside, Dinah, as with meditation, or a commitment to yoga or whatever such practice you may choose, it is here you will find truth. It can hurt, Dinah. It can hurt to understand you have built your entire existence on a lie: that you have invested much energy and emotion and intellect into creating a belief of who you think you are, of what you think you have achieved, and then..."

Tony paused, studying Dinah intently, watching her responses.

"...and then," he continued. "You discover it is all untrue and your world is exploded and there is nothing you can do about it. Your mind is shattered, your spirit broken and your ideas and opinions, your thoughts and views, all turned to dust."

Into Dinah's mind an image of the Tower card from the Tarot flashed before her. The sixteenth trump in the Major Arcana depicts a burning tower with orange red flames licking a blackened sky. It represents the inevitable crumbling of everything built on shaky or shallow foundations. As the structure is destroyed by the flames, dark smoke fills the air and desperate figures leap from the burning masonry in a futile attempt to escape. The card speaks of the unavoidable collapse of false ambition and expectation, a time of transition when anything built on unrealistic hope collapses around us.

Tony smiled. "Dinah, from here on there is no turning back. From this moment, you are changed and life will never be the same again. And it is a good thing. You have discovered, much to your dismay, that you have been existing in pain, and unnecessary pain at that, pain of your own making."

"It sounds brutal, Tony," said Dinah, disturbed by his words. "You make it sound dreadful. Hell on earth. Surely it doesn't always have to be such a traumatic awakening? Surely there can be opportunity for a peaceful, joyous path?"

There was a sparkle in his eye. He had reached her and he knew it.

"There is, Dinah, if you are of a certain type. But for most of us, we will do anything to avoid having to confront ourselves, anything to avoid taking responsibility for ourselves, anything to not have to face our inner state and the dream we have created about ourselves, our thoughts of who we think we are. It's human nature, Dinah."

Something was touching her. She was all in a muddle and yet something in what he said was speaking to her soul. Her mind resisted, but her soul was listening.

By now they had reached a fork in the path. One path led into the woods and the other along the river.

"Which way?" said Tony amiably. "You choose."

Staying near the water felt better and Dinah pointed to the lower path.

"It is always your choice, Dinah, remember that." Tony continued walking, but Dinah stayed still. When he realised she was not following he turned to face her. "To live your life around what you perceive as someone else's view is not wise. Society tells its story about what is and what isn't, and then you join in with your own story of what it is you think is required of you. That sounds like confusion and fear to me."

"Fear? I'm not afraid!" Dinah was cross. She hadn't asked for a lecture, hadn't wanted him to begin his preaching, telling her how it is, how he thought she was.

"Courage is needed on this path, Dinah." The urgency in his voice was unsettling. "It is not a path for the non-committed. Courage is required to allow the illusion to drop away. You will lose everything that is not authentic, and that can be painful, but when it is all gone, you will find everything you have been looking for is right there, as it was all the time. You just didn't notice. You were too busy playing out your story, your idea of how you think things are."

There was a bench ahead of them on the edge of the path and Dinah went to sit down, tired. On the other side of the river a small wooden shack was bellowing smoke from its chimney. She wondered who might be inside. Tony's words were grating now and she wasn't entirely sure why. She felt annoyed though, like a stubborn child who doesn't want to lose an argument. It wasn't comfortable.

"You're not hearing me, Tony." Even to her ears her voice sounded petulant. "I'm sorry, but you talk of stepping out of the story as though it's the easiest thing in the world and something only cowards are unable or unwilling to do. But you don't have anything that brings you into contact with the everyday. You teach your yoga, you live your yoga. For me, I have children and they need me, they need me to be emotionally involved with them. I have to guide them through this world with all its material concerns and issues. A child's world needs an adult. I can't just float away in a bubble and leave them to find their own way."

"I have children, Dinah." He caught her flash of surprise. "Three, all at school and while it's true my wife takes care of most things, I play my part. I simply don't allow myself to become immersed in it."

"You're married with children?" gasped Dinah. His words shocked her. Standing abruptly she backed away from him, her cheeks flaming red.

"I must go," she blurted, flustered. She didn't wait for a response. She was struggling to breathe and horrified. Not wanting to look at him, Dinah began walking, fast, nearly running, back along the towpath.

Of course he's married. She stumbled. Why wouldn't he be? Her breath was coming short and shallow, disbelief echoing through her. "Angels, help! He acts as if he is free, single... and I just assumed, because of how he is, how he is in class..."

"Dinah!" He was behind her.

"Angels, make him go away," she breathed.

"Dinah, wait!"

He was alongside her now, but made no attempt to touch her or stop her. "I'll walk back with you."

Keeping her head down, Dinah hurried on, not wanting him to see the effect his disclosure had had on her. They quickly arrived back at the gate where they had met.

"I'll see you at class," mumbled Dinah, moving past him, but as she did he pulled her into an embrace. Everything in her recoiled, but for some reason she couldn't find the strength to pull away, she was a waxwork, dead in his arms, helpless, until at last he released her.

"Yes, at class," he grinned. He sounded happy, pleased about something, and anxiety washed through her. He was enjoying it she was shocked to realise. He was actually enjoying her pain and confusion.

Turmoil ripped through her. One minute she was on a country walk deep in conversation, and the next she was in pieces. Just like that. He held her hands tight, refusing to let go.

What does he want with me? She tugged her hands in frustration, but not until she looked up and met his eyes did he loosen his grip. The briefest flicker of pleasure crossed his face before the mask came down again. There was no pretending now. Something had been wrong with Tony all along, and now here she was, unwittingly entangled.

"You can trust me, Dinah." He squeezed her hands, his eyes holding hers, before he casually turned and strolled towards his car. Watching him go, Dinah stood frozen and forlorn.

"What have I got myself into, Angels?"

Tony got into his car with a swagger. There was a slight pause, presumably as he put on his seatbelt or adjusted the mirror, perhaps to get a sly glance of her stricken face, before the engine started up. There then came the sound of scraping gears and his car pulled away. She could see him quite clearly as the car turned. He didn't look over or wave, but Dinah stayed watching until the car had completely disappeared and then, trembling, she began to walk home.

"I wish I'd never met him," she told the Angels. "The way he is in class. The intimacy, the touching, the way he strokes my skin, the way he looks at me, speaks to me. He invites me out walking, shows me his most special place on the moor, Angels. He stood by me as I cried, watched me. He held my hands and he speaks to me of things that make my heart dissolve, and yet he's married."

Crossing the road she made for the alley towards home. "He's a yoga teacher. He's told me he teaches yoga above all other teachers. So why so cruel? Does he not realise what he does? The effect he has on his students?"

But inside, Dinah knew the truth was that Tony was perfectly aware of his actions.

At the bottom of the alley she collided with a man causing him to drop his newspaper. He scowled at her as he bent to retrieve it, and was clearly about to tell her off, but something in her face stopped him and he hurried on without a word. Barely registering the incident,

185

Dinah merely rubbed her shoulder and went on her way. All she was aware of was a very real turmoil inside her and a stabbing disappointment. She saw unhappily, that he had been playing with her, with all of them, all along.

"He's married with children!" She was struggling to grasp the truth of it. "What an earth has he done to me? Why did I think he was interested in me?" Thank God, she was nearly home.

Tripping up the steps to her house, Dinah searched for her keys. Locating them in her jacket pocket she fell through the door, slamming it behind her and heading for the sitting room where she collapsed, dejected, on the sofa.

The Tower card flashed in her mind.

The answer is not in this life… just a murmur. *When you witness what has gone before, from a place removed, then the healing will occur.*

She must go back again, back into the past to get to the core of this irrational pain. She needed to know why? Why such a strong push and pull for such a man, why such powerful emotion that defied all reason.

* * *

There was laughter coming from the sitting room when Tony got home. With a sigh he dropped his keys onto the hallway table.

"Hello?" he called.

The laughter stopped, but there was no reply and he didn't bother to go and see who was here. Emily probably had friends round, or her sister. Olivia seemed to spend more time at their house than she did at her own, not that he minded. It kept Emily out of his hair. Tony surveyed the mess in the kitchen. It was as though a tsunami had just passed through. The cupboard doors were ajar and dirty dishes were piled in the sink. The plates left on the sideboard showed they'd had spaghetti Bolognese for lunch and there were curls of grated cheese on the floor. A surge of annoyance flushed through him as he started clearing up. Just as he finished wiping down the counter, the sitting room door swung open, followed by footsteps going up the stairs. Tony marched into the hallway. She was already halfway up.

"What have you been doing here?" he demanded, annoyed. "The place is a mess. Food everywhere, all over the floor and where are the girls?"

Emily had make-up on, Tony noticed. Smoky-grey eyes and glossy pink lips and her blonde hair was straightened. She was wearing perfume too. "We had lunch and then went shopping, Tony. The girls are at your mother's for the afternoon. She said you were to phone when you got back and can you pick them up later."

She carried on up the stairs. "I'm going for a shower. Olivia and Nancy are in the sitting room and we're going out." Tony watched her disappear round the landing. A few moments later he heard the sound of running water.

"You'll need to give the girls supper," she called down, appearing again at the top of the stairs. "And you'll have to go to the shops as there's not much in."

Tony quickly considered his options. "I'm holding a meditation at Siobhan's tonight. It's important. You'll have to go and get them." He had no intention of missing this evening. Four other women from class were coming, too. They needed him.

"Sorry," called Emily, indifferent. "I have plans. And anyway, I'm not going to sit around at home while you're out with your groupies."

Tony's jaw tightened. "They are not groupies. Don't be ridiculous." His voice was ice.

The click of the bathroom door closing left him at the bottom of the stairs scowling into thin air. There was no point arguing with her. She had no respect for what he did. She was completely unable to see past the drama, past the chaos.

She's so immersed in the world, and content to be there, he thought. Never wondering if there's anything more.

It was tiring, but in many ways it suited his purpose. She looked after the girls, taking care of their activities and school, and that left him free to get on with his teaching. Their marriage had always been more of an arrangement as far as he was concerned. Emily worked hard at the bank and by the time they met, when she started coming to his classes, she was already forging herself a lucrative career. In the beginning she had embraced the yogic path, claiming it opened her eyes to the truth of life, to the truth of being human. They had practised at home together, attending workshops, visiting the ashram in India. It brought a meditative still to their daily lives and when they married, Tony stopped working as a surveyor to pursue his dream of teaching yoga full-time. Emily paid for the trips to India and supported him while he set up more classes. But when the children were born things had changed. It was as if she had no time for him and no time for yoga. Gradually, her practice fell away. She was losing her path and there was nothing he could do.

The sitting room door opened and Olivia appeared, glass of wine in hand. Her short blonde hair was slicked back and she wore a plunging black dress that showed off her curvaceous figure. Of the two sisters she was the more attractive, but with absolutely no spiritual awareness whatsoever. There was so much story swirling around Olivia, in her love life and work and day-to-day doings, that being in her company for too long made his head pound. Also, she did not like Tony and never had, and the feeling was entirely mutual. She shot him a frosty glare.

"Tony."

"Olivia." His voice was just as curt.

"So, we're going out tonight." Her tone was challenging and it irked him. "She deserves some fun, don't you think, seeing as she works so hard looking after the girls and at work."

The implication being that I do nothing, thought Tony. He didn't say a word.

"Don't try to spoil it." She met his stare head on.

Tony smiled. "You're very aggressive aren't you, Olivia?" His voice was low, cutting. "I have neither the intention nor desire to disturb your plans." The look on his face said anything but. "Although I notice you do not give me the same consideration. Go and enjoy yourselves by all means. I hope you have a wonderful time."

With a shake of her head, Olivia returned to the sitting room and quietly closed the door as Tony went back into the kitchen. Picking up his phone he searched for his mother's number. She would have to have the girls until ten.

Upstairs Emily was wandering about in their bedroom. Very rarely did she complain about his relationships with his students and he was usually easily able to deflect her accusations, to turn it back on her for not understanding, for being too caught up in her own story, or being paranoid and trying to taint what he was doing. There had been a brief period when he had held the meditation evenings at their house, in the front room, while Emily took care of the children upstairs. At that time, Carmel had been his main focus, a vivacious, pretty girl with long dark hair and soulful eyes. Unfortunately, despite asking her to stay upstairs, Emily had come down for a cup of tea just as he and Carmel were holding hands in the kitchen.

Of course, Emily had made a terrible scene, completely destroying the loving energy of the group. She had ordered them all out of the house before turning on Tony ferociously, flushed with anger, accusing him of taking advantage and insulting her under her own roof.

"She just doesn't get it," sighed Tony, reaching for a mug and pouring some water. "She's so absorbed in herself and how she believes things should be that she misses out on all the beauty on offer."

He hadn't held any further groups at home though, not since that night.

Twenty-two

As usual Tony was positioned cross-legged on his mat at the front of the hall and paid her no attention at all when she entered. With trembling hands, Dinah rolled out her mat, and unable to resist glancing across at him found he was looking right at her, a blank, penetrating stare. He was talking to the woman with auburn hair, the one who most forcefully vied for his attentions, and the two of them appeared deep in conversation, leaning into each other so close their heads were nearly touching. The woman had one hand on his knee and they looked so intimate it made Dinah feel like a voyeur just watching.

She knew her mind and emotions were chaotic. It almost felt as though she was in love with him, but it wasn't a love she understood. It was confused and dark, and didn't seem to make any sense. She knew that to continue coming to class would end in disaster, but still couldn't quite let go. Intuition told her she would be a fool to ignore his behaviour. His words and actions never seemed to match and his arrogant, controlling attitude was too ingrained for him to change. Yet she also knew she was entangled in the strangest way, that something was holding her prisoner and that her yearning was too strong to simply walk away. If it was love, it was doomed.

When she lay down and closed her eyes, Dinah found she could barely catch her breath. Her chest was heaving, her heart pounding, and to her dismay there was nothing she could do to calm herself, not even a little. Focused breathing proved useless. All previous certainty about coming tonight now evaporated and she berated herself for being here. A voice told her to just get up and leave. Just stand up, roll up your mat and go. Finish. Another voice said if she left now without getting to the truth, she would never be completely free of him. The etheric cords would endure between them because their energy was still connected. Sighing, Dinah knew that to find the truth of the situation, she needed to stay at class tonight.

"He's reeled me in, Angels. I was hoodwinked and I allowed it to happen, and all the time I thought I was in control."

However, no amount of self-talk, could take away the fact that she pined for him and that there was still a glimmering, ridiculous hope for romance. The revelation that he was married with children should have put an end to it all, but it seemed her heart had a mind of its own.

Sadness weighed her down, along with disappointment and feeling a fool. Tonight, Dinah was determined to find an acceptance that he had no feelings for her in any way. To him it was just a game, a flippant distraction of playing with others' feelings to entertain himself and give himself a boost. She was just another female yoga student who had fallen for his charms. Great balm for his ego, she thought bitterly.

He was talking now, she realised, as his voice pulled her away from her chaotic thoughts.

"We must always go to the silence. It is the silence inside which holds the answers we have always been looking for."

Succumbing to the rhythm of the words she gratefully dropped into the quiet place inside.

"The breath is our life energy, our life power. Everything can be gained through attention to the breath. Focus on the breath and you will discover yourself. All else is simply of no consequence."

Moving through the ancient yoga postures was a gift, stilling Dinah's cluttered mind as her body flowed gracefully of its own accord. Halfway through the class, however, as she was stretching into downward dog position, she felt him coming towards her.

He always knows when I reach this place, she thought. He never approaches until I've dropped so deeply.

She felt like a fly in a spider's web, desperate to escape, but the more she struggled the more entrapped she became. Tony placed his palms on the back of her waist, gently stroking her skin, his hands warm, his touch easing away her resistance. Despite herself, Dinah stretched in ecstatic delight. "Angels, every time he touches me I lose all reason."

"Tantra" – the word pinged from inside.

Oh! She tensed under his fingers. It was like someone had turned on the light. Tantra, of course!

The insight hit so clearly she was stunned she had not picked up on it earlier. Tantra, the ancient esoteric path rooted in India, known for awakening dormant kundalini – the source of sexual energy – which lies coiled at the base of the spine. Dinah knew that for some Tantrikas the sexual aspect of this potent spiritual practice becomes the focus, and suddenly she saw exactly what Tony was doing. It explained why she was so drawn, while knowing something was decidedly off.

He's woken his kundalini! That's why his energy is so strong. And he uses it to seduce and enslave.

Tony leaned the length of his body against Dinah's back and all thoughts disappeared as the stretch deepened. Their energies were merging, the boundaries between them dissipating. Never had she felt such intensity, and it was all coming from this disaster of a man who made her feel so wonderfully alive, and yet tortured her heart and mind. They stayed together for what seemed a long time, breathing slowly, relaxing into each other, so natural, so beautiful and yet tainted. Tony eased himself from her, steadying her with his hands so she wouldn't tip over at the change in balance.

"This is an opportunity to let yourself melt into the asana." His voice sounded unsteady as he instructed the class and Dinah wondered if he was as overwhelmed as she at what had just happened between them. "Nothing else is needed, no effort, no force. Just be."

The earlier self-mastery was gone and he was struggling to regain his composure. Dinah called for the Angels to help both of them. She longed for him, ached for him and yet was repelled by him too. It was all too confusing.

Tony instructed the class into the next posture and sneaking a look at him as she adjusted her position, Dinah saw her own confusion and pain mirrored back at her as their eyes met. She quickly looked away. When they sat for meditation, Dinah couldn't meditate. Every time she tried to drift inside she could only feel a void in her heart, a dull empty ache that made her want to scream. It was uncomfortable and disturbing.

Taking a breath she shifted her position and once again tried to focus on the peace. It was then she felt the air move in front of her, ever so slightly, barely noticeable, and then someone was gently taking her hands. Without opening her eyes she knew it was Tony and her heart pounded. But as they sat, as the seconds passed, the energies began to settle. Warmth flowed into her, emanating from him, quieting the pain and softening the turmoil. Cautiously Dinah opened her eyes and found him looking at her with something in his eyes she had never seen in him before. The façade was gone and in this moment it was a meeting of souls, a recognition of something deeper, something beneath the drama and chaos and clashing of wills. Now she understood that he was suffering too.

But why so much pain between us? Such longing, such discomfort?

He was her mirror and through him she saw her own yearning and her own aching heart. Until now she had not been able to see it, he had not allowed her to see it, but in this solitary moment, understanding passed between them. And with it a realisation was surfacing.

This connection had to end. It was strong and deep, but not pure. Tony squeezed her hands and she understood that he also understood.

As they held each other's gaze, unflinching, Dinah saw he could not give her anymore. He seemed somehow incapable of feeling, incapable of loving in the way she knew was possible. He wanted vulnerability from those around him, but was unwilling to be vulnerable himself.

"Help me let go," she prayed silently.

Angels were gathering, a protective force field keeping her safe. "The sacredness of life only becomes apparent when you release all expectations and desires. Relinquish control. Surrender will set you free."

Is surrender so easy? wondered Dinah. Something told her it was not.

* * *

The following morning, Dinah was in the coffee shop at the bottom of her road. It was quiet and she'd managed to get the squashy sofa

193

in front of the fire. She was seeing Ambrika later, but for now she settled back into the sofa, stirring her tea and gazing into the flames. Life was a whirl at the moment on all levels.

"Mind if I join you?"

Before she could respond the woman was sitting next to her, placing a pot of tea on the table next to Dinah's. It was the woman from the pub, the one Nathaniel was having trouble with. Dinah was immediately wary.

"I'm Cassie, we saw each the other night. You were with Nathaniel." She smiled warmly. "You're Dinah, aren't you? Nathaniel told me about you. How do you know him?"

Her enquiring smile stretched from ear to ear, as Dinah's guard came slamming down.

"Err... Hi Cassie. I'm sorry, I don't want to be rude, but I don't really want company today." She spoke calmly, but her heart was thudding in her chest. The woman made her irrationally anxious. Cassie's smile froze and a flicker of irritation crossed her face, before she hurriedly concealed it.

"I saw you here and thought it would be nice to get to know each other, that's all," she persisted. "Seeing as we're both in here and have a mutual friend." The way she said the word friend, implied that Nathaniel was far more than that to her. Dinah was struggling to quell a growing urge to flee.

"Cassie, I really don't mean to be rude," she repeated. "I'm sorry, but I came in here to be by myself."

"Oh..." Cassie looked hurt. "I was only trying to be friendly, I mean, me and Nathaniel talk all the time on the phone. I'll admit, when I saw you together the other night, I did wonder if you were an item, but the way he was with me afterwards as we walked home together, and then later that night, made it clear you weren't serious."

Dinah flinched and Cassie smiled secretively.

"I just thought it would be nice to get to know each other." She reached out and softly touched Dinah's knee.

"She's lying." The words came into Dinah's mind quite spontaneously.

"Why?" she asked Cassie.

"Why what?" There was an edge to the woman's voice.

"Why do you want to get to know me?"

194

"Because you know Nathaniel, and me and him have history. We're good together, we have fun" – she paused – "in the bedroom especially." With some effort, Dinah managed to keep her expression neutral, despite her growing horror.

"He can't get enough of me," she whispered. "I'll admit we went through a bumpy phase. He chased me for ages, you know how he is, and then when we started falling in love, he got scared and backed off a bit. Men!"

She smiled conspiratorially and Dinah flushed. Whether Cassie was delusional or not, she wasn't sure, but she was certainly hitting a nerve.

"We're great now though. Back to the way it was before." Her eyes didn't leave Dinah's for a moment, but there was something more; Dinah was becoming aware of some kind of intrusion. With a start she realised the woman was entering her energy field, getting into her psychic space.

Silently, she called for Archangel Michael to surround her and noticed Cassie flinch and move back a little, as if sensing something amiss.

"Yes, we've worked it out together," she carried on. "I do think he has that pattern though, don't you? You know, chase and then run. It was quite up and down with us, but it's made us stronger. Now we both know where we stand and it's good. We're quite similar, you see."

Dinah did see. She was sure the woman was lying blatantly about Nathaniel, but the question was why.

Is she dangerous? Dinah wondered. What is it?

The energy coming off her was incredibly strong. Dinah shivered. The woman clearly had no intention of leaving her alone and the only sensible option seemed to go.

Dinah stood up and forced a smile. "I'll leave you to your tea." Trying to do up her coat, her fingers fumbled with the buttons. The woman had her jangled.

"Oh." Cassie looked hurt again. "But you've barely touched yours. I was only being friendly, what's wrong?" For a nanosecond, Dinah paused. Was she misjudging her? But one look at the woman's face and she couldn't get out of the coffee shop quick enough.

Poor Nathaniel, was Dinah's first thought as the door shut behind her. Whatever it was that she'd seen in the other woman's eyes, it wasn't nice. How did he get caught up with her?

She suspected that Cassie did not take rejection lightly. The woman was unbalanced, that was clear, but Dinah couldn't stop herself from replaying what she had said.

Did they really meet up after I left the pub? The thought left her ice cold. And does he run when things get deep? He wouldn't be the first to be afraid of intimacy and where does that leave us?

The woman had expertly awoken all her insecurities and as she headed to Ambrika's house, she couldn't shake off a gnawing anxiety.

* * *

For the third time in as many months, Dinah was lying on a rug on Ambrika's floor. She was already nervous and the feeling was increasing as the seconds passed, making her question whether it was wise to go back again, to keep raking over the past. Would it be better to leave things alone?

"What's coming, Angels?" The only response was a touch to the side of her cheek.

Ambrika was speaking softly and Dinah was falling into herself, a flurry of colour and visions passing beneath her eyelids until at last she settled into Lizzy's tired, frail body.

Things had moved on. Some time had passed since she had fled the women in the market.

The little wooden house was in darkness. It was dusty and smelled of wood smoke. The only light came from the embers of a burned-out fire in the hearth. In the middle of the room, a rough wooden table was covered with bowls and bottles. Lizzy was kneeling in front of the fire, blowing into it, trying to reignite the flames. As she stared deeper, familiar faces and images were appearing. The salamanders.

They spoke in wispy singsong voices. *Don't be afraid, the time is near.*

A pang of fear shot through her, immobilising her, all except her knobbly hands, which twisted anxiously. *The darkness is gathering.*

Dinah stirred. "Something bad is about to happen," she told Ambrika in a flat despairing voice.

Lizzy was frightened, she was praying. "Dear Lord, give me the courage to face what lies ahead." They were coming for her. She had known that one day this would happen, that it could not be avoided, but now the day was here all her strength had vanished.

"They say I'm a witch," she whispered. "They suspect me of dark practice."

The accusations came from all directions and she knew that other innocent souls had died as a result of such gossip. She was almost surprised she had escaped for so long. Those using natural magic were demonised for their gifts, as people became fearful of links with the devil. But Lizzy had continued her work, increasing her entreaties to the Spirits, asking for the strength she needed.

"I can't run. I'm too old." A tear ran down on her wizened cheek. She was scared.

Tipping her head she listened. She could hear distant voices, like the rumbling of low thunder. Her terror intensified.

On the rug on Ambrika's floor, Dinah was agitated.

"Dinah, tell me what you see," urged Ambrika, but Dinah couldn't speak.

The old woman bowed her head before the blackened fire. She was trembling, fervently calling God, beseeching Him for the courage to meet her fate with dignity. She used many different names to address the Creator. Dinah realised she was invoking different aspects of the Divine.

The atmosphere was already changing, warmth engulfing Lizzy's body, lightening and supporting it. It was as if she was locked in a dream world of sorts, Divine energy protecting her from the harsh reality. Her panic was subsiding and in its wake a sense of soft calm was emerging. From within this serenity three huge golden Angels appeared. Standing side by side, their faces the essence of all-consuming love. The old woman trembled even more, but now it was with awe, and Dinah understood that during this lifetime she had not known the Angels. She had worked with the Spirit Guides and nature spirits – the elementals.

But Dinah knew them and recognised the tallest Angel straight away. It was Azrael, the Angel of Death.

"We are here." The great Archangel soothed. "Do not be afraid, little one. Allow us to lift away your fear. We await your most joyous return."

"I don't know what to do," the old woman whispered.

"Reach for us. Keep looking upon us. They will come and you will put up no struggle, no fight. Your soul is tired. It is your time to rest now, your time to come home."

Voices came from outside, loud, angry. They were at the gate. Light from their torches flickered under the gap in the door as heavy footsteps thundered down the pathway, then banging at the door. But inside, calm and peaceful, Lizzy was floating.

"Come to us, child, talk with us now." Many hundreds of Angels were surrounding her, and all she could see was their magnificent light, beaming down upon her, making her smile with wonder.

The door crashed open and many men poured in, brutal, bursting with rage and self-righteous judgment.

"There," cried one pointing at her as she crouched by the hearth. "Get her!"

Another, his face red with anger, grabbed her tangled hair in his fist. There was only a moment of searing pain, the briefest agony as he dragged her from the floor by her hair. The Angels called louder and she was lifting, breaking free.

"Come child," they laughed. "Look to us and see your God."

A fist struck her face, but as the blood spilled, splattering the ground red, she was no longer of her body. Beneath her shuttered eyelids she was in a different world, watching in wonder as streams of golden light poured down around her. Lizzy was already crossed over.

Someone shouted. "Now you'll pay for the harm you've done us." The maddened screams came louder now, and Dinah watched from above, as her crazed tormentors hauled her outside by the hair, scraping her roughly on the hard, cold ground.

Amidst the chaos she was aware of a man. His arms folded as he observed the scene. He was almost out of sight, hidden by the shadows, yet, to Dinah his face appeared clear and close, his priest's gown filling her with dread. It was him. A man of the cloth, he was the one who had brought about the madness. Through cunning use of words, through position and preaching he had everyone fooled.

Dinah knew too, that he had taken care to protect himself, to keep himself above reproach. It was his henchmen who would dirty their hands with her blood, not he. It was they who would kill, leaving him beyond rebuke.

There was a jolt of recognition. She would know those eyes anywhere. Only this time they were filled with menace and fury. Dinah was horrified.

The mob was slathering for blood, a pack of hunters after a fox. Some of them she had helped in the past with their ills and woes. The fire torches flickered fingers of red and orange onto the twisted, snarling faces. Dinah shuddered. She could feel the malevolence seeping into her bones, the darkness of their intentions. They wanted to inflict pain and hurt. She would never have got away.

"Witch! Witch!" the chanting began. The rocks began to fall, heavy and sharp, bludgeoning the frail old body. It crumpled. Dinah was witnessing the scene from up high. The crowd was being swept along by the vicious forces of destruction, beyond reason and incapable of rational thought. There would never have been any other outcome other than death, and, with this acceptance of her fate, her soul embraced the Angels. They were still calling, beckoning her to them, to the lighter planes where the spirit soars free.

Drifting somewhere between heaven and earth, Dinah looked down on the scene unfolding below. The need to watch right through to the end was strong, despite the anguish and despair she felt for the old woman, for herself, for an innocent being so mercilessly stoned to death. The Angels were reaching for her, softly calling her away from the crumpled heap of flesh and bones being pummelled to pieces below. She couldn't leave. Numbness and disbelief held her there. Even though the Angels soothed and caressed, calling her to them, she could not quite manage to pull away.

Dinah could hear Ambrika questioning her, asking her where she was, what was happening to her now. The crowd, now sure their prey was dead, was dispersing. And Dinah saw that all that was left of Lizzy Norreys was a bloodied mass of rags and flesh, skin and bone, spilling into the earth. The trauma held her spirit where it was, caught between worlds. The old woman who wanted to help those in pain, help those who suffered, who held nothing but love and a desire to serve in her heart, had been betrayed and murdered by those she had so tried to help. Something was touching Dinah's hand. She flinched and moaned, trying to move away before registering it was Ambrika.

"Dinah, breathe," she murmured.

Tears wet Dinah's face as the anguish of a life of mistreatment and abuse fused into a hard ball of pain. And then something split, deep inside, in the pit of her stomach. She moaned as it burst, then as it fizzed and spat, as the burning spread through her. It had a life of its own, gathering momentum, no longer controllable, hot, painful.

Someone's howling! thought Dinah, and her scalp prickled at the sound, a never-ending primal, tortured scream, going on and on and on. When will it stop? She tried to move and only then realised, with a shock, that the scream was hers. It was a cry of deep wounding, of rejection and abuse of humankind by fellow humans, the pain making itself heard by anyone who was willing to listen.

Ambrika was willing. A soft hand stroked her arm and Ambrika's voice floated into her consciousness from far away, but gradually getting clearer and closer. Turmoil racked Dinah's body, flurried thoughts pacing through her mind. She was suspended in time, stuck and unwilling to leave, watching the miserable scene from so long ago that had so broken her spirit.

As she watched, an old wooden cart came trundling down the lane and halted by the body. The driver was a splotchy red-faced man with a stomach that hung fat and heavy. He climbed down from the cart, cumbersome and slow, and ambled to the heap of skin and bones lying discarded in the dirt. Standing a moment he slowly shook his head surveying the bloodied heap at his feet. Then with a sigh he bent down and scooped up what had once been Lizzy Norreys, and with a tenderness that belied his rough appearance, gently placed her in the back of his cart. Dinah saw him heave his bulk back into the driver's seat and with a flick of the reins that made the animal jolt they headed off into the night.

Silence.

Then a voice broke through. Again, Ambrika. Softly whispering gentle mantras to assist Dinah's journey back to this world. As Dinah listened the pain was lessening and she found she was clenched into a foetal position. Her body's attempt to ward off the blows.

Ambrika asked her a question. "What do you need to find peace for that beautiful old woman?"

"Acknowledgement," said Dinah immediately. The response came straight from the depths of her soul. "From the people who understood the work I did, the ones I helped. I need to know I didn't die in vain."

"There were many who were sorry," soothed Ambrika. "They were scared and didn't want to be accused themselves. Many were dismayed and frightened by what happened that day and their souls are here now. They want to help you move into the light. Tell them, what can they do?"

"A burial," replied Dinah. "I need a burial with a blessing read over my grave."

"Let's go back then," whispered Ambrika, "and complete the healing by changing the outcome of the past."

A crowd gathered in the graveyard, mostly women and children, and the corpse wrapped in rough cloth was resting on the shoulders of six strong men. They walked slow and unhurried towards the group. The body was Lizzy's, and the atmosphere was one of sorrow and regret, for a life lost and injustice carried out in the name of God. Dinah's spirit lifted at the sight. Some of those gathered were weeping, some stood shocked and trembling, others pale and still, but their love was strong, bathing her broken soul. Two young men came forward holding spades. They began to dig. It looked difficult work, the ground was hard and dry, but they didn't stop until the hole was large enough for the body to be lowered into the ground. The men covered it with earth and a priest read a blessing, solemn, serious. Dinah watched in gratitude as he made the sign of Jesus, the sign of the cross, over this her final resting place.

Fresh tears trailed down Dinah's cheeks, but now they were tears of acceptance, of wanting to move on and leave the bitter past where it was. To forgive those who acted out of fear and hatred, to understand that they did not understand, to offer love and peace in reply to brutality.

"Dinah, I'm going to bring you back." Ambrika's voice startled her.

"I'm already here!" Dinah opened her eyes, which were red-rimmed and sore, and blinked at her friend, aware of a lingering horror at what she had seen. "I feel sick." She clutched her stomach.

"Take it slowly, there's no rush. That was a lot to take in."

"No, Ambrika," she gasped. "You don't understand. The man, the priest who called for my death, who organised the whole thing. It was Tony – my yoga teacher here in Porrick. It was him!"

Twenty-three

The phone wouldn't stop ringing. Someone was determined to get through and refusing to give up, the caller simply hanging up and redialling every time it clicked to answerphone. The sound was grating and intrusive, demanding to be answered and on the fourth attempt, unable to ignore it any longer, Tony lowered out of his back bend and flew into the hallway to snatch up the handset.

"Yes?" He barked.

"Ah Tony, lovely to hear your gentle tones, so soothing to the ears."

"What is it, Emily?"

She was laughing. Tony was infuriated. Of course it would be her. Knowing he was home and having no qualms about interrupting his preparation for tonight's class. He practised at the same time every day, for at least an hour, six days a week. Starting with pranayama breath work he would then stretch and bend in whatever way his body guided, followed by at least half an hour meditation.

"I thought yoga brought about calm and peace? You must be doing something wrong surely?" The smile in her voice made his stomach knot, but he refused to be goaded.

"And I ask again, Emily, what do you want?"

"I'm working late tonight." She was suddenly business-like. "Till at least seven, so you'll need to pick-up the girls from afterschool club at five and look after them until I get back."

Tony stiffened. "Class is at seven. I can't exactly take them with me while I teach, can I?"

"Oh," – she softened slightly – "I forgot. Well, I don't know what to suggest. I'm needed in the office and as the main breadwinner in our household, it's important I show willing. So just this once, Tony, I'm asking you to sort it out. Can you do that?"

"I think I can manage," he bristled, his voice dripping with sarcasm.

It clearly went over her head though, as did most things he said these days, as she was now talking to a colleague in the background.

Eventually she came back on. "Got to go. See you later."

Click. She'd gone. Replacing the handset angrily, Tony racked his brain. It was either Olivia or his mother. He called his mother.

"Kate's here," yelled Daniel. Dinah hadn't even heard the doorbell. She was in the kitchen mashing potatoes. If Kate was here it must be time to go because she always arrived right on time. "Angels, stay with me," Dinah sent out, hurriedly dishing spoonfuls of mash onto the plates. She was anxious. She hadn't been to Tony's class since venturing back to their shared past life. She'd completely withdrawn, staying away to try and regain some clarity.

Recently though she'd been feeling a pull to go back, just one final time. Initially the thought filled her with horror, but it was becoming apparent she needed to do it to fully show herself he had no power over her other than that which she gave him herself. Tonight was a closing gesture, a shutting of doors to honour a sundered connection and clear any residue. The conclusion to this particular story was here and this was the lifetime which would bring an end to the hideous cycle in which they'd been caught.

She thought of Nathaniel and her heart softened. Something felt different with him. When they talked on the phone it was easy and natural but it didn't feel clear, as though a part of her was still somehow locked into Tony.

"This has gone on too long, Angels. And maybe when Tony is out of my life, I'll finally be clear for a true, healthy love."

Setting the gravy jug down on the table, Dinah called the boys for supper and went to greet Kate.

From the other side of the room, Tony's gaze followed her every move without even the smallest trace of embarrassment. This made Dinah automatically uncomfortable. The heat between them was still there, but she no longer felt so at his mercy. Standing at the front of the mat, she put her hands together under her chin in prayer position. Not an empty gesture by any means, as she suspected she would need all the prayer she could get this evening. Refusing to be distracted she closed her eyes and focused on creating as much psychic distance between them as she could muster.

I will see this through! she told herself sternly, with a confidence she wasn't feeling.

To undo the effects of their shared karma and genuinely resolve the conflicting feelings, Dinah knew she must behave with dignity and grace. Running away would serve no one. Any emotional charge would only draw them together in later incarnations to re-enact the same drama all over again until they were clear.

Until one of them, or ideally both of them, was able to transcend the human experience and offer love and forgiveness instead of resentment and bitterness, they would continue to unwittingly come together in an attempt to heal the wound. They needed an ending that would close this chapter once and for all.

Tony was delighted Dinah was back. He'd been wondering where she was. What kept her away? This woman had him dangerously distracted. He had no idea why it was so strong, why he craved her company so keenly, or even why he felt slightly scared of her. The past few weeks when she hadn't been in class he'd been quite disappointed and this surprised him. It was new territory and worried him a little, that maybe she was actually getting to him, starting to throw him off balance. There was no indication where they were heading, as she kept her thoughts and emotions well hidden, and it was only this reticence on her part that stopped him pursuing a more intimate relationship.

Watching her take off her jumper and shoes, he smiled and then frowned. Something had changed!

There was a peculiar energy about her, but he couldn't decipher what it was. It was uncomfortable, though. She seemed more distant, more out of reach somehow. Tony tried to tune in to her, but to his confusion he found it wasn't so easy, that he couldn't get through. What was going on?

Nobody had made Tony feel so unsure since before he had discovered the yogic path back in his early twenties. The feelings he had around her were in a different league to anything else, so much so it slightly scared him. Even meditation was proving more difficult of late, as she often appeared in his thoughts, distracting him by flitting across his mind's eye. No matter how long he sat, she wouldn't seem to go. And the way he felt when he thought of her was extreme to say the least, as though he was on fire, bursting with heat. Tony smiled.

I'm in charge here, Dinah, he sent out. *I am the teacher, not you.* She didn't move. Total stillness. He needed to regain some control and so getting to his feet he confidently greeted the class, instructing them into the standing pose of Tadasana – feet apart, arms at the side of the body, palms facing forward.

When Tony deliberately positioned himself directly in front of her and stared into her face, he saw her eyes were ever so slightly open and was pleased to see a pale red flush creep across her cheeks. *Ahh, not so unaffected!*

He decided to try and break some of her composure and so deliberately guided them through some intense, dynamic postures. Dinah was struggling to keep up and when he saw the light sweat forming on her back and forehead he started holding each pose for longer. Her arms were trembling as she stretched out, fingertips reaching, a fierce look of concentration on her face.

"There's no need to push," said Tony, affectedly. "Release all effort and let go."

He started to slow the pace down now, intending a softer, more sensual quality to the postures so the students would naturally open, so Dinah would have less resistance. Casting a glance in her direction, he saw she was in trance, languishing in the delicious stretching of her body. The room was getting hotter and with each deeper stretch she was dissolving even further. Perfect.

Skirting the edges of the hall, Tony adjusted some of the students' positions on his way round, slowly but purposely heading for Dinah. And she knew he was coming, he could feel it.

When his hands first made contact with her flesh, where her top didn't quite meet her yoga pants, he felt the warmth of her skin, slippery with sweat under his fingertips. He began to massage her, firmly rubbing right up to her bra strap before trailing his hands down her spine.

You're not so responsive tonight, he thought puzzled. There's resistance. Are you playing with me, Dinah? Tony wasn't sure, but repeated the movement anyway, increasing the pressure and gently building into a faster rhythm. He sensed he was starting to have an effect on her, but now he was more fascinated by the effect she was having on him, by the charge building between them.

He knew nothing further would ever happen. He was married and he'd already worked out that Dinah was not one to play that particular game. At the same time he didn't want to end this thing with her just yet – it was too much fun and she made him feel alive and alert in a way the other girls in the class didn't – although they were more than obliging.

He was ignoring the other students, focusing entirely on her, and was delighted to feel her body responding. Tony liked that he had this effect on women and that he could do this to Dinah in particular, even if it was just for a brief time during class. Gradually he began to slow his movements, before finally trailing his fingers across her sweating skin and coming to a halt.

Pleased with himself and feeling powerful, Tony abruptly left Dinah and went to the student directly in front of her. The woman was pretty with a long dark ponytail and wearing tight yoga clothes that accentuated her figure. She looked up and smiled as he took her arm to stretch it higher, while pulling her to rest against him. The look in her eye said she liked the attention and so wrapping his arm around her waist he tenderly stroked her bare tummy.

Watching from behind, Dinah felt sick with herself and her treacherous body. The woman was clearly delighted. She looked ready to melt, eyes shining as she gazed up at the teacher.

Just like I was, thought Dinah, unable to look away.

When Tony eventually got up he turned unexpectedly and stared straight at her, his face expressionless but his eyes taunting her, piercing and triumphant. Quickly Dinah averted her gaze, horrified all over again. The man was poison.

Now he was moving away and she couldn't stop herself looking over again, even as her heart lurched when she saw he was approaching the auburn-haired woman – his faithful friend, lover – who knew? Simultaneously, repelled and fascinated, Dinah watched as he ran his hands down the woman's thigh, squeezing the taut hard muscle before stroking upwards again. Their eyes were fixed on each

207

other and Tony smiled, his hand quite blatantly gliding across her chest.

Dinah shivered. The woman in front of her was watching the scene as well, disappointment etched on her face. He wanted them jealous that he was touching others in the way he touched them. He liked the game. He liked causing hurt. Feelings didn't matter.

The pain he inflicts, she realised, agitated, makes him feel more important, less worthless! Well, no more! The time had come. Tonight was the night – it was now or never.

A whisper entered her mind. "There is nobody who can hurt you in truth. Even in the midst of severe emotional pain, inside you are always whole and peaceful. The more you buy into your emotions, the more you choose to buy into pain and suffering, the more pain and suffering you will experience."

Sitting for the final meditation only served to make Dinah even more anxious. What Tony was doing was wrong and it grated on every part of her. Under his manipulation woman turned against woman, sister against sister, in a misguided attempt to see each other off and claim his undivided affection.

The class was finished and Dinah swiftly rolled up her yoga mat. She felt surprisingly calm and sure of herself as she approached him. She was ready. Tony was by the door talking to a dark-haired woman, who was clearly having trouble with her back as he had his hand resting there. The woman was facing away from Dinah, but her fitted pink Lycra pants and matching top showed off her toned body to perfection. Their conspiratorial murmuring carried across the hall and when the woman suddenly turned slightly, Dinah saw with a jolt it was Cassie. She stopped short. Now she and Tony were staring at each other, laughing softly, while Tony stroked her back.

Dinah saw she was not the only one taking in the show. The auburn-haired woman was also staring at Tony from the far side of the hall. The expression on her face of was of utter desolation. This only enraged Dinah even more.

"Tony, can I speak with you please?" she spoke out, clear and confident. She strode towards the couple. He didn't acknowledge her, deliberately ignored her as he carried on stroking Cassie's back. Cassie shot Dinah a wry smile.

"Tony, can I talk to you!" Only when Dinah was practically on top of them did he shrug apologetically at Cassie, wanting her to know that he too was irritated by the interruption, and turn to face her.

"See you next week, Tony." Cassie fluttered her eyelids at him as she coolly picked up her bag. Her voice was suggestive. "I'm so glad I've found you. Thank you."

She smiled into his eyes before pointedly smirking at Dinah.

When Tony faced Dinah, he didn't bother trying to hide the sensuous glint in his eye.

"Yes, Dinah, how can I help?" he asked smoothly.

They were alone in the hall now, even the auburn woman had gone.

"I want to know what you think you're doing with the women in your class?" Her tone was steady and serious.

"I'm sorry, Dinah?" Tony sounded amazed and was staring at her as though she was completely mad. "What are you talking about?"

Sudden fury bubbled inside her. "I mean, Tony, all the touching and stroking, the massaging and mind-games! The hand holding and country walks - you seem to go way beyond the call of duty for a yoga teacher! What about your wife?"

His face froze. He no longer looked sensuous and warm. He looked annoyed and slightly dangerous. "I don't know what you're talking about."

"I know how Tantra works, Tony. I understand how energy can be used to lure people..." She paused. He was still. "You're married, Tony, married! You've got women fawning all over you in class, you tried to pull me in, too, but I've woken up and I see you, you know I do. And I know exactly what you're doing."

"Know what I'm doing?" His laugh had an edge. "You're hysterical!"

"You're on an ego-trip, Tony." Dinah was hot with indignation and embarrassment at how he had played her. "You're using yoga and what it brings out in people to boost yourself. You're using your position as 'teacher' to hook women in, to make yourself feel good, while in reality you take away all their power."

Dinah was amazed at her boldness, and at how articulate she was when usually she would stumble for words. Everything about him

209

suddenly appalled her, and she was appalled with herself for walking into it. Taking a step back she saw the draw she'd felt towards him wasn't anything to do with love, it was toxic and it was about being hooked in. It was just a game between the two of them as they played off each other. Pure illusion.

"I would never abuse my position in that way!" His voice was raised and his face flushed. When he came towards her, although he felt threatening, Dinah didn't move.

"Yes you would," she shot back. "And yes you do, and you know it. That's why you're angry, Tony. I've named your game and you don't like it. I see you and you're scared!"

His face contorted. "How dare you question me!" he snarled, white spittle frothing at the corners of his mouth. "Who do you think you are speaking to me like this? You're just a silly little girl, Dinah. You think you know it all, but if you can't cope with my class you shouldn't be here—"

"It's not about coping, Tony," she cut him off. "It's about integrity and honesty. Two qualities of which you know nothing."

She had a powerful urge to kick him hard in the shin.

"You're no Yogic master, Tony, no guru, no spiritual teacher. You're just a bully, addicted to power and games and unable to control yourself!"

"Get out!" He spat the words out like bullets. A flush of red shot across his cheeks as he started to yell. "Get out now! There's nothing for you in my class." He was looming over her, shaking with rage and suddenly seeming much bigger than before as he pushed her towards the door with his body. He didn't feel safe at all, his eyes glittering with rage. Was he going to hit her? Dinah backed away as an urgent voice called inside her, "Leave, Dinah. Go now."

Almost running to the door, she plunged into the fresh air. He was shouting after her, "You need a bloody psychiatrist! There's no place for you here! Mad woman!" Then the door slammed shut with an almost supernatural force.

Dinah stopped and gulped for air. Standing on the side of the pavement, out of the way of any passers-by, she felt sick as she clung to the railings. His mask had well and truly come off now and she had witnessed the monster beneath. There was no going back.

Tony. The archetypal wounded masculine, and until now she hadn't been able to see it. The man was damaged and venting his anger on the world, wielding his power over others and over women with vengeance. The change in him had been instantaneous, from warmth to demonic anger in seconds. The caring, wise teacher of a few months before was gone for good, the man who had gently held her hand, had vanished. She shuddered with shock and upset. "Angels, help!"

Furiously marching home, Dinah saw how in Tony's company she'd always felt anxious and wonderful at the same time, uplifted and alert, but also worried and confused. And every time she'd managed to find a reason to excuse him, while all the time he'd been playing the age-old game of hot and cold, pursue and reject. She'd talked herself into believing in him, in his worthiness and caring heart, rationalising all the humiliations. Well, not anymore!

By the time she got to the bottom of the High Street she was calmer, and it occurred to her how odd it was that Cassie had suddenly appeared at Tony's class.

Good luck to them! She was unable to suppress a small smile.

Twenty-four

From the foot of the hill it looked a long steep haul to the top. The moor was bleak. It was early February, not cold exactly just dull and heavy, with leaden grey clouds skirting across a white glacial sky.

The place was deserted. There were no other cars in the layby and nobody else around as far as the eye could see. When Dinah opened the hatchback, Sophie shot out, tail wagging, delighted to be free. She'd been whining excitedly ever since they had turned onto the moorland road some twenty minutes earlier and as Dinah began the steep trudge up the path she called her to follow. The ground was hard and the higher they went the more vigorous the northerly wind became, whipping her hair against her cheeks and buffeting her clothes.

The revelations of her past life with Tony and the subsequent row had left her shocked through and she was worried for Nathaniel too. Cassie seemed to be everywhere. The gnawing feeling was back, as well as a small niggling voice that wondered if perhaps there was some truth in what Cassie had told her in the coffee house.

Way above her on the crest of the hill, the brooding stones of the tor loomed over the surrounding countryside. The Dartmoor tors were always an impressive sight, huge piles of granite rock standing as an eternal monument to times gone by. There were so many power places scattered over the moor, but this particular tor was Dinah's favourite. Continuing up the well-trodden footpath she found herself falling into a natural rhythm of walking meditation, one step after the other, each one requiring full awareness of every movement and breath. Occasionally she would pause, acknowledging a deepening within her. "If anyone's watching, Angels, they'd wonder what on earth I'm doing," she sent out, glad to have the place to herself. That she was alone suited her purpose for coming.

By the time she was halfway up, her cares and worries didn't seem quite so important. Things just didn't seem to matter so much in the vast outdoors. Out in the raw of the elements the upset of recent days was being blown away by the wind, with her only concern being her footsteps on the land and the bracing air filling her lungs. Dinah breathed in the ruggedness of the moor, taking in the desolate sky, and wide rolling hills spiky with gorse and sleeping heather. Where the land sloped downwards, huge rocks and boulders tumbled down the hillside as if strewn by some giant hand, and along the valley floor a small river flowed, swollen with water from moorland streams. The sacredness of this landscape was tangible.

As she neared the top she held her arms aloft, palms open to heaven to receive the Divine Energies. Directly in front of her was the tor. It never failed to inspire her, to re-awaken her to the insignificance of whatever it was she was struggling with, and she nodded a blessing to it as she passed by. Today it was not her intended destination.

Over the brow of the hill a cluster of Dartmoor ponies huddled together, heads hung low with only each other to shield them from the weather. Behind them was the ring of standing stones. Dinah's belly pinged at the sight of it. This was why she had come.

Sophie charged ahead and Dinah followed behind, breathless and exhilarated from the exertion of the climb. There were twenty stones in total, each about four foot high and some fallen over. Erected by a long-ago people in accordance with sacred geometry, the stone circles were originally built to gather and amplify the natural energies of Earth. All over the world such rings stand in silent testimony to a time when Nature was still revered. Yet even nowadays, they held the residue of ancient worship and ritual. To her, such places acted as powerful portals into the higher spiritual realms, holding formidable forces within their confines.

Marching to the nearest stone, Dinah placed her hands on it, running her palms across its bumpy surface before pressing herself against it. These were the stone people, anchored in the ground, solid and rooted – the Guardians of the records of Mother Earth. The stones had been calling her incessantly during the past few days, pulling her to them until at last, this morning, she knew that she must come. Slipping her coat from her shoulders to the ground, Dinah was left in only a white shift dress, a flimsy cardigan and leggings. Goosebumps prickled her arms, but undeterred and sensing a solid connection with earth would be needed, she kicked off her shoes and unpeeled her socks, feeling the cold damp earth between her toes. Instinct led her to the centre of the circle, where she placed both hands over her heart and stood barefoot and shivering, wondering what to do next. She was relieved no one was around to see her, especially as a light rain had begun to fall, a soft mist sprinkling down on her. They would think she was crazy, on her own, half dressed in the middle of the moor… although she knew she wasn't the only one to visit the stones this way.

"Thank you, stones, Angels, for bringing me here," she whispered tentatively.

Every now and then as she gazed around the circle she would catch rainbow prisms of light flickering around the stones. She relaxed her physical vision to concentrate instead on using her inner eye. "I see you. Have you come to play?" she called into the wind and rain. Nothing.

With a sigh, Dinah stamped her feet harder into the earth and changed her hands to prayer position. She might as well do something while she was here and so she faced East and bowed her head to honour the Easterly direction, the direction of the Sylphs and the direction of Air. Then she turned South towards the direction of fire and bowed again, before facing West for water, and finally North for Earth. Something was changing in the circle. The air was quivering, emanating around her as a damp charge rose from the soil, prompting her to crouch down close to the ground and burrow her hands into the grass.

Waves of humility and gratitude pulsed through her and she sent blessings into the earth, thanking the four directions for their protection. The rain was heavier now and the wind stronger. "Where are you?" she cried, alert to both inner and outer worlds.

From nowhere, frenzy.

Suddenly she was engulfed in a haze of multi-coloured orbs of sparkling energy, jingling on her skin, darting pulses of excitement. The Sylphs, the elementals of the Air, had descended and were making themselves known, gleefully whipping about her until she was laughing and disorientated. It took her a while to regain her bearings, but as she recovered from the surprise of their chaotic appearance, she could hear whisperings in the wind, murmuring voices and distant laughter. The Sylphs are quick and playful and can easily sweep a person off their feet, so Dinah made sure to stay with the solidness of the stones and the earth underfoot. Only by staying grounded was it safe to commune with the Sylphs, without fear of being carried away into the realms of the Air oneself.

"Hello…" called Dinah, excited. This was her first encounter with the Sylphs and it felt wonderful, such lightness, such freedom. She beamed wildly. The rain was beating down now and the wind blasting about her, but she wasn't cold any longer, she felt alive and free and overflowing with happiness. With her hands to her ears, she listened, certain she could make out voices whispering in her ears and mind, or was it only the whistling wind?

"Is that you?" she giggled. "Sylphs, give me a sign? Are you wanting to speak with me?"

Immediately, the wind got up even more at the same time as hundreds of tiny little feet tapped on her skin, like hundreds of tiny invisible spiders they were dancing on her arms and shoulders, through her hair, all over. The lightest of touches, the subtlest of signs and yet she knew it was the Sylphs, that they were connecting, daring her to join them. The wind thrashed her dress around her thighs and clutching it as best she could, Dinah screamed with laughter and began to dance, too. They were urging her on, surrounding her with whirling prisms of light that spun before her eyes and made her giddy, and what began as slow steady movement soon escalated into a wild twirling dance of release.

She skipped and spun, twirled and leaped completely oblivious to how she looked and when she could dance no more she sank to the ground. "Sylphs," she sent out as she caught her breath. "You summoned me here, what must I do?" There was a definite sound of whispering. She waited, patient and still.

A voice made her jump. *Sorceress of the Divine heart, we need your prayers, you keep forgetting. Mother Earth needs you to remember.*

Dinah was thrilled. "I hear you," she spoke into the wind. "No, I haven't been connecting as often as I should. I will, Sylphs, I promise." The energy bubbling in the depths of her stomach was like a mini-volcano, compelling her back on to her feet again. Like a puppet with someone else pulling the strings – she couldn't stay still.

Let your body lead. Surrender. Come with us to where your heart truly belongs.

So, with wet hair flattened against her cheeks and a dress soaked through and dripping, Dinah stretched to the sky and tried to touch heaven. She no longer minded whether she was alone or not, an army of people could have tramped over the horizon and she would not have cared less. The physical dimensions were left far behind and she was lifting away, departing for higher planes.

Remember the truth of who you are, Dinah. Humanity keeps forgetting what it is. The voice spoke gracefully and fluidly. *The world is transforming and it is time for the Mortal Custodians of Earth to reclaim their spiritual power.*

"What must I do, Sylphs? Help me understand."

Tell people, Dinah. Be a light that leads the way. The Earth needs purification, the atmosphere is choking. They must learn to treasure their world.

"What else?"

Honour the Air and you honour life itself. Cherish the birds and the insects who fly, keep their world sweet. Send your love into the air, Dinah, and pray for the planet. The more who love Earth, the stronger she becomes.

The voice was soft but grave and Dinah's dance began to slow.

God gave humanity the gift of Earth, and it is for humanity to choose if they wish to save her.

The dance had stopped and Dinah stood still, ears straining.

Gaia becomes evermore toxic. It cannot be ignored any longer. She yearns to cleanse and heal, but instead more poison comes. Humanity does not understand that all of you count in this battle, and a battle it has become, a battle to save your sacred home. The time is coming when Earth will no longer be able to support you.

The voice was insistent. *Each of you has the choice of how to live your life – taking only what you need or living in greed and excess.*

All Dinah's attention focused what she was being told. "Sylphs, what must we do?"

Man and woman are imbalanced and this has brought the world to its knees. It is the Feminine who will bring the balance to save

Earth. But she will have to be loud to be heard, to be fully understood. When equality is restored throughout your world, Woman will bring forth the qualities Earth needs to adjust the frequencies, the qualities of nurturing and softness, harmony and peace. This alone will save your planet.

There was a short pause and Dinah could hear the wind muttering, many voices chattering before the lone voice spoke again.

Earth is dying, Dinah.

Dinah blanched, fear clenching in her stomach. "I don't understand. Is it too late?"

A whisper now: *Remember. The masculine and the feminine must unite. This will bring about the healing. The male and female must make peace to save the Earth Mother. All of you are responsible, each and every one of you.*

They had gone. She could feel it and she was left standing sombre and chilled and rooted to the spot. Her dress stuck to her skin, she was cold and the joy of the earlier dance was most definitely gone. Something warm nuzzled her hand and looking down, Dinah saw Sophie gazing up at her expectantly.

"Well, Sophie," said Dinah, sadly. "Now I know."

* * *

Someone was tapping his shoulder. "Hey Nathaniel. How lovely to see you." The silky voice made the hairs on the back of his neck stand on end even before he felt her press closely behind him, followed by a hand sliding onto his shoulder.

When he reluctantly turned around it was to find himself face-to-face with Cassie, watching him closely, a look of satisfaction glittering in her eyes. He'd become adept at avoiding her in the town, some sixth sense warning whenever she was near so he could go the other way. But on this occasion he hadn't seen her coming. He'd only nipped to the corner shop at the bottom of his road because he'd run out of milk, but foolishly he'd stopped at the newspaper rack, distracted by the headlines. Without saying a word he flicked her hand off his shoulder and refolded the paper he'd been reading, placing it back on the shelf before moving past her with a tight smile. He had to pay for the milk, but then he could escape.

Except that Cassie stayed exactly where she was, hovering, waiting for him to finish, her eyes boring into his back. Taking his change Nathaniel made for the door, but she stepped smartly in front of him, blocking his way.

"I'm in a hurry," he snapped, trying to step round her.

"I just wanted to say hi, I haven't seen you for ages," she purred. "How've you been?" Her eyes darted about the shop, a strange smile playing on her lips.

"Look, I'm in a hurry and quite frankly I don't think we've got anything to talk about."

A spark of anger flicked in her eyes. "Well I do! We've got a friend in common and I wanted you to know that I had a great chat with her." She pushed herself forcefully into his chest and brushed his hand with hers, her eyes fixed on his face.

Nathaniel flinched and leaned back, slowly shaking his head. "You just don't give up do you?" He was exasperated.

The face she pulled as he took hold of her shoulders and firmly put her to one side so he could get past reminded him of a frustrated toddler. She glared at him as he regarded her scornfully. "And don't bother to say hi if you see me again." He made another attempt for the door.

"It was Dinah!" blurted Cassie.

Nathaniel stopped short, eyes narrowed. "What are you talking about now?" He didn't want Cassie to know she'd got to him, but his heart pounded at the mention of Dinah's name.

"Oh. She didn't tell you? That *is* strange!" Now she was smirking, her rapidly changing emotions moving so fast Nathaniel couldn't keep track. She tipped her head to one side. "Yeah. We had coffee together and a *really* interesting chat. All about you as it so happens."

Sensing he must keep this conversation brief and that it was important to give nothing away, Nathaniel stared at her. "What do you want, Cassie?"

"I just thought you should know that me and Dinah talked, that we got a few things cleared up, that I told her my side of the story—"

Seeing the look on his face, she stopped short.

"There are no sides," roared Nathaniel, exasperated. He rubbed his forehead wearily. "Because there's no story other than the one you make up in your head!"

At this, Cassie's mouth twisted before settling into a thin hard line. "That's not what Dinah thinks! Not now I've filled her in on you and me and our amazing sex life." She grinned nastily from ear to ear and lowered her voice. "You better behave with me, Nathaniel! We go to yoga together now and next time I see her I might just tell her how you call me non-stop, how we meet all the time for mind-blowing sex, how I came with you to Spain..."

Something inside him snapped and grabbing her wrist, Nathaniel yanked her towards him.

"Don't touch me!" she hissed, struggling to make him let go, but he only tightened his grip.

"I want this to be clear once and for all," he said loudly and clearly for the whole shop to hear. He was shaking with fury, his spittle flicking on her face. The cashier looked up in alarm and a woman who'd been browsing magazines behind them, quickly moved away, sensing danger. "If you ever see me around, and I'm telling you nicely this time, I do *not* want you to acknowledge me in any way, and I will not acknowledge you." Cassie nodded vigorously, squirming, trying to back away but trapped by the shelves behind her. Nathaniel was determined to leave no room for misunderstanding. "You are walking on very thin ice with me, Cassie, and if I have to tell you again – if I so much as see you again – I won't be so pleasant."

With a grim expression he dropped her wrist, leaving her to rub it where his fingers had dug into her. "And you stay away from Dinah! Understand?"

"Get away from me," she hissed. "You're mad." But her shoulders slumped making her appear small and defeated.

Nathaniel left the shop. He sincerely hoped that would be the end of it. Cassie was clearly unwell, but what an earth had she done to Dinah? Worried, he took out his phone and pulled up her number.

219

Twenty-five

Since the confrontation with Tony – the one that was meant to have freed her from his grasp – Dinah was becoming inexplicably more wretched with each day that passed. She couldn't understand it. Their dynamic was explained and she had clarity around their unfortunate relationship, but she was still troubled by a nagging sensation of something having been left undone. What had she missed? She understood that they had met again because of the shadow of shared experience from other times, that it was a soul connection borne from a desire to heal, and that the invisible threads drawing them together were urging forgiveness. But confusingly, even though she now knew about the brutality of their past, even though she had seen his dark side with her own eyes, a longing still pulled at her heart and tainted or not, it was strong. It hurt and the hurt made her angry. Somehow she must find a way to emotionally disentangle or she would never know peace.

It meant only one thing – there was deeper work to be done!

So Dinah closed off from the world. She cancelled all engagements in her diary, switched off her phone and blanketed her computer with a cloth. Going out for food or shopping, she kept her head down and kept to herself. How long this would take she didn't know, but she couldn't be disturbed by anything or anyone; it would only pull her out of the healing. The garden brought her solace, pottering amongst the flowers and shrubs was a comfort, and, as Dinah worked outside, weeding and hoeing, tidying and pruning, previously unknown waves of injustice and pain rose unbidden to the surface. Seeds of hate and resentment were cocooned deep within her, hidden in the depths of her psyche where they had been able to incubate and take root. Just out of conscious awareness they had grown stronger and stronger, darkening her perspective on life.

Of course the Angels stayed near, holding her as her shadow-self revealed an unexpected sorrow. The Angels whispered encouragement day in day out, assuring her she was on the right path, on her way to the light once again. "Forgive and walk free," they urged.

A few days in and Dinah was on her hands and knees in a flowerbed yanking bindweed from the soil when she felt her Angel strongly by her side. Stopping what she was doing she knelt back on her heels just as a sharp ache cut through her heart. "Owww!" she exclaimed, wincing and rubbing her chest. "God help me! When will this be done?"

"True forgiveness can feel difficult and painful at first." Her Angel closed around her, sheltering her in its wings, holding her away from the world in a ball of warm light. "As if you are giving in or opening yourself to further hurt, but the truth is that by holding on to anger, it is only you who suffers. Let go of the pain and be healed."

The days passed and Dinah decided she quite liked this self-imposed isolation. It gave her space to really take care of herself and the boys, while avoiding any harsh energy from the outside world. Worryingly, however, Tony was still in her head and there seemed no sign of him shifting anytime soon. It was frustrating.

One morning, when the boys had left for school, she slumped at the kitchen table. "What has he done to me!" she cried, fists curled into balls. "He's like a dark Lord, manipulative and in my head – what must I do to break free?" The horror of the previous lifetime was paling into insignificance compared to the complexity of her feelings in this one. She was horrified by his lack of empathy and the way he encouraged women to idolise him, but she couldn't seem to banish him from her system. In despair Dinah sank to the floor.

Immediately the air chilled. Her Angel was holding her and she found herself viewing the entire Tony drama from a place of detachment, as if watching a TV show with characters and plots, which aren't real.

"The battle between light and dark exists in all men and women," murmured her Angel. "The soul urges compassion and forgiveness, but the ego resists, holding on to anger and the need to control no matter how painful. Focus on peace within yourself, set your intention and trust it will come about. It is your choice to let yourself heal."

Returning to the physical world the Angel's words echoed in her mind and she began to pray, asking God to release Tony from her soul and her soul from Tony. Over the coming days, Dinah repeated the prayer like a mantra. She hadn't seen Tony since their row, but he was appearing in her dreams, always potent, always leaving her tired and drained.

Meditation only intensified the resentment in her heart. Nothing was working and she felt a long way from forgiveness. On the fourth day, with still no sign of recovery, she knew something more was required and it occurred to her that maybe psychic manipulation was being used to bind her to him.

"It would be the easiest thing in the world for someone with the knowledge and power he seems to possess."

Dinah implored the Angels for help. Staring at her reflection in the bedroom mirror a surge of courage moved through her. "I've had enough!" she cried. "I take back my power!" A spark fluttered in her heart. "I take back my power!" louder this time. "I have suffered enough and I take back my power!" She was starting to believe herself – a thrice-spoken affirmation being an effective way to clear stuck energy.

"I am light," she carried on as her mind started to quiet.

"I am love." She hugged herself tightly.

"I am divine." She forced her mouth into a wide smile.

"I am light. I am love. I am divine."

"I am light. I am love. I am divine."

She was on a roll. The energy was building. She visualised a ball of white light around her body and breathed it in, directing it to her heart. In the mirror her reflection smiled hopefully back at her. The forlorn sensation she had been carrying was going. It seemed that by embracing the pain process, without denying or trying to stifle it, she had created enough space for it to pass through. Leaning into the mirror, Dinah kissed her reflected self playfully on the lips as behind her a vast blue light appeared.

Archangel Michael had come. He was wielding his golden sword of truth and Dinah knew just what to do.

"Archangel Michael," she whispered. "Please cut the negative cords between me and Tony, sever any toxic ties or thought forms between us, at both ends, in all directions of time, so we can be free of each other once and for all!" She stood poised.

Tony was beside her now, holding his hands out to her beseechingly as if asking her to go to him. Dinah blanched. Between them ran threads of sticky grey, glistening cords of attachment connecting them to each other, linking them heart, mind and body. One in particular sprouted from her belly and into his. At least six inches across, it was a hideous thing – a heaving tendon throbbing in a solid gnarled mass – indicating a karmic tie from not one lifetime together but many. Before Dinah could react a wall of blue came down about her blocking Tony from view. Michael stood between them. The strength of the cords explained the complexity between them, the depth of psychic connection. "This is why it's so painful," she gasped. "The cords bind us tight even as we try to break free."

The Archangel rested his hands on Dinah's heart and as he did her mind went blank, leaving only a silent black space inside.

Out of a stark horizon rose the great pyramids of Giza, wavering in the heat, pointing majestically into an azure-blue sky. Around her a vast expanse of empty desert stretched, arid golden sands tinged orange by the sun. It was nearing sundown. *Today is the celebration of my twelfth year*, Dinah heard quite clearly. *My initiation.* She was a young girl, standing alone in a darkened doorway watching the sun move closer to the Earth. Only when it skimmed the horizon, causing streams of golden light to flicker over the dunes, did she go through. The Great Temple chamber was alight with fire torches, wisps of jasmine smoke rose from huge golden bowls, perfuming the air with a thick heady scent. A mass of people were gathered, a sea of reverent faces lit by the glow of the flames. They fell silent as she passed, as she headed for the Altar towards the woman, the shimmering Goddess, who waited. The girl trembled with nervous excitement. *Isis waits for me.*

The embodiment of the Divine Feminine, Isis stood tall and commanding, draped in golden finery, with deep brown skin that shone with luminous light. Raven black hair fell to her waist and wide almond eyes flashed with crystalline light. As Daughter of the

223

Sky Goddess Nut and the Earth God Geb, Isis is a Goddess of Magic and Nature, a Queen of Healing and Medicine.

Not a breath of movement disturbed the chamber as with a beating heart the girl knelt before Isis. The Goddess towered over her, silent and still, and the girl trembled as she reached to take her hands. As they touched, in the moment of contact between mortal and immortal, the girl juddered, shot through by a blast of scalding heat that coursed through her palms, up her arms and into her body. They were fusing as one, she and Isis merging together and the girl moaned, rigid, head thrown back, body arched, paralysed by the force searing through her. It was terrifying and it was incredible. When she began to lose consciousness two women came forward to hold her, two priestesses, one each side, propping her up as the current flowed, as molten fire purified every cell of her being. She wanted to scream but couldn't, wanted to writhe but was held still, trapped inside of herself as her body burned. Only when Isis released her hands did it stop.

The girl slumped onto the cool stone floor, breathing hard, gasping as a slow, tender warmth swirled inside her, making her giddy. She was cleansed. *Initiated as a Temple Priestess, a healer in direct lineage of the Great Goddess.* For the first time the girl raised her head, curious to look into the face of the Goddess, but Isis was gone, and all that remained was a deep burning love inside her.

A woman came to her side. It was her teacher, and with a start, Dinah recognised the soul of her present-life father. The woman was pressing something into each of her hands. A green crystal sphere in one and into the other a snake made of gold with eyes that glowed bright. *Initiation gifts, blessed by Isis. The tools I will use for healing.*

Three rings appeared, three circles, and a boy, hovering on the fringes of awareness, just out of reach of her inner vision. Irritation swelled inside her. *The Three Healing circles of Mind, of Body, of Spirit.*

Now she was older, a young woman standing in the middle of a circle of people. *I am High Priestess of the Circle of the Healers of the Mind.*

Dinah felt herself swathed in long turquoise robes that swept around her feet, while on her head a golden headpiece was lavishly studded with crystals and gems, curving over her forehead and reaching to her third eye. *I am a teacher of healers.*

A young man approached, the boy of before only grown big and strong. *A gifted and powerful healer, who follows his own path, ignoring the ways of tradition.* Animosity bubbled inside her. *He walks a fine line between healing and manipulation and it is a source of great conflict and aggravation, which already disrupts our circle.* Those eyes, so familiar. Dinah's heart dipped, even as her Angel drew near. Tony.

"Yet he admires you, Dinah," her Angel murmured. "He would like your respect, but feels only your disapproval and contempt. It makes him afraid and the fear makes him angry."

Dinah sensed she was viewing the original connection between them, forged long ago from a mutual desire to help and to heal. And more unpleasantly, she also sensed that she had not treated him well at all, that she had been dismissive and controlling, scathing and scornful, while piling all the blame onto him. The truth twanged in her belly and she was overcome by a bitter remorse. *I was a High Priestess, initiated by Isis in the art of healing, and yet I showed him no regard, expecting obedience and devotion, refusing to see his dissatisfaction and distress.*

He was older now, handsome and more confident, with angry, intelligent eyes, all-knowing, all-seeing. "He came to resent you for your lack of deference towards him, for your authority within the circle," her Angel went on. "You were unable to prevent him from going his own way and felt responsible for his fall from the light, and fall he did. At this time in the cycle he was not yet evolved enough to turn away from his shadow and the circle was corrupted beyond repair."

The Priestess that Dinah had once been began to murmur.

He presses for change. Defying the elders, challenging their leadership and questioning Isis herself. He wants power and supremacy and believes that men should rule, giving no thought to the feminine, to how this will affect the energies and of the consequences for the Earth. And he is not alone. He is one of many who feel this way as the gulf between male and female widens. Across Earth this period marks the beginnings of the downfall of women. Dinah saw him standing in the midst of a large crowd, a leader amongst followers. *He speaks fluently and skilfully, making grand promises, as with charisma and cunning he gains support within the circle, flattering the men and seducing the women. We are no longer united. There is a division of loyalties and uncertainty is rife.* Dinah watched as the circle crumbled, as healer turned against healer and the conflict spread into the other healing circles, and then out into the wider community.

The sorry scene was fading and now Archangel Michael was cutting the cord that protruded from her tummy, feigning playful exertion to demonstrate how strong the tie between them was. In spite of her dismay at the part she had played in things, Dinah couldn't help but smile. As the Archangel severed the last thread between them she felt the final cut of release.

Falling to her knees, Dinah prayed for help to forgive and heal the sordid past.

"Dinah," came the whisper, "mental and emotional healing can be immediate, when you accept that the pain and suffering you experience, you choose to experience. When you accept Divine order in everything around you and realise it is as easy to choose joy and peace as it is to choose pain."

* * *

Turning on her mobile for the first time in days, a stream of messages and texts pinged into Dinah's phone, most of which were from Nathaniel. A pang of guilt stopped her in her tracks when it dawned on her she'd given no warning or explanation for her mysterious lack of contact. She was on her way to a kirtan concert on the other side of town and so sent a quick apologetic text saying she would call him the next day. There was no time to dwell – the concert was starting any minute.

Inside the building shoes had to be removed and from the number of neatly arranged boots, trainers and sandals covering the reception floor, kirtan was popular in Porrick. It was also just what she needed after all the recent revelations.

The metal staircase leading down to the concert room was narrow and steep and Dinah clutched the handrail as she went, descending cautiously until she emerged at the bottom into a large open space.

Wide-eyed she looked around the room. The walls were swathed with gold and silver fabric adorned with twinkling fairy lights, and oriental carpets covered every inch of floor. Huge squashy floor cushions lined the edges of the room and were filled by people lounging and chatting, all come for an evening of devotional chanting. Dinah was excited. Kirtan never failed to touch her.

Spotting a vacant space near the front she started to pick her way towards it, but faltered halfway across when her skin started prickling and she felt unexplainably anxious. Something was wrong. Quickly closing her eyes she tried tuning in to the energy in the room, but there were so many people and so much activity that it was impossible to pinpoint anything particular.

Taking a detour to the washroom Dinah went into one of the cubicles and sat awhile to catch her breath. Such an extreme reaction left her perplexed. What was going on? After splashing cold water on her wrists she came out again, but the door hadn't even properly swung shut behind her when Tony's face flashed in her mind's eye, accompanied by another sharp bolt of anxiety, so unexpected that she gasped. Three steps later and she collided hard with someone. They both stopped short, alarmed and apologetic, and then both stepped back in horror and headed in opposite directions. She hadn't looked directly at him. She hadn't needed to. Tony. With all ideas of being near the front now abandoned, Dinah quickly sat down on the nearest cushion she could find. She was shaking, her breath coming in short intermittent gasps as panic mounted in her chest. Without even having to turn and check she knew exactly where he was in the room – to her left by the far wall. It was as though she'd gone back in time, feeling him in exactly the same way as she used to and just as intensely.

The musicians were coming out now, each paying their respects to a golden statue of the Hindu elephant god, Ganesh, which had pride of place in the middle of the stage. Unable to will herself to calm, Dinah fervently asked Ganesh in his capacity as Remover of Obstacles, to take away her anxiety. On stage the musicians were settling down with their instruments – bansuri flutes, a long-necked sitar and an array of hand-drums – while an older man with long hair slowly, slowly prised open the harmonium resting in his lap, sending a single elongated note reverberating out into the room. The audience went quiet and he started to hum, deep and low, his voice echoing off the walls, bouncing back into the room. The concert had begun.

From then on was a blur. They were immersed in music and immersed in chanting, as following the wallah's lead they sang, moved and danced the night away. The combination of hypnotic music and rhythmic Sanskrit chants carried them all to a more beautiful place, where dramas fall away and inner peace is restored. Time passed and it didn't seem five minutes to Dinah before the musicians were thanking everyone for coming and packing their instruments away.

Resurfacing from her inner depths she knew immediately that his eyes were on her and without thinking turned to look his way. Their eyes clashed and she jolted. It was like electricity going through her. It was all there in his eyes. Sadness flooded her body and she wanted to cry, knowing unexplainably that he was experiencing the same. Just the two of them locked into each other, neither one able to look away as the unexpressed and unspoken colluded to hold them together. Then Dinah was aware of someone else, an unsettling disturbance. She frowned, awkward, only now noticing the familiar auburn-haired figure sitting next to Tony. The woman was staring at him, at first puzzled and then irritated as she followed his gaze and saw Dinah. It was the woman from his yoga class – the most devoted of his students and his most adoring disciple. Disappointment poked Dinah's heart, even while the hairs on her arms spiked. The woman pulled Tony's arm possessively, trying to break the spell, demanding he look at her. Tony frowned, seemingly startled by the intrusion and then promptly looked away as the woman smiled sweetly up at him and squeezed his arm. It was a gesture of ownership and Dinah saw Tony flinch slightly. With a breath she averted her gaze. Time to go.

The musicians were welcoming members of the audience to come and speak to them, and Dinah saw Tony's auburn-haired friend make her way to the stage. Without another thought, Dinah picked up her bag and made for the staircase. She felt his eyes following her until she had disappeared up the steps.

The entrance lobby was empty and she hurried to locate her shoes. It was a relief to finally push open the outside door and walk free into the cool night air. This one unforeseen encounter had brought up all those feelings she thought she had left behind – the magnetic pull had come flooding back. And yet there was something else too.

It's peace, she realised with surprise. And relief! I'm relieved! Something major had shifted. She didn't hate Tony nor resent him, in fact she felt indifferent towards him, and his female companion too. Dinah could have kissed the ground.

"I'm free!" she cried, not caring who might hear. "It doesn't hurt any more. Thank you, Angels! Thank you, World!"

She practically skipped all the way home, leaving something behind that had kept her stuck for a long, long time. Longer than most people could possibly imagine.

Back in the concert hall, Tony sat frozen. He had known she was going to leave before she even got up and went. He'd seen the look in her eyes as she took in Siobhan next to him, the knowing, the relief, and he liked to think a little sadness too, and sadness was what he felt now. He'd watched her tread up the stairs, felt it when she opened the main door and flinched when it slammed shut behind her. A part of him wanted to go after her, to tell her how he really felt – the confusion and fear, how she stirred things up in him he would rather stay buried, how absolutely out of his depth he felt with her, and how without her in his class a light had gone out, a small but significant light extinguished, and that he didn't know how to get it back without her.

A warm hand brushed his neck and Siobhan snuggled into him. Tony stayed exactly where he was.

Twenty-six

It was already half past twelve and Nathaniel was meeting Dinah at one. He'd been relieved to get a text from her the previous evening and then a call today apologising for being out of touch and asking if he wanted to walk by the river. She told him she'd been doing some inner healing work and would have called last night but was at a kirtan concert. These aspects of her world still baffled him.

Stepping out of the shower he caught sight of his reflection in the mirror and grinned at himself. Cassie had had no effect and life was starting to become interesting. Drying himself roughly with a towel he mused over Dinah. There was a frailty to her, a vulnerable side that made him feel protective, although he knew she would insist she didn't need protecting. He also suspected that trust was an issue for her, and that gaining her trust was something that would only come with time. "And maybe for me, too." He rubbed his hair vigorously. "Have I ever really trusted a woman? Have I ever really let a woman into my heart?" He knew he had not.

If he were honest, the thought of truly opening up to another person, of exposing all the fears and insecurities and the parts about himself he didn't like so much, scared him. But aside from the niggling tribulation, there was also elation and, dare he say it, hope. Dinah made him excited about life. "Tread carefully though," he warned his reflection. "Don't go too fast or you'll wreck it."

By the time he'd finished getting dressed he had fifteen minutes to get there. It was warm and sunny out, a perfect reflection of his mood, and so grabbing his sunglasses he set off.

When Nathaniel arrived, Dinah was standing hands in pockets at the entrance to the meadows. His heart thumped at the sight of her. She was in jeans and a tight grey cardigan and as usual her hair was escaping from her ponytail and blowing around her face. For a moment he just watched. A small brown dog suddenly emerged from the tangle of undergrowth, soaking wet with mucky paws and carrying an old tennis ball in its mouth. It came pelting straight for him, a flurry of fur, water and mud. He guessed it must be Sophie. She came charging over, jumping up, trailing muddy paws down his jeans.

Dinah rushed over. "Sophie! Get down!" She ordered sternly, but the dog paid no attention. Only when Dinah grabbed her by the collar and firmly pulled her off did she stop.

"Oh no! Your jeans!" cried Dinah, dismayed.

"It's fine. Don't worry, I like dogs," said Nathaniel, brushing himself off.

"She's so naughty! She knows not to jump up and does it anyway," said Dinah, exasperated.

Nathaniel just smiled. "I really don't mind. It's only mud." His eyes caught hers and they both fell quiet. His eyes plucked at her soul, reverberating inside like the strings of a violin in the hands of an accomplished violinist. She had never experienced such relaxed attraction with a man, and it was so completely different to the uptight anxiety she felt around Tony. She had turned a corner. She could feel it. Changed from the inside out.

They strolled along the riverbank chatting and laughing at Sophie's antics as she darted in and out of the water. When they got to the gate into the next field, Nathaniel stopped. "I'm sorry about Cassie." He frowned as he turned to face her. "Did she upset you?"

Dinah squeezed his hand. "It's not your fault. Don't worry."

"What happened?" He tensed. "She cornered me again, saying she'd spoken to you and then I couldn't get through to you, you weren't taking my calls…"

"I know, sorry. I've had my phone off recently, I should have told you."

"So what did she say?" His eyes searched hers.

The emotion that suddenly surged up inside Dinah caught her by surprise. To her mortification her voice wavered. "I've come across her before, but this time I was in a café and she just barged in. I couldn't stop her. She was bragging about the two of you, how you chased after her, how great in bed you are together, that sort of thing."

She dabbed at her eyes. "Oh! And how you had great sex with her when I'd left you after the pub."

"That's a lie!" Nathaniel was horrified. "All of it! She followed me from the pub, was all over me. I had to tell her to get lost. I've told you the truth about her, how she won't leave me alone. If I could go back and not sleep with her I would. You must think I'm a complete sod."

"I don't think you're a sod." Dinah was relieved that she really did believe him. "I hoped she was lying, but I did wonder."

"She's crazy." He was furious.

"There must be an imbalance somewhere. It didn't feel right at all. I was worried about you though, she seems very persistent."

"Don't worry, I can look after myself." His voice softened. "I was worried about you."

They smiled at each other and Dinah felt a renewed fluttering of hope. She hadn't realised just how much Cassie had got to her, how much she actually cared.

"Can we talk about something else?"

"Yes!" said Nathaniel gratefully. He opened the gate and they went through.

"What about you?" said Dinah. "I don't really know anything about you other than that you're in property and from London. What about your family?"

Ahead of them, Sophie was playfully dropping her ball on the ground every so often before darting back to retrieve it whenever they got too close.

"She wants us to chase her," laughed Dinah.

By her side she felt Nathaniel darken and she glanced at him, puzzled.

It was a moment before he actually replied. "Yes I have one brother and two sisters." He looked stern and Dinah waited, practically holding her breath.

"Our childhood wasn't great," he suddenly blurted out. "And that's putting it mildly. My father left after my youngest sister was born. I was seven, but hardly remember him and it was a good thing he went by all accounts, although it didn't feel that way growing up – he was a deadbeat." The pain in his voice shocked her.

"I'm sorry Nathaniel, I didn't mean to pry, I didn't realise..." Her voice trailed off.

"It's fine. It's just I never talk about it, that's all." He smiled at her but it was tinged with sadness.

"I'd like to tell you, if that's okay?"

She nodded, concerned.

"There were four of us kids and Mum wasn't interested," Nathaniel continued. "There was no money and she didn't care about us, so we looked after ourselves pretty much, and because I was the eldest I felt responsible."

His eyes flicked over at her, gauging her reaction, and Dinah caught her breath at the anger in them. "That's awful," she whispered.

"Looking back I think there was some kind of mental health problem." Again his eyes were on hers, alert, perceptive. "She could be kind sometimes, but there was always an undercurrent, as if she was constantly on the edge and could crack at any minute. She used to fly into rages." He trembled involuntarily and Dinah saw the pain etched in his face. "Sorry, I've never told anyone all this before." He rubbed his forehead. "Her anger was unbelievable – outright fury. She'd rant and shout and screech at us. Blamed us for ruining her life, for driving Dad away, but when she'd calmed down, she'd be sorry and apologetic, mournful almost and she'd start to drink... So, for us, childhood was something to get through, something to survive. It wasn't happy."

Putting his arm around Dinah's shoulders, he pulled her close into him and she wrapped her arms around his waist. "You don't have to tell me if you don't want to."

"I do want to. Like I said, I just don't talk about it usually. My childhood is something I've put behind me, but it was grim... I was jealous of other kids, with their dads and mums, looking after them, taking care of them."

Dinah's heart ached for him. "I'm sorry."

"It's okay. It has made me stronger. I've made my own way in life and learned that I have to rely on myself."

She squeezed him tighter, wanting to take away the hurt.

"Anyway, the four of us managed, we had to. Mum pretty much left us to our own devices. She died years ago. No loss."

He stared across the river, a shadow falling across his face.

233

"Me and my sisters and brother are close, even though we live miles apart. Lou lives near Newcastle, married with children. Sam is the youngest and lives in the South of France. She's an artist, bit of a hippy." He sounded proud. "Chris is a chef. He's the only one of us still in London. I rent a room off him and stay there when I go up. And me, well if you listen to my sisters, I'm a wheeler-dealer."

She was pleased he was smiling again. "I started small in property – buying flats, doing them up, renting them out or selling them on. I've worked really hard all my life, all hours, taken the opportunities that came my way. Work has been my saving grace."

He looked at her. "I've never married and I don't have children."

"Do you want to?"

"I don't know. I've never found anyone I wanted to marry and I'm not sure about marriage anyway, why it's necessary exactly?"

"Relationships though?" asked Dinah, curious.

"I've not always behaved well, Dinah." Nathaniel stared at the ground. "There have been plenty of women where it meant nothing and maybe I wasn't as respectful as I could have been, but there are others with whom it was different, where there was more to it. I was with Sally for six years from eighteen, and then I met Amanda through my work. We hit it off straight away. In the beginning, she didn't want the marriage and baby package, she liked to work hard and enjoy the money."

"Oh. What happened?"

"When our friends started to marry and have children she decided she wanted that too. The problem was I didn't. We were together for ten years, had a house together, a dog." He paused. "She wanted a ring and babies. She was quite insistent – demands, ultimatums the lot. In the end we broke up."

"Right," said Dinah.

"Yeah." His mouth hardened into a line. "She was very angry by the end. Said I wasted her time."

"Did you love her?"

Nathaniel hesitated. "I don't know. She could be difficult. It was great to begin with but then something changed. We stuck it out, probably for longer than we should have. I cared about her, but I don't know if it was love."

"What about Sally, or anyone else? Have you ever loved?" Dinah found she really wanted to know.

"I'm not sure." He sounded confused. "I've dated since then, had a few shorter relationships, but nothing serious…" He trailed off. "And then I met you. At nearly forty and for the first time in my life, I'm wondering…"

Dinah's heart lurched. Over his shoulder she saw Sophie hurtling up the river path, ears flapping.

"Well?" Nathaniel had stopped.

"I don't know what to say." She looked at him squarely. "Nathaniel, have you heard about the dance of relationship?"

He shook his head, bemused. "No."

"The dance between men and women?"

"No," he repeated.

"It's a dynamic that can play out in couples."

He looked blank.

"It's a fear of intimacy really, of being emotionally vulnerable," she tried to explain. "A relationship begins, but one person is usually more interested than the other and does everything they can to win over the object of their affection. But as the other starts to fall in love, to be won over, the pursuer finds their desire lessening, their feelings changing. The person they are chasing is no longer indifferent or running away, they are open and reciprocating romantically. But the hunter suddenly discovers they aren't so interested after all. They have ardently pursued for so long and now they are getting what they want they don't want it, so they start to withdraw. The more their lover comes towards them, they retreat, maybe now regretting ever having chased at all, wondering what an earth they found so appealing in the first place."

Nathaniel's raised his eyebrows. "You think that's what I do?"

Dinah pressed on. "Their lover now detects the partner withdrawing and it triggers their own fear of rejection, of not being good enough, of being abandoned. They panic, wanting to get them back, but nothing seems to work. The more they chase, the faster the other person runs away until at last, resigned, they give up! And it's only then that their lover, sensing the loss of interest and withdrawal, starts to feel interested in them all over again and to want them back. Only the first partner is now feeling better and so isn't bothered, and so the dance starts all over again. It's cat and mouse – chase, reject – and it gets played out emotionally and mentally, as well as physically, in established committed relationships as well as newer ones…"

Seeing the expression on Nathaniel's face, Dinah paused. He was slowly shaking his head.

"Dinah, I've just opened up, told you things I've never told another soul and you tell me this story. Is that really what you think I'm doing? Pursuing you until you give in and then as soon as you succumb to my wicked ways, I'll be off?"

"It had crossed my mind." Folding her arms and hugging them into her she looked him right in the eye. "People play unconscious games in love all the time."

"And I thought I was cynical!" A small crease at the side of his mouth showed he was trying not to smile. "That's not what I'm doing with you. Unconscious or otherwise."

Before she could say another word he took her face in his hands and kissed her.

When they pulled apart, Dinah was giddy. "It's strange how I feel with you," she whispered, almost a confession. "Like I know you so well."

Nathaniel took her hands. "That's how I feel, too." His voice was gentle as he rested his forehead against hers. "Like I've known you for ever and could tell you anything." The air thickened between them – magnetic energy drawing them together.

This was new territory. The removal of masks so soon, such an early offering of openness and vulnerability.

But he's had so many women, argued a quiet voice in Dinah's head. Can he really be trusted? You've children to think of. Is it wise to let someone in who's told you, no matter how sweetly, that he's been a philanderer?

Dinah's chest burned. "Do you really want love, Nathaniel?" she asked, her voice unsteady. "I mean are you ready for it, really ready to open your heart?"

He stared into her eyes, serious, and then with her hand in his he began walking briskly back up the path the way they had come, gently pulling her in his wake.

"What are you doing?" said Dinah, laughing as she tripped along behind him.

With a turn of his head he grinned at her. "Dinah, there's something between us. You know it. And it's special. We'll work it out. Come on." He was tugging her hand.

"Come where?"

"To my place." He stopped so abruptly that she bumped straight into him. He was staring at her, waiting for a response, the wanting in his eyes making her body burn.

"I can't come now," she said, breathlessly, half dismayed, half relieved. "The boys will be back from school soon – I need to get back."

"Ah, of course." He looked apologetic.

"Sorry," said Dinah, squeezing his hand. "I just can't right now."

"It's okay. I don't mean to push you. I want to do this properly." But even as he spoke the words he was questioning if that was true. What if he was playing a game without realising – if he actually wasn't ready for love in the way Dinah was asking to be loved? He felt suddenly uncertain. "Let's get back then." He started striding up the path again, disappointed with himself and unable meet her gaze.

Following behind, Dinah exhaled hard. She knew if it hadn't been for Daniel and Luke she would have gone back with him without a second thought and who knew if that would be a good idea or not.

Twenty-seven

Everything was quiet as Dinah walked through the back alleyways to Yoga Space. It was still early and the town not yet fully awake. Today was the first day of the year where the touch of spring could be felt. The sun shone bright even though the pavements were skimmed with frost and there was promise in the air, a hint of hopefulness for good things to come. Dinah hadn't worn gloves today, nor a scarf, and after the long winter months it felt good not having to wrap up against the cold.

In the market square however the scene that greeted her as she passed was one of bustling activity. The shouts of greeting and camaraderie among the stallholders echoed around the square. The traders were used to early starts and chatted noisily, some still setting up their pitches, calling to each other as they unloaded their goods from big white vans, everything from vintage furniture to Indian clothing, artisan breads and cheeses, oriental carpets and local veg. Two women laughed loudly as they struggled to secure an awning, making those in the vicinity smile. Everyone seemed happier now the sun had come back, the return of the light awakening the earth and shaking off the slumber of winter.

Outside the Golden Gateway the red-headed assistant was precariously clutching a takeaway coffee in one hand while sifting through a bunch of keys with the other. She looked up as Dinah neared.

"Lovely day," she remarked cheerfully.

"Yes, spring at last," replied Dinah. "Winter seems to have gone on for ever."

Locating the appropriate key the woman unlocked the door so it swung open. "It's the relentless rain that gets to me." She bent down to retrieve her bag from the pavement and headed inside. "But at least the sun's out now." She glanced back at Dinah. "We had a delivery yesterday, by the way. I put a book aside for you – on the unification of the Divine Feminine and Masculine."

Dinah's eyes widened.

"It's here if you want to have a look. I had a feeling that's all." She disappeared into the darkness of the unlit shop.

"Thank you!" Dinah called after her. "I can't stop now, but I'll pop back later."

"Sure. See you later."

"See you." Dinah was pleased. The perfect day for our workshop, she thought.

Today she and Ambrika were hosting a special one-off group. Inspired by the Sylphs, they were offering an invitation to heal the inner Masculine and Feminine to bring balance to Earth. They were going to connect with these archetypal entities through the subconscious and collective unconscious – the etheric realm where all thought forms, ideas and human experiences are stored.

Turning into the cobbled street which led to the yoga studio, Dinah was in good spirits. Tipping her head to the two stone Angels who stood watch at the entrance, she felt behind the largest plant pot for the key.

"Hello?" she called as she pushed the door open. Silence. Peter was nowhere to be seen. He'd obviously already been and gone. The group wasn't starting until eleven and it was only half past eight, so there was plenty of time.

Dinah was excited about the day ahead. Since conversing with the Sylphs she had withdrawn from the world. While Daniel and Luke were at school she had sat in silent meditation as insight and guidance had filtered through, bringing clarity and direction. What they would be doing today felt important – a crucial missing key which could restore harmony and balance to the chaos and consequences of the patriarchy.

They had decided on invitation-only for this workshop and the response had surpassed expectations, with twenty-four people accepting, including Nathaniel.

After the confusion of the past few weeks, Nathaniel was a beacon of hope for Dinah, and his response to today would be telling. How he reacted would indicate whether or not they had a chance of going deeper into intimacy.

In the main studio the wood-burner was already lit and next to it Dinah was grateful to see Peter had left a stash of logs in a basket. Taking pride of place on the altar was a vase of greenery and fresh spring flowers, many still in bud.

Dropping her bags on the floor underneath a woven wall hanging of the blue-skinned Hindu deity, Kali, Dinah paused. Often portrayed as a fearsome warrior wearing a necklace of human skulls around her neck, Kali is nevertheless a kind, compassionate Goddess who liberates souls by destroying the illusions of the ego. She was a fitting Guide for the day ahead.

The room was slightly musty, probably from the last yoga class, and so Dinah opened a window to let in some air before taking a bundle of dried sage from her bag. As she put a match to the herbs she felt satisfied to watch the plume of fragrant white smoke billow into the air. Starting at her feet she wafted the smoke around her in a circular motion all the way up to the top of her head, repeating the action three times before moving on to sage the room. As she walked the periphery of the room in a clockwise direction, she blew the smoke forcefully into each corner, praying as she did, asking God to help everyone who came to break through their unconscious blocks. When she had walked the room three times she put the still-burning sage in a ceramic pot on the altar. The space felt clearer already. Now music was needed.

There was a pile of CDs next to the small stereo, and after selecting one, Dinah sighed as the soothing strains of Gregorian chant spilled into the room. Taking a small red velvet pouch from her bag she emptied the contents into the palm of her hand – eight black tourmaline chunks and eight clear quartz points. These she placed at intervals around the edge of the room, one of each next to a candle, alternately black and white. The stones and the flames would create a grid of protection to prevent negative energies or entities from entering the space. From the wooden cupboard in the reception area she pulled out the stack of meditation cushions, positioning them in a ring around the main room. Lastly she lit two fat candles for the altar – one black, one white – to represent the yin-yang, feminine-masculine energy they would be honouring today.

Dinah was pleased as she surveyed her work. The room was purified, she was purified, and it was not even half past nine. As she settled down on one of the cushions she allowed herself to gently let go of the outside world, releasing all thoughts as she took solace in the inner landscapes and drifted into meditation.

It seemed as if only seconds had passed before Dinah, alerted by noise coming from the hallway, was spontaneously brought back to the present. As awareness of her body and surroundings increased she saw to her surprise two rods inside her – one black, one white – quite distinct and twisting around each other up her spine, entwined into a single column. She recognised the Caduceus immediately from yoga, where this powerful sacred symbol represents the kundalini energy.

As clear as day it ran from below her tailbone, the root chakra and the lowest energy centre in the torso, right up to the base of her skull. The origins of the Caduceus, also known as the staff carried by the Greek messenger God Hermes, lie in ancient Egypt. The Egyptians used it to bring balance and harmony between opposing forces right up until the time of the demise of the Feminine. That she was seeing the two interwoven rods of dark and light, male and female, was a good omen surely? The flicker in her heart centre affirmed her hopes and she knew the symbol bode well for the day ahead. Signifying as it does the integration of the inner polarities and the unity of duality, in one word the Caduceus speaks of wholeness. As above, so below. Exactly the state they wished to attain.

More movement in the hallway encouraged Dinah fully out of meditation. She could hear Ambrika talking to someone, and getting to her feet she went through to greet them.

When Nathaniel arrived at the yoga studio the shoe rack was already full and so he left his boots on the floor before going through to the next room.

Here he found a number of people sitting on cushions in a large circle as they chatted. There was strange music playing and streams of white smoke curled from a small pot in the centre of the room. A man was hunched over it muttering either to himself or the smoke, Nathaniel wasn't sure, as at the same time he wafted it over his head with his hands. With dark skin and long dark hair woven through with feathers, he had the distinct appearance of a Red Indian.

Nathaniel was uncertain about today anyway and this peculiar spectacle only served to exacerbate his doubts. He was now wondering why he had come at all. When Dinah had told him what Ambrika and she were planning and asked if he might want to join them, he had initially been curious. His interest was piqued and so he had agreed. However, during the following days he found he was worried about it without exactly knowing why. By the time he woke up this morning he knew he would have to force himself to come.

There were a few familiar faces from the town dotted around the room, but straight away his eyes went to Dinah. She was wearing an orange shawl loosely draped over her shoulders and talking to a woman with straight black hair, who he recognised as Ambrika. Dinah looked beautiful and when she turned towards him, Nathaniel was gratified to see her face light up. They went towards each other and he clasped her hands in his.

"I'm glad you've come," she whispered. "It means a lot."

"It's great to see you," he smiled softly.

Ambrika came beside them then and touched Dinah's shoulder. "Dinah, we should begin." She stared at Nathaniel. "Hi, I'm Ambrika." She offered her hand.

"Nathaniel," he replied.

The woman seemed to scrutinise him intently as their palms met before eventually returning his smile.

"Of course you are Nathaniel. I feel as if I know you already!" The knowing twinkle in her eye perplexed him, but before he could consider its meaning, Dinah pointed him to the cushion next to hers. Obligingly he went to sit down.

As Ambrika locked the door, Nathaniel felt the atmosphere in the room shift tangibly from relaxed to one of heightened expectancy.

Next to him Dinah cleared her throat. "So, we've an exciting day ahead of us," she said softly, beaming at everyone as the room fell silent. "Today is about healing the inner masculine and feminine. Two aspects which exist in all of us no matter what our physical gender might be; we all hold the masculine and feminine qualities inside – in our psyche, our soul and in the collective unconscious." She paused to give time for the information to sink in. "*But* because of life experience and social conditioning," she continued, her voice more serious now, "both collectively and individually, in this lifetime and those past, we've become imbalanced – the Divine Masculine and Feminine is now masked by the wounded masculine and the wounded feminine – like a mirror layered in dust. We need to clean away the dust to allow our truth to shine through. With things as they are presently, these two aspects are often in conflict. They're at loggerheads with each other externally, but more significantly internally, inside of us, with one dominant and in control and the other repressed and seething.

All around him people were nodding, but Nathaniel was confused. He couldn't really grasp what Dinah meant, what it was she was actually saying.

"Through working with the nature elementals," she went on, "I have learned it is this imbalance only which is the root cause for all the devastation we are inflicting on the Earth, the animals, the birds, the sea creatures *and* each other. It is this imbalance only, this disparity between masculine and feminine, which is the core seed of *all* humanity's problems and suffering. Once this fundamental imbalance is addressed and healed, then our psyches will heal, and then our behaviour in the world will adjust – quite naturally for the better, without struggle or striving. We will become enlightened, if you like. And all that's required is to address our inner wounds – and I know that sounds huge but it is a service to the world for us to focus on healing ourselves, to be brave enough to face ourselves and heal our fears. It is the hidden inner wound that causes us so much anguish, which keeps us locked in darkness, because when we deny our hurt and suffering, when we pretend it isn't there, either consciously or subconsciously, that is what causes us to act out on the world around us – to relentlessly abuse our planet and to abuse other species so mercilessly." Her voice quivered. "Like a horror film, we treat our fellow sentient creatures as objects, things to be used, controlled, destroyed, tortured or eaten according to our arrogance, greed and deluded belief of superiority."

Nathaniel listened in awe. There were tears in Dinah's eyes and serious sad expressions etched on the faces of those around him.

"The Patriarchy has wreaked havoc with us as a species and in turn with our planet – the very foundation of our existence. We destroy our planet, we destroy us, and we cannot feign ignorance any longer. The time has come when we must take responsibility, when it is imperative as human beings for us to change our ways, and fast. It is the wounded masculine and the wounded feminine, which absolutely has to be brought into line, before we destroy ourselves. It is the integration of these two polar opposites, the balancing of ourselves within and without, which I am told is crucial to our realisation of oneness. And our realisation of oneness is what will save both ourselves and the natural world."

Dinah stopped, looking across to Ambrika who sat on the other side of the circle. Nathaniel frowned in concentration. He wasn't sure he was getting it completely but something inside him was responding. He felt something – he just wasn't sure what it was.

Now Ambrika began to speak. "The Feminine has been repressed for many thousands of years," she said, her voice strong and sure. "I believe that apart from a few isolated pockets, the time of the Minoan civilisation in Crete and Ancient Egypt was the last time man and woman truly lived in equality. The Minoans declined around 1400 BC, so that's nearly three and half thousand years ago!"

Gasps emanated from around the group.

"As the patriarchy evolved," Ambrika went on, "Woman was forced into retreat and both male and female quickly descended into their shadow, because when one goes down so does the other. They do not exist separately. Woman has learned from her experience down the centuries that only subservience or beauty, sexual appeal or manipulation, will ensure her survival. Sister was pitted against sister as Woman learned how to play the game, but all the while, deep down, she resented and blamed the masculine for what she had become. In the last century the feminine has begun to rise once more. Movements such as the suffragettes broke through the ceiling that had been imposed on Her, catapulting Woman back into knowing that she could indeed retrieve her power.

"There followed a period of adjustment. In this stage of the earthly cycle, Woman subconsciously believed that in order to be seen and taken seriously, she must meet the masculine by becoming masculine herself – approaching him in a way he would recognise. Women became more male in their approach to the world, with many iconic female figures displaying the wounded masculine qualities of force, aggression and dominance in order to gain acknowledgement. Or, we resorted to playing the siren, again an aggressive role with its own agenda, where we often used our sexuality as a way to secure a place in the world; tempting men with our bodies and the art of seduction. This is a betrayal of ourselves and leaves us still burdened with the wound of our ancestors. This wound rests heavy on all our shoulders, haunting our every move, and until it is uncovered and healed, women will never fully step into their true Divine Feminine power. By playing this game we remain small and controlled."

As Ambrika spoke, there were mutters of agreement from those gathered.

"As women reclaim their power and rediscover their true nature they will most likely find within themselves a resentment of the masculine energy, a subtle yet powerful distaste for men, which is understandable given the oppression the Feminine has endured. But now is the time for forgiveness and healing. As the Masculine must now embrace the Feminine, the Feminine in turn needs to embrace the Masculine. Woman needs the Divine Masculine energy with all Her soul and yet frequently pushes it away. Or we only see the wounded male, thus attracting men who treat us badly or control or disrespect us."

"I've noticed this," a disembodied voice piped up. It was a man with a kindly face and tousled brown hair. "How often women are drawn to men in power, or charismatic good-looking men, who nonetheless behave atrociously towards them or devalue them. I've never understood it. It's as though women don't want to be respected and treated with love, as if they prefer a perpetrator. Why?"

"It's low self-esteem, surely?" said a fair lady in flowing purple trousers. "Ingrained beliefs and conditioning from our own experiences and that of our ancestors – that this is all we are worthy of. I myself had that pattern, repeatedly falling for misogynistic men over kind, respectful men. They were all I wanted and the source was my own lack of self-worth. I see it in my friends and peers too. It's deeply embedded in our psyche, because of what we have endured. Is it that beneath our bravado, we simply don't feel worthy to stand next to men as equals, or to allow men into our lives, who will actually treat us well?"

The man with the kind face nodded. "The majority of men are not misogynistic. I most certainly am not and we cannot lay all blame for what has happened during the past however many thousands of years solely at the feet of men. These qualities are in all of us – men dominate women, women dominate men, men suppress their inner feminine and women suppress their inner masculine. The mix comes in many forms."

"I think you're right," said Ambrika. "Men abuse women and women abuse men. We are in this together and the road to healing begins inside."

"I don't agree with that," said a voice. It was a woman, maybe early thirties, and she looked cross. "I'm Lydia." She smiled apologetically. "I just feel that men still feel and behave superior in all ways as far as I can see. It might not be as obvious as a few years back but it's damn well still there… maybe just more hidden, more covert."

Everyone in the room was silent.

"I've just removed myself from a terrible relationship." The woman warmed to her subject. "I thought he was the nicest guy I'd ever met to begin with. Thoughtful, gentle, kind. He took me out to dinner and brought me flowers, phoned me, texted, held me, told me how he would always be there for me. How right we were together." She sighed. "I fell for it hook, line and sinker, despite considering myself quite savvy around people's characters… but fast forward six months and the dinners stopped, the phone calls, the romance. All he wanted was a counsellor and sex. Someone to offload on and to prop him up. Someone to advise him when he needed it and to help him grow. I felt swamped by him and all his stuff and I now see it was completely one-sided. He was using me – maybe unconsciously but using me all the same. I kept giving him the benefit of the doubt, giving him permission to treat me this way because I could see the potential of what we could become and because he kept fooling me with clever words. I stuck around far longer than I should have until I was completely diminished – a shell of who I used to be. When I first met him I was confident, happy within myself, happy in my own skin. By the time we finished I was a wreck. Self-esteem on the floor, doubting myself, wondering if it was me, feeling utterly exhausted and yet pining for him. He's a nice guy but I think even the nicest guys have a misogynistic streak, without even realising that is what they are doing. I felt as though I was drowning in all his stuff, all his woes and baggage. Somehow he managed to get in and take me over without me even realising.

"And still it was hard to walk away – painful – but I did, and during that period while I was disentangling, the conversations I had with other women proved it isn't unusual. Women accepting far less than they deserve in relationships. I know there are lovely kind men out there, but it amazes me how still it's so ingrained in our society for women to sell themselves short in relationships. It's incredible how little some women are prepared to accept – even nowadays! And I include myself in that."

She folded her arms.

Dinah smiled gently. "I see that, too. I've experienced that, too. The strongest most self-assured women can fall prey when they fall in love."

"Yes!" exclaimed Lydia. "Women need to remember themselves when they fall in love. They must put themselves first – always. Remember their sacred selves and what they deserve. Self-love first – always! I think we let our emotions get the better of us, whereas men tend to compartmentalise. We wear our rose-coloured glasses because we're so desperate to find Mr Right. We've been fed this illusionary fairy-tale of 'the one'!" She scowled.

"The reality of romantic soulmate love, or twin flame love, is so rare, so unusual. I think most people are dealing with far more mundane relationship issues. And women need to say 'No! No more!' I've met so many men who when it comes to emotions are wounded boys in a man's body. We don't *need* men any more like we did in the past. Women can get their own jobs, support themselves, rely on extended family and friends for emotional support and love. Raise our children alone if needs be. If men won't treat women with respect and love and care, then they shouldn't be allowed to get involved with a woman at all!"

For a moment everyone was quiet. Lydia looked around the group and when her eyes fell on Nathaniel, he shifted uncomfortably.

Ambrika leaned forwards on her cushion. "I still think it is a two-way thing," she said, soothingly. "Women are learning to stand proud and strong within themselves, not aggressive, mind, although the anger might be justified it only hurts ourselves. If somehow, some way, we can find compassion then it would benefit all of us

247

and speed up the process of balance between the sexes. And men are adjusting to this new Woman. One who refuses to be put down, to be used, treated like a servant or prostitute or seen as inferior in a way. Woman is now demanding more from Man emotionally and mentally, than ever before. And He too is also trying to find his way."

Lydia's face softened slightly. "I did feel compassion for him. I knew how much he was struggling in life, but it was the way he treated me which hurt."

"I understand," said Ambrika, sympathetically. "Men and Women don't always treat each other well, but often it comes from a place of ignorance rather than a conscious desire to hurt."

"Equality between these two aspects of the self – Masculine and Feminine – is the answer we seek as a species," said Dinah. "As more of us balance our inner male and female we attain a state of inner harmony where enlightened consciousness is more easily within reach for the rest. The more of us who drop into inner peace, the easier it is for others. It may be a process, but we have to start somewhere. The energies are noticeably speeding up and the wholeness of each individual will lead to wholeness of our species. When we find balance between the masculine giving and the feminine receiving, we will spontaneously apply this to ourselves and also to the natural world, which at the moment is suffering in a way we can barely comprehend. At the moment it is just take, take, take. Across the globe we have lost touch with our planet and it is because the Feminine is ignored and dismissed. By giving Her back Her rightful place within the individual, the individual will get back their connection to truth and to Earth."

More nods of agreement.

Ambrika pulled her cushion further into the circle. "Whatever occurs today," she said, "will unfold as it does. To begin with though, can we make the circle smaller?"

Everyone shuffled inwards until they were shoulder to shoulder.

"Let's hold hands and go around and introduce ourselves – and if you feel inclined, say a few words on what the Divine masculine and Divine feminine, or the wounded masculine and feminine, means to you. We will be meeting both today."

Most people only gave their name and where they lived, but when it came to an older man with ruffled grey hair and gold spectacles there was a momentary pause. When he spoke he seemed agitated and his hands shook. "Hello, I'm John," he said, his voice trembling. "It's because of my mother that I'm here today." He stared downwards into his lap. "She was a cruel woman. There was no love from her to me. Either she ignored me or belittled me, smacked me for the smallest thing and constantly criticised me. I grew up feeling hated by her."

His eyes were damp with tears and Nathaniel felt something break inside him as he listened.

John continued. "I've been married three times, but I'm ashamed to say that under my usual caring, kind nature, I sense a real distrust, almost a dislike, of women, and it came out in my marriages, ending them all. I know it stems from her. I would do anything to change it, I'm not proud of it and I'm hoping today will provide some answers, something to help shift this fear I carry…"

As his voice trailed off he hung his head causing the woman next to him to put an arm around his shoulders. When it was Nathaniel's turn he was flustered.

"Hi, I'm Nathaniel…" He stopped, at a loss for what to say. All eyes were on him. Dinah squeezed his hand. "I hadn't thought about any of this before, but I know how John feels." His eyes were drawn to the man who had spoken so openly. "I think I might be the same as you and I never realised. I don't always see women well and I think that's why I treat them as I do – using them for sex or to just have someone there, so I wasn't completely alone. I've never given myself fully to a woman. I always hold back."

His eyes found Dinah's and he felt a terrible weight of sadness.

"My mother was terrible. She didn't care about me, about any of us. We practically had to fend for ourselves after my father left and she treated us as if we got in the way of her life. I thought I was okay. I thought I'd found some kind of understanding, but now I know I'm not alright and I'm not sure I ever have been. I just buried it and kept moving."

He looked down at his hands, ashamed.

When he eventually looked up again, his eyes caught Lydia's across the circle. She looked sad. "I want to forgive her. I want to find a way to make peace with her." He took a breath. "I want to make peace with women."

A hush came over the room. Dinah leaned closer to him as if offering comfort and he was grateful.

A clever-looking woman with a melancholy air raised her head. "I relate to this as well." She was talking to Nathaniel. "What you say touches me, right here." She put her hand on her heart. "My relationship with my father was very bad. He controlled us, all of us. He was violent and angry. We were petrified of him – my mother, my sister, me. My mother wasn't strong enough to stand up to him, to stand up for us. He crushed us all and other than abusing us, he pretty much ignored us. It's definitely scarred me. Left me damaged and broken." She dabbed at her eyes. "I know what it has done to me, to how I perceive men, how I am with men. We all need to heal. We all hurt."

When Ambrika spoke her voice was gentle. "Children are so vulnerable to the adults around them and of course it has an impact. But we can heal; it is possible, with compassion for ourselves and a gentle approach. I think all of us carry wounds from our childhood, and all of us carry trauma somewhere within."

The atmosphere was subdued and heavy. "I think now it's time to begin. Dinah would you invoke the Angels, Guides and deities to help us?" she said. "And if anyone would like someone specific to join us, please do call them."

She closed her eyes and everyone else including Nathaniel followed suit. Dinah's hand clasped in his was warm and comforting. He sensed her take a long deep breath.

"Dear Goddess-God," she said clearly. "Thank you for bringing us together and helping each of us discover the Divine Feminine and the Divine Masculine within, for our healing and unity. We call on Archangel Michael for protection, and Jesus for guidance and support. We call Goddess Isis, for healing, wisdom and feminine power. Amen."

Silence.

Ambrika spoke. "I invoke Goddess Persephone, of dark and light, and Sekhmet for strength and wisdom."

A man's voice: "I thank Jesus, for embodying the Divine Masculine and the Divine Feminine as one."

"I thank Babaji for blessing us with his presence," a woman.

"I honour Brigid."

250

"Gautama Buddha."

"Thank you, St Therese."

"Boudicca, for her fearless warrior spirit and Ganapati for removing our blocks."

"Quan Yin, for compassion."

"Pan and Faunus."

The invocations flowed, and Dinah was delighted at the diversity of those being summoned. Hindu deities, Christian saints, Pagan gods, Angels and elementals, the list was exhaustive, and not until everyone had finished did she continue.

"If you arrange yourselves so you are comfortable, sitting or lying, we will prepare to first meet with the wounded parts."

Nathaniel lay down, stretched out on his back with his hands on his stomach. As he closed his eyes he wondered what was coming next.

"I will summon the wounded feminine first and then the wounded masculine," Dinah continued. "While we wait for her, focus fully on the breath, releasing into your body, surrendering to the ground and to the female."

Nathaniel was starting to drift. Dinah lowered her voice. "We thank the wounded feminine for gracing us with her presence, for speaking through our hearts, our minds, our souls. For helping us to understand."

Now she was muttering so quietly he could barely hear. The words were fading, his mind letting go as he started to drop into something, noticing strange feelings and sensations inside him. The music was playing still and as he focused on his breath and the lullaby of Dinah's voice, he found he was sinking down. The sensation was surprisingly strong. Dinah sounded further and further away as she continued to call in the wounded feminine, and with every hazy word she spoke it seemed he was dropping deeper and deeper. As he did so he was gradually becoming aware of an uncomfortable feeling knotted in his stomach. It was getting stronger and stronger and he was struggling to breathe – it was almost too much. In panic he pulled his mind's attention back to his breath, trying to slow it, deepen it. He realised it was fear he was feeling inside him – no it was more than that, it was terror. Festering and bubbling and within it a vast aching despair the like of which he had never experienced. It was a bottomless grey void of powerlessness and hopelessness. His chest was heaving, his body trembling, and the depth of this pain, of this utter brokenness, was overwhelming. Nathaniel wondered what was happening to him. He felt absolutely crushed – worthless and frozen.

Then from out of this void he noticed something emerging. It was faint at first but as he waited, feeling more and more agonised with each passing moment, he heard a plaintive female voice murmuring, whimpering. Then without warning a howl – loud, which startled him with its force.

I am lost. Nathaniel knew the voice wasn't him; even though it was inside him it was definitely coming from elsewhere. He was simultaneously awestruck and horrified. *I have no power in this world. It has been stolen from me, crushed out of me. I have been beaten down, forced into submission and to survive I had to take refuge in my shadow.* The voice was desperate and made him want to flee, but he was trapped with it. *You use me!* A scream deep inside.

Nathaniel was falling. Crashing downwards into a desolate dark pit with no escape and he simultaneously felt terror and rage coursing through him. The voice was strong now.

Man took all my choices from me. He disempowered me and left me no option other than submission or death – there was nothing in between for a long time, and I hold Man responsible for my descent – and for the conflict between sisters. I hold Man responsible for my demise.

This woman was angry.

His whole body was taut, rigid with fury and he knew it was the rage of Womankind. He felt the humiliation and degradation as if it were his own, the hopelessness, the terror and despair. He was living the female wound.

You were supposed to hold and support me and yet you became my persecutor. I wanted to help you, to teach you my truth so you would benefit from the beauty of my gifts. But it was futile. I was forced to meet you in a way you would know. I had to either let you use me, or become cunning in order to protect myself, or make myself bow to your will to keep myself safe, or I would die. All of these are the death of the Feminine. Man killed me – broke my spirit and battered my body.

The words pelted his heart like gunfire.

I was either the mother, the spinster, the wife or the whore, and you despised me for it, even though the hands of creation were your own. But know this, beneath my persona of acceptance lies loathing, and my compliance masks hatred. You abuse me, disrespect me. You seek power over me, but I will fight you at all costs. I will do whatever it takes to break free.

Shame racked Nathaniel's body. He was desperate to get away from the stabbing, angry accusations, but it was all inside him. There was nowhere to go.

The oppressive weight was only interrupted by Dinah's voice drawing him away from the turmoil within. She was calling in the wounded masculine and the mood was changing. Nathaniel started to ache all over, plagued with sorrow and remorse. He was entering a void of guilty regret and a feeling of being completely misunderstood. He was entering the domain of the wounded male.

The masculine was responding. *Sister, I hear you and I weep for you.* Again the words came of their own accord and all Nathaniel could do was listen. *I feel your pain. Woman has been hunted, forced into submission and treated as inferior. But it was not all men who took part and there are many men, many of us, who always recognised your gifts and valued you, many who cried at the barbaric treatment you endured at the hands of our brothers. It is not all mankind that wished you harm, many abhor what has happened, abhor the destruction of our sisters and feel only horror at the devastation of your state. But we also feel your disdain and your rage and it reviles us. We long for your love and you refuse us. You pull us to you while pushing us away and it is as if you do so joyfully. Punishing all of us, when not all are to blame.*

For the first time in his life Nathaniel clearly saw the truth of the world – of men and women – the scale of mistreatment and abuse, which permeates the entire planet, infiltrating every culture and every race. It was overwhelming. And there was an uncomfortable understanding that he too had played a part.

The male was imploring. *There is huge imbalance in the world. Woman was beaten down, while Man reigned over her. But she is rising again and as you reclaim your power, I long to help you, to support you and love you. Yet I feel your rage and hatred. Your refusal to allow me to fulfil my masculine role breaks me and then I feel useless and dejected.*

Moving further into the depths of the collective wounded masculine, Nathaniel felt uncomfortably hollow.

Without my role of supporting you as I am meant to, in loving you as you deserve, there is nothing left for me and I am bereft. You punish me for the crimes of the past, for the crimes meted out by our ancestors. The world is changing, but now it is you who seeks to disempower me, to discard me, and make me small. You may well succeed, but it will not bring peace, just more imbalance and chaos. I need your love, respect and trust, as you need mine.

For a moment the wounded feminine was silent, thoughtful.

Nathaniel was uncomfortable. The tension which simmered inside him was almost unbearable.

When eventually she spoke it was just a whisper.

I want to love you – her voice had softened a little – *I long to trust you, but I have been burned and it will take time for me to know you are sincere and speak truthfully. I have to adjust and will need understanding and compassion to reconcile with my history, to reconcile the experience of my mothers before me. If you give me this then we may yet find a place of equality, a point of balance between us both.*

The masculine was quiet, but Nathaniel sensed his glimmer of hope.

I can give you what you ask. I can give you time, and while I wait for you to come back to me, I will hold the sacred space you need to heal and will ask nothing of you. When you are ready to meet me again, of your own free will and with love in your heart, then I will be there to meet you as we were meant to meet. I will honour and respect you and I only ask for that from you in return. Only then can the horror of the past patriarchy, and the horror of a future matriarchy, be healed. Only then will we find unity once again, standing side by side in Divine light.

Twenty-eight

From somewhere outside a sound beckoned. Nathaniel drifted upwards to answer, emerging from some deep inner pool. The sound was clearer now and he recognised Dinah talking to the group. It was the most peculiar thing. He was back, but he couldn't say where he had been exactly. When his eyes flickered open, he saw everyone around him looking as groggy and disorientated as he felt. The woman next to him was hugging herself tightly. From her reddened eyes he knew she had been crying and it seemed she was not the only one. There was a resonance of despondency and shock in the circle that was palpable. Nathaniel touched his cheek. It was wet.

The only people who appeared unaffected were Ambrika and Dinah. For some reason it reassured him to look at them.

"Welcome back!" said Dinah, flexing her feet and stretching her legs in front of her. "I think that was strong, more than I expected. Is everyone back?"

People were nodding, some still with their eyes closed.

"That was the most difficult part – meeting the wounded parts of ourselves and of the collective unconscious. We went deep together." No one spoke. "The Angels want us to know we are safe to do this work. They are applauding our efforts."

A few people smiled.

"Try to stay in the depth, to stay connected. We've come to the easier, more uplifting part, where we meet with the whole parts – the Divine Feminine and the Divine Masculine."

Nathaniel was still not quite in the world. His eyes were unfocused and heavy, his mind blank. He couldn't think, but there was a spaciousness inside him, a lightness that hadn't been there before. After a bit of shuffling everyone was becoming still once more. He closed his eyes again.

255

"Focus on the breath," Dinah was saying. Even the music sounded somehow sweeter, more poignant as it carried him inwards to a place of beauty and peace.

"In surrender, it is always the breath."

This time, Nathaniel realised he was actually watching himself float down. He was fascinated as he passed through layers and layers, as some strange part observed his own mind as if it were separate to himself, like the screen of a television with thoughts and images flipping across it. Quite unexpectedly he understood that he was not his mind and knew that what was going through it was just a jumble of ideas, opinions and perceptions, not always based in truth.

"I'm not my mind!" The revelation astounded him.

Lower he went, incredulous at all the sensations in his body, and suddenly he also knew that he was not his body. Nathaniel bathed in wonder as he felt his own vastness, his own limitlessness.

"I am not my mind. I am not my body. I am not who I thought I was. So who am I?"

He no longer knew where he was or what was what, but some part of him was listening to Dinah invoke the Divine feminine, inviting her to come forward. Something, somewhere within himself, was alert.

From out of a glorious haze of perfection a female presence emerged. A woman was near. No, she was everywhere, engulfing him in shining light, embracing him.

I am the Goddess of creation. I am the Divine Feminine. I am Shakti, the life force. I am the dance, the song and the beating heart of the sacred feminine, in all forms.

The murmurs were the most dulcet of tones.

I am compassion and wisdom, intuition and patience. I am acceptance, nurturing and forgiveness. I am the cooling flow of the Moon, healing and kindness, gentleness and fertility. I am rebirth. Passive and receptive, strong in the knowing that all that is due to me will come. Through receiving, I give. I am unconditional love.

Nathaniel was resting within her, in a place of such softness and tenderness that he barely understood. She was holding him, supporting him, and he knew only that he never wanted to leave this place, that he was immersed in something wonderful.

It is love, she said. She was smiling.

Nathaniel was shy. "Aaahh, it's *your* love," he replied.

Her Love poured into him, seeping into every part of his being until he was overwhelmed, awash in it, lost in it. It was too big, too huge, too much and he knew that he'd been longing for this all his life, that his entire existence so far was designed to bring him to this one precise moment. "I've never known this before," he said, his heart burning.

I am always with you, inside you. I was waiting for you to look to me. I never leave. You are my child.

Nathaniel trembled. It suddenly hit him. He did know Her – he knew who She was. "I do know you. I remember. You are the Mother. And you are my Mother." Tears wet his cheeks. He was crying. The feelings kept at bay for so long, so tightly dammed up, were bursting forth, all the longing and pain he'd ever known spilling out of him, his tears falling on the parched land of his bruised heart. He was a river of feeling and emotion, his heart split open from the inside out. "I forgot you," he told Her, and again she smiled.

And then he saw his own mother, her face right up close, and she was crying, too. He felt her pain and distress, her fear and bewilderment. He saw her as a young girl, innocent and carefree, filled with hope and dreams for her future, and his heart broke again. Nathaniel was dissolving. The shell of hardness he'd carried for so long melting under the brilliant glow of Her understanding and compassion. It was like walking free from a prison he hadn't even known he was in.

The energy of the Mother was receding. Now he found himself resting in silent stillness. He was only roused by a voice. Dinah! She was thanking the Divine Feminine and calling in the Divine Masculine.

Nathaniel felt his body start to tingle, a new force was coming through and fresh tears clouded his eyes, he couldn't help it. For the second time Nathaniel was wrapped in a veil of gentle strength, but noticeably different to before. This time he was pulsing with vigour and energy, all the while feeling peacefully calm.

I am Father of the Universe. The commanding male voice came from nowhere and made him jump. *I am the Divine Masculine. But I am not what you may think.* The words strummed through Nathaniel, making his bones hum. *I am benevolence and courage, intellect and*

257

logic. I am Shiva. I am the heat of the Sun. I am support, action and transformation, order and calm. I am thinking, direction and balance. I am encouragement and the material plane. I am giving, and through giving I receive. I am humility. I am unconditional love.

Nathaniel felt like a little boy before an authoritative male presence.

I hold you in the world, ever watchful. Under my care you are protected and safe, and no harm can befall you. As you journey through life, I stand ready to catch you whenever you fall. I am all around, everywhere, with all my love. My power lies in the knowledge of my goodness and the certainty of my strength. When you know me fully, there is no desire to battle or force, or harm. No need to take that, which is not freely given.

Never had Nathaniel felt so safe, so held and protected.

"I didn't know you as a child," he was crying again. "I wanted you so much. I dreamed of you, longed for you, but I couldn't find you. You weren't there when I needed you the most."

The voice was kind. *You look for me externally, but I am to be found within. Seek inside. I am always with you, waiting for you to look to me. I never leave. You are my child.*

And there was his father – a drawn, gaunt figure with hunched shoulders, a despairing air, and a look of utter desperation in his eyes. Nathaniel saw he was begging for forgiveness. He was shocked.

"He's got no hope. He gave up on life and on himself. It wasn't that he left us – he left himself." A heave of pity swelled in his chest for the ruined man in front of him. "He couldn't see what he had and he couldn't see the love in his children or in the world. He was crushed."

And here was his father as a child. A little boy, who so wanted to be good and be loved and yet was hit and criticised by his parents. He had floundered right from the start. Nathaniel was horrified, and his heart opened to the man so long absent from his life. Something broke under Nathaniel's ribcage and he winced, and then as if a switch had been flicked, warmth spread across his chest. "I forgive you, of course I do and I'm sorry for the life you had to bear."

His father looked up and smiled.

The Feminine was coming through again and the Masculine was meeting her. They were merging, embracing inside of him. They had

258

become one. United. The sheer force of love Nathaniel could feel coursing through him was incredible. It obscured everything. He was embraced and loved and held in a way he had never realised was possible.

The beautiful energy was dissipating and Nathaniel flinched. He wanted to bring it back, to make it stay, but found he couldn't move. Music was playing, and as he listened the chords were getting louder. His body felt heavy, like lead weight.

"As we come back to our bodies, stay with the breath," came a disembodied voice he knew was Dinah. "Returning safe and sound, breathing deep and when you are ready you can open your eyes…and smile."

A big grin immediately spread across Nathaniel's face and he blinked his eyes open. Around him people were chuckling.

Dear God, he thought. What was that?

The music was loud now, a clear female voice singing a strange hypnotic song.

In the middle of the room, stood Dinah. Her eyes half open as her lips moved in time to the words. One by one others were getting up to join her and soon Nathaniel was the only one left sitting. Tentatively he stood and began to move his body, feeling his way into the tempo and taking heart from the fact that nearly everyone had their eyes shut. During the next few songs the music evolved into an African tribal beat and everyone was stamping their feet. The woman in purple trousers began to whoop, a wide grin of happiness stretched across her face as she lifted her arms to the ceiling and kicked out her legs, and then it wasn't long before they were all at it, Dinah included.

Nathaniel was bemused to find himself in a room full of people who were wildly flinging themselves about, yelling, howling and shrieking. It made him feel awkward, even though they seemed to be having the time of their lives.

As the last drumming beats faded into silence, everyone came to sitting again. Nathaniel followed their lead and the room was still.

"So," said Dinah, "I'd like to share something. I went deeper than I was expecting. We had lots of company with us, Angels and Higher Beings, so many different energies – the room was filled with light.

What came through for me was the realisation that when I think of the beloved, of Source, that I myself, still subtly perceive a masculine figurehead and it surprised me. I saw that my own view of Source is off balance, that I see the feminine as slightly lower down than the masculine. It is social conditioning I know, but I was quite shocked at myself!" She folded her hands in her lap.

"That resonates with me!" A young woman in glittering gold dress leaned in. "I feel that in me, too. That I have this distorted view of Goddess as coming slightly below God."

Ambrika interjected. "Given the nature of the patriarchy, I think it's to be expected. We are human after all and we've had it drilled into us that the Divine is masculine in form. The ancient nature-based religions, who worshipped the feminine, were practically wiped out across the world in an attempt to eradicate all residue of the Divine Feminine."

People were nodding.

"These beliefs that we've been fed are ingrained. The whole of society told us it was so, both overtly and covertly – our parents, teachers, authority figures, religions – and we accepted it as truth. Now we know it isn't truth, but still it takes awareness and perseverance to break these thought forms, to see them for the lie they are."

"But that's a dualistic view too," said the man with feathered hair. "That God and Goddess are separate, that man and woman are separate. Surely we must go beyond that now? Recognise our oneness and the oneness of the Creator? Until we heal our sense of duality, our schizophrenia, we will remain fragmented as a species. To become whole we must reconcile these splits within our psyche."

There was an air of quiet contemplation within the circle. To Nathaniel it felt a long stretch until the next person spoke.

"I had an insight about how the shadow masculine plays out in both men and women," said a slim man who was covered in tattoos. "I saw how the masculine shadow takes through force. Anything he wants he takes. He wants a luxurious life, and notice it is 'wants' not 'needs' – a large house, shiny cars, maybe many shiny cars, holidays in faraway places – *but* he doesn't value these things. He takes them for granted as his 'right'. He is entitled and wasteful and ungrateful, plundering the planet to feed his wants and although Earth has given what she can and is running low, he still takes more, without replenishing or nurturing."

There were murmurs of thoughtful agreement.

"And I have an analogy," the man went on. "The shadow masculine wants a woman, but if she doesn't want him, if she is unwilling to give, he takes her anyway – he rapes her. The masculine shadow of humanity wants material luxury and although Gaia is unable to give at the rate we demand, we rape her. We are raping the earth, as brutally as a man rapes a woman."

He looked earnestly around the group.

"I saw that as the Feminine retrieves her power that the masculine must listen to Her with respect. The future of humanity depends on this co-operation."

As Nathaniel listened to the man he considered his own lifestyle. In his work he built using eco-friendly methods and tried to limit the impact of their developments on the surroundings, but his personal life was a different story. He realised how little attention he paid when he heard of the annihilation of another piece of rainforest, meadow or the Arctic. How little thought he gave to animals becoming extinct or being hurt and abused. How he just skimmed over it all, filed it away as if it were nothing to do with him.

"We are greedy and spoiled!" He surprised himself by speaking out. "Taking mindlessly with no trace of conscience, assuming that recycling our waste, reusing plastic bags and fitting eco bulbs is enough, that we've done our bit and the rest doesn't concern us because it's out of our hands." He felt embarrassed and ashamed.

Dinah clasped her hands together. "It's common to believe the bigger picture has nothing to do with us as individuals. How much easier to lay the blame elsewhere, or wait until an organisation or Government does something first. But when the individual admits accountability in all areas of their life – work, home and leisure – when we take responsibility for ourselves and make informed choices in our day-to-day lifestyle – *then* the world will start to shift even faster into healing and into the new paradigm."

Ambrika was nodding.

A middle-aged man spoke up from the other side of the circle. "There was so much anger, when I met the wounded parts. It made me question whether there can ever be genuine reconciliation between the sexes."

"I think it comes down to forgiveness," responded a woman with plaits.

"It's easy to pay lip service to forgiveness," said an angry voice. Everyone turned to see. It was the man who had spoken of the damage done to him by his mother. He had removed his glasses and his cheeks were flushed red. "But it's not so simple in practice. When someone has really wronged you, or is still causing you pain, forgiveness can be a devil to find."

"I agree," said Dinah. "With both of you. Forgiveness can prove an elusive quality, particularly when you are angry and hurting. And yet that shouldn't prevent us from trying to drop our pain and resentment, our judgment and self-righteousness. The darkness can only exist in the unconscious, and when enlightenment start to shine within, there can be no capacity for harm towards anyone or anything, even towards someone who has wronged us."

Nathaniel was puzzled. "What does that mean?" he said, confused. "How do we forgive some of the barbaric things that happen? How do we forgive someone who has caused real suffering?"

There was a hush as Dinah stared at him thoughtfully.

"Well for me it means to try and follow the example of Jesus. He was persecuted and murdered for his light because he knew his own divinity. The embodiment of the Divine Masculine and Feminine as one. Yet still he offered forgiveness, even as he was degraded and stripped, even as nails were driven into his flesh – 'Forgive them, they know not what they do.' Jesus knew those souls, his persecutors, were not yet awakened, that they were unconscious, unaware of the truth of their actions. They did not understand the implications – like a child pulling the legs off a spider or hitting another child – they are operating from a place of unawareness. Is this not the very meaning of the light and the dark? The light is consciousness, awareness; and the dark is unconsciousness, non-awareness. When you stand in the light, there is only forgiveness and compassion for those who still suffer in the dark."

"And how do we get this light?" questioned Nathaniel. "And how are some conscious and others not? And if this is the way of things, then those who are unconscious will continue with what they do and nothing can be done."

"Not true!" cried the woman with plaited hair. "Meditation is the answer."

Dinah nodded. "Yes," she agreed. "Possibly the only answer. In meditation we become aware of truth, of the light and love that we are. Meditation shows us directly, so we know for ourselves. We don't have to believe someone else or take another's word for it."

"Exactly," interjected Ambrika. "Meditation shows us the magic within, and when you know this magic, compassion is natural and forgiveness becomes obsolete, because you understand there is nothing to forgive, that a conscious crime by its very nature is simply not possible."

An air of contemplation fell upon the group.

When Dinah glanced at the wall-clock she was amazed to see it was already two. "It's time to finish up!" she gasped.

To close they toned the Om and then shanti, sending the holy vibration of Creation and the mantra of peace out into the world.

Nathaniel felt like a different person, as though he'd been on a journey through a tunnel and was still coming out the other end. He felt quiet and reflective and wanted to be alone.

As Dinah was talking to the woman with plaits and as it didn't look as though she'd be finished anytime soon he decided against waiting. Instead he touched her arm and when she turned gently pulled her close to him. Dinah's eyes gleamed and in response Nathaniel felt heat burst through his chest.

"Thank you. That was amazing," he said, his voice just a whisper. "I'll call you later."

A sudden charge shot between them and for a moment they were both still.

"Speak then." She squeezed his hand.

Reluctantly, Nathaniel released her. As he left he only looked back when he reached the doorway. Dinah was in conversation again, but as though sensing his gaze she glanced over. When their eyes met a knowing smile was exchanged.

Twenty-nine

The smoke quickly fogged Dinah's bedroom. She had already smudged the sitting room and hall with sage and this was the last room. But the most important, she thought with a smile. Taking the Tibetan bells from the bedside table she struck them together, listening for the chime to fade away completely before striking them again. Nathaniel was due any minute and, although it was unspoken between them, they both knew what lay ahead. It was the first time he had been to her home and Dinah wanted the energies as auspicious as possible. With that in mind she had carefully positioned black tourmaline tumble stones on the carpet around the bed for protection and tucked clear quartz points under each pillow to amplify good energy. A swathe of sheer purple fabric covered the mirror. She was so engrossed in what she was doing that the shrill ring of the doorbell jarred right through her.

When she opened the door she found Nathaniel on the step with his hands in his back pockets. If she didn't know him better she'd have thought he seemed shy. "Hey," he smiled awkwardly. "Hi." Her smile matched his. The sight of him made her chest burn. From thereon neither spoke. They didn't need to as the energy between them took over. They made slow progress, stumbling up the stairs towards the bedroom, leaving a trail of clothing as they went. And as they fell onto the bed the outside world disappeared. It was just Dinah and Nathaniel and the touch of skin on skin.

When Dinah next checked the clock, it was almost three. "I must get up!" she cried, bolting upright in alarm. "The boys will be home any minute!"

Nathaniel merely kissed her arm and snuggled closer. "I'd like to meet them." His words caused an unexpected twang in Dinah's belly. She had always been slow to introduce romantic partners to her boys, only because she never knew if it would work out or not, and so far it had been not.

She was conscious of Nathaniel's scrutiny as her mind ran through a myriad of possible responses, but he didn't give her a chance. "You've got a nice home," he said, tactfully changing the subject. Glancing round he nodded at the various oil paintings hung on the walls, dark and yellowed with age.

"They were my great-grandmother's," said Dinah, following his gaze. "She was a collector. They're quite good I think."

He stared at her and squeezed her hand. "It's okay," he said quietly. "With us I mean. We can go slowly."

Dinah was visibly relieved. "I want you to meet Daniel and Luke, I do. It just seems a bit soon."

"It's fine," he smiled. Her frown was still there though and he stroked her forehead, trying to smooth it away. "I'll go and get our clothes." Throwing back the covers he disappeared out of the bedroom.

Dinah called after him, "I've been thinking." Her voice was high. She could hear him walking about before he returned with an armful of clothes.

"What about?" He deposited the clothes on the bed.

"How right from the start you seemed so familiar. So comfortable. Like I knew you already..." She paused, taking a breath. "Do you believe in reincarnation, in past lives?"

"I guess. Maybe." He seemed bemused. "I'm not sure."

"Well, I'm pretty sure... I mean... I was wondering, that's all..."

"About us?"

"Yes."

When his head reappeared through the top of his t-shirt, Nathaniel was grinning. "I like it – that we've known each other before."

"Well, it depends on how we knew each other," said Dinah. "Sometimes, as it turns out, previous incarnations aren't always so nice."

"It's an interesting idea. I've certainly met people who seem familiar. They're comfortable, like you said, and then others I take an instant dislike to for no apparent reason. With you though, there was something as soon as I saw you. There was this draw I couldn't ignore. It felt fated, meant to be... I don't know." There was a

265

twinkle in his eye as he bent to kiss her mouth. "I've got a meeting online at four and your boys will be back any minute so I better get moving."

"Okay."

"You're beautiful, Dinah." His voice was so filled with love that she flooded with warmth.

While he sat on the bed to put on his socks, Dinah slid her arms around his waist, tucking a leg either side of him, resting her cheek against his back. "Nathaniel... will you come with me up to the moor, to spend the night?" She paused, taking a breath. "To journey, like we do in the workshops, to go back and find out if there's anything between us from a previous life? It feels right up there, fitting somehow. We can sleep out under the stars, under the moon..."

Nathaniel turned towards her. "Well, sure. If it's important to you, then why not? It would be fun. We could make a fire, take some food." He cupped her face in his hands and kissed her on the end of her nose. "I need to go. We'll talk later, okay?"

Their eyes locked and she nuzzled his hand.

"Today was beautiful, Dinah. You're beautiful."

"You are, too," she said, and meant it with all her heart. Whether she was ready for true love or not she was committed to finding out, and willing to expose herself to all the possible hazards of truly loving another. Suddenly, Dinah knew she was prepared to take the risk. Nothing else would do.

* * *

In the shadowy half-light of April's budding full moon they picked their way through the rocks and stones and scrub of the moor. The stream was out of view but they could hear it gurgling nearby. It was a cool spring night and Dinah pulled her coat tighter around her. Nathaniel reached for her hand and she nestled into him. It was the first time she'd brought him up here. The knowledge of this moorland space was one blessing she could be thankful for from her encounter with Tony.

This landscape was as familiar to Dinah as her own home. Yet with only moonlight to guide them, which distorts as much as it reveals, she was cautious in finding her way. She didn't want to take a wrong turn. The trees made shadowy, twisting shapes, as they stretched into the darkened sky. Twigs snapped and cracked under their feet and every so often one of them stumbled over a stone or tripped on a tree root. The network of paths crisscrossed ahead presenting a myriad of possible routes, each with its own particular journey and eventual destination.

So many options, thought Dinah. But which one will take us to where we want to go, which one leads to the clearing?

It was a challenge at this late hour in the dark to find the right one. Looking to the moon she asked the Angels for help and immediately, as if lit by beams of moonlight, one particular path stood out from the rest.

"You alright?" Nathaniel squeezed her shoulder.

"Yep, all good."

Dinah had deliberately chosen a full-moon night for their foray back into the past. The energies were far stronger at such times, making it easier to open – to transcend mundane reality and journey into the world of spirit. Even so, the moon appeared especially large and bright tonight, a majestic white disc radiating magical energy to Earth.

"Everything's different by moonlight," whispered Dinah, to herself. "Transformed into something else entirely. The paths I take in the day seem more secretive at night-time – everything is either shadow or light."

"As long as we don't get lost," said Nathaniel, wryly. "I don't want to be wandering around on the moor for the rest of the night."

"We won't get lost," she said, confidently. "And, if we do, we just wait for sunrise. What's the worst that can happen?"

"True. And we've got each other for warmth."

Dinah was quietly on full alert, using every particle of intuition to find her way.

The moon only partially lights up the dark, she thought. Not revealing the whole picture. So much stays hidden in her light. That's her gift. Inviting mortals, so ensnared in their lives, to stop and look around more carefully. To pay attention and take the time to see if things are really as they appear, or if through naivety or apathy, we are allowing ourselves to be fooled. She gives just a hint of how things are and then it's down to us to navigate a safe passage.

In the midst of her musings, Dinah was pleased to recognise a curve in the path ahead and then a bit further on a small tree on the side of the track, its trunk and branches so forcefully windblown that it was destined to stand forever at a tilt. "We're nearly there," she exclaimed, excited. Nathaniel pressed her hand. "There's my tree," she pointed out, the sight of it filling her with warmth.

Whenever she saw the oak after a period of absence she felt like a small child reuniting with a favourite friend. And while many would only see a trunk and branches, bark and leaves, Dinah recognised the soul of a tree, as a sentient being with a spirit of its own. To commune with a tree is to commune with the Otherworld, and to hear its sacred heart is to be blessed by the Divine. The oak trees are home to the Oak-men – wise beings possessing the qualities of strength, courage and patience. The Oak-men offer a gateway to the Otherworlds, a portal through which the parallel worlds become more accessible to seekers who are considered worthy.

It was something of this that Dinah wanted to share with Nathaniel. They had pledged a commitment to each other to seek sacred union and since then she had felt with growing certainty that the reason they felt as if they knew each other so well was because they already did. Tonight she hoped to uncover the past. And there was no better place she could think of to take such a voyage than under the protective canopy of the sacred oak.

She spoke to the Tree with her thoughts. "I've brought a friend – Nathaniel. He is trustworthy. We would like your help." A light breeze swept through the leaves. "Can you please watch over us as we journey, lead us and guide us, so we can find out what has gone before?" Her belly fluttered. The tree-spirits had granted consent.

Just a few steps from where they stood, the fire she'd made earlier with Daniel and Luke was waiting to be lit. The three of them had come up that afternoon to gather rocks, sticks and branches, and after all their hard work she had surprised the boys with a packet of marshmallows and a thermos of hot chocolate. They'd lit the fire then and toasted the marshmallows on sticks. On the way home she'd dropped the two of them and Sophie at a school friend's house for the night, which had given her time to prepare for the night ahead. She had used candlelight and soft music in her ritual, bathing in salted water, massaging purifying oils into her hair and skin, and praying.

Nathaniel was already kneeling by the fire, carefully arranging the scrunched-up balls of newspaper dripped with candle wax they had brought with them, before stacking kindling on top. Once satisfied, he struck a match and put it to the paper. The match flickered and went out. He struck another and again put it to the paper. Again it blew out before it had a chance to catch.

He struck another match, this time cupping his hands to protect the flame, but still it blew out. Dinah knelt beside him to help shield the flame. As he struck the match she called the salamanders to help them and no sooner had she asked than the paper caught and started to burn. Nathaniel began stoking the fire. Dinah arranged their bed for the night with the groundsheet Nathaniel had brought in his backpack, along with sleeping bags, a thick fleece blanket and a couple of small cushions. The fire snapped and crackled, flames reaching into the night sky, bathing everything in an orange glow.

Dinah took Nathaniel's hand. "Sit here." She touched one of the cushions. "Get comfortable, and rest your eyes into the flames, until they want to close. Focus on your breathing and its rhythm."

She took the other cushion and they began to settle – softening into the night, into the sound of the fire, the stream, feeling the earth humming beneath them, breathing in the cool air, relaxing, dropping down.

"Watch your breath, soft and quiet," murmured Dinah. "Always come to the breath. You can ask the elementals to help – earth, fire, water, air." She began to mutter quietly, some kind of prayer or incantation and as Nathaniel listened, he found he was floating. Gently bobbing up and down – sinking, disappearing, resurfacing. They were drifting together underwater – him and Dinah – all the sounds merging, her voice becoming a part of him, silently dropping down through the layers.

Dinah wandered through the dark. It was pitch black and her arms were stretched before her as she felt her way, alert, vigilant and aware of Nathaniel following somewhere behind. She couldn't see a thing, but her mouth was working of its own accord, her lips forming strange words of an unfamiliar yet well-known language. These sounds she made would prise open the past. They were the key that would open the fissure through which they could slip.

She noticed a mist rising from somewhere beneath her, vague at first and then quickly thickening into a white gold haze, completely engulfing her and obscuring everything around her from view. She was breathing it in and it fizzed inside her, like a laser searing the cells of her body. It bubbled and spat. Looking down at her heart she was surprised to see there were shadows over it like bruises and that it was tightly encased in black oily strands, glistening like a spider's web, strangling the life from her. These strands were all the upsets and resentments she had collected over the years and meticulously stored away. Bitterness and trauma left to harden into a shield of pain. The extent of it shocked her, even as she felt the light building inside, pulsing stronger and brighter, dissolving the black until it shone through her skin, streaming through the cracks and scars of everything she had endured. She was aglow from the inside out and she saw Nathaniel in her mind's eye and knew he was experiencing the same.

The light swirled from within them and around them, streaming from their bodies, from their hearts and meeting between them as a sphere of light. They were immersed in golden light and then suddenly it changed. The light had formed into an inverted pyramid, which pointed down into Earth and completely encased them. Then she saw it overlapped a second pyramid, bigger, pointing up to the sky. She could feel herself throbbing and Nathaniel too. They were pulsing into each other. Surge after surge of mounting pressure, not unpleasant, but strong, making her body shake.

She wondered how Nathaniel was faring as the energies sliced through her, stacking on top of each other, a furnace of fire, almost too much, on the edge of too much. She was just hanging on. Dangling, suspended, nails gripping the edge of the cliff. *How much more can I take?*

And then, with a sigh, they passed through. They were back in the stillness – released to the place where the curtain is lifted and love is all there is. Their souls returned, reunited with the cosmos as a single drop of rain dissolves back into the ocean – adrift and in peace.

It was in this moment that Dinah knew quite suddenly why it was she and Nathaniel had met in this lifetime. She was being allowed to see and now she was spinning around and around as images flitted through her mind, voices calling – hazy and indistinct. One minute laughter, the next shouting, disembodied cries, a child calling, a man talking, and then the mist came down and she was alone in the quiet. Silver exploded in Dinah's brain and she wondered if Nathaniel was seeing as she was. *My love. Where are you?*

Thirty

The landscape was grey and cold as she walked along a deserted country track, her breath billowing white as she hurried home. Open farmland stretched in all directions, the fields ploughed ready for winter, the monotony of turned earth broken only by pockets of subdued woodland. Overhead a darkly ominous sky suggested a storm on its way, but despite the melancholy she was in high spirits, singing cheerfully to the world. She had just come from her beloved, where they had met down by the river.

The scene was familiar and Dinah strongly sensed having been here before as a visitor from another time. It was the strangest sensation of déjà vu, more akin to that of a recurring dream, repeating over and over and over. *He loves me and I love him*, the young woman crooned. *We are betrothed and we will marry.*

The heavy cloak slung across her shoulders fell so low that only the hem of her dress could be seen beneath its folds. The hood was down and her golden hair curled into a bun on the back of her head. "Who am I?" whispered Dinah.

Flora. The name murmured through her soul like the softest breeze, stirring long-forgotten memories which Dinah strained to recall. It was only when Sheila's house in London flickered into view that she remembered being Flora, but the delight at remembering was short-lived.

The scene was moving on regardless and Flora was hurrying towards a small copse up ahead, a shortcut to home. But someone waited there hidden amongst the trees. A figure hovered on the edge of Dinah's awareness and then a man appeared in her mind's eye, pale and thin with rasping hands.

"I know you!" Repulsion washed over her and her flesh prickled. The man was much older than Flora, older even than her father, and yet he wanted her as his own. He yearned for her, craved her, and

272

despite her resistance and her father's refusals, he was persistent. He would not give up. The man was a bully and the force of his dominating energy made Dinah recoil. When she looked into his eyes she saw them vengeful and lit with lust.

He follows me, sighs Flora, her voice forlorn but soft as flowers. *He watches when I meet my love and it angers him, even as I refuse him time after time. His rage at being spurned knows no bounds and in his obsession he is set on revenge. I cannot escape him.*

Dinah understood the man had some social standing and was of seemingly good repute. Yet as an animal instinctively senses evil, Flora had always detected the simmering malice within him. She knew with absolute certainty that behind closed doors he was capable of great cruelty, noticing how his servants cowered around him, the fear in their eyes, and the way the local children froze whenever he passed them by. And she had seen how he treated his horse.

He had called for her at their family home one day, only to be informed that she was indisposed. Peering out of the window, heart beating, hidden behind the curtain, Dinah saw his scowl as he left. She shivered as she watched him mount his horse and then as he began to beat the life out of it. Holding the reins tight he brought the whip down again and again as the sorry animal flattened its ears and whinnied in pain. Only when its flesh was laid bare and pink and the blood ran had he loosened the reins, digging his heels into the horse's flanks, and galloped away.

Tears run down Flora's face. *Here is someone who will not rest, not until the unwilling object of his desire is brought to submission.*

Flora doesn't see her attacker. She is halfway through the copse as he lunges from behind. She crashes to the ground, cracking her hip on a rock. *Yet I know it is he. His ardour and fury makes him strong and he pins me down, bunching my skirts, forcing under my clothes. My bodice rips. His sour tongue fills my mouth. I am choking. I cannot breathe and I bite down hard. 'Bitch!' He slaps me and for a moment I am still, stunned, as he heaves on top of me, stifling me with his weight, grunting as he tugs his breeches, grinding his mouth onto mine. And I fight then with everything I have. I am a madwoman, deranged, scratching and screaming. His skin under my nails, I rip at his face, I tear at him and hit and kick with every measure of strength I possess. When my knee slams between his legs, it stops.*

Time is still and he rolls from me, groaning, clutching his groin. He is sighing and wheezing, but I don't stop to see. I'm up and I'm off and I run for my life.

She is frantic. Gasping for air, crying as she runs with clothes torn and hair unravelled, stuck with mud and leaves. She does not go home, instinct takes her elsewhere, to a friend who will help.

A woman's face appeared to Dinah, clear as day with a flash of red hair and piercing blue eyes. Ambrika! Dinah was delighted.

She worries for me, whispers Flora. *She never says as much, but I see it in her face.* She sounds hollow, defeated. *He is not in control of his senses and will never leave me alone.* The woman tends to Flora, who sobs and whimpers. Her face is smeared with blood and she is shaking, unable to catch her breath. The woman speaks soothing words, calmly rubs balm onto Flora's wounds, into her cuts and bruises, helps her re-pin her hair and fix her clothes. She strokes Flora's head and tells her the dress is torn beyond repair, but that it will see her home.

Something bad is coming for me. Dinah was overcome with foreboding, her heart warning of dreadful things. *I will not escape again. He will have my skin to be sure.*

The mist came down around Dinah and within it things were shifting, moving onwards. When the haze evaporated she was indoors and it was night-time. Everything was quiet. She was in a bedroom, and a grand one at that. Something was pressing across Flora's body and she realised she was in a bed, a four-poster, and that the weight bearing down was the covers.

"Where am I?" she asked.

My bedroom, comes the whispered reply. *It is late, but I do not sleep.*

The drapes around the bed are open, and with the embers from an earlier fire still glowing in the grate she can see something of the room. The walls are oak-panelled and an ornate patterned carpet runs the length of the floor. A large lattice window is swathed in flourishes of rich material.

Flora is hot and restless and Dinah senses her unease. *I am scared.* Sleep eludes her and foreboding nags her belly. *They come for me. He makes sure of it. Nothing can prevent it.*

Daylight. Footsteps outside the bedroom door followed by muffled voices. A knock. *Mama?* Flora is shaking. She has not slept and she cannot breathe. *No. It is the maid come to wake me, but I see fear in her eyes. She tells me hurry, be quick. I cannot stand and she helps me, pulls on my clothes as I gape at her, as I stumble and fall. I feel her pity. Her terror.*

They are outside now, Flora standing outside her family home, hurriedly dressed, half-undone as dread squeezes her chest. The morning is cold and she shivers. Big hands take hold of her, big man hands with thick fingers that dig into her flesh, preventing her from moving, making sure she cannot run.

I'll have bruises later. They hold me prisoner already. I see my family and I feel their eyes on me. A sad, lost voice from long ago. *Mother is beside herself and more than anything I want to go to her.* A tearstained face. *Mother, why are you crying?* Quiet brother. Quiet sisters. There were raised voices. *Father is angry. He is shouting, but I don't hear the words, I only see how his mouth opens and closes. He is getting redder and redder and I want to touch him, to tell him to stop. I've never seen him like this and it scares me – he is usually such an even-tempered man.* There is a scuffle. Angry voices. One man. Two men.

I see the carriage then, drawn by two horses, sombre and dreary. The carriage has come for me and the fingers dig tighter into my arms, yanking me forward. The horses snort and stamp their hooves, streams of white air blow from their nostrils as Flora shakes with fear. *I do not want to go. I tell them I do not want to go, but they ignore me. When I fall they do not wait for me, they do not let me find my feet. They drag me, both arms wrenched, aching with pain. I'm done for. My only hope is my beloved will come for me. That he will not rest until he finds me.*

As they near the carriage, one of the men grabs a fistful of her hair and pulls, twisting the roots from her scalp. Despite the searing pain, Flora made no sound, and Dinah understood: Flora has pledged silence. *I am mute. I will show no fear, nor pain. I will not allow them such pleasure.* The hands, rough and strong, force her into the carriage and Flora hits the floor, but manages to kick one of the men on the shin as she falls. He swears and spits in her face before slamming the door and sliding the bolt. She is captive. *They say I am insane,* she weeps. *They say the mad must be incarcerated.*

The carriage pulls away. As it jerks and bumps over rough hard ground, Flora drags herself up to peer out of the small window. She sees her family watching, huddled together, distraught. Her mother is bent double, clinging to father, himself white-faced and trembling. Her brother and sisters are still, arms locked around each other, faces etched with shock. And then through the damp, cold air, she catches sight of a pair of eyes and she freezes. He is standing apart – triumphant, gloating, as with a cynical smile he quietly doffs his hat to her.

Tony.

Dinah felt the stab of injustice slice through Flora, felt the knife blade of bitterness plunge deep as if into her own belly. Flora heaves, fingers clutching at the window, heart pounding as white fury tears her soul. She knows now how he told people in the town, people of influence, how she'd attacked him whilst he was out walking. His voice was oily and laden with self-righteous indignation. "She is a lunatic. Possessed. Scratching and hissing like a wild cat till I had to beat her from me. Look at my face! See how she went for me! Everyone knows how she is," he snorts viciously. "How she talks to herself! Mad. Feeble-minded. For all our sakes she must be restrained."

Hot rage ravages through Flora as Dinah's breath comes shallow and fast. "Flora, no," she cried out, wanting to warn her, forgetting the story is already told and that the past cannot be undone.

Flora's screech cut jagged through the morning air. *May you be damned and your soul go straight to Satan,* she shrieks. They all still, not just him. She was crazed and she will not stop. *I curse you to hell for all eternity, that you be plagued with sorrow and tormented with ill luck, that no good will ever come to you for what you have done to me, and know that throughout eternity – I will never forget.*

Her chest heaves and it is only as her screams fade that Flora sees the maid crossing herself, that she takes in the harrowed expression on her father's face, the fearful bewilderment on her mother's. But Flora only has eyes for her tormentor. She watches his victorious smile grow wider and the glee in his eyes glow brighter, and she crumples to the floor.

You see, he told them I was a mad woman and I gave him the thing he needed to seal my fate – for everyone to see. Her voice was faint, resigned. *He convinced them I attacked him, that I was not safe. It wasn't difficult. I was already known for my strange ways and I was put away from the world, shut away because of him.*

Dinah moaned.

Now Flora is huddled in the corner of a small dim room, down on the floor, whimpering, clutching her knees, which are pulled up under her chin. Her hair hangs limp around her face and her eyes flicker vacantly as she rocks backwards and forwards, backwards and forwards, a relentless sad motion, seeking solace and comfort where none can be found.

Dinah saw her hands, raw and bleeding, scratched by herself in frenzied agitation. Her fingers restless, scrabbling and fidgeting, driving her nails deep into her palms, into her arms, her face, until the blood ran.

Dinah felt cold and frightened. She writhed uncomfortably as the madness and anguish that festered inside Flora seeped into her. Flora was skin and bone, her pale skin blackened with bruises, her hair straggly and unkempt. *I spend my days alone in a cold, damp room waiting for my beloved to come for me.* Her voice was barely audible. *It is his face I hold on to and the memory of his touch. I wait and I wait and I wait for him to come. But my beloved never comes and as the years pass my love turns to disappointment and later the disappointment becomes disillusion in love. By the time death claims me, disillusion has frozen into betrayal and hatred.*

Flora's presence was heavy now, a weight pressing down on Dinah, stifling the air out of her until she could hardly breathe. *Unjustly imprisoned and with no way out,* a mournful whimper. *My beloved never came for me. Freedom came only with death.*

Something let go of Dinah and she was falling, but she no longer cared. He didn't come! She had no room for any other thought. Her heart twisted in pain and her mind spun. "You didn't come for me!" she yelled, accusing. Falling, falling. She wrung her hands, not knowing which way was up and which was down. "Where were you? Why didn't you come for me?" Angry, icy fingers squeezed her heart.

"Answer me!" she screamed into the black. "Nathaniel! Answer me now!"

Without opening her eyes, Dinah could feel him beside her. She had crashed through the nothingness back to the Earth plane and they were sitting in the clearing by the tree. She was reeling. She wanted to rage and cry, stomp her feet, and the force of her wrath shocked her. Why didn't you save me from him? she screamed soundlessly at Nathaniel, her chest heaving with tragedy, at the pain of witnessing the damage caused by another soul's relentless interference. Shaking and breathless, Dinah tried to calm herself as hot tears trailed down her cheeks. The twisting of her heart was so sharp it made her gasp for air, overcome with sadness and regret. An innocent young love torn apart by one man's sense of superiority and desire for revenge.

The relentless foreboding figure who had persecuted her through the ages, invading her life, her thoughts, her dreams and visions, destroying her happiness, stealing her joy. Tony. Always, Tony! He was the root cause of all her fear in this lifetime and she was overcome with fury and bitter resentment. But this time I got away!

Blearily, Dinah blinked her reddened eyes open. The fire was almost out. It was crackling feebly with only a small tinge of orange glowing among the ashes. Shuffling onto her hands and knees, she crawled closer to it, piling on more twigs and logs before blowing into the embers, breathing life back into the flames. It was only when she sat back again that she noticed a solitary light flickering high in the trees. As she watched it grew bigger and brighter. Then more lights were appearing, getting stronger and closer, until dazzled, she had to turn away. They were Angels, hundreds of them and they were encircling her and Nathaniel, offering protection, showering them with love.

"It is a soul tie, Dinah." Her Guardian Angel was gentle, nestling nearer until Dinah was immersed in heavenly warmth. "Your souls agreed to reunite to clear the darkness created during earlier incarnations. When you understand that each of your souls longs for peace and forgiveness, that in truth it is your deepest and only desire – then you will discover the divine joyfulness you seek."

The Angel's words were a comfort, but Dinah was distraught. "Why should I forgive?" she questioned. "Why should I let the perpetrator off the hook? I was an innocent! I did nothing wrong! I fought against one man's rape, and I fell in love with another. I trusted my beloved to come for me and he never did." Anger burned inside her. "He never came for me..." She stopped, inhaling hard as her heart pulsed painfully. It was as if she was shattering inside, as though she was breaking apart right from the core of her being. She clutched her chest, stifling a howl.

A noise stopped her short.

"My love, there was nothing to be done."

Dinah stopped, ears pricked. "Nathaniel?"

"I was only a peasant, a farm worker, and he had position, influence, prestige. I tried to fight for you, as much as I could, as much as my status allowed. I wanted to free you, we all did, your family and I. We never did forsake you, but the opposition was cunning and merciless. There was little we could do. There was nothing to be done." His voice echoed the despondency of Flora's last words. "My heart broke when I learned what had become of you, that you had been taken, that you were gone, and from then on I lived a solitary existence, surviving day by day with no future to speak of without you. I merely lived out my time on Earth, waiting for the blessed release of death when we would be together again."

The loud crack in Dinah's chest startled her, as did the splintering sound that followed – something was being released. But there was no time for reflection as she was lifting away again. Tired of the struggle, she willingly succumbed, trusting the Angels to keep her safe. A kaleidoscope of colour fanned beneath her eyelids, flashes of patterned lights spinning too fast to catch until things finally began to steady and slow, and she emerged into an entirely different landscape altogether.

The terrain is hilly and rocky and surrounded by water. A scorching sun beats down and in the distance a vast triangular stone structure reaches high above the trees and vegetation. It is a temple. *The land of the Sun and the Moon. My people live with awareness of Spirit.*

Now she is inside the temple and it is dark. The gloom is only relieved by the light of a fire burning in the centre of the room, which is being stoked by a man in a simple cloth tunic. As Dinah peered into the shadows she realised she was standing on a raised platform and that the space was crowded with people, all facing towards her. There was a peculiar hush in the room and a charge of

279

expectancy, as if they were waiting for something to happen, and Dinah guessed some kind of ceremony or initiation was about to take place. The faces around her were dark-skinned and when she looked at her hands she saw she was dark, too, and that she wore a finely woven blue robe embroidered with gold. The blue was like nothing she had ever seen, a colour of such richness and vibrancy, of such shimmering depth that it appeared mystical. The embroidery that ran around the hem, the sleeves and down the front was of ancient sacred symbols, painstakingly sewn. Her hands were slim and dainty and painted with dark purple and red ink – detailed designs running from each fingernail, across the backs of her hands and under the sleeves of her robe.

Standing next to her were three other women, each dressed as elaborately as she – one in green, one in red and one in gold. *My Temple Sisters.* In front of them a group of boys were kneeling before an older man with long grey hair – the Priest and spiritual leader. The boys were about twelve or thereabouts, naked to the waist with their heads bowed so their straight black hair fell over their faces. Today was their initiation and the sister dressed in green was dipping a smooth wooden cup into a golden pail filled with dark liquid, and giving it to each of the boys in turn to drink from. It was a herbal elixir, prepared according to sacred law to induce a state of higher consciousness. There was magic in the air.

Only then did she notice the musicians gathered before the platform and hear the music emanating from the instruments in their hands. Each musician held a crude clay pipe in their cupped hands that they were blowing into. The ensuing sounds were so extraordinarily high-pitched they were almost painful to hear. The notes so exquisitely beautiful as to be of another world, echoing off the walls of the temple, splintering the mind and piercing the soul. Music so alluring that one was instantly carried away, and Dinah felt herself, as a Temple Sister, sliding in and out of trance. She was resisting though, as if wanting to stay present. *There is reason to be cautious.*

Dinah's heart flexed as from behind the musicians a man appears, bare-chested and stocky, his arms flung dramatically upwards as he stamps on the ground. On his head an exotically feathered headdress flutters with plumes of yellow and red, and three thick red stripes run across the bridge of his nose. His straight, black hair is cut with a razor sharp fringe and his entire torso and arms are decorated with the same intricate markings which cover her hands. *The Medicine Man!*

Dinah felt anxiety. Something about this man perplexed her. Deep love and utter hatred was fusing inside her, and she knew the woman, herself as Temple Sister, was afraid of him. The Shaman was already deep in trance, hands flicking and weaving, lips moving silently as he chanted inaudible sounds, but the longer Dinah watched him the odder she felt. She knew that as a Temple Sister, she did not like nor trust him. He was a danger.

When the pipes stop, his chants become gradually louder until, with wild rolling eyes and stamping feet, he is shouting, his voice harsh and guttural. The crowd is starting to join in and as the Shaman speeds up, Dinah recognises he is inducing a state of spiritual frenzy under guise of prayer. The air in the temple is stifling, and still they shout louder and faster, stamping their feet until the ground shakes, until Dinah can feel her head starting to go. *The energies are too strong. What's happening?*

She is nauseous and woozy and sweat pours down her back and chest. Suddenly the Shaman halts abruptly, and immediately the crowd stops too. Everyone is watching him, waiting for instruction, and he turns to face her with an arm raised and a single finger pointing upwards. Nobody moves and she watches in growing terror as, deliberate and slow, he lowers his hand until that one ominous finger is pointing directly at her. Fear shoots through the sister as all eyes turn to stare, the energy of this accusation and contempt jolting into her body.

Everything went black.

I hated him from the start, without knowing why, without good cause, and my hatred ran deep. From childhood to adulthood, I tried to bring him down, using my sacred position as Temple Sister to destroy him. I told the elders he was not to be trusted and I was relentless; whispering in their ears, claiming he was false, doing everything I could to turn the people against him. But he discovered my ploy.

My accusations ran away with me, becoming more and more dangerous until I could be ignored no longer and a meeting was called. He was confronted, forced to explain himself – to prove he was true. And of course I should have known. It could not be avoided. They told him it was I who was causing the trouble and I was brought to stand before him, to stand before my tribe. And still I lied. We stood side by side as I lied my way through, falsehood after elaborate falsehood spilling from my lips. I could see the confusion in him. Feel his confusion as I made up tales of his manipulation, of his false intentions and desire to lead the tribe alone with the help of the powers of the dark.

The woman is coughing now, she is starting to choke, and Dinah feels hands tightening around her neck, squeezing the air from her body. *So he came for me. Stealthy and quiet so no one could hear but me, so no one could hear me cry out. His hands around my neck, filled with loathing as they tightened.*

And then there was nothing – only a limp, lifeless body and a regretful spirit.

Dinah was horrified. "You strangled me!" Shock and disbelief jolted through her. "Nathaniel! You murdered me!"

Thirty-one

She was a weightless cloud orbiting the material planes as Angels held her close. It was peaceful here and calm. Drifting in the space where time ceases to exist and the illusion is revealed for what it is in truth. "Ahhhhhh…"

But now she was dropping again, tumbling through the realms until she lands in the body of a small thin girl. *I laugh, but it doesn't feel nice.* She is standing in a dirty narrow lane of tall squashed houses, some brick, some wood, but all decrepit and ramshackle. The roofs are bowed and broken, and the tops of the houses lean toward each other, shutting out the light, and seemingly closing above her head. Dirty rags drape from every window, while street fires belch out noxious fumes, almost but not quite disguising an underlying stench of rotting waste. Dogs bark, babies cry and puddles of putrid water pool around her feet. Her skin is pale but blackened with dirt, the same as the children she plays with. Someone is crying and Dinah turns to see a small boy, thin and dirty like herself, crouching on the ground while the other children taunt and throw stones at him.

He tries to be our friend, brags the little girl. *'But I won't let him. I tell my friends stories about him and we all run away.*

Dinah knew the boy. She could see it was Nathaniel and watched him, unable to smother the glee in the little girl, in herself, as one of the bigger boys punches so hard that his nose spits blood. He falls backwards, sprawling on the ground as tears streak his filthy cheeks. The children run off. All except the little girl, who just stares at him. She sees only too well the desperation in his eyes, the pleading. Laughing spitefully she runs after her friends.

"I enjoyed my revenge."

The scene was receding and once again Dinah was spinning down the centuries, a horrified spectator and reluctant witness to her own misdeeds.

There is music and dancing. The barn has been cleared of hay and is lined with thin wooden tables, the floor covered with straw to soak up the spills. Rough white cloth covers the tables which are laden with food; tureens of steaming soups and stews, trays of mutton and pork, boiled hams and vast plum puddings. At one end of a table a portly man dressed in breeches dispenses ale into metal tankards, while at the other, a woman hands out cups of tea from a metal urn. It is a merry scene, everyone eating and drinking, dancing and laughing. *Harvest Home.*

Dinah is aware of being in a cumbersome body with the rough reddened hands of someone used to regular manual labour. *I am the scullery maid at the big house. A woman of no beauty or station.*

She is sitting by herself, slightly apart, on a three-legged stool in the corner of the barn. Her blouse is itchy and makes her want to scratch. A young man appears in the barn doorway with fair hair and melting green eyes and the maid swoons. *He works in the stables and is liked by many – mothers and daughters both.* The maid's heart pounds and she feels quite faint. She is in love with this man but only from afar. *He has always had my heart, but pays me no notice. Just this morning I heard him talking with friends as I went to fetch water. They were loud and when I heard it was he I crept closer, being careful not to be seen. I stayed hidden, listening as they laughed, as they talked about the party, about which of the female servants they'd be after tonight. Someone said my name and I froze, scared. I left then, to get on with my work, but the sound of his laughter, disbelieving and scornful, rang in my ears all day long.*

The man was taking a tankard of ale and when his cup was full he turns to offer the woman behind him a drink. It is the parlour maid, Alyce, a slight pretty girl. Jealousy and humiliation meld inside the scullery maid.

Then the world went grey and Dinah was adrift again. 'Dear God, when will it end?' she moaned.

A new time, a new place and she is queuing at a well – an older woman with a bucket in her hand in a desert town. It's dusty and sparse and a gnarled old beggar man is pestering people for coins, while ahead of her a dark-skinned man with a rough grey beard wears a red and white keffiyeh.

Dinah regards the beggar. He is pulling at people's clothing, with matted hair and only a tatty tunic covering his skinny frame as he demands money for food. His voice is rasping and a shiver of recognition washes over her, contempt blistering in her belly. When her turn comes to draw water she steps forward and lowers the bucket into the darkness. Something tugs at her clothes and when she turns she is repulsed to find the beggar clasping her skirts, holding out a bony, calloused hand. Up close he is even more grotesque and the woman recoils. His grin is sly and reveals rotting brown teeth. She is disgusted and shakes him off before returning to get water. The tugging is stronger this time, more persistent and so she pushes him away harder, making him stumble. Now he is angry, and comes at her shouting, gripping her wrists, demanding money. Although she tries to free herself, he is stronger than he looks and in the ensuing tussle she nearly drops her bucket down the well. Her disdain gives way to fear. The man in the keffiyeh intervenes, takes hold of the beggar by the scruff of his neck and violently shoves him away: "Go! You are not wanted here." The beggar hits the ground in a cloud of dust and the woman thanks the man for his help. As she plunges her bucket into the well, she knows he lies still on the ground, watching her, cursing her.

A moan of horror in Dinah's head. "Oh, Nathaniel!"

Thumped back to the physical world, Dinah bent to the earth, pressing her palms flat into the ground. There was comfort in its solidness, in feeling the grass and leaves, and she pressed down harder. She was stunned.

"What a horrible tangled dance we've led, an unending cycle of darkness, of tit for tat, pursuing and tormenting each other through so many lives. Both unable to find forgiveness inside of us, never understanding or trying to understand, only vengeance and betrayal and cruelty!"

Once upon a time their love was innocent and pure, but she had seen how in their careless, unwitting hands, it had warped into a relentless cycle of hatred and destruction. Regret engulfed her. "We were borne from love, the only real power that exists. Eternal, unconditional love and still, we managed to destroy ourselves.

285

Where is the light between us, Angels? Why has it always been so awful?"

Love from the Angels poured into Dinah's wounded heart and she gratefully received the healing, her cheeks wet with tears as a whispering breeze moved through the trees. *The battle between light and dark exists within, but love can never be extinguished. Forgive and walk free.*

"But did he see what I saw, Angels? Does he know what we once were to one another? And what we became?" Inwardly, she was sobbing, her heart contracting with both sorrow and love as beneath her the earth cracked apart. She was plummeting down, spiralling into the crevasse, falling through layers of soil and rock. Down, down, Dinah fell, descending into the shadowy realms, where fear and horror lurks, a hidden place filled with anger and self-hatred, recrimination and despair. This was somewhere she didn't want to go – a place she had avoided as she hurtled through life, a most secretive place that until now had been buried in the depths of her psyche. But it had not gone away. It was waiting, biding its time until it could resurface to shatter her world. The urge to flee, to scrabble away engulfed her, but try as she might she was heading straight for it and there was no going back. The only way was through. *Breathe, Dinah,* whispered her Angel.

And so she tried to stay brave. She met the waves of pain as they came for her, as they washed her away and pummelled her to the ground until she lay quaking and bruised. It gripped her so tight that she shook uncontrollably, tears pouring down her cheeks, her mind wired taut – an unquenchable sea of grief.

And then suddenly the turbulence was passing.

The chaos was falling away as she fell into still, empty nothing, dropping into the black, into the quiet womb of the Earth. Here, the ferocity of feeling was subsiding and in its wake, just ahead of her, a pinprick of light – a hazy glimmer of faraway bright. Her breath was steadying and the panic settling. Calm was emerging and Dinah found she was synchronising with the pulse of the land, throbbing in time to the soul of the Universe. She was empty, transparent, made of nothing and yet filled with everything. "I am merged with creation." The thought surprised her. "No, I am creation!" Her Angel cocooned her and she was reverberating from the inside out. *Listen to love.*

Dinah shivered. She was cold. A wind had picked up and was blowing on her skin, urging her to reawaken to the physical plane. Out of trance she found she was hunched over herself, folded in two with her forehead resting on the ground. Without moving she turned her head towards where Nathaniel was sitting, pressing her cheek into the earth. Blinking groggily she opened her eyes ever so slightly, just a slit, as the sound of leaves rustling in the trees and the water gushing in the stream nearby told her the world was still here.

The fire had gone out.

She stared at him. He had hurt her beyond anything she could have imagined; deserted her, humiliated her, betrayed her, killed her. Yet she was not by any means blameless.

He was sitting motionless, quiet, his eyes still closed. Dinah was grateful. The man before her was not the man she had known then, and the woman she was then was not who she had become. She felt clear and light and for a moment closed her eyes.

When she next looked over at him it took a moment to register that he was staring back at her. "Are you okay?" He sounded concerned and a pang shot through her. Dinah sat up.

"I hurt you." It was all she could say.

"I hurt you, too."

She was relieved to detect love in his words. He stretched out his arms and then his legs, wincing in discomfort. "So..." he smiled, a small wobbly smile. "We've been here all night, Dinah."

For the first time she noticed the dark giving way to the light. "Yes." She hugged herself and shivered again. "What did you see?"

A slight frown crinkled his forehead and she waited. When he did speak his voice was gentle. "I saw that we've been through a lot you and I, and yet we're still here, trying. I saw that we haven't given up on each other, despite everything."

Their eyes locked.

"What now though?" she whispered, slightly afraid.

Tentatively Nathaniel stood up, and moving slowly came to sit by her side. As he slid his arms around her waist he gently rested his head on hers a moment before softly kissing her cheek. Dinah felt so warm and safe in his arms she could have wept with relief.

"I didn't know what I was asking of you to come back with me," she apologised. "I wasn't expecting any of it!"

He squeezed her tighter. "Dinah, I'll do whatever it takes to make you happy."

She squeezed him back then, her heart warm through with love. "Thank you."

Her eyes must have spoken for her heart because he kissed her then, and she kissed him back. Too many broken relationships had left Dinah jaded about love, about the very notion of romantic love. Yet the Angels had brought them together. And here she was, back with her true love, teetering on the brink, on the edge of something wonderful. Two separate souls in two separate bodies, united by what lay in their hearts.

The morning sun reached over the hillside as tired and peaceful, Dinah and Nathaniel slowly made their way back to the car. The grass was damp with dew; a white mist enveloped the horizon, shielding the moorland hills from sight.

They were quiet as they drove back to the town. Lost in thought, caught in the mystical moment between two worlds, between a night in the wilderness, of magic and revelation, and the transition back to the everyday.

Porrick was deserted. Nathaniel pulled up outside Dinah's house and turned off the engine.

"What exactly happened for you last night?" ventured Dinah.

He hesitated and then smiled. "I felt love," he replied, his voice no more than a whisper. Dinah caught her breath. "And I saw us hurting each other. I saw us tormenting each other, over and over, brutal. I want to leave that behind, to move ahead, a clean slate."

"You really believe we can leave it all behind?" Her voice mirrored the softness in his. "That we can make a go of it? Despite everything you've seen?"

"Yes!" He was adamant. "That's in the past. Last night showed me I do know what love is. I've known all along. I love you, Dinah."

Her heart lurched at his words. "I love you, too. I have all along."

His face shone. "You are my beloved!"

Taking his head in her hands, she kissed him. "Will you come inside? Stay with me."

With a smile, Nathaniel pulled the keys from the ignition. "I can't think of anything I'd rather do more." He opened his door.

"Nathaniel, wait a minute." Dinah touched his arm so he turned to face her. "Are you okay for us to take things slowly though? I don't want to kill the relationship by rushing."

He stroked her cheek. "Dinah, it's fine. I'm with you on that and I'm not going to force anything. You need space, you've got it. We can go day by day, no pressure from me. We're in this together and I'll do whatever I can to make you happy and to make us work."

Their eyes locked and he squeezed her hand. "Come on. Let's get inside. I'd do anything for a cup of tea!"

Acknowledgements

Thank you everyone who encouraged me while I was writing this book. To David in particular for your incredible patience, support and encouragement. I would never have finished and got to this stage without you. To my boys for putting up with me during this (very long) process and for being the wonderful, grounded amazing people that you are. To my mother and sister for your ongoing encouragement and support, and for picking me up when in the middle of one of many, many episodes of crashing confidence. And to my friends, who encouraged me and those who read my words and gave feedback, particularly the early drafts... Jo, Izzy, Sandy and Mark, Sarah, Damaris, Mel, Kat, Jan and Nicky. Cheriefox.com your cover is fabulous and I am so grateful.

Printed in Great Britain
by Amazon

46627631R00172